The Year of Durocher

A Novel by Theodore Jacobs

Published by International Psychoanalytic Books (IPBooks)
25–79 31st Street; Astoria, NY 11102
www.IPBooks.net

ISBN: 978-0-9851329-6-5

Library of Congress Control Number: 2013900216

For Mickey, Ellen, Annie, Nina and Jenny

Each friend represents a world in us, a world possibly not born until they arrive, and it is only by this meeting that a new world is born

---Anais Nin, 1937

Chapter One

When the unspeakable happened in the summer of '48 and the Giants brought Leo Durocher over from Brooklyn to manage our team, I knew that this was not going to be my year. My own Pearl Harbor had not struck yet, but for us Giant fans the deal that installed the despised one as our team leader ranked right up there with Japanese diplomacy.

"They might as well have brought in Hirohito to run the club," my friend, Mel Schleifer, said.

After that we measured all acts of infamy on a ten-point Durocher scale. When Doreen Mandelbaum pulled a number on Mel, accepting a date for a drive-in movie and then, like a nervous Greyhound passenger, insisted that he keep his hands glued to the wheel, we gave her six out of a possible ten. For out-and-out deviousness and treachery, Myra Herz earned an even seven points. Not only did she refuse a date with me on the pretext of having to go to her East Hampton house for the weekend, but that Friday night she brazenly appeared at the Thalia Theatre with some nerd from Dalton where I caught them, *in flagrante*, on line for *The Maltese Falcon*. A compromise seven and a half (I held out for eight, Mel argued for parity with Myra) went to Corky Kravitz for finking out on a Saturday night rendezvous and keeping me waiting in the rain outside Tip Toe Inn, our late night hangout, for more than an hour.

We gave out only one ten that year. It went to Cara Rosenhaus, otherwise known as Tokyo Rose, a sputtering flame of mine whose capacity for loyalty was such that she might have earned a lower score if she had gone to bed with Durocher himself. As it was, she got involved with a character from Brooklyn who, for out-and-out *chutzpah*, beat Durocher and Stanky combined. What happened that last year at my school, Harmon, between her, me, and Stan Schneiderman, the Flatbush firebrand, constitutes as sorry a tale as the great Mel Ott's managerial record. In fact, for pure heartache I have to rank it on a par with my first glimpse of Leo the Lip in a Giant uniform.

My troubles began with Cara—or more precisely, with Cara on one side of me and Stan Schneiderman on the other, like two arms of a pincer. I was never certain whether this particular alignment of forces, the Luftwaffe ahead, Rommel to the rear, constituted a North American extension of Third Reich power or whether it represented just one more example of God's spitefulness against me for quitting Hebrew school. My experiences with Rabbi Ruven, Jehovah's emissary to the Upper West Side, rather inclined me to the latter view. Not only did he send me an angry note addressed to Jonathan TD, short for Jonathan, the defector, when I didn't sign up for Hebrew school that year, but when he spotted me lighting up an Old Gold outside Whelan's drugstore, accused me of having become the kind of no-goodnik who likes to make a public display of breathing in poison gases but who has managed to inhale nothing of Jewish values.

It was true that I'd been having trouble believing in God—the idea that a Beneficent Being was looking on while Myra Herz and Corky Kravitz went unpunished and the mad owner of the Giants continued to make lunatic trades gave me problems—but when it came to my first encounter with the Cara-Stan cabal, I became convinced that an invisible hand was at work. If there was a Jehovah—and some days I thought there just might be some mysterious purpose in the Durocher move—there could be little doubt that I had been fingered by Ruven to receive a hefty dose of the punishment he meted out to the unfaithful. Sometimes I had the idea that the entity people called God was not a solo practitioner or even a mom and pop affair, but a vast department with long-reaching tentacles like the CIA or the IRS and that each year certain groups of sinners were targeted for special sting operations. The Cara experience convinced me that this had been the year of the Yom Kippur cheat, the self-abuser, and the worshiper of the graven images that appeared each month in *Esquire* magazine, and that my being all three accounted for the special punishment that had been visited on me.

Long afterward, when I talked of these things in analysis, my analyst told me that I was a good example of a Fate neurosis. By this he meant that I am the kind of person who has a talent for slipping his head into a noose but who blames his troubles on fate; on having been born in the wrong century, in the wrong country or to the wrong set of parents—in short, on an unlucky roll of the dice. Although I resisted that label, I had to admit he had a point. For years I was convinced that if I had come into the world not as myself but as my friend, Andy Konigsberg, who lived in a nine-room penthouse at the Century and whose father owned the Brass Rail restaurant, life would have been very different for me. For one thing, I would not have been mixed up with girls. Andy warned me to keep clear, pointing out that women ate money for breakfast and quoting his father to the effect that it was the wives, not the husbands, who went for the á la carte vegetables and whipped cream desserts and whose pocketbooks were keeping him at Harmon.

Andy himself was doing very well as campus representative for *Time* and *The Saturday Evening Post* and, seeing me headed for trouble, offered me a partnership in his latest venture, importing toy soldiers from Israel.

"The Israeli army is the hottest item on the market right now," he explained. "If they *shtup* the Arabs a couple of more times, you'll be looking at collectors' items."

I told him I did not think that the project was for me. I had no head for figures and, in any case, I was not up for business. The idea of putting all of my energies into trying to hustle a dollar and, at the same time, having to guard my flank against the likes of Mitch Sternheim who sold Turkish cigarettes from cartons stashed in his locker and who, sensing we had a good thing, would try to pressure us to reveal our Israeli connection, had no appeal for me. This kind of cat and dog existence had been my father's life and it had brought him nothing but long nights of insomnia.

"You're an idiot," Andy declared. "You're going to end up with more pain in the *kishkes* than you can dream of, and for what? So that you can keep another Bess Myerson in style and win the Bergdorf big spender award? When the honeymoon is over and you are looking around to borrow a spare pair of testicles, maybe you'll wake up and realize that there is only one thing to remember: cash is king."

I probably should have listened to Andy. We might have branched out into a Woolworth-type chain and made our fortune. But I didn't. Something lunatic in me kept me on a fool's path looking to women for my salvation. It wasn't really the *Esquire*-type, though, that I was seeking. It was a straight-shooter like Ann Rutherford, an actress whom I'd been in love with since third grade and who seemed to me the perfect woman—not only pretty and smart, but able to appreciate guys like Mickey Rooney and me, who, though short, were gutsy. On a lark I wrote her a couple of letters, and although this effort cost me dearly—when she didn't respond I lost Carl Hubbell, the southpaw ace of my baseball card collection, to Mel on a bet that my strategy of enclosing a self-addressed envelope would elicit an answer—for years she remained my ideal.

My analyst thought my problem was that I was into repetitions and that I had never really gotten over the hurt I experienced in the fifth grade at the hands of Edie Metzger, a black-haired beauty who had an air about her of only-child entitlement. For a while she seemed to favor me, and once, in homeroom, even slipped me a couple of passes to Palisades Amusement Park that her father had supposedly gotten from Meyer Lansky himself, but it didn't last. In the end, she dumped me for turdy Eric Kaiserbaum, whose family was Kayser Hosiery and who showed up at a Purim party with a Haman costume from F.A.O. Schwartz.

I took some lumps, too, in seventh grade when, foolishly, I became entangled with Dory Silverman, a brilliant pianist who took lessons from a woman who had once taught Leonard Bernstein. We went hot and heavy for a couple of months, and after the time we had, on impulse, dashed into Kresge's and bought rings to exchange, I took it for granted that I would be her date at the annual Tavern on the Green party thrown by Dory's piano teacher. Suddenly, though, everything fell apart. In the lunchroom one noon Dory slid in beside me, offered me half her peanut butter and jelly sandwich, and told me it was over. She had decided, she said, that our relationship was a mistake, that she had not known that I couldn't carry a tune, and that she was really in love with Charlie Bardoff, the zit-faced concertmaster of the school orchestra who caked himself with acne cream before every performance and who, according to rumors, had already been spotted by scouts for the Philharmonic.

The doctor thought that these setbacks had something to do with what happened later and with my having become involved with Cara, but I don't think so. As far as I am concerned, my having met her was a matter of the purest chance. It happened at the Harmon football field on a gray Friday in October when we were playing Ryder, a prep school from Brooklyn with Manhattan pretentions who, to beef up its line, imported two- hundred-pound ringers from public schools in New Jersey and Long Island. Cara should not have been in the stands that day. She hated football, and even at Finley, her own school, rarely attended a game. She had come over from Finley to our side of the hill as an act of loyalty to her boyfriend who, at the time, was modeling for *Redbook*. The magazine was doing a piece on fall fashions, wanted photos of blond, waspy Ken Masters in Scottish sheepskin, and chose Harmon with its stately buildings rising just behind the grandstand as the location for the shoot.

As for me, my being on the field was a pure case of wishful thinking on the part of our coach. Although as part of my neurosis I had been playing at football for years, I had never achieved the stardom that at the age of twelve was predicted for me. At that time I was co-captain with Duke Shulz, a ferocious Bronco Nagurski-type, of the Cavaliers, an afterschool sport group to which, as a city kid, I was sent to get fresh air. We played our games at Van Cortlandt Park, the vast expanse of meadow at the foot of the Riverdale hills against teams composed mostly of neighborhood West-Siders, outfitted like their doormen, in half uniforms. Since I was a fast runner and in other sports a good athlete, they designated me tailback in our single wing attack. We had no set plays, but when we took possession of the ball, Marv Kraus, our lanky quarterback who stood over five feet tall and had a release as quick as Sammy Baugh's, would size up the opposing team through an opening left discreetly in our huddle and give one of us the nod.

I lived in dread of carrying the ball and tried to avoid Marv's eyes, but when he spotted a weakness in the defensive flank and a chance to sweep an end, I usually got the call. At the snap from center

I was already on the move, heading for the sidelines with a sprinter's
speed and keeping my free arm at the ready to stave off the ultimate
danger, a helmet in the groin. Terror gave me wings, and sometimes I
could turn the corner and chalk up a substantial gain: Often, though,
I'd be trapped by a fleet-footed linebacker, who, spotting my give-away
glances as we shifted into formation, had diagnosed the play. Then,
out of panic, I would reverse fields, dash like a Broadway purse-
snatcher for the opposite side, and look for someone I could lateral to.
Against the Rangers, a group of predominantly Riverside Drive kids,
we set a team record, pulling off a quintuple lateral on a single play,
and though we ended up losing five yards, we gained a reputation for
razzle-dazzle.

Perhaps it was my success with the Cavaliers—in my last
game for them I not only scored on a seven-yard sweep around left end
but, in a play that became the talk of the league, added the extra point
with an unprecedented plunge off tackle—that motivated me to go out
for football in high school. The idea, though, of my actually carrying
the ball against teams like Fordham Prep and All Hallows, whose
squads were manned by bigger and stronger editions of the Irish
toughs who used to fall on us in Riverside Park, pummel us for having
killed Christ, and steal our football, was too alarming even to dream
about and I switched my position to wide—very wide—receiver.

Since, as it turned out, my skills were pretty much limited to
speed of foot and a couple of shifty moves that I had learned as a
matter of survival, I never rose beyond the mediocre—and for a senior
rather shameful—status of a junior varsity player. Until that last
year. Then, three weeks into the season, the two varsity ends went
out with injuries and, desperate for bodies, the coach summoned me to
his office, handed me a varsity jersey, and told me that I would be
starting the next game against our arch rival, the Ryder School.

At Harmon this caused something of a hubbub. The sports
editor wrote that my elevation recalled the rise from obscurity of Don
Hutson, the great Green Bay Packer end. Ron Stedman, an arts
columnist, likened the opportunity I had been given to an understudy
walking on for the great Maria Callas. In the hallways and
classrooms I kept a low profile, assuming an air of nonchalance, and

pretending to be untouched by the sudden glare of publicity. When alone, though, I felt a pitch of excitement that threatened at any moment to spill over into palpitations. All that had happened seemed quite incredible, the plot of a dime store novel, but as I dressed for the game the reality of the situation bore in on me. When we lined up against Ryder I would be at the left end position. There was no escape now. My destiny, which had begun innocently enough in the bosom of the Cavaliers, was spinning itself out now in a test of fire.

As soon as the P.A. announcer called out my name, a responsive cheer arose from the crowd, half encouragement, half derision, such as greets a utility infielder when, after sitting out a hundred games, he finally takes the field.

As I positioned myself for the kick-off, hands on knees, weight forward, I wondered how it can happen that a nightmare can slip away from its dream moorings and enter our lives and, for the first time since I left Ruven's temple, I found myself looking skyward and mouthing an appeal for safekeeping to whoever was up there.

Whether it was because I was embarrassed by this weakness and afraid that spectators in the stands could see it, or whether I somehow intuited that against my wishes my father had decided to drive up to Harmon and had slipped into the stands, I was never sure, but quite suddenly I felt impelled to turn my head and look at the crowd.

Problems with my father had been going on for a long time but had come to a head that morning when he announced that he was planning to come to the Ryder game, to be there for my varsity debut. This I did not want to happen. First of all, just knowing that he was in the stands, watching me, evaluating my performance, would make me uptight and put additional stress on my marginal talents—the last thing I needed that day.

Besides, at that point I felt angry at my father, angry and saddened by the distance that had developed between us. When I was small he was my hero, the pioneer from far off Canada who as a gusty teenager came to New York, made his way alone, and eventually built himself a business. Besides he knew people—actually had friends— who had joined the famous Royal Canadian Mounties and were in on the capture of dangerous criminals. As I grew older, though, I came to see that he was a dreamer, someone whose intriguing schemes evaporated with the morning light.   And his head-in-the-clouds approach to life was a source of endless aggravation to my mother.

Not only was his hardware supply business sinking fast under the weight of his all-thumbs management style, but the IRS was threatening prosecution for an unpaid, and ignored, tax bill.   In typical fashion, my father's plan to solve these problems, one that for months became the subject of nightly dinnertime lectures, was to launch a line of two-spout kitchen faucets.

"It's revolutionary," he declared, "right up there with anything your Mr. Edison could come up with. Just think, two spouts to do dishes. A couple of pots filled from the sink before you could say Jack Robinson. Wait. You'll see. In a year every housewife in Brooklyn will be after her hubby to get one."

When he carried on that way, my mother would just look at me and say nothing, but the meaning of that look was clear. She'd heard that kind of talk for years and she had come to regard my father's moneymaking schemes to be about as realistic as a Coney Island huckster's pitch for a cure-all tonic.

She was critical of him as a parent, too.

"He loves it that you are a ballplayer," she said.   "It's his favorite topic at the corner bar. He can't stop talking about his boy who just made varsity. But try asking him for a few bucks for a piece of equipment or something, and you'll soon find out just how far his interest goes."

On that score I did not know what to believe. I suspected that what my mother said was true, but this was not an idea I wanted to test out. I did not want any more disappointments, any more hurt, at the hands of my father. I still had hope, in fact, often daydreams, that we'd return to what we were, to the buddies we'd been. But these days his private worries—despite his insistence that everything was shipshape, I sensed that he himself feared that all would come crashing down—caused him to lose himself in fanciful schemes, in money making ideas that never came to earth.

When we had company, he would come alive—he liked to play the genial host—but otherwise he either kept to himself and perused trade magazines or was on the phone exhorting one or another of his ineffectual salesmen to contact one more prospect. For a couple of years I tried to get him to take me to ballgames or even to the park for a catch, but he put me off so often with excuses about work that had to be done or bills paid that I finally gave up. Occasionally, though—it happened maybe once or twice a year—he would surprise me with tickets to a Giants game. Then we would take the subway to the Polo Grounds and sit side by side in the bleachers. But we didn't talk much—I suppose we didn't know what to say to each other—and although I tried, I never could quite overcome the hurt I felt over the months of disappointments that preceded these sporadic attempts to reach out. Probably because my resentment grew with each fresh disappointment, over the years I came to adapt my mother's distrust of my father. I became suspicious that the overtures he made toward me—from time to time he would come into my room and try to start a conversation about our team's prospects or about a game that we'd just played—were insincere and that, as my mother claimed, he was using me to puff himself up. So I kept my distance, and although I understood that he was making an effort to be closer to me, I remained wary.

When he heard about the promotion I'd received, I knew that he'd want to be present for my varsity debut, but the thought of his sitting in the stands, watching my every move, just made me too nervous.

"I don't think you ought to come, Dad," I said. "Just knowing you are there throws me off. I don't want to have to worry about that."

"Not to worry," my father replied. "Worry is the last thing you should have from your father. If you don't want to see me, it's no problem. I can be strictly incognito. This I know how to do. Believe me, you wouldn't even know that I am in the house. And this judging business is another thing not to worry yourself about. I don't judge. This you should know. Whatever happens, I'm proud."

"I appreciate that, Dad," I replied, "but I'd rather you not come. Maybe another day."

He heard me, but I wasn't sure he'd listened. I didn't put it past him to convince himself that I didn't mean what I said, that it was really my mother speaking. And it would be like him to tell himself that a boy needed his father at a big game, needed his support, and that he owed it to me to make the trip up to Harmon.

As I scanned the stands looking for a familiar bald head, I saw that the crowd was composed mostly of Harmon students in a Friday afternoon celebratory mood; ties loosened, jackets open or shed entirely, and spread haphazardly on the wooden benches. Some sported maroon and white banners or Harmon buttons larger than a coat lapel, sold by a vendor with an overflowing wicker basket who, like a genie, appeared mysteriously at our games. Scattered in the stands were perhaps a dozen young women, primarily girlfriends and relatives of the players, but also including a cluster of adventurous spirits from Finley who came over to Harmon to meet boys. There were a number of pretty faces in the crowd, but my eyes were drawn to one—a girl in the first row with rust-auburn hair, an animated manner, and from what I could see, a distinctly Hepburn profile. She was holding on to the arm of a jaunty Alan Ladd type who, as I watched, leaned over and nibbled popcorn from her hand. There was something about that scene that disturbed me—Mel said that it called up atavistic memories of Dory Silverman feeding pieces of bologna sandwich to Charlie Bardoff—and until I was brought back to the moment by Jim Conway, the assistant coach, who barked at me from the sidelines that if I preferred to sit in the stands he could get me a ticket, I kept turning my head to look at that couple.

Even after the whistle had blown, Lenny Stein had gotten off his usual shaky line drive, and I was charging downfield in pursuit of the ball, I found it hard to clear my mind. Pictures of the girl, like after-images, played in front of me, her elegant profile, her bright laughter as she scooped a handful of popcorn, the open unselfconscious way that she rested her head against her boyfriend's shoulder; I could not rid myself of these images.

Lenny's kick sailed low and struck a Paul Bunyan of a lineman in the chest. It bounced off his pads, was juggled by meaty hands, and fell to the ground. Like a pirouetting elephant, the giant whirled, pawed at the bouncing pigskin, and, managing finally to snatch it from the turf, shoveled it towards a green-shirted figure that suddenly appeared beside him. It was Schneiderman himself, Ryder's shifty halfback, with moves like Tuffy Leeman, who took the toss. Weaving his way along a seam between converging bodies, he scooted forward for a dozen yards. Then, coming up against a wall of maroon jerseys, he made a quick cut to the outside. In front of him a fierce brontosaurus-like creature, breathing smoke in the cold air, ran interference and looked for someone to devour. As I moved in from my flank position, sizing up the action and hoping to arrive in time for the pile-up, the dragon spotted me. Lowering his helmet and making a straight run for the groin, he charged. I saw him coming, braced myself and shifted into the interference-repellent stance that I had been taught and that I had practiced in front of my bedroom mirror all week, feet firmly planted, weight forward, arms extended and wrists flexed. In my head I heard the coach's voice barking out instructions like Pat O'Brien playing Knute Rockne, keep on your feet; fight off the blocker; turn the play to the inside.

What happened after that I'm not sure. Mel said that from the sidelines it looked as though I had tried at the last moment to avert the block with a matador-like pivot, had lost my footing, and had hit the turf like an axed steer. I recall only feeling a sharp pain in the rump as I struck the ground, hearing thundering hoof beats passing overhead, and catching a glimpse of Schneiderman's back as he sped past me and turned up-field. When the whistle blew, Ryder had the ball on our forty-yard line where Schneiderman, swinging wide to avoid a kamikaze lunge by Lenny Stein, had stepped out of bounds.

Our coach's reaction to the play was swift. Before I could get to my feet, Wally Buckstein, a tangled-foot klutz who rushed the passer like Grandma Moses and who had been diagnosed by specialists as a closet case of Down syndrome, was on the field grinning his mongoloid smile and waving me to the sidelines. I was out of the game.

The coach said nothing as I passed him on the way to the bench, but he looked at me with the scorn of Vince Lombardi sizing up a free agent from Yeshiva University. I knew what he was thinking, that faced with combat, at the point of taking a hit, I had chickened out. I imagined him cursing himself for putting me in the lineup, for being fool enough to think that I was varsity material, and for not listening to Brad Greenfield, our inside linebacker who, after watching me play defense in practice, had suggested a quick option to the Chess Club.

I wanted to protest, to defend myself, to point out that the latest Movietone Newsreel showed a clip of Mel Heine, the Giants' all-league center, employing the same maneuver that I had used and that my problem was not guts, but footwork. I said nothing, though, and for what seemed like endless time, I sat alone at the far end of the bench, wrapped in misery and feeling the dead weight of despair.

What hurt most was the knowledge that I had let the team down. The players, the student body, even the coaching staff had hoped that, despite marginal talent and a Gandhi-like aversion to physical aggression, I might yet rise to the occasion.

As I sat staring at a patch of cleat-scuffed grass, an image of the grandstands behind us and of the people who had witnessed my ineptitude rose up to torment me. Beneath the helmet that I still wore to hide my face, I could feel a fresh wave of heat color my cheeks. I found myself hoping against hope that my father had not shown up, that he had listened to me and not been present to see my shameful performance.

If he was seated in the stands, attired in his Hickey-Freeman topcoat, accompanied by Arnie Sugarman, company treasurer, who, during the football season, fancied himself a scout for the Giants, what could he be thinking? I feared that in his mind I would be finished, relegated to that bottom-of-the-heap compartment that he reserved for buffoons and has-beens, and which housed the likes of Maxie Baer, two-ton Tony Galento, Senator Bilbo of Mississippi, and Napoleon "Nap" Reyes, the Havana Hurricane, who handled ground balls like Toots Shor and who, in an act of sheer perversity, the Giants had installed at third base.

In the tumult that followed the opening play, I had forgotten about the girl in the stands who had sparked my tachycardia, but now an image of her floated in front of me like a close-up on a movie screen. I saw her laughing, snuggling close to her snooty-looking boyfriend and, with her free hand, feeding him popcorn, like Hepburn in bed with Tracy. I winced. What must someone like this pretty, vivacious, quintessentially East-Sider have made of my buffoonery? I pictured her bursting into laughter at my pratfall, then, catching herself, quickly covering her mouth to conceal her mirth. No doubt she thought me a clown, a junior varsity Buster Keaton, plucked from that sorry squad and installed at left end as some kind of perverse practical joke.

Before the kick-off as we stretched and pranced in front of the crowd, I pictured meeting the young Hepburn after the game. In this scenario I haul in the winning pass with twenty seconds on the clock and we come from behind to win by two points.

As I trot to the sidelines, mobbed by a throng of students, I spot her. She has come down to the field to join in the celebration. For an instant our eyes meet and she nods. It is the slightest of contact, the barest movement of her head, but that moment has meaning. A connection is made, and the two of us know that somewhere, perhaps across a crowded dining room at Tip Toe Inn or on line for smoked fish at Barney Greengrass, the Sturgeon King, we will meet again.

Sitting head in hands on the bench now, and recalling that fantasy, I felt doubly foolish. Doubtless by now, with less than a minute left in the first quarter, the girl had completely forgotten me. Or, if she remembered anything, it would be an image of the comedian, Number 86, feinting left, spinning right, and hitting the ground like a wet turd; an image that, despite her Park Avenue breeding and Finley-girl manners, would surely evoke fresh chuckles. There was no question now of my meeting her. I did not dare. Although sitting on the bench I had made a point of keeping my back to the stands and my helmet on, I feared that she might still recognize me.

My only chance for redemption was to get back in the game. Since he had given me the hook, the coach had not so much as glanced in my direction. He was putting the freeze on me, letting me rot in solitary as punishment for making him look to be about as shrewd a judge of talent as Horace Stoneham, the mad Giant owner, himself.

My only hope, I reasoned, was to put a whammy on Buckstein, give him the evil eye, and, using body English from my spot on the bench, somehow psyche him out of the game.

At that point the score was 7-0 in favor of Ryder, Schneiderman having scored on a slashing run off tackle, and now they were threatening to score again. With Schneiderman toting the ball on his hip like flashy Glenn Davis, they moved inside our fifteen on two back-to-back drives and only a fumbled snap from center and a tipped pass leading to an interception prevented another score.

Now I concentrated on Buckstein and used whatever spells I could remember, voodoo chants learned from our Haitian maid, mouthed silently so the coach would not hear, a special stare, baleful and menacing, taught to me by my grandmother who used it to put a *K'en a hora,* an evil eye, on the next-door neighbors, *chutzpahniks* who had bought themselves a Cadillac Eldorado.

Buckstein got called for two penalties in a row and the last one, for grabbing Schneiderman's jersey in a futile attempt to keep him from racking up a big gain, blew his mind. He rushed the referee and if Marc Baum, our outside linebacker, hadn't managed to pin him to the ground and sit on his head, the nitwit might have done serious damage. Still the coach did not pull him and I became alarmed that my spells seemed not to be working. On the very next play though, trying to put a bear hug on Schneiderman, the galoot stumbled, fell over himself, and could not get up. He lay on the ground like a sick porpoise, the sudden victim of a pulled hamstring. Stu Fencher, the sophomore manager, who had taken Red Cross and doubled as team trainer, ran onto the field and after a quick examination, declared Buckstein *hors de combat.* Now Martin had no choice. Without looking back at me, he barked my name. I leaped up and started for the field, giving both coaches a wide berth as I headed for the huddle.

"Don't forget to report to the referee, Brains," Conway called out after me and, as an echo, Coach Martin added, "And don't let me see any of your artsy-fartsy maneuvers." I was stung. My ears burned. I hoped that no one in the stands had heard him. It took no skill to translate that remark. The coach regarded me as the next thing to a fairy—a Jewish wide receiver. In those days the Harmon student body was predominantly Jewish, and although he never came out openly and said so, it was clear that Martin was less than enthusiastic about coaching a squad of boys, all of whom had the latest protective gear from Davega and all of whom wanted to play quarterback. More than once I heard him muttering in the locker room, asking the Good Lord for a switch to Fordham Prep, and one time, confiding to a visiting colleague, he likened being a football coach at Harmon to leading a platoon of Italian infantrymen.

I worried that the opening play had confirmed his view of me as one of those Jewish non-contact types for whom the tough head-to-head combat of football brings out the essential mama's boy. Thinking like that made me mad, and as I lined up in my crouch, my eyes on the quarterback, watching his hands for signs of the snap, I mouthed epithets at the coach for harboring such ideas. The opposing tackle, who stood six-foot-three, weighed two-thirty, and was nicknamed Stretch for his ability to cause opposing linemen to be carried out on stretchers, thought I was uttering curses at him. He shifted his weight in my direction, lowered his helmet, and muttered a bone chilling threat.

"You are going to eat those words, Number 86," he growled.

I knew then that I was in for real trouble.

The next play, an end run, meant the offensive tackle had to clear me out of the way. As the ball was snapped, Stretch raised his hands to his chin, fanned out his elbows like ox handles, and prepared to send me off to Mt. Sinai Hospital. For an instant, as he charged, I was paralyzed. I saw this tank rolling toward me, knew it would crunch me like a field mouse, and could not move.

"Arms out, for Christ sake, Jonathan, fight him." Distantly, like a thin echo from another world, I heard Conway shouting at me. Then, instinctively, without thinking and without knowing what I was doing, I acted. As the monster bore in on me, arms sweeping upward in an effort to decapitate, I grabbed his helmet along both sides, yanked him forward, and executed a leap worthy of a springboard diver that hurtled me over his head. I was clear in the secondary. A guard had pulled on the play, and, along with the fullback, was leading the interference. They headed straight for me with

Schneiderman cradling the football in one arm like Doc Blanchard, gliding three yards behind. I braced myself and held my ground. Then, all at once, I had an idea. Recalling photos I'd seen in *Life* magazine of the human torpedoes that the Japs used against us during the war, I rushed forward and, taking rough aim, flung myself at the feet of the two blockers. I fell short and they nearly jumped over me, but I continued to roll forward and caught their legs. Cut down from below, both fell hard, and the three of us ended up in a tangled heap, with the lineman trying to grind his cleats into my face. Now running unprotected, Schneiderman tucked the ball, put on a burst of speed, and tried to turn the corner. Marc Baum and Manny Fried, our other linebackers, were there, however, and between the two of them, grabbing and pushing, they drove him out of bounds. He had gained only two yards.

"Aw right," Martin called out between cupped hands. "Aw right. That's stripping the interference."

"Let's do it again," Conway added.

The block I'd thrown had knocked the wind out of me and I was just getting to my feet when Schneiderman passed me on his way back to the huddle.

"Neat one," he said. "You are playing us smart, 86. But we are going to have to pay you back for that one."

Ryder huddled and broke quickly, lining up in their usual single wing formation. The quarterback barked signals, but even before the snap I sensed what was coming. They were going to run the same play and this time stuff it down our throats. Watching from the bench, I had seen this pattern. Ryder considered itself a far better team than we, a bit like USC playing Columbia, and they fully expected to grind our noses into the Riverdale dirt. It galled them to be thwarted, even for a play, and when we somehow managed to hold for a down, it was odds on that their quarterback, furious, wanting to stick it to us and admonishing his linemen to kick butt, would come back with the same call.

In urgent need of a fresh strategy, but having none, I crouched down and waited for the onslaught. But then, like a telepathic message sent directly from the brain of stout Steve Owen, coach of the

Giants, I recalled a pro football magazine article in which he described a surprise defensive maneuver that he had taught his linemen.

It struck me that what worked for the Giants ought to work for me. And it did. Feinting to my left as the ball was snapped to get Stretch headed in that direction, I suddenly pivoted, took off toward the opposite side, and slipped past him. Schneiderman had the ball, and coming from behind him as he started around end, I caught him by the jersey. He drove a straight arm to my face, but I hung on, kept pulling, and the two of us went crashing to the dirt.

After the whistle, I stayed down—my head felt like a battered pumpkin—but Schneiderman jumped up, agile and unhurt, and started back toward the huddle. Then, seeing me still on the ground, he stopped, extended a hand, and pulled me to my feet. He seemed to be looking me over, taking my measure. Then he grinned.

"Gutsy playing, Number 86," he said and trotted off.

Schneiderman's words had a strange effect on me. I felt good, as though I'd been pulled to my feet by Coach Martin himself and told that I'd done well. As I walked back to the line, I puzzled over this reaction. Who was this Schneiderman, anyway, I wondered, and why should a remark of his mean anything at all to me? I knew something about him, of course. Whenever anyone spoke of Ryder they spoke first—and last—of Schneiderman. And not only in football. He was a true triple threat athlete, perhaps one of the last of that breed, who played three sports and excelled at all of them.

Until I actually saw him in person, I had imagined Schneiderman to be a big, rangy fellow, six-foot-two or -three and close to two hundred pounds. He wasn't. He was no more than 5'9"— roughly my height—and thin. He was wiry, though, and very fast, and there was something about his body, perhaps its lean toughness, that gave the appearance of strength. In competition he had a quality— no one could define it precisely—that made him dominant. Opponents knew right away that he was the team leader, the one they would have to shut down to have any chance of winning.

Still, for me there was something beyond all this. Schneiderman had become a presence in my mind, someone who, quite irrationally, I thought about a good deal. In basketball, although I'd played against him a few times and pretty well knew his moves, I worried days before a Ryder game that he'd come up with something new, completely outplay me, and make me look like a fool. And knowing that he'd be doing his stuff on the football field that afternoon, carrying the ball and displaying his fancy footwork, I'd had nightmares about him. In my dreams he breezed by me, untouched, out-feinting me and grinning as he headed for the end zone. Outmaneuvered, missing tackles, and falling all over myself, I watched with horror as my face was transformed into a likeness of Buckstein.

I did not know exactly what it was about Schneiderman that made me uneasy, but somehow I found him intimidating. Perhaps it was his combative quality or the fact that he appeared self-confident and brash—the Leo Durocher of our prep school league. I was never quite sure, and even though, on the evidence of what had just happened, he seemed a decent enough guy, I found it difficult to shake this feeling.

Late in the fourth quarter Schneiderman scored again on a slashing run off tackle and Ryder had a two-touchdown lead. They missed the extra point try when their quarterback overthrew a pass, and with three minutes left in the game they led 13-0.

Then, striking suddenly like an Israeli commando squad, we scored. On the kick-off, Mike Sternboch, our return specialist, who took bets in school as a local agent for Jimmy the Greek and had been known, at the sign of an approaching teacher, to cover the thirty yards from the locker room to the john in under two seconds, fielded the kick on the fifteen, stumbled, righted himself, found a crack of daylight between onrushing tacklers, and, racing along the sidelines like a bookie on the lam, crossed the goal line untouched. Lenny Stein's extra point attempt sailed three feet under the bar nearly knocking the glasses off Andy Potsalis, the school janitor, who was repairing a broken drain near the bleachers, and the score was 13-6.

Ryder came on strong, marching to our twelve, but on a critical fourth and two we pulled a safety blitz, sacked the quarterback, and took over on downs. Hank Rudovsky, a reserve tackle whose job it was to be a courier from the bench, appeared in the huddle with instructions from the coaches. We were to go all out. During the weeks we had rehearsed a few new plays, including some tricky stuff for dire emergencies, and now we had the word to start pulling the rabbits out of our hat.

In one of these maneuvers, which we dubbed Sleeping Beauty, I was to play the leading role. Prior to our launching it, my job was to pretend to be injured, drift to the sidelines, and still inbounds, lie down and make myself inconspicuous. Then when the ball was snapped, I would race downfield and be open for a long pass from Goodstein, our quarterback.

After we'd failed on two consecutive running plays, Goodstein drove a stake into my heart by calling for the Sleeping Beauty stunt. In the huddle, he looked at me. "Make it good, Jonathan," he said. "We need this."

We'd gone over that play just once in practice, not believing, I suppose, that we'd ever really use so desperate a maneuver, so I had only the vaguest idea of what to do. If it was my fate to turn into Sleeping Beauty, though, I told myself, I was going to do my best to pull it off.

As our team lined up, I limped toward our bench on the left sideline as though I was leaving the game. My eyes were glazed, my stare vacant. As I reached the edge of the field a few feet from the bench, I stretched out on the ground just inside the playing field.

As I lay there, something caught my eye. I glanced to my left and saw the young Hepburn was standing on the sidelines just a few feet from me. I had no idea why she was there. Most likely it was simply to have a better view of the action, but I couldn't help thinking that maybe she'd had it with the popcorn munching boyfriend and was scouting for new faces.

In any case, when she spotted me on the ground, she turned toward our bench, started waving her arms, and pointed toward me. She thought I was injured and could not get up. Desperately, I started making shooshing sounds, and when I caught her eye, raised my head and put a warning finger to my lips. For a moment she seemed confused. Then, understanding, she nodded and put an answering finger to her own lips.

We had made contact and, more than that, we had formed a silent pact. That seemed an omen, a sign, that somehow, in some way, the two of us were linked.

Now I strained to hear the count. At a distance I could see Goodstein crouching over the center, his head turning left and right as he scanned the defense and barked out the signals. I listened for seventy-two, the snap number, and when I heard him call it and saw him begin to back pedal, I took off. I sprinted down the sideline for thirty yards and then looked over my shoulder. Pressured by two elephantine linemen, Goodstein was rolling left and trying to find throwing room. Just as his pursuers closed in and he was about to be driven out of bounds, he stopped, whirled and let the ball go. The pass was high, flying skyward in my general direction, but it was a fluttery toss, a last ditch *brucha* heave, and I could see that it was going to come down short. Keeping one eye on the ball, and maneuvering to get under it, I tried with the other to scan the field. Someone was streaking towards me. I could not see who it was, but I didn't have to. I knew it would be Schneiderman. Caught off guard, he had not spotted me until I was well down field and in the clear. Now he closed in, covering ground like a rocket launched from the Ryder secondary. I looked up, hoping against hope that the ball would reach me before Schneiderman did. At the same time, I was terrified that if I did make the catch, the guy would put a hit on me that would send me straight to an orthopedic unit.

The ball descended, struck me in the chest, and desperately, like a wino grabbing a handout, I clutched it. I was facing up field, toward the passer, and now, hugging the ball to my gut, I pivoted and started to drive forward. As I did, a rocket struck, ripped into my midsection, and smashed me, like an iron spike, into the ground. I hit, bounced, and hit again. My elbows and forearms landed hard against what in the baseball season was the infield dirt. The football squirted loose. Stretching an arm from beneath Schneiderman, who was sprawled on top of me, I tried to pull it back under me. I could not quite reach far enough to grasp the ball, though, and I managed only to poke at it. It began to roll toward the pitcher's mound. Schneiderman spotted the loose ball and tried to go after it. Our arms and legs were tangled and I could feel him pushing away, trying to free himself. Sprawled on the ground, flattened beneath him, I knew that if he broke loose, he'd make the recovery.

There was only one thing that I could do. As Schneiderman tried to get to his feet, I reached behind me, grabbed what I could, and held on. I had gotten hold of a piece of jersey just above the waist, my hand hidden beneath the thrashing of limbs. At first Schneiderman seemed not to realize what was holding him back. He bucked and wriggled, trying to rise and dart forward. Then he spotted my hand. He cursed—one of the few curses I'd ever heard him utter—and with a quick karate chop that I thought had broken my wrist, freed himself from my grip. Then he was up and moving. Tracking the football, which had hit the rubber, bounded back in our direction, and was rolling end over end, Schneiderman threw himself on it. I had gained my feet and was a step behind. Schneiderman's body covered the ball, which disappeared beneath him. He had recovered the fumble. I saw this and, instantaneously, the flash thought occurred to me that the game was over; Schneiderman had beaten me out. Then, without thinking, propelled by something inside, I dove, helmet first. I landed on top of my opponent, my helmet catching him at an angle between his shoulder and jaw. I heard a crack, bone on hard plastic, and his head dropped to the side. The ball did not come free. It remained out of sight, hidden by his body. He did not move.

The referee ran over, waved his arms, and blew his whistle. The play was called dead as players from both sides, pushing and jostling, surrounded us. Tapping me on the shoulder, the official gestured for me to get up as he reached in between us and searched, like a ferret, for the ball. Finding it beneath Schneiderman and pulling it free, he turned towards the stands, indicated that Ryder had taken possession, and pointed toward our goal, signaling that it was first and ten for the visiting team.

When, after a few seconds, Schneiderman did not get to his feet and seemed scarcely to move, the Ryder trainer and two coaches ran onto the field. They turned him over, knelt to look at his eyes, and then pulled at his waistband to loosen the pressure around his midsection. I stood to the side, scared and numb, able to see only the

backs of the crouching figures. After another minute, Schneiderman
rose slowly to his feet, shook his head several times as though trying
to knock out cobwebs, and then, refusing assistance, trotted off the
field to applause from the scattering of students left in the stands. As
he passed me, he raised his head and looked straight into my face.

"You like to play rough," he said. I said nothing. I could think
of nothing to say. Later, my head filled with replies that I could have
made: It takes one to know one. The kettle's calling the pot black,
original quips like that, but at the time nothing came. In thirty
seconds the game was over. Like an old pro running out the clock and
not wanting to risk a fumble, the Ryder quarterback took the snap and
immediately fell to the ground, clutching the football to him like a
newborn baby. By the time he rose, called another huddle, and lined
up behind the center, time had run out. Roger Spencer, the math
teacher who doubled as official timekeeper and was holding a
stopwatch inches from his nose, fired a cap pistol on the sidelines to
signal that the end had come.

I headed for the bench, moving slowly and loosening my helmet
strap, but keeping my head gear on. As I approached the sideline,
Coach Martin brushed past me on his way across field to play the good
sportsman and congratulate his opposite number. He looked straight
through me and said nothing. This didn't surprise me. What was
there to say? Schneiderman had hit me and I had not been able to hold
on. More than anything, I wanted to do well and had ended up the
goat. As a kid, I couldn't imagine what it was like to be Mickey Owen,
whose bonehead play cost the Dodgers the '42 World Series. Now I
knew.

I thought again of the girl and the view she must have now of
klutsy Number 86. Having come down to the field from the stands,
she'd had a good look at my goof, the way I managed to botch Sleeping
Beauty and hand the game to Ryder. I was tempted to look around for
her, try to catch her expression, and see if my worst fear had come
true; that the connection we'd made, signaled by a shared glance, a
momentary meeting of the eyes, had been shattered by her
disappointment in me. But I did not dare. I was not prepared to
absorb another blow.

Instead, I avoided all eyes and walked straight to the water bucket where I managed to hide my head for a few minutes. Finally, when the bench was clear, I headed for the lockers, waited until the shower room had emptied out before ducking under the water, and then dressed as quickly as I could. Mel awaited me outside. He fell into step with me and we walked in silence across the field. Finally he spoke, first clearing his throat like a nervous frog.

"You made three tackles and had two assists," he began. "Not bad for a rookie in his first game."

I said nothing.

"Actually you turned in a very creditable performance," he persisted. "Everyone expected Schneiderman to run all over you, but you held your ground. You gave as good as you got."

"Forget it, Mel, will you?" I protested. "I fumbled and Schneiderman recovered. That was the ball game." Mel had no ready reply.

"True," he finally said, "but who could take a hit in the *kishkes* like you got and hold on to a football? It's not a physiological reaction. When a person takes a shot in the guts, the hands automatically spread out to protect the intestines. Just watch next time some little old lady gets zonked by a yellow cab. You'll see what I mean. It's an instinctual reaction."

"A receiver's job is to hold on to the ball," I snapped, "even if he's hit by a Mack truck."

"That's jock talk," he snapped back. "Pure jock lingo, straight out of some boot camp manual. Brutes who talk like that have left the human race long ago. They couldn't hack it as people. They've become bison and rhinos, thick-skinned critters with hides that can stop bullets, and they want everyone to follow suit." We were starting down the long hill to the subway. I didn't answer. Mel made one more try.

"Don't forget that some of the greatest names in football had off days," he said. "Did you know that in 1933 Sid Luckman fumbled on the three yard line against Princeton and in '36 Ken Strong dropped a touchdown pass that cost the Giants the championship?"

I was not going to be assuaged.

"I don't care," I said. "I blew it. We would have had the ball on the fifteen, with a chance to win it."

Mel shook his head.

"Not likely," he replied. "Not with Schneiderman in there. In the last quarter he was cutting up our line like it was made of Junket. The only way we could have beaten them was if you had finished the job and broken his skull."

"I probably should have done just that," I muttered half aloud. We were at the bottom of the hill now, across from Benny's, a hole in the wall luncheonette, where we often got sodas to fortify us for the long trip home. Mel put a hand on my shoulder and leaned close to me. "Jimmy the Greek made Ryder a ten point favorite," he said. "We beat the odds and I made a few bucks. Come on in and I'll buy you an egg cream."

"Thanks, Mel," I said. "I just don't feel up to it right now."

He nodded and started into the store. At the threshold, he stopped and looked back.

"Are you upset about your dad?"

"What?"

"His being there. At the game."

"What are you talking about?"

"You didn't see him? He came in just after the kickoff with that Oliver Hardy character he hangs out with."

"I had no idea."

"Yeah. Most of the game they were standing alongside the bleachers at the far end of the stands, pretty much out of sight."

Mel's words struck me like a blindside tackle. I felt shocked; shocked and angry. My first thoughts were of my father's obstinacy and his insistence on going behind my back and having his own way. I had told him plainly not to come, that I didn't need anything to add to my nervousness—I already feared that I'd end up playing like Buckstein on pot—but no doubt telling himself that despite what I'd said, in the end I'd be glad that he made the effort to show up, he had simply disregarded my wishes. And he had been rewarded, not only by seeing his son give away the game, but by witnessing a performance that, around our league, made me a choice contender for goat of the year.

"Lucky you didn't see him," Mel put in. "If you had spotted him in the crowd, you probably would have developed a lot worse case of fumbleitis."

I winced, and seeing that his words stung, Mel tried to assuage me.

"You know, J, your dad's a big fan of yours, during the game I overheard him talking to his sidekick. He was singing your praises, describing all your good moves."

"With fans like that, I don't need Schneiderman to knock me on my ear."

Mel then reached out and touched my arm.

"Go home and get some sleep, Jonathan," he said. "You need to forget everything for a while. I'll call you later."

I climbed the steep stairs to the subway platform and boarded .a train that waited with doors open to begin the long trip to Manhattan. Alone in the car except for a prune-faced woman whom I recognized as a Finley Latin teacher, I slumped into a seat, and out of a mix of depression and exhaustion, dozed off. Dreaming of jousts and tournaments and gladiators being hacked to the ground, I did not stir until, like a sleeper responding to an inner time clock, I came to at the 96th Street station. Making a run for the doors as they began to shut, I managed to hold them open and squeeze through. Then, with the practiced hand of a veteran straphanger, I pulled my book bag free before they could close on it.

Chapter Two

For weeks after spotting the girl in the stands, and especially after what happened the night of the game, I asked myself, how long does it take for such a person, or, in this case, two new people, to dismantle your world?

For me it was a matter of minutes, twenty-one to be exact, which I calculated this way: a total of two minutes—with Coach Martin watching my every move I didn't dare take a second more—stealing glances at the girl between plays; a nine-minute live encounter with her that very night and, for shock value—this was right up there with spotting Bacall buying toothpaste at Walgreens—ten minutes of conversation with young Durocher himself.

For hours after the game, flash images of the Finley girl's face played in front of my eyes and each picture set off a burst of palpitations. I worried that my preoccupation with the girl, whoever she was, could be damaging to my health, but Mel reassured me that biology doesn't work that way.

"The immune system is not only about bugs," he said. "It guards against any kind of foreign substance, even if it's from your grandstand Garbo. Immunologically speaking, your Miss Finley is a newcomer, a stranger at the gates, a potential invader. Right now your T cells are on the move, defending the home turf and keeping the lady at bay. By my calculations you've got about a month before she sets up shop in your *kishkes* and starts real trouble."

Even though what Mel said made sense and came from reliable sources—he was a long-time subscriber to *Scientific American*—I felt in my guts that this time he was off base.

This was not about science. It was about mystery, magic, the making of miracles. How else can you explain that combination, that magical amalgam; the rust-red hair of Rita Hayworth, the fresh complexion and dancing eyes of Linda Darnell, and the feistiness of Hepburn herself? Faced with such a creature, an amazing specimen even to the veterans at Central Casting, I felt totally paralyzed, as vulnerable as the kid without antibodies who lives inside a bubble at Mount Sinai.

When you add to that the shocking experience, on a par with encountering Durocher checking out at Zabar's, of finding myself face to face with Schneiderman that very night, it is amazing that it took as long as it did—this one-two punch threatened to put me on the canvas faster than Louis finishing off Two-Ton Tony Galento—for my world to collapse.

That whole night was a total surprise. I expected to go nowhere, to be in bed by nine and, based on the previews I had on the subway ride home, to dream horrible dreams.

The entire trip downtown was a nightmare. The whole way I was tortured by images, agonizing reruns of the play that cost us the game: my fumble after making the catch, Schneiderman falling on the ball, and my final, futile lunge, helmet first, helmet cracking bone, at his curled body. I could not get this scene out of my mind. Each time I replayed it, I was assailed by feelings of remorse known only to the likes of Mickey Owen and Wrong-Way Corrigan.

This was one of my biggest problems. I could never simply write off an error, let it go as an unfortunate mistake. Instead, I held on to every miscue, every bonehead move I ever made. For months on end in ninth grade I tortured myself by endlessly reliving that night of horror with Corky Kravitz when, trying to make out with her at Mel's house, I failed repeatedly to penetrate her crossed arm defense and ended up mired in an armpit.

This trait, this need to claw at myself, came directly from my mother, one of a coterie of left-wing West Side ladies who read *PM*, idolized Max Lerner, held auctions for the Lincoln Brigade, and, over lunch at Schrafft's, plotted the overthrow of Franco.

Feeling as stricken and betrayed by Stalin's flirtation with Hitler as we Giants fans did by the Durocher deal, my mother for years thereafter berated herself for her moment of weakness when, swept away by admiration for the Soviets, she impulsively sent a box of freshly baked rugelach to Uncle Joe himself.

To my surprise, though, when I stretched out on my bed and closed my eyes it was not the game-losing fumble I thought about or the klutzy pratfall, or even the shock of Schneiderman slamming into me like a heat-seeking missile. I thought only of the girl in the stands, of her high-cheeked profile, the elegant swan-like neck, the flowing rust-red hair that, catching the sun, seemed to be tinted with gold, and of the contagious smile, beamed for the moment at a Park Avenue wasp, but raising hopes that it might one day cast its glow on an up-and-coming West-Sider.

What troubled me, and struck at my guts like a sharp right to the breadbasket, was the thought that I might never see her again; that we'd had our one encounter in life as happened when, waiting on Eydie Gorme the summer I clerked at Ben's Florsheim Shoes, I wrapped the sandals she bought, handed her a receipt, and watched her disappear from my life.

What worried me, too, was a long-standing problem of mine— my shyness. I feared that even if the impossible happened and I found myself sitting hip to hip with the girl at a Chock-Full-O-Nuts counter, my inclination would be to turn aside, pretend nonrecognition, and to let the moment pass. Whoever she was—and I imagined that she was part of a wealthy, East Side Finley set whose families ran international companies and golfed at elite country clubs—I felt instinctively that she was out of my league.

This was just the kind of problem—Mel called it inherited inferiority traceable to a fear of the Cossacks—I had been struggling with for years. Just a few months before, at a Knicks game, when Corky Kravitz slipped a hand into my trouser pocket and whispered into my ear that she needed a hot dog, I made a beeline for the refreshment stand and ordered a frank with all the trimmings. And a month before that, at a Harmon mixer, when Myra Herz suggested that we cut out of the dance, head downtown, and park in an empty lot at the Riverside boat basin, I took her up on that idea and, seizing that rare opportunity to indulge my passion, lectured her on the fine points of racing sloops, catamarans and day sailors.

Now I worried that if I ever met the girl again at a Finley mixer or some such event, my embarrassment would be such that I simply could not speak; that if I tried, I would be about as articulate as Harpo on a blind date and would end up making as big an ass of myself as I did in the Ryder game.

The thought that she might recognize me, might remember Number 86 toting the football like Chaplin juggling a hot plate, and behind cupped hands break into a poorly concealed chuckle, was simply too much to bear.

And I realized, too, that even if I employed a disguise and tried to pass myself off as a chess club nerd, complete with yesterday's smelly shirt, sooner or later my cover would be blown and Miss Finley would find me out. Then the game would be over; she'd want nothing to do with me. Although one always hears about forgiveness—the need to forgive and forget—the sad truth is that goats—big time goats—are never really forgiven. History will bear me out on that.

Nearly ten years after dropping the third strike on Tommy Heinrich, Mickey Owen had his bathing trunks ripped off by Dodger fans at Coney Island, and the year before that, more than two decades after the fact, Charlie Root, the star-crossed Cub pitcher who fed a historic home run ball to Babe Ruth, was assaulted in a Chicago men's room for daring, after so cruelly letting the Cub fans down, to show his pecker in public.

Under these circumstances I thought it best to lay low, come down with a disabling case of intestinal flu, and stay away from Harmon for a couple of days. I knew, too, that at all costs I had to avoid reading the *Hilltopper*, the muckraking school newspaper that assailed our losing teams with the zeal of the *Daily Worker* taking on General Motors.

Managing to stay home, however, would require some careful planning. The next morning I would have to appear sick enough to persuade my mother that I needed to remain in bed and not so sick that she would send for Dr. Bass, the Benjamin Spock of the Upper West Side who, within seconds, would expose me as a malingerer.

At that time Mel was into subliminal perceptions and he devised a plan to influence my mother by means of covert communications.

"She'll never know what hit her," Mel said. "Before you know it she'll have you tucked up and in bed with strict orders to stay put for at least two days.

"What you need to do," Mel added, "is to create certain links in your mother's mind. First thing tomorrow morning you complain of stomach cramps. Then, casually, in the next sentence, you throw in the phrase, the people's virus, such as 'this stomach flu has gotten to be so common it's practically become the people's virus.' Unconsciously a connection will be activated in your mother's mind, she will associate you with the suffering Soviet population and treat you like a casualty from the Battle of Leningrad."

Although I had some question as to the effectiveness of this approach—in recent years my mother had become quite ambivalent about Moscow—I said nothing. I did not want to start an argument with Mel, and, in any case, I had to contend with a more immediate problem. My father had come home, and now, at the dinner table, I would have to look into the face of someone who had been witness to my shameful performance.

It was not that I feared his criticism. On the contrary, I knew that if he mentioned the game at all he would find something to praise. Focusing on some minor success of mine, perhaps on the play in which I caught Schneiderman from behind and hung on to his shirttails, he would cling to that bright pearl of memory and explore its every facet like a jeweler appraising an heirloom. In fact he did pretty much that.

"I came to your school today," he began when we were at dinner, "but you didn't notice, you didn't see anything, isn't that right? Your first time with the A-team, this I didn't want to miss, but the whole time we stood in the back. Sugarman came, too, but I told him right up front that we could not sit. 'If Jonathan spots us in the stands, this could cause a lot of aggravation,' I told him. 'Something like that can go straight to the *kishkes*, we have to be strictly invisible.'"

I just looked at my father and said nothing. I didn't have to; my silence spoke for itself.

"You played one hell of a game," he went on. "Sugarman said so, too. The way you took down those Ryder blockers, my God that was a sight. Just took their legs right out from under them. Where did you ever learn something like that? And that catch of yours. Right in the open. When I saw that ball in the air and you out there alone, I told Sugarman to pray because only a pro could catch such a ball. But you did it and you made a big gain."

"I fumbled, Dad," I said, "and we lost because of me."

My father shrugged. "It was your first time with the A-Team," he said. "Next game, you'll see, will be a different story."

There was nothing more I could say to him. This was my father. He couldn't—wouldn't—face anything negative, any setback, any disappointment. He needed to paste a smiling face over every trouble, every problem he encountered, and this included the big troubles he was having at work.

Although in the past year his business had come apart at the seams, was slipping like an unstoppable mudslide into bankruptcy and, out of pure aggravation, Sugarman had shrunk to under two hundred fifty pounds, my father carried on about Ruth, the bookkeeper, who, despite having fibroids and having to contend with a diabetic mother, had gotten the invoices out on time. The fact that, at that point there were no more than a handful of customers left to bill, the business was fast becoming a mythical entity, and that Seidman, his main competitor, was cutting the legs out from under him, my father never mentioned. These unpleasantries he did not like to think about. Instead, he went on about Ruth's devotion, her bulldog determination, which he compared to Churchill's, to see a task through to the end, and his plans to order in a deli spread and honor her as employee of the year.

When it came to dealing with the IRS, his approach was consistent. For years he had been in trouble over payroll taxes, falling months behind in his payments, and then trying, like Leslie MacMitchell, NYU's ace miler, to make up the ground with a last-minute sprint for the wire. Sometimes he made it, making a payment at the eleventh hour, but in recent months he had come up short.

Reminded in due time of his obligations by the government, my father had been summoned to the Office of the District Chief. Demands were made, dark words spoken, and the specter of indictment and prosecution raised for him to contemplate. To this confrontation he reacted by becoming a devoted fan of his inquisitor.

"He's quite a man, this chief," my father declared when he returned from the IRS office. "A no-nonsense person. He laid out everything, recited all the rules and regulations by heart. This is a man of learning, you can tell. And Jewish. An individual like this is just who we need in the mayor's office. In a couple of weeks, when things get straightened out, I'm going to propose a run for City Hall. And I'll offer my services, offer to help him out. In my business you make quite a few connections."

To such schemes my mother reacted with near psychosis. Raised in marginal poverty, the daughter of a withdrawn man whose habit it was to sit alone in darkened rooms, she was an anxious woman for whom the fantasy of losing everything, of being dispossessed from her home, and of being cast into the world as a street person, constituted an ever-present threat.

That evening my father treated our loss to Ryder like an IRS audit; he acted as though it were a non-event. Describing the incredible open field catch I had made to my mother, he made no mention of the final score or of the fact that I had coughed up the football and handed the victory to Ryder. Realities of that kind were not on his agenda.

He had much to say, however, on other matters. Holding forth like a university lecturer, he instructed my mother and me on a number of centrally important issues, anti-Semitism in the borough of Queens, the cause of enmity between Arab and Jew (at heart they were too much alike), and the fundamentally paranoid nature of the Russian people, a discourse that prompted my mother, like Molotov at the UN, to leave the table.

Although relieved by this clear avoidance of my humiliating goof, I also felt confused and hurt by what seemed to be my father's total indifference to what he knew—must have known—was a painful experience for me. And yet, at the same time, I understood that this was his way of being tactful. He did not want to embarrass me and add to my state of misery by mentioning a game-ending performance that, for sheer ineffectualness was surpassed only by the base running skills of a big Ernie (the schnoz) Lombardi, the Giants' elephantine catcher, who looked, and ran, like Jimmy Durante.

It was not solely for my sake, though, that my father said nothing. For reasons that were never clear to me—perhaps it was because he felt that he had fallen so far short of his own expectations—he carried within him a feeling of shame about himself that quite readily extended to any family members who suffered a setback in life. He never wanted to speak about, or even acknowledge, such troubles.

If he had continued to talk about the game, he would have had to acknowledge in some part of himself that, far from showing signs of becoming that *rara avis*, a Jewish pro-football prospect, his son had actually been the goat, the anti-hero, whose skills resembled, not a varsity lineman, but those of Manny Diaz, the spastic delivery boy with cerebral palsy who, in the Central Park touch football league, was thrown in as wide receiver for the short-handed Carnegie Delicatessen.

I thought of speaking out, of breaking the ice and of forcing my father to face the truth (perhaps as a start to facing other truths), but I could not bring myself to do it. He looked too content at the moment, too secure in his denial, as he tackled the sensitive question of American Jews' support for the anti-Semitic Soviet Union. Instead, I begged off from dessert, made my excuses as an exhausted athlete, and returned to my room.

I was stretched out on my bed with the lights out, trying not to think, when Mel called.

"How are you doing?" he wanted to know. "Have you taken your emergency cyanide pill yet?"

"Not yet. I didn't want Coach Martin to have that much satisfaction."

"Not to worry. He's already gnashing his dentures. Finley has refused the trade. They think that they are getting a bad deal.

Conway tried to sweeten the pot by throwing in Buckstein, but they wouldn't bite."

"There is always the chess club."

"Actually Conway looked into that, but it's no go there either. Steinmetz, their manager, worries that someone with your coordination is liable to trip over his own rook."

"Well I'd better get to the cyanide."

"Have you thought about a headstone inscription? How about something pithy like 'Giving up the ball, he gave up the ghost.'"

"Not bad, but it doesn't quite capture the essence of me."

"You're right. We need something that reflects the complexity of your personality, your despair at not being Don Hutson, and yet your remarkable ability to carry on despite this deep wound. How about something like, 'Although not a Hutson, neither was he Flotsam.'"

"My mother would object to the reference."

"I'm just trying to be appreciative. I have every confidence in you, Jonathan. I have no doubt that in next week's game you will recover every one of your fumbles."

"I'm practicing. Schneiderman has agreed to come by and bat me around for a couple of hours to toughen me up."

"Great idea. The coach will be impressed by your attitude. In another year or two he might let you off the bench."

Mel was silent for a moment. Then his voice turned serious.

"How are you holding up, Jonathan?"

"Okay, I guess. A bit low, I just want to forget this whole stupid afternoon."

"It's not only the game, is it?"

"Not really. I still get spasms in my gut when I picture that football squirting loose and, when I doze off, I dream that my fingers are covered with glue and a football is stuck to them so tightly no one can rip it out. But right now that is not what is bugging me."

"It's the girl in the stands, isn't it?"

"I'm insane, Mel. Certifiable. Could you please call up and reserve me a bed at Bellevue? I keep seeing that face in front of me and her reaching up and pecking at the cheek of that fruitcake she was with. It's pure torture, and the craziest part is that I have no idea who either of them is."

"You are absolutely right, Jonathan. You are mad. There is no doubt that this is early dementia praecox. You have all the signs. Being in love with a phantom is pathognomonic. Whoever she is, this lady is already causing big trouble. Are you sure that you haven't seen her before?"

"Never."

"Not in the subway? Walking on Broadway? On line at Zabar's?"

"Nope."

"Well we've got to do something to relieve your misery. You look as though you just found out the lady has a thing for Buckstein. I'm going to make some calls. Maybe I can find out who she is. I have some good friends at Finley. They may know. She's a blond?"

"Reddish hair; auburn."

"And a distinctly Hepburnish profile?"

"You've got it."

"Okay. You get some sleep. While you are dreaming of her, I'll see what I can come up with."

I tried to stop him. "Forget it, Mel," I said, raising my voice. "I don't want to know. I don't want to know anything about her. I just want to erase this whole lunatic day." But he had already hung up.

I closed my eyes and tried to sleep, but intrusive images; the grandstand, the girl, the wasp boyfriend, Schneiderman motionless on the ground, pressed in on me and kept me awake.

An hour later, almost to the minute, Mel called back.

"Her name is Cara Rosenhaus," he announced, speaking rapidly, in conspiratorial tones, as though he were an undercover agent who'd been getting the low-down on the Nazi super who ran our building.

"She's a junior, plays the flute, and lives on Park in the nineties. The father's got money. He owns a big furniture store in Harlem, the kind that sells a complete living room to *schvatzers* for five hundred bucks, charges twenty percent interest, and repossesses half the *dreck* they sell. He fancies himself a liberal, though. He's a big Democratic fund-raiser and also twists lots of arms for the UJA. As for Cara, she's got a reputation as a live one. She's smart, feisty and opinionated. She's into politics, organizes marches, and does the whole liberal-radical bit. There's an older brother who writes poetry and won't have anything to do with the furniture business. My sources tell me that your gal is ambitious, competes with *frere* Henry to be Daddy's favorite, and will go all out when she wants something. My spies say that she took this mannequin, Ken Masters, away from his long-time girlfriend with a campaign of pure ego massaging. The word on him is he's got looks, a great body, and zero personality. It flatters her to keep him around, but the smart money says that she'll dump him in six months, maybe sooner if *Redbook* gets tired of his *goyisher* puss. Anyway, it's a sure bet that sooner or later this kind of anti-establishment-type will do an about-face, turn against this wasp in sheep's clothing, and look for the opposite; a Woolworth kind of guy like you.

"Besides, with a free spirit like Miss Finley you have a distinct advantage. How many guys would be willing to get out on a football field and act out their wish to be Sleeping Beauty? She'll love the gutsy way that you've come out of the closet."

"I try to be creative, but there weren't too many fans out there today who appreciated my act."

"Nonsense. You've still got plenty of boosters. There's me, your mother, the entire Ryder team, and now this new lady. It's amazing the way you found her. How in the world did you manage to spot the one girl in the crowd who's got a reputation for adopting losers and guys with fumbleitis?"

"It's intuition. One look at that face and I knew that this was someone who had it in her to love a physically challenged wide receiver."

"I get it. Your eyes spotted Hepburn in the stands and your unconscious saw a Salvation Army lady."

"It was the popcorn. The way she fed it to the idiot boyfriend touched a chord."

"Of course. Any woman who can be that nurturing to a tight-ass wasp has got to be a saint. Looks like this time your intuition has zeroed in on a real find."

"Except that she's already been found. The whole game she was climbing all over Mr. Fashion Plate. Obviously she's into him big time. I'll probably never see her again."

"That is exactly the attitude I expected from you. If it were up to you, this entire story would end right now. You would simply give up, not pursue this dream girl of yours, and she would disappear from your life faster than Eydie Gorme vanishing into the crowd on Broadway. Well, this is not going to happen. Not only are you going to see her again, but you are going to see her tonight. In fact, in an hour's time Miss Finley Heartflutter will step out of your dreams and into your sieve-like arms."

"What the hell are you talking about?"

"Just what I said. Knowing that you'd pop cyanide before you'd make a move, I contacted my Finley connections, called in some markers, and got us invited to a Park Avenue party thrown by none other than the infamous Cara Rosenhaus herself. So dig out your best Sears finery and meet me downstairs in half an hour."

"You are totally insane. Do you think after today's fiasco that I am going to expose myself to that bunch of vultures? Those Finley faggots hate Harmon. Once they spot me, they'll be doing Buster Keaton pratfall imitations all night."

"You've got it wrong, Jonathan. For the Finley crowd, anyone who brings down Harmon is a hero. For them you are a prize, their secret weapon, the perfect mole; a guy who looks for all the world like he's playing for Harmon, but who manages to set up scores for the other side. Once they find out who you are, these Finley girls will be all over you, including, no doubt, the lovely Miss Finley herself."

"I appreciate what you've done, Mel, but I am not up to personal appearances tonight. I am too beat to get out of the sack, and, anyway, I have a bunch of nightmares on hold that I have got to deal with."

"Excuses. You are retreating, Jonathan. It's the Cossack phobia. Are you going to cut and run because you are afraid of a little competition? While you are under the covers dreaming of stiff-arming Schneiderman and prancing into the end zone, Cara Rosenhaus will be on her living room couch wrapped in the arms of a stiff prick from *Redbook*. Are you going to lie there like a wimp and let this happen?"

"Actually, I was waiting for the right moment to rush over there, break down her bedroom door, and catch them in flagrante."

"Don't be an ass, Jonathan. An opportunity like this doesn't come along very often. It's once in a lifetime. This could be the real thing. You've got a chance. Either you get off the bench and into the game, or you'll spend your life tortured by images of beautiful women reaching up to kiss an endless stream of no-name wasps. And I'll tell you something else. In a situation like this even a retard like Buckstein would be out there giving it his best shot."

Mel knew what he was doing. He was a natural psychologist and, intuitively, he understood what would get to me. While it is true that out of pure fear I was ready—all too ready—to abandon the project, the very thought of being beaten out by Buckstein, of sitting on the bench while the galoot got into the game and tried to put his spastic moves on Cara Rosenhaus, was more than I could bear.

"You're smart, Mel," I said. "You know that insults will get you everywhere."

"For friends you do what you have to do," he replied. "But let's get going. We don't want to be late for the party."

"A half hour," I said. "I'm staying no more than a half hour. Just long enough to say hello."

"Hello is good," Mel replied. "Hello could be the start of something big."

Chapter Three

If you know Manhattan, no doubt you know upper Park Avenue; block after block of stolid, white and red brick apartment buildings manned by doormen with freshly scrubbed faces in dark gray uniforms, many Irish who, like sentries, guard their respective entrances and, with a fine sensibility, honed over many decades of service, sniff out West-Siders and other undesirables.

Cara lived in the most venerable and grandest building in the area, an imposing castle-like structure with a circular driveway and an interior courtyard containing in its center a grassy oval which, in spring, sprouted random daffodils.

Like all entering vehicles, our cab had to stop for clearance at the guardhouse. With a clipboard in hand, an elfin figure, a uniformed Barry Fitzgerald, checked our names against a master list of invitees to Cara's party. At first puzzled, then perturbed by not finding our names on the list, the guard attempted to cover over his anxiety with nervous chatter.

"Must be here, gentlemen, must be here. These eyeglasses are a new prescription, don't you know, and I'm having a devil of a time reading the print. But let's take a good look again. You were invited of course. Yes, well then you've got to be here."

Then, finally, just as the cab driver, sullenly patient, head resting on arms at the cab window, began to grumble aloud and in the back seat I experienced rising panic, he found us, two pencil-scrawled names—first names only—added at the very bottom of the list.

"Is it Mr. Melvin and Mr. Jonathan then," the guard asked, his voice, now restored to cheerfulness. "Down below here they've added two names, Christian names only, but I suppose that is because you are very good friends of Miss Rosenhaus?"

"Very good," Mel called out from the rear of the cab. "Very old friends."

"All right. Very well then. Go right ahead and enjoy your evening, gentlemen."

"How does it feel to be an afterthought?" I asked Mel once we were inside the lobby.

"Don't be so sensitive. We made the list, didn't we? In life that is all that counts. The fellow who graduates last in his class at Harvard is still a Harvard graduate and the world will treat him as such. Being in the right place at the right time is the name of the game. Besides, don't forget that, list or no list, you are a somebody. Never forget that. When that apartment door opens, this Finley crowd is going to see the genuine article, Harmon's first string varsity end."

"And Ryder's most valuable player."

Mel shook his head.

"Don't think that way. Celebrity is celebrity. Name recognition counts. After a while, people don't remember whether you were a hero or a goat. You are a name, a personality. And that is guaranteed to bring the Miss Finleys of this world knocking on your door."

The elevator came, operated by a tall, silent figure with white gloves and West Point posture. On the sixth floor the doors opened, and with a gesture of his head the operator indicated that the Rosenhaus apartment was to the right. Without hesitancy, like a member of the family, Mel strode the few yards to the door and rang the bell.

Cara herself answered, and right then I knew that I was in big trouble; that when it came to haunting my dreams and messing up my mind, the girl who stood in front of me, lithe, spirited, radiantly beautiful, would give Leo the Lip a run for his money.

Up close she was even lovelier than I imagined; tall—perhaps five-foot-six or -seven—with deep, Sinatra blue eyes, rust red hair swept up from her face, and a smile reminiscent of the young Garland greeting soldiers at a USO dance.

"Hello, there," she said brightly, stepping toward us and holding out a hand to Mel. "Great to see you. You are?" her face flushed. Clearly she had no idea who we were and she was embarrassed.

Mel came to her rescue.

"Friends of Myron Klutsky. I believe he called?"

"Myron, yes, of course. Dear Myron. We've been buddies since second grade. Played ring-a-leavio together. I'm so sorry he couldn't come tonight. But, yes, he called and asked if he could invite two Harmon friends. I told Myron he didn't even have to call. Just send them over, I said. Any friends of Myron are welcome here. He knows that." Cara's smile widened and her face took on an impish look. "Even if they are Harmon boys."

"We appreciate that," Mel said.

Cara continued to stand in front of the door, seemingly carried away by her own thoughts.

"Actually it's a coincidence that you are here," she said. "I happened to be at Harmon this afternoon for the game. Most of my friends hate Harmon, say you guys are a bunch of stuffed shirts, but the truth is they can't stand it that you can beat the pants off us in every sport and you send more kids to the Ivy's. Personally, things like that don't bother me. I've got a lot more important things to hate. I tell my friends, if you are going to hate something, hate a society that has homeless people sleeping on the streets and permits thousands of kids to go hungry at night. That's what you should hate.

"Anyway, I felt bad for Harmon. They had a chance to win, but they blew it. With a couple of minutes left, one of their guys fumbled the ball when he got hit, Ryder recovered, and that was it. The game was over. It was a real shame. I felt terrible for that poor fellow. He looked so sad. I felt like giving him a big hug."

Mel looked at me, his face breaking into one of his idiot grins. Then he reached out, slipped an arm behind my back, and gave me a shove forward.

"Now is your chance," he said to Cara. "Here he is, the very man you've been speaking of, Number 86, who, unfortunately, lost the ball but came within a hairsbreadth of scoring the winning touchdown."

Cara looked at me, then looked at me again, inspecting me, as though she could not believe that this short fellow in front of her, a gate-crasher, foisted on her by that jerk Myron Klutsky, could be the same player her heart had gone out to; poor Number 86, poor Sleeping Beauty, who had come so close to turning certain defeat into a fairytale triumph. Then, suddenly, she came toward me, gave me a hug that made me feel the strength of her arms, and lightly, with tenderness, planted a kiss on my cheek.

"You are wonderful, Number 86," she said, "you are a very courageous man." Then taking a step back, she appraised me once again.

"Are you really all right? No broken bones, no broken head?"

"Except for having to live with a perpetually red face, I'm fine," I replied.

"Oh no, don't say that. The fumble wasn't your fault. Not when someone steams into you like that. This Schneider fellow must be one mean guy."

"The worst," Mel put in. "He's a crazy Kamikaze-type. He'd torpedo his mother if she caught a pass in his territory."

"Well, we won't worry about him," Cara said. "We'll leave him and his Ryder cronies to their nasty ways." Cara turned, faced the door and took both our arms. Then the three of us, looking like a debutante flanked by her two escorts, crossed the threshold and entered the apartment.

For the moment I was too discombobulated—Cara's behavior had thrown my heart into what felt like a dangerous tachycardia—to take in much. All I could see was what seemed to be a noisy crowd of your prep school East Hampton kids, a flood of blazers and short skirts, and a couple of circulating waiters in stiff white jackets passing out canapés to the crowd. From another room I heard somebody at the piano playing "Stardust." The flash thought occurred to me that this was not my world; that this was alien territory, and that sooner or later someone like me, whose father could barely earn a living and whose clothes featured strictly bargain basement labels, would get the boot.

With the two of us still in tow, Cara headed toward a bar set up in the corner of a vast living room, a museum, really, with Picasso and Manet drawings on one wall, a dark, tumultuous Jackson Pollock on another and, in between, a small colorful Delacroix oil. On the floor was a thick pile beige carpet, on top of which were scattered several rich, multicolored Oriental rugs.

At that time in my life I had not been inside the Frick Mansion on Fifth Avenue, but this is what I imagined the inside of that venerable home to be like, walls covered with masterpieces from antiquity onward and, in each room, elegant Persian carpeting lending a soft glow to the surroundings. I wondered what it would be like to live in an apartment like this and to have a father who, for a hobby, collected world-class art.

"First thing, we'll get you fellows a drink," Cara was saying as she ushered us to the bar. The small, baldheaded man who attended it, kept nodding at Cara and smiling a welcome smile at us.

"Richard here will take care of you. Just tell him what you want. We have everything, but I'm partial to Richard's special brew. He has a secret recipe that I can't pry out of him, the old skinflint, but it works. It's a totally amazing drink. Have one and I'll be right with you. In the meantime, make yourselves very comfortable." Cara then turned to Mel, "Why don't you circulate a bit?" she suggested. "You'll probably see a number of familiar faces." Then, leaning close to me, "Stay put. Don't move. I want to spend time with you."

As though given orders by some feared authority, like John Terman, our headmaster, who once threatened me with suspension for removing my clip-on bow tie in assembly, or Coach Martin, who, with the special snort that he reserved for suspected mama's boys, barked at me to hold my ground and strip the interference, I remained fixed to the spot where Cara had left me.

Sensing that I needed a drink—perhaps from long experience he recognized the tell-tale signs of another stricken youth falling into Cara's grip—Richard handed me a glass of his special brew. Cara was right. It was delicious, smooth, slightly citrusy, easy going down, its powerful wallop masked by the fruity taste.

As I stood there, waiting, straining to spot a familiar face among the whirl of figures in there, Mel sidled up to me. He had wandered off into the den to peruse a group of African sculptures, and even at a distance I had heard the low, admiring whistle that he reserved for things exceptional. Now he was back.

"Let's put them to the test," he said, gesturing toward the crowd standing like asparagus stalks in the living room. "We'll see how long these blue stocking types can hold out against the locker room scent of real Harmon men."

Mel was no athlete. In fact, more than anything, he reminded me of a penguin with glasses, but when he went to parties he dabbed on an aftershave that smelled like Bronco Nagurski coming off the field in 100-degree heat.

"It never fails to get you to third base," Mel had told me. "It's the call of the wild. I'm working on a more pungent version that will get me to home plate."

"Why don't you just go on ahead and look around?" I said. "I'm tired from today and right now I'd prefer to keep a low profile."

Mel gave me a suspicious look. He knew that, ordinarily, the last thing I would want would be to be left alone in a room full of strangers, but he said nothing. He sensed that something was afoot and that I needed space.

"I'll go ahead and scout the crowd," he announced, "sample a bit of East Hampton's best. If you hear me massaging the ivories and you care to join me, come on over. We'll do our thing."

To attract girls, Mel and I had worked up a party routine. A gifted jazz pianist, Mel would launch into a medley of Gershwin and Porter numbers while I half sung, half talked the lyrics, all the while steeling myself against the possibility that another Dory Silverman, perhaps now in the form of Ms. Finley herself, would blow me off for not being able to carry a tune.

Mel's playing, relaxed and easy-going, invariably attracted a bevy of pretty girls, young model types who surrounded the piano, swayed to the music and, moved to sing along, usually managed to drown me out.

After about a half hour of playing—before he sat down Mel would slip on a pair of sunglasses a la George Shearing to arouse maternal feelings—he could pretty much have his pick of the ladies. Then, taking a final sip of the whiskey that he kept at the ready, Hoagy Carmichael style, and sprinkling on a bit more of the Nagurski cologne that he carried in his pocket, Mel would rise from the piano bench, take the prettiest girl by the arm and, with a wink at me, disappear into a bedroom.

I had no such luck with women. The girls who hung around me were usually the best friends of the pretty girls; plain types, either short and plump or elongated scrawny numbers. The former variety, a distinctly heavyset girl, blond and husky, a female version of Mike Hadressian, my old history teacher who played for the football Giants, now approached me. She appeared from the kitchen area, found an opening in the crowd, and making a beeline for me, called out my name.

"Jonathan?"

I wanted to go into hiding.

"Yes, hello."

"I'm Debbie. Cara sent me over to keep you company. She's busy being a hostess, but she told me to tell you not to move. She'll be right here."

"I'm glued to the spot."

A thought occurred to me that Cara knew how to limit the competition. I wondered how many other offensive guards she kept in her collection.

"Cara says you are from Harmon," Debbie was saying. "Aren't you living dangerously?"

I motioned for her to keep her voice down.

"I'm incognito," I said. "I'm pretending to be a visiting chess maven."

"Actually you look the part, a little shaggy-doggish if you know what I mean. But you've got to spill some of that drink on your shirt if you want to look authentic."

Then Debbie came real close and, stretching her face toward mine, lowered her voice to a stage whisper. "I hear that you are a football player and that you lost the game for Harmon."

I looked behind me.

"You must have the wrong man."

"No, no listen. It's all right. At Finley we are into losers. We are Earl Browder fans. We root for the Philadelphia A's. We would not know what to do with a winning team. We'd probably boycott it as part of the military-industrial complex. Anyway, Cara says that you remind her of Gregory Peck."

"Really?"

"Yes. You know, sad eyed, a little forlorn, living under a cloud. Cara thinks that you feel out of place here, that you are like the character in *Gentleman's Agreement*. He tries to pass, but he doesn't really fit in."

"She told you that?"

"Uh-huh. Cara's sharp. She's a real quick judge of character. But don't worry. She's very much drawn to depressed types."

"That boyfriend of hers doesn't look depressed."

I had spotted Ken Masters in the living room, tall, olive-skinned, cigarette in hand, holding forth in front of a group of Finley students and every once in a while glancing over his shoulder as though he were looking for Cara.

"No he's not. That's just the point. He's different. He's what in psychology class we call an Oedipal out, a girl's effort to escape from her father. Ken's a lightweight. He's good looking, Park Avenue, pseudo-sophisticated. He entertains Cara, lifts her spirits, but she is really drawn to the melancholy type."

"You mean if I give away more football games and feel low enough, I may really be in business?"

"Definitely. Oh very definitely. Even now you may qualify. She's already spoken of you as Harmon's Hamlet. Just be yourself, and you may be in line to be Cara's next. We'll see. If by the end of tonight she invites you to the East Hampton house, you know you've got a leg up."

"Is that the test?"

"One of them. It's a touchstone, along with an invite to a family dinner. See, one thing about Cara is she's into family approval. Not that she'll admit it. She acts the free spirit who couldn't care less about what anyone thinks, but the truth is she very much wants the thumbs up from her brother, Henry, the one she's always mocking as an egghead nerd, and from her capitalist father. A word to the wise: no matter what she says about them, no matter how much she puts them down, don't go for the bait. Don't trample on their image. They're her secret heroes."

"That's good to know. Thanks for the tip. You're a real fount of information, Debbie."

"Well you see, I'm her Boswell. I follow her around. The shenanigans amuse me. At first I didn't like the role, resented it, too much in her shadow you know. But now I get a kick out of being on the inside. I'm her confidante. She listens to me. You know how Harry Hopkins had Roosevelt's ear, gave him the real scoop about what's going on? I'm like that. I'm what in politics they call a gray eminence."

"I see," I said. "Well you certainly are a good person to know."

Just then Cara arrived, looking harried. A strand of hair had come loose and fallen over her face and she was trying to blow it back in place.

"Sorry," she said. "Everybody has a problem. Everyone has a story they have to tell me, but do they listen to what I have to say? Of course not. No one listens. Have you noticed that no one takes advice? They can't. People are into doing themselves in, wrecking relationships. There is nothing you can do about it. My brother, Henry, he's a perfect example; he wrecks every relationship, says its biological, and probably for once he's right. I think the human race is doomed. Are you upset with me? Has Debbie here been entertaining you?"

"Absolutely. She's been filling me in on the scene. She's a regular Boswell."

"She is, she is. Debbie takes in everything. She is the perfect recording machine. I can't remember what day it is. I don't know what I'd do without her. And she's a clairvoyant. She's like Nostradamus. Just yesterday Debbie told me that someone new was going to come into my life, didn't you, Deb."

"I had a premonition, but I had no idea it would be Gregory Peck."

Cara frowned at her friend. Then, shaking her head, she turned to me.

"I don't know what I'm going to do with her. She's such a blabbermouth. She can't keep a secret. She told you, didn't she?

What am I supposed to do with a confidante who can't keep a secret? I hope that you don't mind the comparison."

"I'm flattered. Gregory Peck's one of my favorites. I like his cool."

"Exactly, the calm, the restraint, grace under fire. It's definitely sexy. Muted sex I call it. It's a turn-on."

Cara then approached Debbie and touched her arm.

"Deb, do me a favor will you? See if you can find Ken. Ask him to go into the kitchen and see if he can calm down the caterer. She's having a tantrum because cook burned her spinach pie." Leaning forward so that her face was close to Debbie's, Cara gave her a kiss on the cheek. One hand now was on Debbie's waist and I thought that she was giving her friend a slight push. Without another word, Debbie nodded and was off. Cara took my arm.

"Let's see if we can find a place where we can sit for a while," she said. "I want to get to know you."

The living room was crowded with bodies, with people sitting cross-legged on the floor, so we wandered into the large paneled dining room and settled down on a small settee at the back of the room.

"I want to know all about you," Cara said.

"I'm not sure what there is to tell."

"Well who are you, really? I don't mean just who are you, but *who are you?*"

"You are interested in the man behind the sex symbol."

"Exactly. The inner you—the poetic you."

"You mean the part of me that can turn a fumble into a metaphor."

"Right. There is something definitely aesthetic about you, the wan look, a touch of the haunted artist."

"Actually, I'm not feeling very well just now. It has been a rough day."

"No, there's something more. Do you paint or write?"

"I do a column called *On the Bench*, for the school paper."

"Satire, I'll bet. Or is it trenchant character sketches?"

"Neither, really. It's more like a bench sitter's view of the world; a second stringer's take on the Harmon scene."

"But you are not a second stringer. You are a key player. After that Sleeping Beauty maneuver you pulled, I said to my boyfriend, 'Keep your eye on Number 86. He's Harmon's secret weapon.'"

"Thank you. I wish that were true."

"It is. It absolutely is. That play was a creative act. I said to Ken, 'Now that is the work of an original mind.' Right then and there I knew that we had a lot in common. For years Sleeping Beauty was my favorite character. I loved the transition, the shift of worlds from the mundane to the magical. My dad and I were into it for God knows how long. I'd go into their bedroom—maybe I was four or five—and pretend to fall asleep and he would wake me up with a kiss. See, he was my prince then. Oh my God, this sounds awful, just like I just stepped out of some kind of Freudian textbook."

"Not at all. It actually sounds quite wonderful."

"You think so? Well, thank you. I am always afraid that I'll come across as a case history. Well, anyway, the point is, I was really into my dad until I grew up and learned more about his business."

"You disapproved?"

"It was a disappointment. I love my dad. He is a really good man—you'll see when you meet him. There's nothing he wouldn't do for his family and he is always reaching out, trying to do something for kids in the city. But he grew up having to hustle for a living, selling whatever he could get his hands on, and he's stuck with that attitude. As far as I'm concerned, he takes advantage of his black customers. He sells them cheap stuff at big prices. It takes them years to pay it off and by the time they've finished paying the stuff has already fallen apart."

"It's that bad?"

"It's pretty awful. I tell him he needs to upgrade, that it would make a big difference, that he'd be proud of himself, that he'd feel like a *mensch*, but he won't listen. He says the problem is the abuse his stuff takes, the tears, the spills, the animals shitting on the upholstery. Yeah, I say, well what do you expect when we treat people like animals and give them shacks to live in? Our society's the problem, the whole dog-eat-dog economic system, but you don't have to add to the misery. If you gave these people something decent to sit on, chairs that lasted more than two weeks, maybe you'd be part of the solution rather than part of the problem. We fight about that all the time."

"You have pretty definite views."

"I speak my mind and Sidney doesn't like it. His face turns red and he looks like he's going to explode. But it's his fault. He taught me to say what I think."

Then Cara turned to me.

"What are you into?" she asked. "Are you a socialist or one of those Harmon-types who walks around with a fat wallet, just marking time until he can get into the family business?"

"A socialist," I replied, "and sometimes left of that. My mother's really into Russia and I myself am an Earl Browder fan."

"My mother's into Bergdorf's," Cara said, "the ultimate consumer, the perfect executive wife. And Sidney, he's a sweetheart, but if he's crossed, watch out, he'll start screaming, acts like a storm trooper. I call him Von Ribentrop. He doesn't think it's funny, but I say if the boot fits, wear it."

Cara leaned closer to me.

"Do you listen to the Red Army chorus?"

"I don't recall hearing that group," I confessed.

"I've got the record," Cara confided. "I listen every night. It's inspiring. They are the voices of the new world. Marx was amazing, don't you think?"

"Definitely one of the smartest."

"Smart is not the half of it. When you say 'smart' I'm not sure that you appreciate the man. The guy was a prophet, and someday the whole world will be transformed by his vision. Do you believe that?"

"Absolutely. No question."

"My brother doesn't. He says people are too selfish. But he's the selfish one. He calls himself a poet and he is always talking about humanity, but he doesn't give a shit about real people. See, that's the problem I have. Everyone in my family is a consumer."

"I can see that would be a real problem."

"What about you? Are you a selfish shit?"

"I hope not, I give to the UJA."

Cara's response, an unsmiling stare combined with a slight and, I thought, disdainful, shake of her head, told me that she didn't think this was very funny.

"Well, I hope you're not," she went on, "actually, I don't think that you are. I can tell things like that. I have a feeling that the two of us are really going to get on, that there are good vibes here. Do you sense that?"

I nodded. "I know what you mean."

Cara smiled. Then she reached out and touched my arm.

"You can do better than that. How about a little enthusiasm?"

I blushed. I felt miserably self-conscious, like a twelve-year-old at his first dance. Cara sensed my embarrassment and her voice softened.

"You're just a little tense," she said. "Who wouldn't be after a day like you've had. You need to relax. Have another drink."

"Great. Do you think Richard can mix up a brew that unties uptight Harmonites?"

"Absolutely. He has handled tougher cases."

Cara looked around, spotted a classmate standing nearby and asked him to be a dear and send Richard over.

"You know, I am thinking of coming to another Harmon game," Cara announced. "I'd like to see you in action again. My boyfriend, Ken, probably won't be interested. He is not much of an athlete. He fences, but mostly it is for show. He thinks it will help him land parts when he becomes an actor. If he won't come with me, though, I'll come alone. I am curious to see what you have up your sleeve."

"Funny you should ask," I replied, "just tonight I was working on a Cinderella play. See what you think of this scenario. Right up to the end of the game I act the part of a drudge. I do nothing but block and tackle, tackle and block. I'm a workhorse, a day laborer, no scoring threat and the other team simply ignores me. Then, in the last minute, our quarterback discovers me, realizes that I am the receiver he's been looking for his whole life, and hits me with the winning pass."

Cara laughed and clapped her hands.

"Brilliant. Absolutely brilliant. I'll be there. Just let me know when Cinderella makes her debut."

Cara slid closer and took my arm.

"After the game will you take me home? I'll be all alone."

"It would be my pleasure."

Just then Ken Masters appeared in the doorway, looking annoyed and agitated. He was tall, with a long torso and there was a stiff, slightly mechanical quality about the way that he moved. With the barest nod to me, he addressed Cara directly.

"I've been looking all over for you. You are needed in the kitchen. The caterer claims she has been sabotaged and won't get out the desserts."

Now it was Cara's turn to look annoyed.

"Can't you settle it, Ken? Do you need me for everything? Look, tell the lady to forget the spinach pie. We'll pay her for it. It was a dumb idea anyway. This isn't a Greek wedding."

Ken looked flustered.

"I think you'd better tell her yourself."

Looking vexed, Cara shook her head and appealed to me, "Are all you men like that?" she asked. "Afraid to ask directions or take on the hired help? No wonder the world is in such a mess." Then, once more, she turned to Ken.

"How is it, Ken Masters, that a heartthrob like you, a guy who can charm the pants off any girl in the junior class, can't handle a lunatic lady caterer? Maybe if you
show her one of your head shots, she'll be so thrilled she'll pack up her spinach pies and go home."

Ken Masters looked like he'd taken a shot right to the midsection.

"I'll see what I can do." He started to leave.

"Oh forget it, Ken." Cara was on her feet now. "I'll handle it. Tell the ladies I'll be there in five minutes." Ken started to leave, then turned back. His eyes took me in with a quick furtive glance. "Also, more people have arrived," he said. "They've been asking for you."

"You know something, Ken?" Cara replied, "They can wait. If they want so much to talk to someone, let them talk to each other.

And if they don't want to do that, maybe you can organize a game of charades."

Without another word, Ken left. Cara looked at me.

"He's really sweet," she said, "but his mother raised him. She crowned him king and he can't get used to not having ladies in waiting dancing around him. I'm doing something called neo-development. I'm trying to give him some backbone. Anyway, we were talking about you and your life. What do you want to do with your life?"

I was caught off guard. I thought that we had moved past the interview stage.

"You know, I'm not sure," I said. "Right now I am just trying to get through the week without fumbling my life away."

Cara nodded sympathetically. "I'm sure you won't," she said, "but don't you want to make a difference do something meaningful?"

"I guess so, but I'm not sure what that could be."

"Well you are still young," Cara said. "Probably in a couple of years you'll find your calling. I've had mine since I was twelve."

"Really? What is that?"

"I'm going to be a senator."

"A U.S. senator?" I must have looked incredulous.

"You just flunked the male chauvinist pig test," Cara said sharply, "you have the same idiot look on your face that my father always has. Debbie calls it male myopia, but I call it male imbecility. Do you know what my father really believes about me—he doesn't dare say it out loud—that I'll end up living a couple of blocks away on Park Avenue and that, if I really hustle, I might get to be president of the PTA."

"No way," I said. "You are definitely Capitol Hill material. You have the drive that it takes."

"Without drive you are nothing," Cara agreed. "But you've got to have a lot more than drive. You have to know in your heart what you are destined to become. Knowing that creates a vision. Then you can develop a plan."

"Sounds like you've thought a lot about this."

"I have. I'm just at the vision stage. Women in this country need a female senator."

"I never thought about that," I confessed. "But when I think of the U.S. Senate, I picture a room full of men. Women don't really have a voice there."

"Exactly. I am glad that you understand that. You have promise. You seem educatable."

"With a good teacher, I can learn fast. And by the way when you get to the planning stage, count me in. I'd love to work on your campaign committee."

Cara leaned over and gave my arm a squeeze. "You really are a sweet guy," she said. "Do you think that you might come out to our East Hampton house one weekend? We could do some strategic planning."

"Sounds good," I said. "I'd be very interested in developing a winning strategy with you."

Somehow these words just came out of me, and having spoken them, I suddenly felt exposed and vulnerable. Cara looked at me and smiled.

"Well I guess we'll just have to see what kind of strategist you turn out to be," she said, "and whether or not you have the winning touch."

Just then Richard brought the drinks and I took a long sip of his special brew. I was feeling dizzy but good, remarkably good. I had a vision of working side-by-side with Cara, developing her campaign—and mine—at poolside, on the beach, or just possibly in her bedroom in what I imagined to be an East Hampton mansion. As Debbie had said, the invitation was a marker. It gave me a leg up, and for a first meeting that was something.

Deborah had come in behind Richard and, spotting Cara, she signaled to her that they had to talk. Cara stood up, conferred with her friend and appearing concerned and confused, excused herself.

"I'm sorry," she said. "Some strangers are at the door. I have to go."

She hurried off with Deborah trailing a step behind. Curious, I drained my glass and, feeling instantly light-headed and dizzy, followed them to the front door.

A group of new arrivals was standing in the foyer, looking aimless and lost, like a bunch of dateless boys on Saturday night, and in the center Cara was talking to someone wearing a top coat that came down to the top of his ankles. I could catch only a few words from Cara's side of the conversation.

"Linda Grinstein sent you over? You know her from camp? She told you it would be okay to come tonight? I heard nothing about that. Do you know that Linda isn't here; that she got sick and couldn't come? What's that, you came all the way from Brooklyn? Well, okay, I guess it will be all right."

Richard was standing protectively next to Cara, but now he shifted into his butler role and began to collect the coats. Standing in the rear, I could not tell who Cara had been talking to, but as the group dispersed, I caught a glimpse of two faces. And, instantaneously, I felt an explosion in my chest, a sudden burst of pain followed by a feeling of panic nearly as strong as the attack that paralyzed me the time in eighth grade when, standing outside Barney Greengrass's appetizing emporium, I almost got caught in a firefight between the police and Dutch Shultz who, believing he was on safe ground, had just bought a pound of Nova for Sunday brunch.

What I saw were two faces that I had hoped never to see again, and I knew then what it was like to be pursued by the Furies. It was Stretch, Ryder's elephantine tackle, and their right guard, a short, round Wallace Beery-type whose favorite play was to ram his palm up into the opposing lineman's nose. And now, walking behind them, I spotted Schneiderman himself, wearing a gray double-breasted suit garnished at the breast pocket by a red silk handkerchief.

They were standing a few feet away from me now, and my first impulse was to retreat to the living room, make myself invisible, and at the first opportunity, slip out the door.

Given what happened on the last play of the game—after Schneiderman got knocked out, Stretch and a few teammates surrounded me, cursed me out, and muttered dark threats of revenge—the last people I wanted to see that night, or any other night, were these two bruisers looking for all the world like Capone hit men. They were heading for the bar, and as they passed by, Stretch spotted me and nudged his buddy.

"Isn't that eighty-six?" he said.

"Who?"

The Harmon guy. Eighty-six. Freakin' Sleeping Beauty. The guy who racked up Stan."

"Mr. Dirty Pool? No kidding. What's he doing here?"

"Maybe this is a freakin' fag party."

"Let's have a look."

The two of them came closer and scrutinized me like vigilantes closing in on their prey.

"Hey," Stretch said, "Are you eighty-six?"

"Were you talking to me?" I replied with as much cool as I could muster.

"Yeah, you. Are you the guy who zonked Schneiderman?"

"I don't know what you are talking about."

I was half hiding behind a chair with a tall back. Stretch walked over, grasped the top of the chair, and leaned over to get a good look at me.

"It's him," he announced. "Definitely. I remember the face. Freakin' Sleeping Beauty. I figured we'd catch up with him sometime." His buddy joined Stretch, and with the two of them moving in on me, I experienced fear of the kind I had not known since the time in grade school when, shipped off to the principal's office for asking Jody Moskowitz to angle her paper in my direction during a math quiz, I waited for over an hour in a state beyond terror for the retribution that I knew awaited me.

"You're the Harmon guy who busted our guy, right?" Stretch asked. He pointed toward Schneiderman who had stopped a few feet away to chat with an acquaintance.

Stretch was definitely working up a head of steam, and I sensed that I had better try another tactic.

"Oh, you mean the accident when I dove at the ball and clipped your friend by mistake," I said, as off-handedly as possible. "That was a shame, a real fluky thing. I hope he's all right now."

"You put a dirty hit on him," Stretch said in a clearly menacing voice. I knew then I was in real trouble. Taking a step back to get out of fist range, I began to apologize, to say how sorry I was about the incident, when, sizing up the situation, Schneiderman moved in quickly to intervene.

"Hi," he said, extending a hand to me. With the other he put a firm hold on Stretch's arm. "I'm Stan Schneiderman. We've just come in."

I shook his hand and introduced myself. "He's the guy, Stan," Stretch put in. "Freakin' eighty-six. The guy who laid on the dirty hit."

"I know who he is," Schneiderman said. He took a long look at me, an appraising look. Then he smiled.

"You pack a punch, Jonathan. I was really kayo'd out there. While I was out, I dreamt that I was in the army. A war was going on, and when I stepped out of my foxhole I got hit flat out by a mortar shell."

"I'm really sorry," I said. "I guess I went a little crazy after I fumbled."

"Situations like that are crazy making," Schneiderman said. "Do you know how many times I've done things like that? And it's always in the last minute of close games. Winning becomes a life or death matter. It's madness. Or maybe we're mad to begin with. Anyway," he added, "forget it. You went after the ball. Things like this happen." Then he grinned at me, "Next time we meet though," he said, "watch your back. I travel with a couple of gorillas."

"I'll do that if I ever get off the bench again."

"Don't say that, Jonathan," Schneiderman replied quickly. "You are good, you have good hands and you are gutsy."

"Thanks," I said. "From you that means something."

Cara now came up to us, smiling and looking very much the hostess. Debbie followed a half step behind.

"Well you two enemies seem to be getting on very well."

"We're not enemies," Schneiderman said, "We're rivals. We play on opposing teams. On the field we butt heads, right Jonathan? Off the field it's a different story."

"Well, I'm glad you feel that way," Cara said. "I hate people who hold grudges and are always plotting revenge. That's the hallmark of a primitive mind. Do you notice it's always the right-wingers, the Neanderthal-types, who are into hatred and retaliation? They are the ones who burn crosses and synagogues. And that is because they are low on the evolutionary scale. In fact, if you study these types you will find out that they are animals thinly disguised as humans.

"Animals don't take revenge," Schneiderman said. "As far as I can tell, that is very much a human trait."

"Yes. Well, for my money these reactionary types are worse than animals. They may look like ordinary folk, but underneath they are the most vicious kind of brutes."

Then without waiting for a response, Cara abruptly changed the subject.

"By the way, I owe you an apology," she said to Schneiderman. She reached out and lightly touched his arm. "I didn't recognize you when you first came in. I had no idea who you were."

"Why should you? There's nothing to recognize"

"Don't be so modest," Cara said. "I hate false modesty, the old saccharine humble pie bit. You are a fabulous player—Stan Schneiderman the one-man band. What you did on that last play, the way you streaked across the field, knocked down poor Jonathan here," Cara took my arm and gave it a quick squeeze, "and made him fumble was an incredible performance. You were a human rocket, everyone says so. No, you are a real star. Once they recognize you, half the girls in the room will fall into your arms."

"That is awfully nice of you to say," Schneiderman replied, "but I don't recognize myself in your description."

"Well then, we'll just have to take you in hand and convince you of the reality," Cara said.

Cara now slid a hand into mine and with the other took hold of Schneiderman's arm. Then, placing herself between us, she moved us toward the door.

"I am incredibly lucky," she said to both of us, "I have two heroes with me tonight. Let's drink to a long friendship."

Holding Cara's hand, I started for the bar but managed only a few steps before a wave of dizziness and nausea hit me. All at once the room was spinning and I felt so sick I could not stand. I slumped to the floor, trying desperately not to vomit. My head throbbed, I poured sweat, and I could not move. To stop the whirling sensation, I shut my eyes—and promptly blacked out.

When I awoke—perhaps a minute later—Schneiderman was kneeling alongside me, holding my head. On the other side, Mel, who had rushed in from the living room when he heard the commotion, was loosening my tie and trying to slip a cushion under my head. I looked up. Cara also stood alongside me barking orders to Ken Masters, who had come in behind Mel.

"Call an ambulance," she said.

Ken looked down at me from what seemed like an enormous height.

"He's not that bad," he declared. "He just got sick from too much booze. He'll get over it."

"He's ashen," Cara said. "He looks half dead. Get an ambulance."

"I don't think that is necessary," Ken retorted. "Look, his color is coming back."

"Oh, for God's sake," Cara cut him off. "I'll do it myself."

She headed for a phone. Someone had handed Schneiderman a glass of water and now he was holding it at my lips, urging me to take a sip. I tried, but a fresh wave of nausea swept over me.

"Thanks," I said, "but I can't. I need to wait a while." Schneiderman nodded and adjusted the cushion under my head.

"Just rest easy," he said. "Breathe deeply. Get in some oxygen. You should be feeling better in a few minutes."

"Thanks," I said. "You're awfully kind." Schneiderman squeezed my hand.

"Forget it," he said, "I'm just trying to keep you in shape for the return match so that I can knock you flat then."

"Once is enough," I said.

The dizziness was subsiding and I raised myself on my elbows to help clear my head.

"Keep that man flat." A woman's voice sounded behind me, and in a flash, breaking through the crowd, two ambulance attendants in green uniforms appeared. They kneeled beside me, one on each side, and someone grabbed my wrist to take a pulse. Both were young, a woman of perhaps twenty with a stethoscope around her neck, and her partner, a stubble-faced fellow a few years older, who was now attaching a blood pressure cuff to my arm.

"What happened?" the woman asked.

I told her all that I remembered.

"Any seizures, uncontrollable movements of the limbs?"

"None," Schneiderman answered for me.

"Any history of heart trouble, diabetes, stroke?"

I shook my head.

"His pressure is okay," her partner announced.

"Probably this is going to turn out to be nothing," the woman said, "Looks like pure alcohol intoxication, but to be on the safe side we ought to check you out at the hospital."

"I really don't think that is necessary," I said. "I'm feeling much better now."

Leaning on Schneiderman I pulled myself to my feet.

"I'll take him home," Mel volunteered. "and make sure he's tucked up in bed."

The woman attendant looked dubious.

"He's unsteady on his feet," she said. "He really ought to be checked out at the E.R."

I was dizzy as hell and still holding on to Schneiderman, but I did not want to go to the hospital.

"I'm really fine," I said. "I guess Richard's brew was a little too good."

Cara stood next to me, looking me over carefully.

"You aren't used to it, that's all," she said. "That concoction carries a sneak punch. You have to grow into it."

I was standing alone now and I started to walk slowly around the room, trying to shake off the lightheaded feeling. Both attendants observed me.

"I guess he'll be all right," the woman finally said, "but make sure that someone is with him at all times. The last thing we want is a fall and head injuries."

Cara placed herself squarely in front of me now, held me by the shoulders, and searched my face.

"Are you positive you are all right?" she asked. "You are not just saying that?"

"No, really. I'm fine."

I wondered what Cara was thinking, whether she was as disgusted with me as I was with myself. I tried to ward off what I was feeling, but the shame of the situation bore in on me and I felt like kicking myself. The one time that I actually got to meet a girl who matched my dreams I managed to collapse on her living room floor like a whiskey-drinking thirteen-year-old. And this following the Ryder fiasco.

Cara stood in front of me, looking me over, but I averted my eyes. I could not look at her.

Gingerly, as though he was assisting a fragile old man, Mel led me out of the apartment and to the elevator bank. Schneiderman had walked with us to the door and now called to me from there, "I hope that you feel much better, Jonathan, if I can do anything, just let me know. I'll leave my number with Cara."

"Thanks," I called back. "I appreciate that."

Cara stayed with us as we waited for the elevator. I kept my eye on the call button.

"I want you to get him straight to bed, no stops, no delays," she told Mel. And then, turning to me, "Jonathan, I want you to promise me that you will get plenty of rest. Sleep late in the morning and take it very easy all day."

"I will," I promised.

Then Cara leaned over and kissed me on the lips.

"I'll call you tomorrow," she said, "I'll be anxious to know how you are."

Chapter Four

Mel called early the next morning to do a post-mortem on the night's events, and to inform me of the true meaning of my collapse.

I had awakened with a headache and I was not up for one of his discourses on mind-brain relationships—he regularly linked eccentricities of the cardiovascular system to unreleased genital engorgement—nor was I in the mood to listen to a report—Mel consulted Freud's Standard Edition as soon as he got home—on the unconscious meaning of syncopal episodes.

I pretty much knew, anyway, what he would say; that unable to face the twin-pronged wish that arose under the influence of Richard's brew; to spirit Cara off to her bedroom and, on the way, to grind Ken Master's head into one of the Rosenhaus' blood red Persian carpets, I had developed acute anxiety, and, as an emergency defense, simply lay down on the floor and lost consciousness.

I was in no mood for this kind of two-bit analysis. I had slept fitfully, dreaming of being wounded in a gunfight and, in any case, I did not want to leave the house. I was waiting for Cara to call.

"I've got a bitch of a headache and I'm hung over," I explained to Mel. "I need to stay in the sack for a couple of more hours."

Mel saw right through me.

"The morning line has it five to two that you don't hear from her," he announced.

"What are you talking about?"

"Girls like your Miss Finley are notoriously forgetful. They don't mean anything by it. That is just their nature. If Cara Rosenhaus actually remembered you this morning, no doubt she would send warm greetings and her sincere wishes for a speedy recovery."

"And if I could remember your name, I'd thank you personally for your supportive words."

"Look, you don't understand. There is no question about what happened last night. Cara was totally into you. You stole the show. From the moment she opened the door and realized that it was actually you, Number 86, the genuine article, the anti-hero himself, you were golden. You could do no wrong. You definitely upstaged the stiff-backed wasp she totes around with her.   The problem is, girls like Cara are short on memories that don't have to do with them. When it comes to other folk, the visual images simply don't stick. Once an individual is out of sight, off the retinal screen, he's gone, erased from the brain circuits."

"As the most forgettable person I know, no doubt, you are speaking from personal experience."

"I'm a student of science, Jonathan.   I speak not from the unreliability of subjective experience, but from proven fact. Repeated studies have shown that your Park Avenue Finley types retain the image of people around them, including lovers, at most for twenty minutes at a time. You can bet that a half hour after we left Cara's place the image she had of you, including the picture of you laid out like a diva on the living room floor, had vanished from her brain, nudged out, no doubt, by Schneiderman and his Coney Island henchmen."

"You are totally mad. What about what happened at the door; the way she spoke, her promise to call today, and the kiss, a smack on the lips, in case you hadn't noticed. What about that? Was that all phony, all smoke and mirrors?"

"That's just the point. At the time, all of that was real, totally genuine. But that was last night. These ladies are not known for their staying power. Their problem is they can't settle in. They are on the move all the time, always looking for something new. And a girl like Cara is a magnet. She attracts guys from everywhere. They show up on her doorstep, bright-eyed, eager, half in love. You have jocks sporting varsity letters, math nerds, even a few pansies who go for her spunk.   They stay a month, two months, until Cara loses interest. Then she moves them out and they drop into oblivion."

"I guess I've made the round trip overnight."

"Not necessarily. On the surface, yes, no question. You fall into the rapid turnover group, but something tells me there is more to this thing than that. I have a hunch that you are holed up someplace in this lady's psyche. Don't ask me why.   Maybe she's getting a jumpstart on giving to the One Hundred Neediest Cases, but somehow you've gotten under her skin. You've touched something in her, probably her soup kitchen side, and she'll remember you. Sooner or later, maybe while she's doing her Saturday rounds at Bloomingdale's, you are bound to surface."

"Maybe I ought to be proactive. I could hustle down to Bloomie's, hang out around the lingerie counter, and when I spot her, do a reprise of last night's performance."

"Too gimmicky, even for a cross-dressing wide receiver. What kind of cover story would you use; that you were really shopping for a new pair of panties? True no doubt, but she'd probably not believe you. No, it's better to wait it out, stay cool, and don't be over eager. Let Cara make the first move. It will make her feel good about herself."

"Okay, but I have no intention of sitting on my duff all day, waiting for a blinding light to go off someplace in this lady's cerebrum. I'll give her until one o'clock to call. After that I'm out of here, and if she wants to see me again she'll have to scour the bench at the next game."

"Don't downplay yourself, Jonathan, your Miss Finley may think she is dealing with a West Side wimp, but she's getting a lot more than she bargained for. How many guys have gone head to head with Schneiderman and come out standing up? You've got some steel in you and that is what you need with someone like Cara Rosenhaus. If she senses weakness, you are finished. She'll want to whittle you down to Ken size, make you another boy doll, but you've got to hold the line. Make her come to you. And don't forget, these liberal Finley girls talk freedom, equality, women's rights, but what they truly want, what they are really looking for, is a Leo the Lip type to keep them in line."

Somehow I felt strengthened by Mel's words and fortified in my resolve not to take guff from Cara, to run the show whatever might develop. And I was determined to keep to the one o'clock deadline. If Cara called a minute after that, it would be too late. I would not be available.

It was just past twelve-thirty when she called. I was in the bathroom putting a touch of Brylcreem on unruly hair before walking out the door when, at a distance, I heard the phone ringing. I dashed back to my room and managed to pick up the receiver before Cara hung up

"How are you? I've been worried about you."

"Cara?"

"Yes, I'm downtown. I would have called earlier but I had to meet a friend for brunch and I got stuck trying to convince her to be a person. I've been thinking about you a lot. How are you making out?"

"Except for an army of elves hammering on my head, okay."

"I'm sorry. Have you tried Bromo Seltzer with a tomato juice chaser? The combination works. It's Richard's own antidote. I had to twist his arm to get it out of him. The truth is, he likes to get people drunk. He gets off on it. It's a power thing. Phallic. Disgustingly male. I've called him on it, told him that knocking people out with a drink won't add an inch to his dick, but he won't listen. Anyway, I'm very sorry that this happened to you. I should have warned you."

"It's okay. I should have watched myself."

"Well, I'm glad it was not worse. For a while there I was terrified. Just when we were connecting, really connecting, you disappeared, vanished. Your face turned pure chalk and the way you passed out, you looked like a goner. We should have insisted that you go to the E.R. After you left, I wanted Ken to go after you and take you to the hospital. But he refused. He kept saying that you were just drunk, that you couldn't hold your liquor. I could have killed him. The fact is, he is jealous, an insanely jealous man—or boy—I should say. He has the maturity of a spoiled five-year-old. But the truth is, he should be jealous. You were a tremendous hit last night."

"I was?"

"Absolutely. Everyone said so. Half a dozen people came up to me afterward. They couldn't get over your guts in showing up here after what happened. People were impressed—Schneiderman, too, by the way. He thinks a lot of you and how gutsy you are. Afterwards he came up to me and asked if you were my boyfriend. I said no, I already have a boyfriend, if you can call him that. By the way, don't ask me why I am with Ken Masters. I can't possibly answer that question. It is a pure mystery. Anyway, I told him that you were first in line if we break up; that is, if you are interested. But I don't know how we got into this. I just called to say hello and to say that I was thinking of you."

I was stunned. Cara Rosenhaus, *the* Cara Rosenhaus was thinking of me. And not only thinking of me and, presumably, my welfare, but putting me on the waiting list to be a boyfriend. Right then and there I wanted to get off the phone and tell Mel, really stick it to him. I imagined relating the conversation with Cara, and watching him crumble, crushed by the realization of how wrong-headed he could be.

"Well, thanks. I'm really flattered. I never think of anyone keeping me in mind except my mother and that is mostly when she is on my case. Actually, I've been thinking about you, too. I wondered where you were, what you've been doing this morning. For some reason, I have a vision of you in ladies apparel at Bloomingdale's."

"You are amazing. You really are. Do you have ESP? I thought of that when you knew just when to pull Sleeping Beauty out of your hat. That is a real gift. Actually, I'm down here helping my friend, Marge, return a blouse. She has trouble being assertive, really big trouble, and not only at Bloomies. Her boyfriend is seeing someone else on the side and she won't say anything. Do you want to know why? She is afraid to lose him, and do you want to know why that is?"

"Why is that?"

"Because she has bought into the myth that females don't make waves, that they have to put up with the garbage men throw at them. Can you imagine anyone today believing that?"

"That is hard to believe. But I suppose for some people it is a pretty fixed idea."

"Well it better not be. Do you know how many hours I've spent with her? But with some of these girls, it is impossible to get through. I've shown her evidence that proves that females are clearly superior beings biologically and psychologically. You know this, right?"

"I've heard that said."

"It is not a matter of what is said. It is what is true. Anyone with half a brain who has kept up with science knows that."

"I guess a lot of people haven't kept up."

"That's just the point. People are ignorant and they'd just as soon keep themselves that way. They have to be pushed to open their eyes. Gender discrimination is going to be a big issue in my campaign."

"No question you'll have a lot to say about that."

"Well I certainly hope so. People don't always like what I have to say. It rubs them the wrong way. And do you know what? That is good for them. Have you noticed that wrong way rubbing is good for people?"

"Actually I hadn't noticed that."

"Yes. Well, it's true. Rubbing against the grain keeps brain cells alive. It prevents dementia. In any case I am going to need a lot of help to get my message out, a lot of support from my friends. Which reminds me, I was totally amazed by your nemesis."

"Which nemesis is that?" Suddenly I had a terrifying vision of Stretch and his sidekick still on the prowl for me.

"Schneiderman, I wish that you could have stayed to hear him last night. You would have been amazed."

"At that point I think I'd had enough of Schneiderman for one day."

"Not that Schneiderman. I'm talking about an entirely different person. You think of him as a jock, right? Strictly macho. An all-American Jack Armstrong with Wheaties between the ears. Well I am here to tell you that is not who he is. Would you believe it, the guy is a feminist."

"Somehow that is hard to imagine. What does he do, advocate for women's rights to watch him commit mayhem?"

"I couldn't believe it either. We talked a while at the party and I couldn't believe what I was hearing. I was just bowled over. I never expected to find a trace of the political in this kind of person, but there he was talking women's rights, victim's rights, the rights of the abused."

"Somehow I think of Schneiderman as more abuser than abused."

"You would, wouldn't you? But it turns out he is immersed in this stuff. Did you know that his father is a DA?"

"He never mentioned it."

"Yeah. As a matter of fact, he has just resigned. Turned out he had a fight with his boss who is a real toad. The guy refused to prosecute a brute of a wife beater who has Tammany connections. Schneiderman's dad couldn't take it and quit. And now Stan is all involved. He is up in arms about the corruption, and wants to organize a protest to expose it. I'm with him on that."

"A rocket and a reformer all in one. Pretty impressive."

"Absolutely. Who would have guessed. You ought to get to know him. You are very different. He comes on as easygoing, not one of your tough talking types. But there is a lot of steel in Schneiderman. Anyone who messes with him will find that out real fast. You are a Harmon boy, a West-Sider, used to the comfortable life. No offense, but they don't breed toughness over there. In fact, I think it would be hard for you to be tough even if you needed to be. But underneath, I mean basically, you two have something in common. There is a kind of sweetness about both of you. I'll bet if you got to know one another you'd end up being great friends."

"You must be dreaming. As personalities we are about as compatible as Louis and Schmeling. But in any case, fraternizing with the enemy is out of the question. That is something the coach won't tolerate."

"It's none of his business. These coaches are Neanderthal men anyway; low level military types who were too dumb or too ornery to make it in the army so they spend their lives trying to turn high school kids into brutes."

"Well, they are pretty good at it. And if you don't show them you've got the killer instinct, they will keep you on the bench until the splinters burning your ass manage to fire you up." Cara made a sound that conveyed pure disgust.

"As far as I'm concerned that is utter garbage. If you want to
go along with the system, that is your choice. Anyway, I just wanted
to see how you were. Don't keep yourself a stranger."

"I'll try not to."

"No, I mean it. Come over and see us. We'd like to get to know
you—at least I would. Ken has a thing about Harmon. He thinks you
are all dullards, cloak and suitor's sons, know-nothing materialist
types without souls. Gogol's dead souls, you know—but that is his
thing. It's a case of the big bucks model trying to make himself out to
be some kind of artiste. It doesn't wash. Anyway, if you'd like to come
over sometime, I can handle him. Actually, someone like you, a man
who's not afraid to let a whole grandstand full of people see his
feminine side would be a good model for him. You could open his eyes."

"Sounds like a tall order, but I'd be glad to try."

"Okay. It's a deal. You'll call then?"

"Sure."

"Promise?"

"I promise."

Cara made sure to give me her number before we hung up and
I should have felt good about our conversation. But I didn't.
Somehow I felt depressed, as though I'd just been handed half a
bologna sandwich and told that I could not carry a tune.

When I found him at lunch, Mel immediately caught my mood.

"You heard nothing?" he asked softly.

"Worse. Politeness, cordiality. And a lot of talk about Ken
Masters." I repeated the conversation. When I finished, Mel simply
stared at me in disbelief.

"You must have been first in line when they handed out tin
ears," he said. "You missed the entire message. This is a woman who
is extending an invitation to you. It couldn't be plainer."

"To do what, help scrub off a little *chutzpah* from that stuffed
goose of a boyfriend?"

"That's just the surface. That's her cover. She's telling you
that right now she is locked in with Masters—probably still living out
her mother's fantasy of capturing a blond wasp, but she is trying to

free herself, and she's asking you to help out, to be the lever that catapults her out of there."

"That's one of the best offers I've had in years. It's right up there with an invitation to another round with Schneiderman."

"Listen, don't knock it. It's an entrée. The lady is giving you a way to get into her world, to start something that could be big. What you need to do right now is just hang out with the beautiful couple. Make friends with Ken. Admire his physique. He'll begin to like you, to ask you to stick around, and once Cara gets to know you and makes the comparison, one of the gutsiest tight ends ever to pull on a Harmon uniform versus *Redbook*'s leading fag attraction, the game will be over. Ken Masters will be headed for the private Potter's Field that Cara keeps for her exes."

"And how long before I follow him to the dumping ground?"

"Listen, this could be a very different story. Most likely Cara's problem is she's unable to make a free choice. She's been tied up with mama's needs and has been looking in the wrong direction. She seems to understand that now. And what if this thing really worked out? Imagine, in five or six years your whole life could change. You'd actually realize your secret dreams. You'd be a bona fide East-Sider, the spouse of a powerful new voice on the political scene, and manager of Rosenhaus Furniture, Harlem's number one name in home furnishings."

"This is your fantasy, not mine."

"Possibly so, but add this to the picture: an East Hampton villa two hundred feet from the ocean and membership in the Bath and Tennis Club, where you spend afternoons lobbing tennis balls at your celebrity wife, doing laps in the pool, and observing the passing scene while you sip tall gin fizzes."

"I hope you find a mate that opens that door for you."

I was annoyed at Mel. I had no doubt that he secretly envied that lifestyle and wanted it for himself—although he would never admit it—but part of me, too, was taken with the picture. And I could imagine myself in white slacks and yachting cap sipping daiquiris on the porch of the club, my West Side roots a distant memory.

I intended to call Cara the next day, and the day after that, but I never did. Mostly I forgot, but in the evenings when I remembered, I'd start to dial her number, get about half way through, and hang up. Then I'd promise myself that I'd call tomorrow.

"It's shell shock," Mel explained. "Your nervous system is sending you signals. After being wrecked by Schneiderman, fumbling the ball, and crimping out at the party, your system is saying, 'enough.' When this happened in the war, guys had to be shipped back from the front. It is the body's way of trying to rescue itself. You've got to wait until you can handle another blow."

I thought Mel was right. I wasn't ready for another smash to the midsection, no matter where it came from—in this case no doubt, from the big galoot, Ken Masters, or possibly, from Cara herself if she turned tail and ran back to him. But whatever the source, I knew I wasn't up for it.

Still, the days were passing and with a feeling of fright I realized that I was losing whatever slight connection I had made with Cara. She was simply fading out of my life and we were becoming, as before, two people from different worlds who had simply never met.

"In your situation, a phone call is too risky," Mel said. "If she brushes you off, or, God forbid, doesn't know who you are—with these ladies this is not an impossibility—you would definitely have a catastrophic reaction. Physical collapse is not out of the question and, who knows, a total breakdown cannot be ruled out. What I suggest is de-conditioning your nervous system. Take a walk across the park. Hang out in Cara's neighborhood for a while. See if you can spot her at a distance. Let your body get used to the sight of her. And if you feel okay, you can say hello. It will be harder in person for her to stiff arm you the way she could on the phone."

Though I was usually cautious about Mel's ideas—he had a way of sliding off into worlds of his own invention—this seemed like a good one. I badly needed to get out of the house and away from my fruitless obsession with the phone, and, one way or another, try to have some contact—even a sighting at a distance might break the phobia—with Cara.

That afternoon—it was Saturday—I set out across Central Park. My plan was to walk the streets near Cara's building on Park and 90th. If I spotted her, or, worse case scenario, caught sight of her and Ken strolling hand in hand, I would follow at a safe distance, periodically checking my pulse and respiration to make sure that no breakdown was in the offing. After an hour of crisscrossing the streets, though, I had still seen nothing. I was tired and about to give up, but I decided, as a final strategy, to board a bus, ride a half mile down Lexington, and come back on the Madison Avenue line.

It was on Lexington and 86th that I spotted them, Ken and Cara, walking north, chatting, not holding hands. At the next corner they turned towards Park Avenue.

I got off at the next stop, headed back uptown, and followed their route. On Park and 90th I spotted Cara, now alone. Apparently they had just said good-bye and Cara was headed towards her apartment building.

Suddenly emboldened—the fact that they had parted and Cara was now by herself seemed like some kind of omen—I caught up with her in the middle of Park Avenue, just as she reached the median island that divides the north- and southbound traffic.

"Cara."

She turned, looked startled, momentarily bewildered. Then a smile, quickly broadening, lit her face.

"Jonathan."

Then taking a quick step forward and nearly tripping over a piece of uneven cement, she threw herself against me.

"I wondered when you would show up."

Chapter Five

There was an old rickety bench on the island, and we simply plopped onto it as though we had been waiting a long time to do that.

For a moment we sat side by side, saying nothing, both still surprised by the encounter, both assimilating what had just happened. I could feel Cara's eyes on me, scrutinizing my face. She remained silent for a few more seconds. Then, abruptly, she sat upright and turned to face me.

"What happened?" she demanded. "You promised to call."

"I know. I tried several times. I couldn't get through."

Cara had a way of looking at you when she knew you were lying; perfectly level, mildly reproachful, patiently awaiting the truth.

"Well, it wasn't exactly like that," I admitted. "I started to dial your number a couple of times and I hung up before you answered."

Cara nodded as though to say she understood that something like that must have happened; that, given my history, she knew a snafu of some kind was inevitable.

For my part I felt ashamed, ashamed and furious at myself for making a totally gratuitous confession. What dark, self-destroying force, I wondered—Mel claimed it was the same one that caused me to squander money on the self-addressed envelope I enclosed in my letter to Anne Rutherford—had driven me to present myself as a suitor who possessed all the sophistication and derring-do of a twelve-year-old playing telephone games.

Cara sensed my embarrassment and moved in quickly.

"Do you know how often I have done things like that?" she said. "I've gone for months agonizing over making a phone call and then, in the end, not making it anyway. In seventh grade I had a crush on this boy, Kevin. Every afternoon at four o'clock I would go home, dial his number, and freeze. He would answer and I could not say a word. Then he would get mad and I would panic and hang up. Finally the police came around to investigate a stalker."

"I guess we suffer from the same hang ups."

"Probably so. I felt that we had a lot in common from the moment I opened the door and saw you there with your friend, Mel. You were standing behind him, looking scared. There was something appealing in that, very Gregory Peckish, only shyer, more boyish. You suffer from shyness, don't you?"

I nodded, but felt uncomfortable. Shyness had always been a problem of mine, but it wasn't something I was proud of and I did what I could to hide it.

"Actually I'm the same way," Cara said. "I put on an act, but half the time I go around terrified that I'm a complete washout, a total nonentity with no clout and no talent."

"I never would have guessed that."

"Nobody does because I'm good at putting on a show. I have been playing at being a bright penny for a lot of years. It's what my father wanted. I used to blame him for everything; for my feeling insecure, for making me think I had the brains of a Rockette, the whole works. But I've decided it's not really Sidney's fault. He is who he is, and if you let him get to you, that is your problem. No, if anyone is the culprit, it's my idiot brother, Henry. Do you know anyone whose ambition is to be Ezra Pound? Not only to write like him, but to be him, obnoxious anti-Semite and all. That is Henry's model. Don't ask me why. It's psychotic. I think he identifies with the Nazi in Pound, admires the viciousness. At one point he wanted to convert to Catholicism and he would have done it, too, only he knew that if he dared my father would have pulverized him into a wafer. The irony is he is talented, he can write. Actually, I used to think that he was better than crazy Pound. But he's full of himself."

Cara went on that way, talking about her brother, calling him pretentious and a jackass, but also clearly admiring him and, I thought, trying still to deal with the hurt he'd inflicted on her.

"The most unbelievable thing," she said, "is that for years this lunatic was my hero. But could I get a smile, a hug, from this stiff? I might as well have been trying to get a hug out of the Fuhrer himself. I'd ask him a question after trying to read his darling Pound and he would look right through me. Or he'd just walk past me, reading some gloom and doom lines from T.S. Eliot, another anti-Semite."

Then abruptly, Cara stopped talking and looked closely at me.

"Are you interested in any of this?" she asked, "or am I just being Henry, going on, boring the hell out of you and forgetting that anyone else exists. I hate myself when I act like that."

"Not to worry. I'm really interested in all of it. And I'm interested in you," I added as lightly as I could. Cara gave me a quick, acknowledging smile.

"Thanks," she said. "I really appreciate that. I guess all I was trying to say is that I know what it's like to feel insecure. I may sound like miss know-it-all, but the truth is I still feel like that dumb kid who was living in the shadow of this genius brother. Maybe that's why I've put so much energy into politics, that kind of thing. That is what spins Sidney's wheels. I've spent my life trying to be his favorite." She paused, then added. "Is that pathetic or what?"

"It makes total sense," I said. "I've been in pretty much the same place myself. As a kid I thought my father hung the moon. He grew up in Canada and he used to tell me stories about the Canadian Royal Mounties. For years I was convinced that he was one of them, on a mission to nail the Nazi super of our building who wanted to cremate us for playing stoopball in front of the building. That idea of him didn't last long, though. When I was about twelve it fell apart. One night my mother scared the life out of me by coming into my room in tears.

"I asked her what was wrong, and she said, 'It's your father. The man is living in another world. He believes in magic, he thinks this family can exist on magic.' Then she took a sheaf of checks out of her pocket and stuck them right under my nose and said, 'Do you see these? Can you tell me what's wrong with them?'

"I took the topmost check and looked at it. It was from my father's business account made out to my mother with the notation 'for household expenses' written on the bottom.

"I didn't see anything wrong, and said as much to my ma.

"'Look again,' she ordered. I looked, still nothing. So she snatched the check out of my hand and held it in front of my face.

"'It's not signed! Don't you see that? He doesn't sign them. Every week he gives me these phony checks. He'll sign it in a few days, he says, as soon as his creditors pay him. Well, I am still waiting, and waiting doesn't put food on my table.' Then she started crying again and I really got scared. I thought she was going to have a nervous breakdown."

"God, how awful," Cara put in. "Is your father really insane?"

"You would think so, but it's not really like that. He lives on wishes and he convinces himself they will come true. A couple of days after my mother broke down, I did what I had never done before. I spoke up. I told him what happened, told him about my mother's upset and about the checks she had shown me.

"'I told him I was really worried about Ma. I said, 'I'm afraid she's getting sick over this.'"

"What did he do?"

"He put his hand on my head. Then he stroked me a few times and told me not to worry, that everything was under control.

"'Your mother is a big worrier,' he told me. 'That's her nature. You have to understand that. The fact is, there is nothing to worry about. Money is a little short now because quite a few customers owe me. Things are tight for them, too, so everyone is short of cash, but they are good for it. In a few weeks everything will be back to normal.'"

"And did that happen?" Cara asked. "I mean return to normal?"

"That was five years ago and my mother has been on the verge of a nervous breakdown ever since."

"And you?"

"I sometimes think I am, too."

"Did you ever speak to your father again, about the situation, I mean?"

"There is no use. When my father makes a promise, he truly believes that he'll keep it. And when that doesn't happen, he'll talk about running into a short delay, an unavoidable delay, and then he'll promise that tomorrow will definitely be the day. As a kid my ambition was to be Carl Hubbell, to pitch for the Giants, so every Sunday when he was home, I'd ask my dad to take me to the park so I could practice my delivery. And every Sunday it was the same story.

"'We'll go later', he would say. 'It's been a busy week. I need a little more rest.' Of course later never came. He'd stay in bed pretty much the whole day. Then, one Sunday, he surprised me. I don't know what happened, maybe he made a few bucks that week, but he was up early, came to my room with a glove and ball, and was ready to go. But then I wouldn't go with him. It was too late. He had disappointed me too often. I told him I had a big test at school the next day and I needed to rest."

"That was too bad," Cara said.

I thought I detected a hint of criticism in her voice, as though she thought I should have been big enough to forgive my father, that I should have gone out with him when he offered, so I felt I had to explain myself.

"You've got to understand what the man is like," I said. "Ninety-five percent of the time he can't untangle himself enough to look even remotely like a parent. And then, from nowhere, out of the blue, he'll act the part of the devoted father; only what he is really doing is deciding, when the spirit moves him, to stick his nose into my life."

"Such as doing what?"

"Taking it into his head to show up at a Harmon game. That's what he did the other day after I told him straight out that I didn't want him there, that playing against Ryder made me nervous enough."

"And he ignored you?"

"You know, I don't think that he thinks of it that way. He probably convinces himself that I didn't really mean what I said; that, underneath, I really want him to come, that I really need his support at a big game like that."

"That's pretty twisted thinking." Cara put in.

"That's the way the man thinks." I said. "That's exactly what gets him into trouble."

I wanted to go on, to tell Cara about the mess my father's business was in and his troubles with the IRS. I felt a need to tell someone, to share the worry and the fear that I felt, but I held back. I hardly knew this girl and I had no idea how she would take that kind of information. Perhaps she would be put off and not want to have anything to do with someone whose father could end up behind bars. So, despite the temptation to open up, I kept my mouth shut.

Cara, though, sensed something, sensed my worry. She was very keen that way. She had a feel for people's troubles and she was quick to respond. She reached out and touched my arm.

"Look, Jonathan," she said, "If your dad is in any kind of real trouble, my father might be able to help. He knows business and he has a lot of contacts. If you think it would be useful, he'd be more than willing to speak to your dad."

"Thanks," I said. "It is really good of you to offer. I'll think about that."

At that point I was embarrassed and I wanted to get away from this topic. I felt that I had talked too much, revealed too much, and made it look as though I came from a really troubled family. Cara recognized my upset and changed the subject.

"I want to ask you something," Cara said, "can I be frank with you?"

I nodded.

"I was going to do something with Ken this afternoon," she went on, "watch some basketball in Central Park. But he got paged by the magazine and had to leave. They needed him to retake some photos that didn't come out right. Would you be interested in coming with me?"

I answered without thinking.

"Sure, okay. That would be great."

As soon as I spoke I could feel my heart revving up. I was stunned by Cara's words. The thought that she wanted to see me, actually to spend time with me sent a shock through my system. It was an idea that I had not allowed myself to think about, in fact a scenario that had seemed as realizable as an invitation to an afternoon tryst with Hepburn herself. On the other hand, the notion of playing second fiddle to big, splashy, Ken Masters, the *Redbook* heartthrob, did not have a lot of appeal. And I was puzzled by Cara's interest in basketball. Why would she want to go to a Central Park pickup game?

"It's supposed to be fun," Cara explained. "Guys from a bunch of schools scrimmage every Saturday. Stan Schneiderman got it together."

"He told you that?"

"He mentioned it to Ken at the party. Actually Stan invited him to play, but that is not Ken's thing. As a basketball player, he is a great fashion model. But Ken wanted to go anyway. He wanted to see Schneiderman in action. Apparently he is a wizard on the court."

"I've played against him." I put in, "he has some decent moves, but he's no Cousy." Cara said nothing but she looked at me as though I was a bratty fifth grader trying to knock down the teacher's pet.

I felt ashamed and I turned away from her, hoping that she had not spotted the rising color in my face. If she had, she gave no clue. She simply carried on with what she had heard about the game, that it was really an all-star affair with some of the city's best players participating, that it was a showcase for high school talent, and so on. But at that point I was not listening. I was thinking about Cara's offer, and as I did, I felt myself becoming upset. Not only was I a last minute fill-in for Ken Masters, but her overture amounted to an invitation to watch Schneiderman put on another show and to join his fan club. Suddenly this seemed like a bad idea, but there was no backing out now without my looking like a total ass. I said nothing and we started out.

Our first stop was Cara's apartment building. Walking alongside Cara, with her elegant profile and glinting rust hair bouncing on her shoulders, I felt distinctly out of place, a West Side bumpkin who was drawing frosty stares from doormen up and down Park Avenue.

Cara was walking rapidly and I felt as though she was pulling me along.

"I won't be more than a few minutes," she said over her shoulder. "I just want to freshen up and change my blouse."

"No problem. I can wait in the lobby."

Cara stopped walking and turned toward me.

"Don't be silly," she reached out and touched the back of my hand. "I want you to come up, sit, relax for a few minutes. Have a drink. I'll give Richard strict orders not to do you in this time."

"Thanks," I said. "I appreciate that. No doubt he's a loyal *Redbook* reader so I'll need all the protection I can get."

Cara said nothing.

We walked another block in silence. At that moment, I felt totally confused and I could think of nothing to say. Who was this girl walking beside me, I wondered, and what was she about? Why had she invited me to come upstairs? Was this a signal that she was ready to fall into my arms, a sign that as soon as the apartment door closed we were to kiss passionately, stumble into the living room, and fling ourselves down on a plush Rosenhaus carpet? Or was I contending with a teaser, one of those Finley spider-lady types who enticed men, played with them for a while and, when tired of that particular game, disposed of them without a thought. After he'd met her that first night, Mel warned me to be careful, that Cara might turn out to be a tease.

"She's definitely a Hepburn look-alike," he said, "but just watch your back. She might have more Stanwyck in her than we know.

"The problem with these girls," he explained, "is that they are totally blind. They will cut you to pieces and absolutely believe that you are benefiting from the surgery. It's a hereditary condition. Their mothers pass it on to them in-utero." At the time I wrote off Mel's remarks as another example of his signature cynicism, but now they came back to me.

We were about twenty feet from the building entrance when Cara stopped and turned toward me.

"Listen," she said, "I have a terrific idea. Why don't you play today."

"What are you talking about?"

"The game. In the park. I heard that you are a terrific player."

"Who told you that?"

"Schneiderman. After you left the party he said that you have one of the best set shots in the city."

"Your friend had too many of Richard's specials."

"No. He was serious. He said that you are a real outside threat. Anyway, I'll bet he'd be thrilled if you agreed to play."

As she spoke, I had a vision of being on the court opposite Schneiderman, trying to guard him but being left flatfooted as he faked me out and breezed past for an easy two points. In this scene Cara is on the sidelines, watching and looking sad.

"I'm really not up for it today," I said. "I think I've had enough of Schneiderman for a while. Besides, I couldn't play if I wanted to. I have no basketball gear with me."

"That is a problem I can take care of," Cara put in quickly. "My brother has tons of gym clothes he never wears. But I can understand how you feel," she added. "Who would want to go head to head with a ballistic missile?"

For a moment her face took on a serious, almost grim, expression, as though she was remembering Schneiderman's explosive hit on me, the way I was spiked to the ground, and tragically, the football squirting loose from my arms. Then, as though suddenly infused by some inner ray of light, she brightened up.

"What if things are entirely different this time?" she asked. "What if you and Schneiderman end up on the same team?"

"Now that's an idea," I replied. "But frankly, if I get to choose I'd rather team up with Attila the Hun."

"Schneiderman's faster," Cara replied. "And he has a better hook shot. The rap on Attila is that he's got lead feet. But I wasn't kidding, this could really happen. We are talking about a pickup game. Players change all the time. You two could end up on the same team. I'd love to see that," she added. "You would make a sensational duo. We'd have to send out for a *Post* photographer to record this historic event."

"All he would catch is two guys trying to knock the stuffing out of each other." I replied. "Not a very pretty picture."

"Well, actually, it could be a classic pose. Dempsey versus Tunney, Louis versus Schmeling, that kind of thing."

"You have a lively imagination," I said.

"By the way," I asked. "Why in the devil do you keep talking about me and Schneiderman getting together? Do you come from a long line of matchmakers?"

"It's a family habit," Cara admitted. "But the fact is, you two could be buddies. Neither of you realize it, but you are a perfect fit. He is Brooklyn savvy and you are Broadway kitsch. You complement each other. You would make an unbeatable team."

I felt a bit offended by Cara's designation of me, which seemed to suggest something put on and artificial, but I said nothing. Cara though, caught my facial expression and she reached out and touched my arm.

"What I mean is that watching you two guys out on the field is like watching two well-oiled parts of a remarkable machine that somehow fell off, got lost, and need to be put back together again."

"I see. Well that is interesting. I can hardly wait to tell Schneiderman that we are really brothers under the skin; that we started life as two parts of the same Rube Goldberg contraption. If he knows this, maybe he'll go easy on a relative."

Cara stopped walking, turned, and stood in front of me so that I could not move.

"Listen you," she said. "I want you to get something straight. Rube Goldberg couldn't invent you even if he wanted to. He doesn't build dream machines."

I looked at Cara and could say nothing.

The surge of excitement I felt in my chest seemed to have a paralyzing effect on me. I just stood there looking dumb. Then, slowly, awkwardly, I reached out to her. She took my hand and we walked that way to her building.

I sat in the foyer of Cara's apartment while she got ready. It was dark and quiet there. In the stillness and dim light the place looked immense and formidable, like a museum after hours. From where I sat, on one side I could see the dining room, insistently formal, with tall, straight-backed chairs and a polished mahogany table, and on the other the living room with its thick carpeting overlaid with richly-colored Persian rugs. On the walls of both rooms I could make out perhaps a dozen carefully arranged paintings, the Rosenhaus collection of modern masters, put together by Cara's father, known on the streets of Harlem as King R.

Cara appeared looking scrubbed and very pretty in a light blue blouse and grey skirt. At times when she let her hair down and it flowed auburn-red over her shoulders, there was an aura of elegance about her, an effect that was enhanced by her high cheek bones and straight back posture, but at the moment, with her low heeled oxford shoes and white socks, Cara looked more like a sophomore cheerleader off to practice her routine.

Motioning for me to follow her, Cara headed for the door. There she handed me a blue and white athletic bag.

"In case you get the bug," she said. "Or you can't stand watching Schneiderman do his thing without you."

On the way to the park Cara kept up a stream of chatter—she had a reputation as a talker—mostly about her father's involvement in city park projects and how that had become his latest obsession.

"He's into playgrounds," Cara said. "He's given the equipment for at least half a dozen. Last year the mayor wanted to put up a plaque at a new one that he's outfitted, but he refused. He said, 'Seeing kids tramping around in my sandboxes is good enough for me.'"

"Is that sincere?"

"I think so. One thing about Sidney, he can be generous. He doesn't hold on to his money. He always has some new charity he's plugging. On the streets he walks around with pockets full of quarters to hand out to bums and winos. He's good that way, but I tell him he's responsible for putting people on the street. He encourages them to buy on credit, fifty bucks down, five years to pay. The fact is, a lot of them can't pay. They get in over their heads, can't make the payments, borrow from the rent money, and end up losing everything. We duke it out all the time. He argues that I couldn't live in the style I do if it wasn't for the store, and I tell him I'd be glad to try, that what our family needs is less possessions and a lot more understanding of how we are treating folks who are spending the little cash they have to get themselves a decent bed to sleep on. We've been battling this out for years and no one ever wins.

"Actually, a strange thing is I got my interest in politics from Sidney. He would have loved to have gotten into the game. A long time ago he ran for City Council and came in fifth in a five horse race. If he had won, he might have had a different life. I guess maybe I'm trying to live out his dream."

Cara stopped walking and turned to me.

"Look, I'm sorry to go on this way. You must think that I'm a total narcissist. Next time we go out I want you to sit me down and put a hand over my mouth if I start in like this. It's the only way to stop me."

Actually, I had thought myself of doing this, of stopping her mouth, but not with a hand. If she went on this way next time we were out, I thought, I'd simply take hold of her chin, turn her face toward me, and end all of her talk with a kiss. Right now, though, I wanted to hear more about Cara's family. I found them oddly intriguing. As she talked, I pictured the cast of characters: King R, a blustery Jackie Gleason-type, brother Henry, a college kid's version of Leslie Howard, thin, self-consciously esthetic, naturally snobby, and the mother—Cara had said almost nothing about her mother—a stylish, dyed blond, well preserved, plucked in her youth by King R from the garment center contingent of grade B models. Privately I wondered to myself if I would ever get to know these people, ever get close enough to Cara to be part of her world.

At that point she had said almost nothing about Ken Masters. I wondered if she was deliberately keeping him out of the conversation, keeping their relationship a secret. In any case, I wanted to know about him and what he meant to her. Were they truly a couple or was he the boyfriend of the hour, replaceable perhaps— this was Mel's idea—by a man of the people.

And how did Schneiderman fit into the picture? Cara had said that he and Ken went back a long way, but how in the world did these two get together? How did a cardboard mannequin get to be buddies with a whiz like Stan Schneiderman, Ryder's version of Leo the Lip?

I finally worked up nerve enough to ask Cara about this, but we were approaching the basketball courts then and she was distracted by spotting Schneiderman. From a distance we could see him in action, dashing up and down the court, spinning, faking, driving for the basket, looking for all the world like one of my heroes, Al McGuire, St. John's legendary ball handler.

"They met at camp," Cara finally replied, turning back to me. "They were summer friends for a couple of years but then lost touch. They got reacquainted at my party the other night and Stan invited Ken to come to the park this afternoon."

So that was the story. I had been told that summer camps can make strange bedfellows—one year at Camp Scatico Len Fierman, our all-league wrestling champion, got tight with Leo Goldbaum, the glee club's prize countertenor, and ended up a cross dresser; but the idea that Schneiderman, the Flatbush flash, would team up with a sheepskin wrapped straw man like Ken Masters was as unbelievable as the rumor, circulating now among baseball insiders, that had DiMaggio been Jewish, he and Hank Greenberg would have been an item.

Afterwards, when I told Mel about it, he said he'd stopped being surprised by pairings of any kind, that he'd learned his lesson years ago when he'd lost a hundred dollars on a bet that Durocher and Ott, the jackal and the lamb, would end up feuding, only to find them hip to hip at Toots Shor's bar one night, arms entwined, toasting each other.

"You can lose a lot of money betting against the unbelievable," he added.

The courts were just north of 96th Street, not too far from Spanish Harlem, and they drew a large contingent of black and Hispanic players who made use of the scrimmages to practice their moves.

As we approached, I saw that a game was in progress. Half the players, Schneiderman's team, wore white tee shirts, while the other half, the Skins, were bare from the waist up. Along one side of the court, scattered among a couple of rows of weather beaten benches, sat a half dozen players, waiting to get into the game.

Cara and I took seats in the first row and watched the action. It was a warm mid-September day, still a couple of months away from the start of the basketball season, but Schneiderman looked to be in mid-season form. As I watched him move with that unmistakable stride of his, a long, easy glide that appeared unhurried but that covered ground with surprising speed, I recalled last year's Harmon-Ryder basketball game and the trouble we had stopping him.

The player assigned to guard Schneiderman would dance in front of him, hands waving in his face, eyes fixed on his legs, trying to anticipate his next move.

Schneiderman would glide to within inches of his man, teasingly hold out the ball, and then, with a head fake and sudden acceleration, sweep by the defender and drive to the basket.

Now he was using the same moves, leaving a bare-chested defender flat-footed as he feinted him out and drove in for a layup. At other times Schneiderman would feint, start to drive, stop, step back, and hit a one-handed jump shot from outside the circle.

These were thirty point games, the first team to reach that number being the winner. That team stayed on the court to take on the next pickup group.

When we arrived, Schneiderman's team was close to finishing off the Skins and we had barely settled into our seats in the stands when he sunk a one-hander from the corner and the game was over. The final tally showed that Schneiderman had scored more than half his team's points.

At the whistle he headed for the sidelines, wiping his face with a towel flung to him by a shapely blond girl in a scarlet blouse and jeans—someone told me later she was a Schneiderman groupie—who had been recruited to handle such matters.

When he was about ten yards from the grandstand, Schneiderman spotted us. Waving and smiling a welcome smile, he hurried over. "Cara, Jonathan," he called, "how great to see you. What a surprise. How terrific of you to come. Is Ken here?"

Cara offered apologies and explained the situation.

"Too bad," Schneiderman said, "I was hoping to get him on the court."

"Not much chance of that," Cara replied. "When it comes to sports, Ken's talent stops at modeling the uniform. But this fellow here"—Cara gave me a little nudge forward—"should be in there with you. If

what you told me is true, we have star material sitting on this bench."
Schneiderman nodded and reached out to touch my shoulder.

"Absolutely," he said, "I know from firsthand experience just how good Jonathan is. Last time we played he scored—what, Jonathan—over twenty points?"

"Eighteen," I said, "and half of those were free throws." Schneiderman laughed.

"You have a modest friend here," he said to Cara. "the fact is, he was great. I think he hit half a dozen set shots from beyond the circle."

"You guys still won," I reminded him. "And you scored over twenty points yourself."

"That I don't remember," Schneiderman said, "but I know it was a very close game and that at the end we had to double team Jonathan to stop him from blowing us out of the water."

He turned to me. "How about it? Can we get you out there?" he asked.

"Thanks," I said, "I appreciate the offer, but I'm not up for it today."

"Don't be a spoil sport," Cara put in. She reached out and took my arm. Her grip was surprisingly strong.

"I really want to see you play," she added. "Stan here does too, don't you Stan?"

"Absolutely," Schneiderman agreed.

"I'm really out of practice," I protested, "I'd look like an idiot."

"No way," Schneiderman said, "no chance of that. You are too good, too much a natural for that."

"Thanks," I said, "but you don't know how bad I can be. Anyway, I'm not really ready. It would take me a while to change."

"No problem," Schneiderman said, "we'll take a break and wait for you."

Reluctantly—I felt strong pressure from the two of them—I picked up the bag that Cara had left at our feet and headed for the locker room.

As I changed, I felt rising fear and rising excitement. The thought of going up against Schneiderman again was triggering tachycardia—I could already feel jumpiness in my chest—but, strangely, I also felt something else; anticipation of the encounter and—stranger still—something like satisfaction in the knowledge that this time, on a basketball court, we would be competing on more level ground.

A few minutes later I emerged from the locker room wearing a polo shirt that could have fit Chairman Mao and baggy white shorts that fell to within a couple of inches of my knees. Cara waved and gave me the thumbs up.

"You look great, Jonathan," she called, "casual chic."

I smiled and waved back.

"Good luck. Break a leg," she added as though I was going on stage.

While I changed, Schneiderman spoke with the waiting players and explained that he had invited a guest, an old buddy, to play a couple of games. If they resented my cutting in that way, no one said anything. Schneiderman was the leader, clearly the dominant player in the group, and without saying so, the others accepted—and seemed to welcome—his authority.

My team was composed of a couple of players from Clinton High who had been waiting over an hour to get a game and two holdovers from the Skins whom Schneiderman chose to stay on. After huddling with his team and whispering some instructions, he came across court and introduced me to my teammates.

There were the two Hispanic boys from Clinton, both about my height, and two lanky black fellows, one a scrawny six-footer, probably no more than fifteen, and, alongside him a bony giant, easily six-foot-six, who warmed up by executing half a dozen slam dunks followed by a leap to the rim where, like a kid on a jungle gym, he hung on for a couple of seconds. Hector, a recruit from the stands who sported sideburns that curled beneath his earlobes, acted as referee.

The teams took the court, each player now crouching in position, and with a sharp toot on his whistle, Hector tossed the ball high in the air between the centers to start the game. The tap went to Schneiderman's team. The Shirts' right guard, a heavy set fellow with no waist and the build of a linebacker, leaped forward, grabbed the ball, and, whirling, heaved it half the length of the court. When it came down, Schneiderman was under it, all alone, steps from the basket. At the opening tap he had feinted left, then sprinted down court. Taking the ball on the run, he sprang forward for an easy layup.

Marco, one of the Hispanics who was playing point guard for our team, shook his head, cursed under his breath, and took the ball out from behind our basket.

The inbound pass went to me and I started up court. The fellow guarding me, an acned Jughead lookalike, came forward and moved in close, waving his arms, two-stepping in front of me, and looking to slap the ball out of my hands. I stopped, pivoted away from him and looked for someone to pass to. A few feet ahead of me I spotted Leon, one of the speedy Clinton High boys, cutting toward the basket and I rifled the ball to him. It never got there. Darting in front of Leon as soon as the ball was thrown, Schneiderman stepped in, picked off the pass, and went in all alone for another easy score.

Now I was doing the cursing. Barely a minute old, the game was all Schneiderman. I determined to slow things down, to move deliberately, to keep my eyes open for Schneiderman's stunts, and to prevent him from stealing the ball—and the game.

On our next two possessions we managed to tie the score with a couple of baskets. I tossed a high pass to Ambrose, our string bean center, who promptly executed one of his trademark dunks, and then, no more than ten feet from mid-court, I hit with my specialty, the two-handed set shot, modeled point for point after the technique of Sid Tannenbaum, NYU's back court wizard, whose number, six, I wore on my Harmon uniform.

On the sidelines, Cara called to me through cupped hands.

"Great shot. Way to go, J." And from out of bounds, before he passed the ball in after my basket, Schneiderman smiled at me and, concealing a hand in front of his tee shirt, gave me the thumbs up sign.

For the next dozen minutes Schneiderman and I exchanged baskets. He scored on a jumper and a running one-hander, and I retaliated with a hook shot from the key followed by another two-handed set shot that swished through the net without touching the rim.

It was 20-18, in favor of the Shirts, when I got hurt. It happened in the backcourt, just after I'd managed to pick off a rebound from the defensive board. Leaping high, I grabbed the ball just over the arm of the opposing center, turned and, seeing an opening, started toward mid-court. I had moved to within a couple of feet of the center line when, from nowhere, Schneiderman swooped in, flashed an arm in front of me, and managed to slap the ball out of my hands. Striking the floor at an angle, the ball took a low bounce and started to scoot away. I darted after it, grabbed at it, and nearly had possession when, coming up from behind, Schneiderman again tried to make a steal. This time, however, as he reached across my body to swipe at the ball, he lost his balance, and stumbling forward, crashed into me. I went sprawling, landed hard on the gravel surface, skinned a knee, and jammed a wrist as I tried to break my fall.

Waving his arms and looking irate, Hector, the referee, gave a blast on his whistle, shook a finger at Schneiderman, and did a dramatic rendition of the body blow that he had delivered. Looking decidedly sheepish, Schneiderman raised a hand to acknowledge the foul. Then, leaning over me, he reached out a hand to help me up.

I shook my head and stayed down. The pain in my knee was searing and I did not know if I could get up. Hector came over to appraise the situation, and from the sidelines the pretty girl in jeans ran onto the court with a bucket and sponge.

I sat up and inspected my knee. The skin had been scraped off, the flesh looked macerated, and the entire area was a mass of blood mixed with dark specks of gravel. The sharp pain had become a stinging throb, and I felt as though I could put no weight on that leg. Realizing that I could not get up to my feet, Schneiderman and Leon, each grasping me under a shoulder, gently raised me to a standing position. Leaning on both, I hopped to the sidelines.

Cara was waiting for me there. She guided the three of us, Schneiderman holding up one side, Leon the other, to an empty spot next to her on a bench and helped ease me onto it. Then she squatted in front of me to survey the damage.

"This is a beaut," she said. "I'll bet you haven't had a skinner like this for a few years."

"Third grade was the last time as I recall. It got me a day off from school and ice cream two nights running."

Cara looked up at me. "I can do better than that," she said.

Schneiderman now kneeled beside Cara to inspect my knee.

"Goddamn, I'm sorry," he said. "I don't know what happens to me out there. I just lose it."

I glanced down at Schneiderman. He looked guilty, guilty and shame-faced, like a fighter whose KO punch has inflicted a serious head injury.

"Look, it wasn't your fault," I said. "We were both going for the ball."

"I guess that's our thing," he replied. "We go for the ball and in the process manage to beat the other guy's brains out."

I shrugged. I didn't know what to say to that.

By then the pain had eased a bit and I was able to stretch out my leg. Cara had gotten a Band-Aid from the bucket and sponge lady and she applied it now with a quick, smooth touch. Then we sat together on the bench and watched the end of the game.

After what happened, Schneiderman was not himself. He played cautiously, passed off a lot, refrained from driving for the basket, and under the boards kept his elbows under control. Still, he managed to hit three long one-handers and the Shirts again were the winners.

At the whistle, I got up. "Let's get out of here," I said to Cara. "I think I've had enough for one day."

"Don't rush yourself," she said. "You're hurt, you've got to take things easy. Look," she added, "why don't we go someplace and sit for a while. Have a Coke. Relax. It will do you good."

At that point I just wanted to go home. I was feeling pretty lousy and all I could think about was crawling into bed, turning on the radio, and shutting out the world. The chance, though, to spend some private time with Cara was hard to resist.

"Okay," I said, "but let's not stay too long."

"We won't," Cara said. "Don't worry, I take good care of the wounded. Say," she added, "how about we ask Stan to join us? It would be a chance for the two of you to sit together, get to know one another."

Terrific idea, I wanted to say. Maybe if we sit close enough he'll manage to do a job on the other knee. But Cara's voice sounded enthusiastic, pleased with her plan, and I thought it best to keep quiet.

"Sure, if you like," I said.

There was something about Cara's need to bring Schneiderman and me together that I did not understand. It was as though she had to be the peacemaker. Or was it that by bringing the two of us together she was trying to mask the fact that it was she who was becoming interested in Schneiderman.

"It's a Chamberlain Complex," Mel said when I told him about it. "She tries to be the good guy, to appease everyone, to make nice so that she won't recognize her own aggression. The lady must have Germanic blood in her," he concluded. "She has a need to take over whatever she can get her hands on."

I didn't want to believe Mel, but there was something about Cara, about her ambition to move ahead on so many fronts, that made me think that he had a point.

I thought then that Mel was speaking out of jealousy and I told him so. "If you are looking for hidden aggression," I said, "You could start with your attitude towards me."

Cara now instructed me to sit tight and keep my leg extended. Walking to the edge of the court, she stopped Schneiderman as he came off. From where I sat I could see him smiling and nodding, obviously pleased at her invitation. Then, taking a few steps in my direction, he signaled to me that he was going to change and would be ready in just a couple of minutes.

He was as good as his word, and shortly the three of us made our way out of the park, me walking gingerly and the others pacing themselves to allow me to keep up. A few blocks away we found the place that Cara had mentioned, a remodeled storefront featuring art nouveau posters, rose-tinted lighting, an espresso machine, and attitude. An unsmiling young woman, pridefully French, showed us to a remarkably small table, not much bigger than one found under a foyer mirror, and the three of us sat, knee to knee, huddled around it like conspirators planning a heist. Schneiderman helped me ease into my chair.

"Are you in a lot of pain?" he asked.

"It's a scrape," I said. "It will be okay in a couple of days."

"Let's hope so," he said. Then smiling at me, he added, "Well, anyway, I'm glad we won't be playing one another soon. I can imagine what you've got in store for me."

"As a matter of fact, you can't," I said. "I'm working on something very special."

Schneiderman grinned. "Well, I'll just remember to watch my back," he said.

"Can you two quit sparring?" Cara suddenly put in. "The game's over. We are here together as friends. The three of us. In fact, I've been thinking that working together we are going to make one terrific team."

"Playing what kind of games?"

If Cara picked up the jab—it slipped out despite what Mel called my Dale Carnegie approach to Cara's take-no-prisoners conversational style—she responded with only mild irritation.

"This is not about games, Jonathan," she said. "It's about work that needs to be done." Cara then turned her back to me and leaned toward Schneiderman.

"Look, I don't want to be intrusive or too personal or anything, but I heard some upsetting news about your family and I wanted to talk to you about it."

Schneiderman looked startled and seemed, instinctively, to pull back.

"What news?"

"I heard that your dad had a blow out with the DA in Brooklyn and got fired."

"Who told you that?"

"I heard it from the grapevine."

Schneiderman now looked angry. His face seemed to tighten up and I thought he might lash out at Cara. As for me, I was stunned by the way Cara was speaking. I could not imagine barging into someone's private business the way she did, especially in a matter that was so sensitive.

"Ken told you, didn't he?" Schneiderman asked, but didn't wait for an answer.

"I should have known the guy is a loudmouth. He always was. And did he also tell you about the corruption, about the kind of guy the Brooklyn DA is? The fellow is strictly Tammany," he went on, "nothing but a stooge for the big boss, DeSapio."

Schneiderman's voice took on a note of bitterness and his expression seemed to hover between anger and pain.

"The police arrested a rapist. It was a clear-cut case," he continued, "and my father was set to prosecute the creep when the DA suddenly claimed there was a flaw in the case. This was totally phony, a trumped up excuse to let the guy go. Obviously DeSapio wanted him released and the DA just caved. And when my father fought him and insisted on prosecution, the DA threw him out, just tossed him out on the street after more than twenty years of service."

"Christ, that is horrible," Cara said. "That is the lowest of the low. Look, we are going to go after this creep. He is not going to get away with shit like this. What is your strategy?"

Schneiderman looked momentarily puzzled.

"I hadn't really thought about that," he said, "but I know that my dad plans to contact the mayor's office and lay out this whole rotten business."

"That's fine," Cara said. "That's a start, but if you think something anemic like that is going to get you anywhere, you are incredibly naïve. If you know O'Dwyer, you know that he will do whatever is good for him. He needs Tammany's support. If they give him the high sign to look the other way, he'll do just that. If you want results," Cara added, "you have to get the media involved. You need to hold a demonstration, picket Gracie Mansion, make a scene so that the police get involved and you get some press coverage. You've got to put pressure on O'Dwyer. That is the only way you'll get the crook out."

Schneiderman was silent while Cara spoke. Initially he seemed to be amused. Then gradually, almost reluctantly, his expression changed to one of respect. "You know your way around this kind of thing, don't you," Schneiderman said.

"It's my other life," Cara replied. "By day I'm a Park Avenue princess. At night I wander the streets looking for picket lines. If I don't find one, I get twitchy. I'm liable to have a seizure."

Now Schneiderman was interested. He appeared curious, amused, bemused. He was leaning toward Cara. I said nothing but felt myself irritated, upset by what I thought was Cara's putting it on, doing a number, and—Mel hit the mark when I told him—spinning a Cara web.

"I started before I was a year old," Cara was saying. "That was my father's union period. He was into the Labor party big time. He joined picket lines at GE and Ford, demonstrated against sweatshops, marched to Washington for John L. Lewis and the CIO, even volunteered to pick grapes at coolie wages to expose abuses. A lot of times he would strap me on his back and take me with him. I was a mascot, a poster child for the union movement. I got to know a lot of Hispanics, Mexicans, Puerto Ricans, Guatemalans, all of them. I'm still a favorite south of the border.

"When he made his bundle, Sidney did a U-turn. He denies it, but it is true. He got greenback fever. Out in East Hampton he started salivating for land to build on. He got stomach pains whenever Christies had an auction. So he left the party, threw down his picket signs, and joined the gold rush. Today he will fire a packing clerk before he will allow a union shop. Can you believe that? He claims the unions have become whorehouses run by pimps and fat cats who want to feed off the minimum wage worker. For my money, that is pure projection. But I guess I got infected early. I'd walk miles for a good demonstration. And if anyone needs a really good organizer, I'm always on call."

"Well it looks like we can really use your help," Schneiderman said.

"Okay." Cara said. She shoved her chair closer to Schneiderman. "Here's what I'd do."

For the next ten minutes, while I sat looking on, Cara outlined a strategy having to do with soliciting supporters, distributing leaflets, organizing a Flatbush rally and a letter to the *Times*—that kind of thing.

I felt out of it. It was not that I didn't care. What happened to Schneiderman's father struck me as thoroughly rotten, a devastating blow that, unlike my father's self-imposed calamities, was not of his own making. And I was glad to do what I could to help. But in the face of Cara's zeal, her run-on monologue, and her huddling with Schneiderman, I felt simply abandoned. And I was hurting.

Finally, after a couple of more minutes of watching the two of them put together what sounded to me like a cockamamie plan, I let my irritation show.

"I'm feeling pretty lousy now," I said. "I'm going to have to get home."

All at once, to my surprise, Cara did a complete about turn.

"Oh, my God," she said. "I'm so sorry, Jonathan. There you are sitting in pain and we are yapping about how to get enough behinds to stage a demo. I don't know what happens to me. I just get swept out to sea with this stuff. It's an addiction. Next time will you please haul me away if I get started like this?" Then she turned to Schneiderman, "Look, I'm sorry to have to go. Jonathan here is in pain. He's been a real stoic just sitting there all this time. I have to get him out of here."

"You don't have to get me anywhere," I said. "I'm fine. The thing is just acting up a bit. I'll be okay when I get home." Cara rose and came to my side. Then we said a quick good-bye to Schneiderman. He wished me good luck and a quick recovery.

"I'll see you out there soon," he said.

"I'm sure you will," I replied. "Just keep watching your back," I added as a mock warning.

Outside, we turned toward Park Avenue and walked a couple of blocks in silence. My knee was burning and I felt agitated.

Suddenly halfway down the next block, Cara stepped in front of me, turned, and blocked my path.

"I don't care for sulkers," she said. "It gets you nowhere. If you have something to say, come out with it. Handling anger this way makes you look childish, as though you were afraid to fight."

I did not move. I felt a sharp pain in the mid-section, as though Marciano had landed a short right to the breadbasket. I looked at Cara. She was standing in front of me, eyes wide, jaw pointed, looking like a pint-sized Durocher taking on the plate umpire.

"I'm not angry," I said. "I was just thinking. I guess my mind was wandering."

"Baloney," Cara said. "You're jealous, pure and simple. Schneiderman kicks your butt good every time you play him and it makes you mad as hell. You don't want his winning any rounds with me. Well, if you've got a problem with him, go after him, but don't take it out on me. If you don't think you are in his class, that's your problem, not mine."

Then, as quickly as it came, the storm was over. Cara fell back in step with me and we walked on without speaking.

"I'm sorry," she said after a bit. "I just can't stand being given the silent treatment. That was my mother's tactic. I hated her for it. My dad and I fight. We can go toe-to-toe, but that's okay. That's much better. If you have a gripe, come out with it. If I think you are off base, I'll let you know. But don't freeze me out. I don't do well with that." Then she took my arm.

"Are you in a lot of pain? I could put in you a cab."

"No, really, I'm okay. I'll put on an ice pack when I get home."

"Good idea. Is there someone there who can help you?"

"My folks will be home."

"Will your mother know what to do? Is she the kind who can handle these things?"

"She can be a caretaker when she needs to."

"Okay, but if you are having any trouble, call me. Promise?"

"I promise."

We were a few yards from Cara's building. The white-gloved elevator man from a couple of weeks back was tending the door, standing ram-rod straight and watching us. Cara moved in closer, pressed herself against me, and looking up, gave me a deep, open-mouthed kiss. I kissed her back hard, trying to wiggle my tongue to meet hers. Then she simply put her arms around me and held me.

"I want you to be okay and to get back on the court. You can go head to head with Stan Schneiderman anytime," she said. "Do you believe that?"

I nodded. "Sure. Absolutely." In fact, I was trying to believe it but the idea of keeping up with Schneiderman, going head to head with him and coming out on top didn't come easily to me.

"All right then." She reached up and held my face between her hands for a moment. Then she let go and headed into the building. At the doorway she turned back.

"I'll call tomorrow to see how you are," she said.

"Promise?"

She made a mock cross-my-heart sign and disappeared. Limping a little, but without much pain, I walked to the corner bus stop.

Chapter Six

To my surprise—Mel warned me that given her history I could easily disappear from Cara's radar for days, if not weeks—I heard from her early the next morning.

I was awake and trying to get back to sleep when she called. A few minutes earlier I had been aroused by the sound of my father shouting into the telephone at one of his salesmen. Sunday morning was the traditional time for them—there were four, like the Horsemen of Apocalypse, who covered four boroughs (my father boycotted Staten Island as territory historically unfriendly to Jews)—to call in with their weekly sales reports.

The news in recent months was cause for alarm. Sales, like a fatigued marathoner, were lagging far beyond expenses, but in predictable fashion—it was not in his nature to hear alarm bells of any kind—my father simply ignored any numbers he did not like. Dismissing the red flagged balance sheet that Sugarman pushed under his nose as nothing but the misguided meddling of pea-brained bookkeepers, my father chose instead to rally his troops. Calling on their loyalty in these Sunday morning phone sessions, he exhorted them to set a new Brooklyn record for hardware sales.

That morning his lecture lasted a good ten minutes and although I managed to drift off during part of it, there was no sleeping through his stirring peroration. And before I could settle down again, I heard my mother calling me from just outside my room.

"Telephone for you, Jonathan."

"Who is it?"

"A young lady. A stranger."

"Cara?"

"Could be. What would your mother know?"

"Tell her I'll be right there."

I jumped up, momentarily debated whether to rush to the bathroom—I was afraid that the pressure from my full bladder would cause me to be abrupt on the phone—rejected that idea as creating too risky a delay, and in the foyer where we kept the telephone slipped into the chair that my father had just vacated. My mother took up a position in the connecting living room where she pretended to straighten pictures.

"Cara?"

"I was thinking about you all night, Jonathan. I was really worried. When you left you seemed to be in a lot of pain."

"I'm okay. The swelling has gone down. Thanks for calling."

"Truth? Are you really all right? You're not just being macho?"

"No, really."

"Are you able to walk?"

I extended my leg and jiggled it in the air.

"Can you hear that sound? That's my leg itching to move. It can't wait to get on the road."

"Really? Can you travel? Could you go someplace today?"

"Absolutely, I could run the marathon, or, if I got in the mood to kick ass, I could challenge your pal, Schneiderman, to a game of one on one."

"I'm calling you, Jonathan, not Stan Schneiderman."

"Right. Sorry. I must have had a bad dream about him."

"If you are really okay, would you like to come out to the beach today?"

"The beach?"

For a moment—Mel, the avid student of psychology, announced that it was the classic syndrome of psychic paralysis, induced in the peasant class by an invitation to the royal palace. Cara's meaning did not register. My thoughts immediately went to Rockaway and Jones Beach, frequent destinations for our crowd on sweltering sunny days.

"East Hampton. Sidney wants to go out for the day. Would you like to come along?"

In a flash, as though arriving from some buried data book, I suddenly remembered the tip that Debbie, Cara's personal Boswell, had passed on to me: that East Hampton was the key, that an invitation to the beach house was a sign that you were in the game and more than that, that you had a shot at being drafted into the big leagues.

Palpitations set in immediately and I found myself unable to speak.

"Jonathan?" Cara's voice seemed to be searching for me. I tried to calm myself, to tame the fierce combination of runaway excitement and primal dread that had taken hold of me. It was a familiar feeling, the same feeling, in fact, that I had experienced in the Ryder game when, lined up in my right end position, hands on knees, in danger of keeling over from a galloping arrhythmia, I awaited the opening kickoff.

"Are you there, Jonathan?"

"I'm here," I managed to get out. "Sorry. I guess I'm not awake yet."

"Well can you come? Do you want to come?"

"Sure. Yes. Okay. I do. I mean it sounds great, like a lot of fun."

"Can you be ready in half an hour?"

"What?"

"Sidney wants to get going. He's already pacing the floor. If we don't get on the road in half an hour, we'll have a certified lunatic to contend with."

I glanced at myself in the tall mirror that stood in the foyer. Slumped in a chair, folded into oversized, sleep-ruffled pajamas, half awake and thoroughly demented, there was no way that I could meet such a deadline.

"I'll be there," I said.

In fact, I was out of the house in twenty minutes, hair approximately combed, my father's cologne splashed on, toting my old Cavalier's athletic bag. This I packed with towel and bathing suit—I opted for a square cut boxer model rather than the bikini number that Mel had given me for Hanukkah—and a change of underwear in case one was needed.

As I got myself ready, dashing from bedroom to bathroom and back again, my mother followed me, insisting on knowing where I was going.

"To the beach."

"Which beach?

"A beach."

"Rockaway?"

"Near Rockaway."

"Who are you going with? Are you going with the girl on the phone?"

"I'm going with a friend."

"I know that you are going with this girl. I can tell."

"Okay. You are right. You are an incredible mind reader. They ought to book you on Ed Sullivan. Yes, I am going with this girl and her family."

"She invited you?"

"Yes, she invited me."

"Who is she?"

"A girl."

"Which girl? Do I know her? What kind of girl?"

"Fat, ugly. You would not like her."

"What do you see in fat, ugly girls?"

"I like them. I'm weird. I've got to go now."

"What time will you be home?"

"Ten, eleven. I don't know."

"Call me."

"I'm late. I've got to run."

"Call me when you get there. Let me know where you are."

"If I can, I will. I'll be fine." I gave my mother a reassuring pat on the shoulder. "See you tonight."

I took fifteen dollars from my desk drawer, all the money that I had accumulated from the hit and run allowance my father gave me—he was good for a five dollar bill on the increasingly rare occasions when a sale actually closed—and did something I absolutely never did—Mel said that this act alone demonstrated that extent of my passion—I jumped into a taxi cab. Telling the driver to step on it as I had urgent business to conduct, I perched on the edge of my seat, money in hand. Heeding my plea, the cabbie made a sharp turn and headed east. Barreling through side streets, we reached Central Park West, sped through the 86th Street transverse, and arrived at Park Avenue in under seven minutes.

Sidney Rosenhaus answered the door. He was a big man, about six-foot-two, thick- limbed and overweight in a jowly sort of way, like a beefy lineman gone slack from being out of training. Standing there in front of me, his large body covering the door frame and blocking most of the light from within, he surveyed me with a quick glance, then nodded.

"This one's good," he called to someone inside. "He made it in under twenty-four hours." Then he turned to me.

"Do you know what it's like to sit in this confounded apartment, sweating a fountain, waiting for a fairy with an Armani overnight bag to show up?"

I stared at the man.

"No, of course you don't. Why would you? You are still a baby. Wait, when you have a daughter who is into a fag model who wears beads and thinks he is descended from the pharaohs, then you'll get it. Then you'll do your own sweating."

Once more Sidney Rosenhaus turned and called back into the apartment.

"He believes it, right, that he's descended from pharaohs?"

"Who, Dad?"

"The boyfriend. Mr. Photoshoot."

"King Tut, Dad. King Tut."

Mr. Rosenhaus eyed me and gave a shake of his head in the direction of the voice.

"Name dropper, that one. You know who we are talking about, right?"

"I think so."

"You can't miss him. He's got a sheep fetish. Goes nowhere without his sheepskin coat. It's his blanky. In ninety degree weather he'll wrap himself up in it just to feel the wool. Personally, I think the guy is into animals anyway."

Then Cara's father moved in closer.

"If you're worried about competition," he confided, "not to worry. A fruit pie like this Ken character doesn't rate. He's not in the game. Don't let the fashion shots fool you. The camera knows how to make him look good, real macho, and the girls go for it. But the truth is, he's a powder puff. In my opinion he doesn't really like the ladies, if you know what I mean. His pecker points the wrong way."

Sidney Rosenhaus laughed at his own joke. Then taking a step back he looked me over once more, now scrutinizing my clothing. Then, reaching out, he plucked at my sleeve.

"Did you sleep in these clothes?"

"Pardon me?"

"Looks like you slept in these clothes. Either that or you hooked them together fireman style so you could jump into them when the princess called."

Again he turned toward the inside of the apartment.

"You've got this one well trained, Cara," he called. "He's got the firehouse routine down pat."

Just then Cara appeared. She was wearing a low-cut gypsy peasant blouse, blue skirt, and sandals. She wore no makeup but her face had a freshly washed glow that made her look prettier than ever.

Cara took her father's arm, gave it a squeeze and, at the same time, shot me a knowing wink.

"I see you two are already in deep conversation. But if I know Sidney here he hasn't introduced himself. Dad," she said, "I'd like you to meet my friend, Jonathan Manheim. Jonathan, this is my dad, Sidney Rosenhaus."

I extended my hand. Slowly, as though coerced, Sidney Rosenhaus reached out. His grasp was light, fleeting.

"Your folks found the reform solution, right?"

"Pardon?"

"Your moniker. You've got the reform Jews way of adding a bit of goy to a name, not too much, just a sprinkle to give it a little class. Jewish families don't use the name John, right? The Catholics have co-opted that one. There is Saint John, John the Baptist, Pope John, a whole slew of Johns. But Jonathan is perfect. It keeps the gentile John, but gives it a little twist. This makes it kosher."

"I hadn't thought of that," I said.

"Well, you learn something every day," Sidney Rosenhaus replied.

Just then Cara's mother appeared from inside. She was pretty much as I had imagined her, a woman who, in her youth, had clearly been a striking beauty and who now—I guessed she was in her mid-forties—retained the fine good looks of a former model. Immaculately groomed, trim in a way that requires diligence, with attractive—not flashy—lemon blond hair, she was simply and expensively dressed.

Bound for the country, she wore a tailored pink blouse and dark blue skirt—I'd seen outfits like this in Bergdorf Goodman's windows—an inventive necklace of square gold pieces that played off, and seemed to add luster, to her blond hair, and highly polished blue loafers, smartly elegant, that must have cost over a hundred dollars a pair.

"Mother," Cara said, "this is my friend, Jonathan Manheim." Mrs. Rosenhaus took in my origins, my genetics, my West Side aura, my Klein's-on-the-Square clothing, in a single glance. She nodded and offered a thin smile.

I imagined that she had instantaneously compared me with Ken Masters and was wondering just what in the world her daughter had in mind.

"Did you have to travel far this morning, Jonathan," Sarah Rosenhaus asked in a pleasant, measured voice, clearly practiced at framing coded questions.

"Just across the park, Mrs. Rosenhaus," I replied. "It took just a few minutes by cab." I was relieved to be able to say that I was from Manhattan, not a borough—say Brooklyn or the Bronx—that clearly would have finished me off with this lady. Mrs. Rosenhaus nodded.

"And your family knows where you will be and that we won't be getting back until quite late tonight? On a Sunday night the trip from the Hamptons can be a bit of a nightmare," she added, again granting me the thin smile.

"Thank you for asking," I replied. "My mother is used to my getting home late from the beach on Sundays."

"Oh, you know the Hamptons?"

"I've been there a few times," I lied. Mrs. Rosenhaus nodded again, noncommittal, like a technician administering a polygraph test. Then without another word she left the room, returning a minute later trailed by Louise, the kitchen maid, and Richard, the brewmaster, each carrying two large bags.

"I guess we are about ready," Cara's mother announced. "You can call for the car, Sidney," she said to her husband who had retreated to the dining room and was gathering up the Sunday *Times* to take along.

Garages in the area were not in the habit of delivering cars to their customers. Standard procedure was for the parking attendant to transport the vehicle to the main floor of the garage where the customer would come to fetch it. With a combination of clout and cash, however, Sidney Rosenhaus had managed to negotiate a special arrangement whereby he paid a premium—and kept mum about it—for delivery service.

When, a few minutes later, we reached the lobby—Louise and Richard took the service elevator with the bags—a spotless black Lincoln Continental was waiting at the curb. Clarence, the leprechaun doorman, was on duty and along with the others, he greeted me cheerily, as though I had become a member of the family. Although this greeting did nothing to change my feeling of being an alien, a barely tolerated alien in this world of service elevators and black sedans, I felt momentarily buoyed by this scrap of recognition.

Trotting ahead of us, Clarence opened both sets of car doors and I was starting to follow Cara into the back seat when Sidney Rosenhaus grasped hold of my arm.

"You'll sit up front with me," he announced.

Feeling instantly alarmed, as though I had been seized by a burly traffic cop, I looked up at him, then at Cara. Sidney Rosenhaus was smiling and gesturing toward the front passenger seat. Cara looked startled, uncomprehending. She moved quickly to her father's side.

"What do you think you are doing, Dad?" she said. "This is my guest. He belongs with me."

"Take it easy, young lady." Sidney's voice was sharp, cautionary. "Just calm down." He held his arms chest high, palms outward, as though he was issuing a silent warning. "I'd like a little

time with your friend. He looks fairly normal. It's a three-hour drive.
I need conversation."

"Mother will sit with you."

"Mother has had twenty-seven years to sit with me. In that
time—you can ask her yourself—I don't think she once mentioned the
football Giants or the U.S. economy. I hear that Jonathan is a football
player and—who knows—maybe he's also interested in what goes on
outside Bloomingdale's front door. Do you read the paper, son?" he
asked, turning suddenly toward me and catching me off guard. I
nodded.

"Most days I read *The Times*," I answered.

"And the business section. Do you look at the business
section?"

"Sometimes," I lied.

"I'm asking, see," he explained, "because on long rides I like to
talk business. It stimulates the bloodstream, keeps the brain focused.
Besides, who knows,"—here Sidney Rosenhaus gave me a
conspiratorial smile and, I thought, a wink—"maybe I'll make a
discovery, find a compatriot, a *confrere*, someone who can appreciate
what I do and knows what it is like to earn a dollar." Cara's father
then turned again to me and seemed in some odd way to be making an
appeal.

"With a son who won't set foot within a mile of my store—says
being any closer fogs his brain—and a daughter who makes a thing of
hanging out with a fairy who poses in undersize jeans to show off his
crotch, chances of my finding a future partner in this gang look pretty
slim."

"Very funny," Cara said. "Well, I can assure you, you won't
find any *confrere* on this trip either. Jonathan here is interested in
politics. He is going to work with me on a number of projects. And
when I get my campaign up and running, he's going to be my right
hand, aren't you Jonathan?"

"I am planning on that," I said.

"Politics. Very good. That's excellent." Cara's father looked
pleased at the news. "I love politics. Next to business—I mean
talking tactics, marketing strategies, things like that—there is

nothing better than a good political discussion." He gave me another broad smile. "This will make my day."

At this point, Cara's mother reached out and touched her daughter's arm.

"Don't get into it with him, Cara," she said. "You know what a mule he can be. If he wants Jonathan up front with him, let him. We'll change seats on the way."

"He is impossible, Mother," Cara said. "The truth is, he's afraid I'll have my hands on Jonathan's crotch all the way out. That's the crotch he's worried about."

"Cara." Mrs. Rosenhaus sounded shocked, embarrassed. "There is no excuse for that kind of talk."

Sidney Rosenhaus waved his wife down. "Easy, Sarah, don't let her get your goat." Then, turning to Cara.

"As a matter of fact, that is not something I worry about," he said. "That is strictly your idea. Maybe you are getting a little tired of hanging out with a fag who only wants the ladies to look and not touch."

With a shake of her head that indicted how pathetic she regarded that last shot, and looking distinctly unhappy, Cara climbed into the back seat. I took my place besides King R.

"So what do you think of Truman?" Sidney Rosenhaus asked as we headed north on Park Avenue toward the Triborough Bridge.

I had no idea where he was going with this, and what response, if any, would keep him calm, keep his eyes on the road.

"Well, he is a pretty gutsy guy," I said. That seemed a safe enough answer. Actually, it was the image of Truman that automatically came to mind: gutsy, the plain speaker who tipped his hat to no one.

"So you've bought the line," Mr. Rosenhaus said. He shook his head in mock despair.

"Shame on you. You are not thinking for yourself. That's the image his PR people want to sell you; Truman the regular guy, the straight shooter, the tough, no-nonsense guy. What they don't say is that this tough guy managed to annihilate a half million innocent people. And do you know why he destroyed whole cities and fucked up the genes of an entire population? Because he's dumb, that's why. He is a dumb man. The guy has zero *seckel*.

"Look, the man sold clothes for a living. I looked up the store record. It stunk. Half the time the place was in bankruptcy. Your tough-talking president couldn't sell a pair of sneakers to shoeless Joe Jackson."

"I didn't know that," I said. "I guess that is not the best credential to be president."

Sidney Rosenhaus glanced at me, and smiled.

"I like the understatement," he said. "I like understated guys. But do you know why the man was bound to go bust, why he never could make it? Have you figured that one? It was because he didn't know his customers. He couldn't read people. So we got ourselves a president who burned up a country because he couldn't read the Japs. He didn't understand that they were finished anyway and didn't need a kayo punch.

"That's one thing I learned from my father," he went on. "To use my eyes, observe people. Find out who they are and what they are really all about."

"He is going to tell you he's become King of the Sharks, because he's studied human nature." Cara piped up from the back seat, "And as a student of human nature he figured out that *schvatzers* in Harlem need furniture to sit on. And he'll tell you how he parlayed that insight into an empire that is singlehandedly responsible for seating half the black *tushes* in the city. Of course his stuff leaves a little something to be desired, but that doesn't bother him. He figures the Stickney people have enough to worry about without competition from him."

With a shake of his head, Sidney Rosenhaus gestured toward the back seat.

"The voice of the people. That is my socialist daughter, God bless her. She means well. She has a good heart and I love her but she doesn't understand what it takes to earn a dollar. You hear her. She finds all kinds of fault with her father, but if she didn't have money behind her, if I wasn't backing her, believe me, she couldn't get to first base with any of her projects."

Mr. Rosenhaus' voice was becoming agitated and, a couple of times, he took his eyes off the road to glance at me. I tried to show an interested face, a sympathetic face, meanwhile feeling rising anxiety at the thought that in the back seat Cara was listening, no doubt trying to determine where I stood, whether I was on the right side of things.

"What I wanted to say before I was interrupted," Sidney Rosenhaus went on, "is that I not only studied people, but I made a point of taking a hard look at myself as well. I figured out that if you want to make your mark, be a somebody, you've got to be brutal with yourself. You can't let yourself get away with a freaking thing.

"When I was young, I was a ballplayer. I played in the Babe Ruth League and was scouted by the Newark Bears. Do you know the Bears, the Yankee farm club? Rizzuto came up through them. Well I could swing a bat and I could have had a try-out with the Bears. They wanted to schedule it, see if I could hit a curve ball. But one morning I looked in the mirror and who did I see? I didn't see DiMaggio or Hank Greenberg, or even the sumo wrestler, big Johnny Mize. What I saw was a poor man's version of Ducky Medwick. Do you know who Medwick is? Not bad with the bat, but a guy who is liable to get zonked on the noggin anytime he goes after a pop fly. That was me. Good hit, no field. So I turned in my spikes and looked around for an honest living. Do you know what I wanted to do? You'll get a laugh out of this. I wanted to build airplanes. How about that for a fantasy? I love airplanes, love flying, but I took another look in the mirror and I didn't see Howard Hughes looking back. And I didn't see a Mr. Boeing either. What I saw was a kid from Hester Street whose father sold junk and who learned the furniture business from the bottom up. So I realized that's what I know. Furniture. I know how to buy from crackers in the Carolinas and sell to *schvartzers* in Harlem. So I came down to earth fast. Just dropped like a shot up B52. And I told myself, forget the dreams. That's it. You're in furniture. No illusions. Maybe I'm a notch above my dad now, but basically I'm in the same line.

"The truth is, my stuff is okay. I don't need anyone to tell me it's not Stickney. But if you take care of it, if you don't piss on it, it will last ten, fifteen years. The problem is the merchandise gets trashed. Trashed like you wouldn't believe. Half my customers are on dope. They will get high and start brawling and slash the sofas; or they will get sick and barf all over them. I sell everything stain-proofed, free of charge, no cost to the customer, but it's like spitting in the wind. Do you know what I mean?"

"I do," I said. "I can see what you are up against, Mr. Rosenhaus."

"For me, this is not human behavior," he went on, "this is subhuman. Your friend back there goes for my throat when I say this, but that is the way I feel. If you are a person, you show respect. You take care of what you have. That is one thing my father taught me. We had nothing in our house, a few beds, some chairs, a couple of dressers, practically nothing. But my father insisted that we take care of whatever we had. 'Take care of our things and take care of your family,' my father said. I've always tried to do that."

"Your father gave you good advice," I put in.

"He was the best," Mr. Rosenhaus said. "He thought straight. He knew what was important."

Sidney Rosenhaus was quiet for a moment, then he shot me another quick glance and took two more of his deep breaths.

"Right now I have a problem with something else," he said, looking straight ahead and seeming to concentrate on the road. "Do you know my son, Henry? Have you met Henry?"

"I haven't had the pleasure."

"Well, you'll meet him today. He's at the house now. Henry's a poet. He writes poetry. Wherever he goes, he is writing poetry or reading poetry. I bet my wife he writes poetry on the can. You are probably thinking what is it like for a huckster like this, a guy who barely graduated high school, to have a son who is a poet. Well I can tell you it feels weird, that's what it is like. It feels damn weird.

"You wonder to yourself, is Henry a good poet? I haven't the faintest idea. Not a clue. The first line of poetry I ever heard, Henry read to me, and I didn't understand a word. But I'm getting more of it now. Come sit out by the pool this afternoon. I'll read a Frost poem. I like Frost. I relate to apple trees and meadows and things like that.

We have a couple of acres at our place and I put in apple trees. You'll see, I have a regular orchard.

"It took me a while—I admit it—to get used to my boy being a poet, but I'm proud of him now. How many street vendors like me do you know who have sons who are poets? None I'll bet."

"I can't think of any right now," I said.

"Well there you go. But the problem, see, is that poets can't earn a dime. If they manage to pull in a couple of thousand a year, they are bestsellers. So I want to provide for Henry. I'm not talking about a handout, understand. I don't believe in supporting the able bodied. I want to be a patron like those Italian princes I've heard about who took care of poets like they were Talmudic scholars. But who knows how long I'll last and when I'm gone, it's over. He'll have no more Italian princes signing checks. So I told Henry you need a business, a little business of your own to keep the cash flowing. Do you know what woven labels are?"

"The little labels inside your jacket?"

"Right. Good for you. You use your eyes. Well every garment has a woven label. Every clothing company, every dinky manufacturer on the street needs labels, good times or bad. The business is a gold mine, an undiscovered gold mine. Nobody thinks about labels. Nobody is rushing out to buy label companies. What I tell Henry is, the business would run itself. You could steer it with one hand and write with the other. But he's not interested. It would be a distraction, he says, would take him away from his writing. You could hire a manager, I say, be an absentee owner and just collect the receipts, but he won't listen. If you see him today," Mr. Rosenhaus added, "maybe you could have a little talk with him, show him the light. He likes young people. Do you know Ezra Pound?"

"I have heard of him."

"Pound is one of Henry's favorites. If you know Pound, you will have an in with Henry."

"Well, I'll see what I can do." I promised.

"Much obliged," Sidney Rosenhaus said, "*Obligado*, as they say south of the border."

Once again Cara's father lapsed into silence, looking distinctly worried as he scanned the roadside for signs for the Long Island Expressway.

"Thirty," his wife called out from the back seat. "Exit Thirty. Sidney. Make sure you don't miss it this time. Mr. Rosenhaus has a bit of trouble reading signs," she explained to me with lowered voice, "he has cataracts."

"I can see perfectly well," her husband muttered, but not loud enough for his wife to hear.

Once on the expressway, Mr. Rosenhaus seemed to relax. On an empty stretch of highway he looked over at me with a quick appraising glance.

"What about your family," he asked. "What are your folks in?"

"My dad runs a hardware supply business."

"Your dad is a smart man," Mr. Rosenhaus declared. "Do you know why I say that? Because choosing that line of work shows that he understands people. He understands human instincts. In business that is the thing that counts. Forget your profit margins, your phony business plans. You make money when you know what drives people, what pushes them from within. Your dad understands motivation. He knows that the human animal builds up and tears down, builds up and tears down. That is what wars are about, the urge to tear down civilizations so that we worker bees can build them up again.

"Do you ever watch kids in a playground?" Mr. Rosenhaus suddenly asked me.

"Not recently," I admitted.

"Well you really ought to do that," he said, "that should be your laboratory. If you want to understand what people are all about, the animal clawing from inside, just watch kids. It's all there. Basic instincts, not dressed up, not camouflaged. What I like is, you see it all raw, the whole cycle of building up, knocking down. And possessiveness. A kid will kill to hold his place on a swing. To watch these kids is a study in warfare. And a study in making a civilization, too.

"Every Tuesday I visit a playground," Mr. Rosenhaus went on. "For a while the mothers fingered me as a pervert, but the cops know me now and let me alone. I've even gotten some of them interested in kid-watching."

"That sounds fascinating," I said.

"Would you like to join me sometime?" King R suddenly asked.

I was trapped.

"Sure. That would be great."

"Well anytime you are interested, give Cara a heads up. She'll alert me and I can meet you in the park."

"I'll do that," I said.

At that point we had been driving for more than an hour and everyone seemed comfortably settled in. But then, as though aroused by an alarm clock, Cara's mother suddenly pushed forward on her seat, stretched an arm between her husband and me, and waved her wristwatch around.

"Time to change," she said, "we are very overdue. Pull over at the next exit, Sidney."

Mr. Rosenhaus looked straight ahead.

"I'll get off in a few minutes."

Mrs. Rosenhaus raised her voice.

"Pull over now, Sidney," she demanded, "we have been waiting for over an hour."

Sidney Rosenhaus looked at me and shrugged his shoulders.

"When you hear that tone my boy, you don't argue. Not unless you want to touch off an atomic bomb. One thing you may have noticed about women," he went on, "when they see two men having a good time together, they want to break us up."

I murmured something that I hoped sounded like agreement. At the next exit, Mr. Rosenhaus pulled off.

A minute later I was in the back seat sitting hip to hip with Cara. She smiled, touched my hand and then, without speaking, held a finger to her lips. Silently she edged forward in her seat and motioned for me to do the same.

Cara's mother's face was in profile. She seemed to be scrutinizing her husband.

"Well, did you have a good visit?" she asked in a muted voice meant for her husband's ears only. Mr. Rosenhaus nodded.

"Very good. He's a good boy."

"Oh?"

"Quiet. A good listener. Takes in what you say."

"That must have been flattering."

"Flattery is not the point. He's respectful. That's a sign of character. The boy wants to learn."

"And?"

"And what?"

"What else?"

"Nothing else."

"What about the family?"

"The father's well off. Runs a successful business."

"What kind of business?"

"Hardware, building supplies."

"I see. And the mother?"

"I didn't ask."

"You never ask about the mother."

"I didn't get around to it."

"When it comes to mothers, somehow you never do."

Sidney Rosenhaus did not reply.

Cara leaned back, stifling a laugh. Then she gave me the thumbs up.

"You did well, J. You know how to read people. Sidney's right, you are a good listener. Maybe that's what drew me to you, that you are interested in learning."

"What do you think I want to learn?"

Cara's face took on a look of prankish innocence. Her hand touched my thigh.

"I wouldn't know, would I?" she edged closer to me.

"You know he's smitten," she whispered. "I can tell. He is already thinking of you as the son he doesn't have. A few more conversations like that and you'll have an offer to manage dinette sets, complete with salary and commission."

"It would be the best offer I've had in years," I replied.

Cara turned so that she could look directly at me.

"We'll have to see if anyone can top that," she said. Then slowly she began to rub a hand across my arms and chest.

"Nice?" she asked. I nodded, then I froze in place. Cara's hand had moved to my leg and was playing over my crotch. Then, without a word she began a light massaging movement. I became instantly aroused and panicked. What if King R spotted us in his rearview mirror or his wife took it into her head to turn around and start a conversation? I had visions of King R stopping the car, coming around to the back seat, dragging me out by my hair, and dumping me, like yesterday's trash, on the side of the road. I wanted to pull away, to remove Cara's hand, but I did not dare. Not only might she take that as a rejection, but it might put an end, also, to any future massages.

Fortunately—I was approaching the precipice and imagined having to scoot out of the car bent over like Groucho to hide the inevitable wet spot on my trousers—we reached the house an instant before Cara propelled me to the point of no return. As we pulled into the driveway, Cara quickly removed her hand, sat up, and tucked in her blouse. "To be continued," she whispered. I slid to my corner of the seat, crossed my legs, and willed the excitement to recede. When, finally, following Cara, I emerged from the car, the sun was bright, almost blinding. I was glad of that because as I stepped onto the asphalt there remained a suspicious contour to my trousers, one that a hawk-eyed mother was all too likely to detect.

At first glance the house was not as grand as I had imagined, not the glistening white stone palace flush on the beach that I had pictured, but a sleekly modern structure painted steel blue gray. Built as a single story home for much of its length, only gradually, toward the rear section, did the building rise to form a second level.

The true grandeur, I discovered, lay not inside, but behind the house in majestically landscaped grounds, cultivated as an apple and orange orchard. This expanse extended from the edge of the pool-cabana area—a Hollywood set in itself—for two acres, finally sloping off and ending in a shallow stream.

Inside I was immediately taken by the contrast with the modest seeming exterior. I found myself not in the plush elegance of the Park Avenue apartment, but in a spare and glistening modern art museum created by someone with an eye for the new and the bold. Around the gallery like space hung half a dozen striking canvases; a Pollock, two Hoffmans, a Rivers, a Rauchenberg and, placed on pedestals between them, a like number of sculptures by Arp, Bourgois, and Smith, among others; all innovative artists whose work was regularly on display at the 57th Street galleries.   I was stunned. It was as though, coming in from the beach wet and sandy, I had pushed open the side door of a summerhouse and found myself in a room at the Guggenheim. Cara was watching me as I started to walk in. I took a few steps, then stopped short. For a few seconds I just stood there, managing, finally, to emit some kind of appreciative sound. Cara had moved into the center of that open space, a continuous living-dining area, and waved her arms in a circular motion.

"This is my father's effort to erase his history," she said, "his attempt to wrench a few hours of pleasure from his five and dime store existence."

"Looks like he's done a damn good job of it," I said.

Cara shrugged her shoulders. "I suppose so," she replied, "but when you are trying to outmaneuver yourself, you have a lot of fancy footwork to do."

Suddenly I thought of my own father and the history he could never escape; not only a bleak and impoverished childhood in a Toronto ghetto but, more importantly, the conviction, as the youngest child in a family that already had too many children, that he was nothing but a burden, a dead weight dropped on that unhappy crew.

In these surroundings I could not help comparing him with Sidney Rosenhaus who, for all the furies that pursued him, had somehow managed to create a universe in which he was king—and this his palace. The comparison made me sad. I felt an urge to say something to Cara, to share with her what I was feeling, but I was not sure that she would understand—or care—so I let the moment pass.

"Henry is here somewhere," Cara was saying. "Probably reading at the pool. Let's go find him. You've got to meet him sometime."

A glass door at the rear of the room led out to the pool area and there, at the far end of the deck, near the diving board, we found

Henry. He was seated with his back to the house, folded into a lounge chair and immersed in a book. Cara called to him as we approached but there was no response. The figure in the chair did not move. It was only when we were on top of him and after Cara had slipped her hands over his eyes and had given him a kiss on the neck that he stirred.

"Really Cara," the slumped figure protested. There was a reprimand in his voice, I thought, a note of exasperation. Then slowly, reluctantly, he rose and faced us.

Henry was tall, much taller than I had imagined—probably six-foot-two or -three, and strikingly thin. He stood before us now, a gaunt figure with a narrow, oval-shaped face that seemed to fade into a receding chin. Thin, silver-framed glasses were perched on his forehead. Seeing him standing there, a book in one hand, a gin and tonic in the other, he reminded me of a Giacometti stick figure, one of those strange, pencil thin sculptures I had once seen at the Museum of Modern Art.

"Cara," Henry said. He leaned down and his sister raised her face and gave him a peck on the cheek.

"This must be your new friend," he added. He took me in quickly, head to toe. Then he extended a hand and smiled at me. It was an open enough smile, but there was something about his manner that was vaguely off-putting, an air of superiority that made me feel that, while talking, he was secretly sniffing my body odor.

"I'm Jonathan," I said.

"Forgive me for saying this, Jonathan," Henry continued, "but I'm so pleased that you look normal."

"Excuse me?"

"Normal. Regular. Not average, mind you. My sister would never consort with an average man. I mean normal looking, regular, someone you can walk down the street with without wanting to hide because you are with a preening idiot. The last fellow she brought around was a strutting peacock; gay, of course, but pretended to be bi. Used my sister as a beard and poor sis here"—Henry patted Cara's shoulder—"didn't even realize it. But I'm not really surprised. My little sister has a penchant for freaky people—no offense. It's an obsession. She collects damaged protoplasm the way other people collect beetles. If you want to make out with her, show her a withered limb or a couple of mongoloid ears. You'll be tucked up in her bed in no time."

Cara stepped forward and gave her brother a little push. He faked reeling backwards from the blow.

"What you are seeing here is King R humor," she said to me. "A perfect copy. My brother prides himself on being totally different from his father; the poet son of a Harlem huckster. But the fact is my brother is every inch his father's son. They both live to be perverse."

"And what about you, my dear," Henry retorted, raising an eyebrow and peering down over his glasses, which he had flipped onto his nose. Without waiting for an answer, he turned to me.

"Cara's a stone thrower," he said. "You've probably noticed that. Everyone is out of step but her. But the truth is, she's the odd one. Just look at her record. No offense, but she's into losers. Don't ask me why. She is just drawn to the type."

Cara seemed stung by her brother's words and she came back at him.

"My brother got his pride hurt because Ken Masters didn't fall all over him. He made it pretty clear, in fact, that he preferred the little sister. Henry is not used to that."

Henry burst into a forced laugh.

"One thing you can say about Cara is she is not short on imagination. That is the bonus that you get for dating her. She will entertain you from her storehouse of fantasies. Has she mentioned the one about becoming a U.S. senator? That's been good for a chuckle. The problem is, she believes these things. And if you don't go along with her, you see what happens. She tries to assassinate your character." Henry then turned to me with a question.

"Do you know *The Hollow Men?*"

"I beg your pardon?" Suddenly I felt panic, as though I had shown up in class without having done my assignment.

"*The Hollow Men.* For my money, Eliot's best work. Better than *The Wasteland.* Tighter, more controlled."

I nodded in agreement.

"It is sawdust heads like this Ken Masters guy that Eliot had in mind. All biceps and abs and, inside, nothing, just six feet of hollow tubing."

Cara caught my eye and with a slight movement of her chin pointed at her brother.

"You've just had a perfect demonstration of why you should never get involved with me," she said. "It's an invitation to being trashed by the Rosenhaus clan, *pere et fils*. They make a thing of slicing up anyone who moves in on their territory. They are the ones who specialize in character assassination."

From nowhere the image of a football squirting out of my arms appeared in my mind and with it an impulse to blurt out the question that had arisen with it.

What do they do when there is no reputation left to destroy is what I wanted to ask, but I thought better of it.

"I guess I'll have to take my chances," is what I did say.

At that moment Sidney Rosenhaus and his wife, Sarah, appeared on the deck dressed in tennis whites and carrying racquets pressed into wood frames. Sidney wore a baseball cap with a cotton sweatband circling his forehead. His wife was dressed in a starched tennis skirt and white socks with red tassels. On one wrist she sported a light blue sweatband of her own.

"How about a game of doubles?"

Sidney was speaking to Cara, but glancing at me. He ignored Henry.

"Right now?" Cara asked.

"Sure. I called the club. They have a couple of empty courts. I'd love a game."

"What about you two playing each other?" Cara asked.

Sidney pointed over his shoulder with his racquet. "Bad back. Hurt it going for a chip shot a couple of weeks ago. I can't play singles for a while."

Cara looked at me, as though for a signal. I suspected that she wanted me to come up with something that would get us off the hook, but I felt King R's eyes fixed on me and, at that point, I had no intention of taking him on.

I looked at Cara, smiled, and mouthed the words, "whatever you want." She did not respond to my message.

"We weren't really thinking about tennis right now," she said, seeming to address both parents.

Sidney took a step toward his daughter and made an open gesture with his arms that seemed like a mute—or was it a mock—appeal.

"Come on," he said, "an hour, that's all. Do something for your poppa. It's the only chance I'll get to play this week."

Cara then turned to me, still looking, I thought, for a way out.

"Do you even play tennis, Jonathan?" she asked.

"I play a little." Actually I was curious about what it would be like to play against King R or, if the teams were chosen up another way, to have him as a partner.

"Okay, then, Sidney," Cara responded, "but just for an hour." This she said with particular firmness, a quality, I came to learn, that was most apparent when she feared being influenced.

"Absolutely," Sidney Rosenhaus replied. "We will stop on the minute."

Then turning toward me he threw out an aside.

"When a dictator speaks, the people listen," he said.

Cara led the way back to the house and into the basement which was furnished as a combination cellar-ping-pong—workout room. At the entrance, she opened a large closet that was crammed with sports equipment. I counted seven tennis racquets lined upon one side of the closet, and from this collection Cara selected two, inspected their grip sizes, and handed one to me.

"You look like a five and a half," she said. "You've got big hands. Do you know how to use them—I mean do you know how to grip a racquet?"

"I have some idea," I said.

I followed Cara upstairs and into Henry's room which was lined floor to ceiling with books. She dug into a bottom dresser drawer, pulled out some white tennis clothes, and tossed them to me.

"You've got to wear white socks too," she said. "You'll be on display. This is a club that used to bar Jews and blacks. Now that the Wasps can't get away with that, they insist on a lily-white dress code."

"Do you really want to do this?" I asked.

"Do you know the phrase, all politics is local?" she replied. "Right now we are in Sidney Rosenhaus country. He calls the shots. As a kid I learned that if you want something from King R—say to back you when a scheme of yours really needs backing—you play ball with him. He doesn't take easily to not getting his own way."

"I gather that," I said.

Ten minutes later we were at the Racquet Club, a surprisingly modest looking place consisting of a small clubhouse with an awning covered patio. On the deck there were two white metallic tables and, at each, four matching chairs. Stretching out in front of this porch was a large expanse of grounds containing half a dozen green composition courts, immaculately maintained.

It was already three o'clock then, but it was still quite hot outside and only two of the courts were in use. At the far end of the complex an older married couple, probably in their late fifties, were engaged in a heated match that, based on the stream of grunts, moans, and gleeful bellows that emanated from that area, sounded like sex in the afternoon.

In the near court, four teenagers were clowning, flirting, and intermittently playing at tennis while Ed Warren, the resident pro, who once ranked fifty-fifth in the world, watched from the patio, ready to give a warning blast on his whistle at the first sign of a house rules infraction.

Sidney Rosenhaus approached me and handed me a racquet.

"What about you team up with Mrs. Rosenhaus," he said to me. "I'll play with Cara."

Cara was standing nearby. She was loosening the screws on her press.

"I was planning on playing with Jonathan," she said.

Sidney shook his head.

"It wouldn't be a game," he declared, "with old people, the first thing to go is the legs. You two would run us off the court."

"But you play all the time," Cara protested. "You know strategy."

Sidney shook his head.

"Not a match for youth," he continued. "There is no fun without competition. I figure fair sides would be the two of us against them." With a slight pointing of his chin he indicated his wife and me. "That should make things pretty much even-steven. Sarah here," he added by way of explanation, "has developed a mean net game."

"It's a matter of survival," Sarah Rosenhaus said. "Coming to net is the only way to keep the King over there off balance."

Cara nodded her approval. "Good thinking, mother," she said. Then she gestured toward me with her racquet.

"This okay with you, J?"

"I'll give it a try," I said.

In fact, the teams were pretty even. Despite his bad back, Sidney Rosenhaus proved to be the kind of infuriating player I knew from the Central Park courts; a bulldog of a retriever. No matter what shot you hit, no matter how sure a winner it seemed to be, he managed to get to it and send it back, often with a teasing lob. Even on angle shots that seemed well beyond his reach, Sidney would lumber over, a bit like a rhinoceros on the move, stretch out his racquet, and just reach the ball before it skittered off the court. The only shot he could not return was a sharp-sliced volley. His wife had figured this out, and she was a tiger at the net, darting here and there to head off King R's return of service and to put it away with a quick, decisive stroke. As she did so, she would pump a fist, let out a victory whoop, and encourage me to come to net and join in the fun.

I am not a consistent player. My backhand is weak and my forehand erratic, some of the time delivering a blazing cross court drive, at others a limp floater that Sidney Rosenhaus took great delight in smashing back at my feet. My best weapon, learned on a Harlem court from a pro who had once taught Althea Gibson, was a bullet first serve, tough to return when it actually came in, but, like my other shots, thoroughly unpredictable.

"Hey who do you think you are, Pancho Gonzales?" Sidney called over to me when my first serve of the set skidded by him. And then to Cara, "You'd better hang on to this one. He knows how to go for the jugular."

"Why don't you sign him up?" Cara called back. "Jonathan is your kind of man. He would be a great partner for you, on or off the court." Saying this, Cara turned to me and gave me an exaggerated wink. I looked back at her with a deliberately puzzled expression and mouthed the words, "don't embarrass me."

Cara turned out to be a surprisingly good player. I had not thought of her as an athlete, but in tennis she had almost perfect form—the result of years of lessons—and a consistent and tactically smart game.

The Sidney-Cara team took the first set 6-4, but in the second, with Sarah Rosenhaus playing fierce net and urging me on, we rallied from three games down to even the score at 6-6. Then, with Sidney beginning to puff and wheeze, we pulled out the next two games to take the set 8-6.

At that point Sidney Rosenhaus held up a hand to indicate that he had had enough and in silence the two teams walked off the court. At courtside Sidney put an arm around me.

"Now that is what I call a workout," he said. "Good for the heart. You're all right," he added. "You've got promise. You are not consistent, but you can play. When you come down again, how would you like to take a few lessons?"

"That would be great," I said. "I can use all the help I can get."

"I'll arrange it," King R said.

"By the way," he asked, "how did you like your partner?" Before I could say anything, he supplied his own answer.

"She's quite a net player. A bulldog. You wouldn't guess it, would you, but when it comes to beating the pants off men, she is unstoppable."

When we got back to the house, everything was prepared for a barbecue. The Rosenhaus' employed a couple to care for their place, a Ukrainian woman and her husband, who functioned as housemaid and gardener. Together they had arranged and decorated a long table in the garden, complete with fragrant candles and freshly picked flowers. The gas grill was open and four prime steaks were set on it, waiting for King R to don his chef's hat and apron and to demonstrate the grilling technique that he had been taught personally by Toots Shor, notorious showman and proprietor of the worldclass steakhouse that was home to the rich and famous. On the table the platters of food created a variegated color pattern that complemented the array of flowers—there must have been a dozen types—that surrounded the house. There was a large salad bowl, fresh corn, steaming mashed potatoes, a medley of vegetables, iced tea, and a ruby-red cherry pie with a lattice work crust.

"Unless we eat right now we'll be on the road for five hours," Sarah Rosenhaus said to me, as we got out of the car, "so why don't you and Cara just wash up and be back here in five minutes?"

"Please don't rush us, Mother," Cara put in. "We've just played two sets of tennis. We're hot and sweaty. We need to take showers and rest for a bit. We'll be down as soon as we can."

Her mother started to argue, then thought better of it.

"Make it as quick as possible," she said, "otherwise we'll be on the road for five hours." Then she turned to me.

"You may have noticed that it is an exercise in futility to argue with Cara," she said. "And if you haven't already learned that lesson, you will. I refuse to get into anything with her. It's been too many years of pointless fights, but maybe you can get through to her. If we are not on the road in an hour, we'll be in traffic until midnight."

Cara listened and said nothing. Then she reached out, took me by the hand and led me quickly back to the house.

"She can be a bitch," Cara said underneath her breath as we approached the front door. "Did you see the way she went after Sidney on the court? She relished every point. The woman is full of hostility. She hates the fact that Sidney and I have lives, that we are real players. All she's ever known is modeling and, by the way, don't get her started on that. She'll go on non-stop about her reign as queen of the cloak and suitors. When that went, when she could not trade on her looks anymore, all she had left was her wardrobe and a basketful of envy."

"That's sad," I said.

"It is," Cara agreed. "And sometimes I feel sorry for her. But when she gets petty and tries to play the Director General so that for five minutes she can feel like a somebody, it gets me mad. She doesn't really want me to succeed. She'll have kittens when my political career takes off. What she really wants is for me to be here with her, keep her company, and share her misery as proof that she is not the only failure."

"That is not you," I said.

"I'll blow my brains out if I ever end up like her," Cara replied.

At the top of the stairs, we were just about to split to go to our rooms when Cara took hold of my arm.

"You did good, Jonathan," she said. "You were a terrific sport. My dad likes you."

"He doesn't seem like such a bad guy," I said.

"Listen, he's great," Cara said. "He was my hero, my mentor. He has had a lot to do with who I am, with what is important to me. He is a terrific guy, but you've got to agree with him. Don't try to cross King R. He has a long memory for things like that." I nodded.

"Next time I'll play on his side," I said.

"Smart thinking," Cara agreed. "Especially for a potential son-in-law." Then, quickly, when she caught the look—instant panic—on my face: "Just kidding. You can relax. You are not going to be shanghaied into this family. It's just that we like you."

"Thanks," I said.

"Now go to your room," she directed, "take a shower and rest a while. If my mother freaks out, I'll handle her. We both need to get off our feet."

With my head throbbing and feeling slightly dizzy, I walked to my room and did as Cara instructed. I was on my bed, trying to take a ten-minute nap, when my door opened and Cara let herself in. With a finger to her lips she crossed the room with two quick strides, slipped into my bed, and held me from behind.

"Let's snuggle," she said.

"Is there time?"

"There is always time."

I turned toward her and we kissed, a long, easy, open-mouth kiss. I felt something I had never experienced before; a loving feeling, a deep, melting tenderness and something like that coming back from her. Cara gently stroked my head and neck, then slipped her hand under my shirt and massaged my chest and abdomen. When her hand reached my navel area, she quickly withdrew it and with quick, sure moves undid my belt and opened my fly. Then her hand searched for my penis, drew it out, and raised her head to look.

"You must have been first on line when they gave these out," she whispered.

I felt myself blush.

"I guess I haven't done so badly."

"I'd say." Then with what seemed to me a practiced hand, Cara gently massaged my testicles and penis, followed this by sliding down so that her head hovered over my crotch and was about to take my penis into her mouth—something I'd experienced only once before when, after downing two margaritas and floating into an atypically magnanimous mood, Myra Herz declared that although it was not my birthday she was going to give me a present anyway—when Sarah Rosenhaus' voice sounded sharp and irritated from the top of the stairs.

"Cara, you need to come now. Your father can't put on the steaks until you both are down here."

Cara made a face at the door.

"The bitch has uncanny timing. She knows just what is going on in here."

"She does?"

"Absolutely. She has a sixth sense for the state of my sex life. Anytime I'm in the middle of things I can count on her to develop an urgent need for my company."

"That's a bummer," I said sympathetically.

"You don't know the half of it. I have had to do it on a park bench just to get away from the woman. Anyway," she added, sitting up and beginning to straighten her blouse, "we'd better go now. Otherwise we'll be in for a non-stop harangue." Then, leaning forward once again, she gave my penis a last, soft stoke.

"I'll be back," she said.

In the garden, Sidney was wearing his chef's hat, a fancy pleated affair, and as soon as he spotted us coming, he arranged the steaks on the grill and called me over.

"I want you to watch this, Jonathan, in case you ever do any grilling. There are two secrets to turning out a great steak. Number one is the meat. Never work with anything but prime. The steaks you see here are gifts from Toots Shor himself. Number two—and this is the most neglected item in the whole business—is the marinade. Never settle for store bought. That will ruin your meat. Myself, I use a recipe—also from Toots—that is top secret. You have to be in his inner circle to get it."

"That must be some marinade," I said.

"Nothing better. You'll see. If you want, I could see about getting you on the list."

"Now that's impressive," Henry put in. He had stopped by for a drink before catching a train to the city and a poetry reading in the Village. "Congratulations. You are the first of the beaus to be let in on this secret. You've made quite a hit with Sidney here, hasn't he, Dad?"

At this Sidney Rosenhaus looked distinctly uncomfortable. He mumbled something about my being a fine boy, then looked away. I didn't know what to say, but felt an impulse to get King R off the hook.

"I would very much appreciate that," is what I did say. And, in fact, I felt strangely honored. Later Mel claimed that it was this offer that drew me in and made me want to be part of the Rosenhaus clan, that, psychologically, it had caused me to link King R with the great Toots himself.

Sidney's performance was as good as his word. The steak was luscious, tender and wonderfully flavorful. I had never been to a great New York steakhouse like Manny Wolfe's or The Palm, but I could not imagine any steak better than this. The whole meal, in fact, was extraordinary; the corn, the vegetables, the sweet and tart cherry pie, all perfectly turned out. I had never eaten a meal quite like it.

There was tension in the air, though. While we ate, Cara's mother kept looking at her watch and, with a kind of silent urgency, pressed us to finish up. Sidney Rosenhaus kept looking at his wife and, finally, half way through his steak, setting down knife and fork, confronted her.

"Will you stop this *noodging*, Sarah," he demanded. "You are giving the whole table heartburn."

"I'm not *noodging*," Sarah Rosenhaus retorted. "The whole bunch of you are dawdling."

Sidney did not argue. He simply shook his head as a silent commentary on his wife's behavior. Then, a moment later, turning to me, he spoke in a conspiratorial voice.

"We have this every Sunday night. Mrs. Rosenhaus gets nervous about leaving, and it affects the family's indigestion. Aggravation will always upset the digestive system," he added.

I nodded in agreement.

"Are you children about ready?" Sarah Rosenhaus asked while I was still eating my pie.

"We'll be ready in ten minutes," Cara answered in a voice both appeasing and exasperated.

Signaling me to follow her, Cara got up from the table and walked quickly back to the house. I followed her up to her room. As soon as the door slammed shut, I grabbed Cara and kissed her hard, my tongue searching for her open mouth. She responded only with a light touch of her lips.

"There's no time," she said, interposing an arm between us and giving me a slight push. "My mother will be barreling up here any second."

Then, more gently, "Look we'll spend a whole evening together soon. I can't relax in this situation."

"Okay," I said.

I did not want my feelings to show, but, in fact, I had not felt as sharp a sting of disappointment since the day my father tore up the tickets we had for a Yankees-Tigers game to protest the shameless behavior of his former hero, Hank Greenberg, who had not only chosen to play on Yom Kippur, but had gone three for four, with two runs batted in.

I recognized, though, that Cara was right; that if we started anything her mother's voice was sure to break in from the top of the stairs, interrupt our doings, and leave me, as regularly happened on dates with Myra Herz, with throbbing groin pain.

On the return trip there was no discussion about the seating. Cara's mother claimed her place beside King R and I slid into the back seat with Cara. As soon as the doors were shut she nestled into me, and in less than ten minutes was asleep. I managed to stay awake, looking out the window at the passing towns, now painted dark gray as the night descended, for perhaps another hour. Then I dozed off.

Cara and I awoke pretty much at the same time, just as we were approaching the Midtown Tunnel.

"You two have a good sleep?" Sidney called to us, seeing in the rearview mirror that we had stirred. "*Gey gezunt,*" he continued in Yiddish, "You should live and be healthy and have long lives. Just make sure you limit your sleeping together to *shluffing* on the way home," he added and chuckled at his own witticism.

"Don't be obnoxious, Dad," Cara called to him.

"Who, me obnoxious," he called back, "you must have the wrong chauffer."

At the apartment building, Sidney turned the car over to the doorman—the leprechaun was on duty—who immediately called for it to be picked up.

"Well we made good time," Sidney commented. And then calling back to me.

"Jonathan, I think you were our good luck charm."

"Thank you," I said.

"Call me Sidney," he went on. "We've broken bread together. We are no longer strangers."

Cara's parents got out of the car, and coming around to the rear, supervised the doorman as he retrieved the luggage from the trunk. I started to let myself out when Cara reached over and grabbed my arm.

"Come here you." She pulled me to her, then slid down on the back seat to be out of sight. I fell on top of her. We kissed two, long, tongue-searching kisses.

"Thanks for coming," Cara murmured in between them. "You are really special."

"You are too."

Then quite suddenly she raised herself up and pushed me off of her. "The Inspector General will be looking in the window any second now."

"Okay."

Quickly we got out of the car. On the sidewalk I said my good-byes to the Rosenhaus family.

"Good to see you, boy," Sidney said. Sarah Rosenhaus nodded.

Now Cara was standing next to her parents. She came forward and we shook hands.

"It was fun," she said.

"Absolutely."

"I'm glad you could make it."

"Me too."

Cara then turned, fell in step with her parents and, as a threesome, they walked into the lobby. The leprechaun followed with the bags.

I watched them go, then headed for 86th Street and the crosstown bus. It was just eleven o'clock then and the night air was still mild, but thick clouds were rolling in and beginning to conceal the stars. Turning toward Madison Avenue, I looked overhead. In the dense atmosphere the street lamps were giving off circles of light, halos, that reached into the darkness, then faded. Using these lights as beacons to help me navigate the unfamiliar East Side streets, I walked quickly, found my way, and feeling strangely energetic for that time of night, hopped onto the number ten bus that crossed the park to my side of town.

Chapter Seven

Mel called me early the next morning. I had told him about the East Hampton invitation and he was eager for a report.

"Well?"

"Well, what?"

"How did Sleeping Beauty make out with the polo set?"

"They loved me. Gave me the VIP treatment. All weekend I drew crowds they haven't seen out there since Sally Rand made an appearance on the nude beach."

"Congratulations. I knew you were perfect for the part. After you've played the role a few more times, we can put you up for Queen of the West Side queers."

"Great idea. And in the parade float I'll be sure to wear the dime store bikini that you gave me. That should turn a few heads."

"Absolutely. It will make you look like you've actually got something down there."

"It's too early in the morning for sibling rivalry."

"Sorry. Dialing your number seems to trigger off my put-down buttons. Actually, I just called to see how you are."

"Not bad for goat of the week."

"Listen, don't knock survival. The first week is always the toughest. I understand the first few days after his goof Mickey Owen nearly took a dive off the Ebbets Field scoreboard."

"I don't blame him. I've thought of asphyxiating myself in Coach Martin's locker."

"It wouldn't work. You'd look better to him that way—less stiff—so he'd stick you in the lineup, figuring if you couldn't stop Schneiderman, you might manage to spook him out."

"By the way," Mel continued, switching to his concerned voice, "how did the East Hampton campaign go?"

"Not bad. We made a landing on the beach."

"That is something. General Ike salutes you. A toe-hold is just what we wanted. I was afraid that Rosenhaus would lash you to his cabin cruiser and dump you back at Rockaway."

"No way. King R and I made beautiful music together. It was a lovefest. After a day with yours truly, the king was ready to make me a VP, with my choice of the dinette or bedroom set division."

"Now that is impressive," Mel said. "What did you do, let him know that you've never read a line of poetry?"

"Actually, he reads Frost. He owns an orchard and he likes to hear about apples."

Then I told Mel about my day with the Rosenhaus clan, my reception by the parents, and all that happened with Cara. He responded with a long whistle.

"That was more than a beachhead. That was a blitzkrieg. You took high ground without a fight. I had no idea that you were such a talented tushie kisser. It was pure genius to get in bed with the father. You sensed where pay dirt was. With girls like Cara, it's the father who chooses the groom. Rosenhaus has already got Barney measuring you for a rental tux."

"I'm not so sure. King R does his own measurements. He schmoozes and measures at the same time. He's the kind that will grill you a steak and have your number before the meat is off the fire. We hit it off fine, but that man keeps his own counsel. With someone like that, you never know where you stand. And Mrs. R could barely keep herself from holding her nose when she was around me. One look at my beach bag and she had me down as a West Side kid, half a step from a Delancey Street Jew. She made it pretty clear that I don't belong in Cara's league."

"Forget her. She's a snob who will look for a Bergdorf label in a jock strap. But don't worry. In this family she doesn't have the vote. Sidney's the mover and he's halfway in your pocket. Show him that you can read a balance sheet and *kibbitz* with *schvartzers,* and he'll be all the way there. In fact, the way I figure it, if you play your cards right, in five years you'll be walking around your own apple orchard."

"From your mouth to Adam's ear."

"But you need a strategy," Mel went on, "you've got to have a battle plan or you'll find yourself stuffing your face with rugelach just to forget that you've been dumped by the Finley firebrand. What you are dealing with here is a case of Popeye without the spinach; a show of muscle, but no real strength to back it up. Cara likes to think of herself as tough—a no-nonsense broad who tells it like it is. When she looks in the mirror she wants to see Bogie looking back. But in cases like this, the tough guy pose is a con. It's her shield, her way of putting on a helmet and shoulder pads so she won't get hurt. Women like this pride themselves on being ready to duke it out with any Wall-Street type who steps onto a Broadway bus, but they can keep the mask on only as long as they have a toady in their corner who services them between rounds.

"That is where big Ken comes in. For years he's been the guy with the sponge and towel, always on hand to stop the bleeding when Cara gets into a brawl. She pretends he is chopped liver, but the truth is she needs someone like that and that is why she's hung on to him all this time. She may not acknowledge it, but she's got a thing for his sheepskin coat. It has gotten to be her blanky."

"How do you fight a sheepskin fetish?"

"With strategy. You've got to insinuate yourself in Cara's unconscious mind. Not rapidly—you are liable to provoke a counterreaction—but slowly. Slow and steady, until you've slipped into the part of her brain that is looking for a good mother, the mother she's always wanted Mrs. R. to be."

"You mean I've got to make myself into Queen of the Cloak and Suitors?"

"Actually, a fag in sheepskin clothing is more to the point. Big Ken has become the mama cat."

"I see. To be in line to peddle *dreck* furniture to black folks, I have to make myself into a call girl or a fairy."

"Actually both. They overlap in Cara's unconscious."

"And how do I manage this?"

"As I said, slowly. First you have to be a presence. A steady presence. Not intrusive, not pushy, but a force. If you lose that place; say you have no contact with the lady for a week, the game will be over. You'll fade fast and the *Redbook* rover will expand into that spot. At that point you can pack it in."

"A presence means what, sessions on her living room couch?"

"Right now you are nowhere near that. You had an East Hampton moment, but that's gone now. You've got to win back that spot by ousting the Sheepman."

"And I do that by?"

"Contact. Steady contact, so you're always someplace in her mind. You've got to be creative. Watch for an opening, then slip in under the mannequin's radar. Use your noggin. Think Sleeping Beauty strategy. If the two of them are nuzzling in the park, lie down on a bench and make yourself invisible until he leaves. Then make your move."

"Do I get my training with the CIA?"

"You've got to do better than those buffoons. This job is four plus on the near impossibility scale. It is right up there with detaching Grace Kelly from Monaco. But think of the prize if you pull it off; an empire in Harlem and a spouse in the U.S. Senate. And not only that. Your dad will be so pleased with you, there is a good chance he'll forgive you for not hanging up your trousers all these years."

"You've got his touch," I said. "You know how to make a sale."

Following Mel's strategy, I tried calling Cara several times that week but could not reach her. On each occasion the phone was answered by a different member of the family and I was told, first by Cara's mother who failed to recognize my voice, then by King R who, with prompting, remembered me as the one with the wild serve and, finally, by Henry who, greeting me as an old pal, kept me on the phone for ten minutes while he read a passage from Pound's *Cantos*, that Cara was out for the evening.

Each time I left my phone number, slowly enumerating the numerals, but by Friday night she still had not called back.

"Not a good sign," Mel said when I told him what was going on. "Either she's slipped back into her sheepskin comfort zone faster than I thought, or something else is going on."

"Like what?"

"Who knows? With this lady it could be anything; a liaison with Earl Browder, a one-nighter with Henry Wallace."

"I am more worried about her *shtupping* the Sheepman on a shoot location."

"Not likely. She's too smart for that. If she was into that kind of thing, she'd be aiming higher, Abe Ribicoff at a minimum. No, my guess is she's gotten all wound up in one of her good works projects; she's probably spending nights bagging free lunches for Harlem kids."

"As long as she's not bagging the Sheepman."

Mel tried to reassure me on that score, claiming that, by his calculations Cara must be in a state of confusion, put there by the East Hampton weekend with yours truly. Mel speculated that, most likely, she had had little prior exposure to a genuine anti-hero, and that, trying to sort things out, she was unlikely to throw herself into the sack with the mannequin. He was pretty convincing, but I worried anyway. And all that night I dreamed of being upstaged by a robot outfitted with a foot-long phallus.

It was during breakfast the next morning that Cara called. My mother answered the phone and with a look that was, and was not, a smirk, handed it to me.

"Your friend."

As soon as I heard Cara's voice, intense, exalted, vibrating with a sense of danger, I knew where she'd been and what she'd been doing. A moment of lucid thinking would have solved the mystery days before, but as Mel pointed out at that time lucid thinking was about as possible for me as hanging onto a football after a Schneiderman rocket strike.

"You're not alone," Mel added in an effort to apply balm to my wounded feelings, "everyone knows that lovers are at war with lucidity of any kind."

"They've locked him out," Cara was saying, "practically thrown him out on the street."

"Who?"

"Schneiderman's father. Can you imagine that? After twenty years of service, they treat him like vermin to be stomped on."

"Where are you?"

"Here, outside the DA's office. Schneiderman's dad got into a fight with his idiot boss and confronted him on his corruption. So Mackel called the security guards and had him hustled out of the building."

"That's terrible. Are you with Schneiderman now?"

"We are planning an action. We want to let Mackel know that he can't get away with this strong-arm stuff. Can you get here in half an hour? We need all the help we can get."

I was about to leave for an appointment with an allergy specialist that had taken two months and endless phone calls to arrange. I'd been miserable with allergies all summer, sneezing and tearing up from the time I awoke, and on high pollen days having trouble breathing, so this was one doctor's appointment—I would have been all too glad to jettison almost any other—I really wanted to keep.

I paused for perhaps a half second before responding to Cara and she immediately picked up my hesitation.

"Are you with us, Jonathan?"

Instinctively I knew what my answer had to be. This was a call to arms for Cara and—I don't think she was at all aware of this—a test of my mettle.

"I'll be there as soon as I can," I promised.

On a Saturday morning it took me the better part of an hour to reach Brooklyn. I found my way to the Federal Office building, about a four-block walk from the subway, and as I approached I spotted a group of people—there must have been close to two- dozen—milling about in front of the entrance. Working in pairs, they had fashioned a number of placards which were attached to wooden handles. One of these, held aloft by a Finley girl with a distinctly philosophic turn of mind, posed a simple but profound question. "Who is the criminal?" it asked

Toward the middle of the group a small, white-haired man wearing a shiny Dodger team jacket displayed a quintessentially Brooklyn sign: "Throw the bum out," it read.

Just to the side of the building entrance Schneiderman was huddled with Cara and her friend, Debbie, who, since I last saw her, had managed to move up the ranks from her tag-along role as Cara's Boswell to her aide de camp. Like an eager production assistant, she carried a clipboard, had a yellow pencil lodged behind one ear, and seemed poised for action.

Cara was at the center of the group, giving orders, while flanking her Debbie and Schneiderman leaned in like members of a starting line-up getting final instructions from a voluble coach overflowing with strategy.

When he spotted me approaching, Schneiderman broke away from the huddle and with that easy ground-covering stride reached me quickly.

"Jonathan." He stretched out a hand and at the same time grasped my shoulder. Instinctually, automatically, I had the inclination to pull back out of the path of his trajectory.

"Thanks so much for coming," he said, his hand still on my shoulder. "Cara mentioned that you might, but I didn't really expect it. I hope this wasn't an awful imposition."

"Not at all. Glad to help. Listen, the two of us go back a long way," I added.

Schneiderman's grip grew tighter.

"A damn long way," he agreed, "and we've covered a lot of ground in that time."

"Well, you have anyway."

"Come on. What about that huge catch you made on that stunt play you guys pulled on us. I had to cover half the field to catch up with you."

"Somehow you managed."

"Yeah, well I can still feel that crack on the head you dished out to get even."

"Next time you'll know not to grab what doesn't belong to you."

"I guess we'll see whether I've managed to learn that lesson," Schneiderman replied with an easy laugh.

Just then Cara called to us.

"Hurry up you love bugs," she pleaded. "We've got to get this thing organized." She approached us, looking all business.

"Stan," she said, placing herself between us and addressing Schneiderman directly, "I want you at the head of the line. You have to be the first guy the public sees. You are standing in for your dad today and all the victims of Mackel's abuses."

Somehow I couldn't picture Schneiderman as a victim, but I kept my mouth shut.

"And you, Jonathan," Cara turned now to face me, "will be the rear marshal."

"I bring up the rear?"

"You guard the back of the line," Cara continued, ignoring my remark. "Your job is to keep order and keep your eye out for any patrol car that may come nosing around."

"You expect the cops?" I asked, trying not to show the surge of fear that gripped me.

"We don't know," Cara replied calmly. "Mackel has half of them on his payroll and I wouldn't put it past him to call them in. And those guys can get pretty nasty," she added

"Do you think they will try to break us up?"

"Could be. They've threatened us at other demos, but we can hold our own."

I wanted to ask more, to find out what Cara meant, but she had already turned away from me and was heading back toward the group, which was assembling just across the street.

"Well, we've got our marching orders," Schneiderman said, smiling at me.

"From Jimmy Hoffa himself," I replied.

"Well, we'd better get cracking."

"Right. You're first in line so I suppose you're the queen bee for the day," I quipped. Schneiderman grinned. "And you are the drone at the tail end of the pack." His voice took on the light, teasing quality that I came to know as vintage Schneiderman. I didn't answer, I just looked at him.

"Listen, you've got a very special spot," he went on in a voice half sympathetic, half teasing, "being rear marshal is an honor. I understand it's reserved especially for Harmon men. Cara knows that you boys have a talent for bringing up the rear."

"I'll watch my rear," I replied *sotto voce*, "and you watch yours."

We crossed the street and joined the group. Cara and Debbie were arranging people into what Cara called "marching buddies," pairing younger and older marchers to form ten couples in all.

"If the reporters show up," she explained, "we want to look ecumenical."

Intercepting us as we approached the line, Debbie, clipboard in hand, directed us to our places, Schneiderman out in front, me stationed a couple of yards behind the last couple, a big-breasted blond who, I learned later, had risked her job as office manager to join us, and a string bean of a girl with a long ponytail whom I recognized as goalie on the Finley field hockey team. The girl held signs in both hands, and when I had assumed my post, handed me one, indicating by her example that I should hold it aloft as a symbol of our commitment to justice and the rule of law. Her sign, self-created, was meant to rouse the citizenry to action.

"Let's shackle the jackal," it read, and was illustrated by a ferocious-looking beast that bore Mackel's visage. Mine, the work of a friend of Cara's who was slated to play the lead in the annual Finley musical production, carried a Brechtian reference, "Mack the Knife lives here," it declared.

Cara stood to the side of the line, a whistle held to her lips, ready to give the signal that would start us off.

"Move smartly," she ordered, "and be spontaneous. Let Mackel and his crew know what you think of him."

"Don't be afraid to sing out." Debbie, standing by her side, chimed in.

"You got it," the skinny white-haired man in the Dodger jacket called back and, waving his arms like the director of a choral group, elicited a barrage of instantly invented assaults on Mackel's character. Cara gave a shrill blast on the whistle, like a referee at a football game, and we began to move, slowly at first, then more quickly as we crossed the street and filled the sidewalk in front of the DA's office. Everyone seemed to be having a good time, shouting, cursing, raising fists, and encouraging the small group of spectators who gathered to watch to join our cause.

I found myself silent. I wanted to get into things, to raise my voice along with the others—I could hear Schneiderman sounding off at the head of the line—but somehow I could think of nothing to say. Cara was walking alongside the marchers, encouraging us, and watching for slackers. As she approached, I made some belligerent gestures and managed to mouth a couple of insults, but, somehow, I just wasn't into it.

Feeling guilty, I compensated by functioning as a hawk-eyed scout, every few minutes sweeping my gaze from right to left and, at intervals, making a full circle to look out for trouble in the rear.

They came, as Cara predicted. We had been marching for less than fifteen minutes when I spotted a police cruiser heading our way.

Nosing toward the line, the cruiser stopped just across the street. For some minutes the two policemen in the car observed us, watching quietly, like Indian scouts taking in the enemy's movements.

After a short while one of the cops, a burly Paul Bunyan type, opened the patrol car door and slowly pulled himself out, looking for all the world like a giant emerging from a clown car. He walked toward us slowly, assessing the situation, and when he was about two feet away asked in a tone, half commanding, half friendly, who was in charge here. I signaled for Cara, and from her spot near the building entrance, she strode forward.

"Yes?"

"We are from the thirty-third. Do you have a permit for this demonstration?"

Cara spoke sharply. Her words were clear, definite, with only an edge of hostility.

"This is a picket line, not a demonstration. We do not need a permit. We have a legal right to picket these premises."

"Is that right? You work here? All these people work here?" the burly one made a sweeping gesture to take in everyone on the line.

"Many of them do. Others are sympathizers. Sympathizers have a right to form a picket line."

The cop persisted. "You work here?"

"My friend works here. I support his cause. I happen also to be the organizer of this strike."

"Oh yeah? You don't like the pay? They want to cut your hours?"

"We don't like the boss. We don't care for his fascist policies."

"The DA, Mr. Mackel? Lady, you are in the wrong country."

"Fascists exist on our shores, too, in case you didn't know it."

Just then the man's partner, a thin-faced Stan Laurel type, joined his buddy.

"They are calling this demo a strike," the big man explained. "Claim that Mackel is a goddamn Nazi."

With his index finger, the smaller man made a circling motion around an ear. "Radicals," he declared, "nutty radicals."

"What does this look like to you?" the first man asked his partner. He seemed to defer to him as the brains of the outfit.

"Looks like a demonstration to me," the smaller man answered. "You don't strike against Nazis. You demonstrate against Nazis, like you demonstrate against the Ruskies over at their embassy." He addressed Cara directly.

"Lady, you have to have a permit for a demo like this."

Cara remained calm. "As I told your friend here, we do not have, and do not need, a permit. You had better call your superior to read you the first amendment."

"No one has to read me nothing and I don't have to speak to no one," the patrolman said. His voice was rising and he was becoming agitated. "We got a call to investigate a demo in progress at the Fed building. That's here. That's you, lady. Our orders are to break it up if there's no permit. If you got no permit, you'll have to leave."

"We are not leaving," Cara said flatly. "We are picketing against injustice and we intend to keep on marching."

"Okay. That's fine. You do that and we'll just have to take the whole crew of you in."

Hearing that, the feisty, white-haired character in the Dodger jacket began to shout at the cops. From his place on the line he had been observing the scene with increasing agitation and now he thrust himself forward.

"Why don't you fellows do your jobs and catch some rapists?" he demanded. "This lady's done nothing wrong. We have a right to be here. You guys are harassing us."

"I don't like your tone," the big man put in.

"I don't give a damn what you like," the Dodger fan put in, as though he was taking on the home plate umpire. "Just because

Mackel pays you guys off to protect his ass doesn't mean we have to take your guff. And don't think you are going to get away with this, either."

"You can't speak to an officer that way," the big fellow warned. He reached for his nightstick and stepped forward menacingly.

"Go ahead, arrest me, you overblown blimp," the old guy shot back. At that, Cara tried to intervene, to hold our man back—later at the stationhouse I learned his name was Max—but it was too late. Placing one hand on a hip, he wriggled his torso and, extending the opposite arm as far toward the approaching patrolman as it would go, he gave the cop the finger.

The big guy was on him instantly, thrusting Max to the sidewalk and pinning his arms behind his back. The partner joined in quickly. Kneeling on top of Max, he dug his knees into his back and cuffed him roughly.

"You kike son of a bitch," the burly one muttered as he shoved Max's face into the ground and applied a choke hold on his neck.

"What did you say?" Cara put in. Standing a couple of feet away, she had heard the remark and now she leaned down so that her face was inches from the big cop's head.

"None of your business, lady," he growled. "You keep out of this."

"This is my business," Cara retorted. "Bigots are my business. What is your name?" she demanded. "I am reporting you as a vicious anti-Semite." She reached over and tried to pull the big guy off Max.

"Quit it," she shouted. "You are killing this man."

The hulk ignored her and, unable to move him, Cara turned toward the smaller cop and gave him a shove. Caught off guard, he tumbled backwards, nearly tripped over Max, and had to stop himself with an outstretched arm. At that point the big one spun around, grabbed Cara, stood her up, and pinned her arms behind her back.

"You are under arrest," he bellowed and then, almost as an afterthought, added, "for striking an officer." The patrolman had his handcuffs out and was about to clamp them on Cara's wrists, which he held now with one meaty hand, when from behind him a rocket struck. Schneiderman had been watching from a dozen yards away and when the cop grabbed Cara, he took off. Smashing into the officer as though he was a tight end who had committed the fatal error of making a reception, Schneiderman cut his legs from under him and the big man went down hard, with Schneiderman falling on top of him. The cop's face hit the sidewalk, skinning his nose and cheek and drawing blood. For an instant he remained down; then he heaved and bucked, trying to throw Schneiderman off.

The partner moved in quickly, his nightstick out, looking for a piece of Schneiderman's skull to crack. Not finding it quickly enough, he grabbed Schneiderman's neck and pulled his head back. Then he brought down his club, striking two quick, bone-cracking blows. Blood poured from Schneiderman's skull, he fell to the ground, then reached up and covered his head to ward off more blows.

Terrified, feeling totally paralyzed, I stood a few yards from the melee. I wanted to act, to do something, but I could not move. But then, when I saw Schneiderman being clubbed, I started shouting.

"Lay off of him," I screamed, "you are going to break his head open." I started to rush toward the cop who had just beaten Schneiderman. Hearing my voice, he jumped to his feet and held his nightstick out in front of him as he spit out a warning.

"Keep out of this," he shouted. "Keep your distance or I'll bust your skull in two."

I thought of launching a diving tackle, the kind of submarine maneuver that I had used to bring down the interference in the Ryder game, but the cop's eyes were glued to me and I knew that if I dared one step toward him he would bring the club down on my head.

"This is brutality," I yelled. "you guys are fascists. I'm reporting this. You're out of control." The words just came pouring out of me. I held up a fist and feinted a move, as though I was going to make a run at the cop. Instinctively he pulled back. Then, seeing I wasn't coming, he started after me, his nightstick held head high, waving it as he ran.

I whirled and took off, covering ground with speed I hadn't known since my days with the Cavaliers. The cop pursued me for about thirty yards, then gave up. Seeing that he wasn't behind me, I stopped at the corner and looked back. The burley one now had

Schneiderman in tow. Using his weight, he had fallen on him, cuffed his hands behind his back, and stood him up. Now he was radioing for backup to help with the arrests.

It came soon in the form of three more patrol cars—they pulled up with tires screeching as though they had gotten a tip that Dillinger was on the picket line—and a paddy wagon to cart the prisoners away. With two hefty policemen on either side of them, Cara, Schneiderman and Max, the silver-haired Dodger fan with the Stanky tongue, were being escorted into the van.

With reinforcements now in place to keep an eye on what was left of the demonstrators, the two cops who had first arrived retreated to their patrol car and stood alongside it for a while, taking in the scene. I was sure they were hoping to catch sight of me in the crowd. They then eased themselves into their seats—both were nursing wounds from the scuffle—and followed the paddy wagon to the stationhouse.

At that point I did not know what to do. I looked back at the crowd. Most of the marchers had dispersed and the few who were left were standing around in clumps, talking, gesturing, looking as bewildered as I felt.

Some part of me told me to join my friends, to find out where they had been taken, and as a sign of solidarity get myself there. But that, I realized, could get me in big trouble. The cop who had chased me would surely recognize me. No question he had it in for me and I had no doubt that if I showed up at the stationhouse he would trump up some charge and have the cuffs on me in no time. I knew it was no big deal to get busted—last year Mitch Sternheim had been tossed in the hoosegow for making book outside Tip Toe and was back at the old stand in a matter of hours—but the idea of actually being arrested terrified me.

What if they threw me in a jail cell for a month and I could not get out? How could I bear the isolation, the hunger—I imagined being famished at night, with no chance for a snack—and the exhausting lack of sleep. Who, I wondered, could even sleep on one of those wooden slabs with a mattress the thickness of a White Tower hamburger? And what if they put me in with some pervert who gave me the choice of humping me or slitting my throat? I'd end up gay, and as Mel would no doubt point out, my only chance for romance then would be to switch goals and, after subscribing to *Redbook*, make a play for the Sheepman.

The only thing to do, I decided, was to keep a cool head, go home and think things over. In the face of this crisis, I needed a strategy, a way of preceding that demonstrated support for my friends, but that kept me out of the clinker.

Nothing I could think of seemed right, so I dialed Mel's number.

"You've gotten yourself in deep this time," he said when I told him the story. "This calls for creativity. If Cara finds out that you got your tail out of there while she and Schneiderman were getting their heads busted, she's not going to be a happy camper. In fact, given the situation, I'd better put in a backup call to Myra Herz. What I suggest," he went on, "is that you beat it back to the stationhouse and roll around in some dirt on the way. You are going to have to look like you've taken your share of lumps."

I knew that Mel was right. I had to get back to where the action was. Our original strategy called for me to be an active presence in Cara's life. Sitting on my duff while Cara was probably locked in some rat-infested jail cell was being no presence at all.

I started for the subway but realized that, in the heat of the moment, no one may have thought to call Cara's parents. I stopped at a phone booth and dialed the Rosenhaus family number—Cara had her own phone—but there was no answer.

They were all at the police station. In fact, Debbie had called them from Brooklyn and they had mobilized themselves like a firehouse emergency unit. The first person I saw when I walked in was King R, standing in front of the sergeant's desk, kibbutzing like he was doing a number on a Harlem customer. Just to his right, in deep conversation with an officer in a starched uniform decorated with gold trimming like a war hero, was a tall, thin gentleman in a gray business suit who seemed to have the easy, affable, manner of a Hank Fonda. This distinguished-looking gentlemen, I learned from eavesdropping, was Schneiderman's dad, the ousted one, who had taken on Mackel and was the source of all of our troubles.

Sidney Rosenhaus glanced my way when I came in but didn't seem to recognize me, or didn't care to. With him I never knew. A few minutes later, though, spotting me again as he left the front desk, he gave me a nod and stopped for a moment.

"Jonathan, right? Ace or double fault, right?" He gave me a playful poke in the chest.

"Hello, Mr. Rosenhaus," I said.

"You involved in this thing?" he wanted to know.

"I was there. Cara was terrific," I added.

Sidney Rosenhaus shook his head and waved a finger in front of my face, like an out of control windshield wiper, "Stupid," he said. "Plain dumb. For a smart girl, she's an idiot. Just got herself in a lot of trouble. If you people wanted action, why didn't you come to me? I have connections."

"I guess we didn't think," I said. "We were outraged, we wanted to take action."

"Outrage will get you nowhere," Sidney Rosenhaus said. "Outrage will get you *bupkus*. What were you trying to do, knock Mackel out of the ring? A guy like that can snap his fingers and send your ass to Riker's Island anytime he wants.

"With someone in his position," King R went on, "you need finesse, a little backstage work to ease him out of this job, slip him into a judgeship."

"I see," I said, "we'll consult you next time."

King R nodded. "If you are smart, you'll do that," he said. Then he pointed his chin at me.

"They nab you? Are you charged?"

"I managed to slip through their net."

Sidney looked at me suspiciously.

"Turned tail?"

"No sir, just hid out."

He said nothing. He just continued to look at me.

"Well, your little lady will be damn lucky if we can get her off this hot seat without her tush getting burned," he said. And he started to walk away.

Before he could move, Schneiderman's father came up to him with the precinct captain at his side.

"Good news, Sidney," he said. "They are going to be released. No charges. No record. The captain here agrees that everybody got out of control. He is willing to let our kids go with a warning."

"We'll remember this, Captain," King R said, reaching out to shake the officer's hand. "If you need anything for this stationhouse, a water cooler or something, you'll call me."

"Thank you," the captain said. "I'll do that. Actually there is one thing you fellows can do for me right now," he said, "keep your kids on your side of the bridge. We've got enough trouble managing our own zealots."

"I know what you mean," Sidney Rosenhaus responded. "I have relatives in Brooklyn. Crazy, every one of them. Dodger fans. Fanatics, you know what I mean? When he was here, they loved Durocher, can you beat that? Adored that madman. A guy like that, you ought to have a police patrol on him around the clock, lock him in the bullpen between games."

"Good idea," the captain said, clearly trying to maintain the semblance of a smile. He glanced at the stationhouse clock. "Well, gentlemen, you must excuse me," he said, beginning to back pedal, "I've got to get back to work. I'll have your people released right away."

A few minutes later a heavy door at the back of the room swung open, and accompanied by a mustached sergeant who served as their escort, the group appeared; Cara and Schneiderman first, then, bringing up the rear and leveling charges of civil rights violations at the guard, peppery Max.

Then, after a brief delay for security checks, the others appeared: Cara's mother, Henry, and—I did not believe what I was seeing—Ken Masters. They had been inside visiting the prisoners, and they strolled out now, smiling and looking at ease, as though they had just been to an adult education lecture.

Watching them come out, Cara's mother chatting amiably with the Sheepman, I was stung by a sudden feeling of betrayal and I could feel my heart beginning to spin into a tachycardia. Sitting on a nearby bench, I experienced a rush of anger that was mixed with utter confusion.

How in the world did Masters get here? I wondered. Who told him? Who made that call?

And immediately I knew.

I searched the room for the quisling, Debbie, Cara's Boswell, or, more accurately, her Disraeli. She was the one who called around. She was the informer. I remembered how at Cara's party she had talked down Masters, made him look like a toady who was at his mistress's beck and call. She had me thinking that she was on my side, that she could be my mole, working from the inside to foment a coup, but I could see now that she was setting me up, pumping me for information that she could then pass on to the mannequin. She was his ears as well as Cara's. In fact, I wondered whether Cara had put her up to playing the double agent.

Then a dread thought came over me, sped directly to my heart, ratcheted up its rhythm, and precipitated a bout of dizziness.

What if Debbie had seen me bolt? She was there. She could have seen the whole thing. That, I realized, would explain everything. No doubt seeing me take off had infuriated her, and she had called the old shoe, Masters, for help. And she probably had a few choice words to say about me when she got hold of him.

At that point my head was throbbing and I could no longer think. I looked around. Everyone seemed to be part of a group of two or three; talking, arguing, going over all that had happened. No one was looking my way and I had the urge to escape then and there; simply disappear and never have to see any of these people again.

Before I could move, Cara spotted me. Breaking away from Henry, she called over to Schneiderman who was talking with his dad, pointed to me, and came quickly to my side. Schneiderman followed her, smiling and looking glad to see me.

"Jonathan, you're here?" Cara reached over, took me by the shoulders, and planted a big kiss on my lips.

"Thank God. We were worried sick. No one knew where you were. We were ready to call hospitals."

"The last anyone knew, that bastard was coming at you, ready to bust your head open, too." Schneiderman put in. Instinctively, he reached for the right side of his own head, which was heavily bandaged. Cara took a long look at me. She seemed genuinely relieved.

"We had visions of you in intensive care," she said in a tone that sounded half admonishing, half frightened, "or bleeding to death in a gutter somewhere."

"I'm sorry I worried you," I said, "actually, I'm fine, slightly bruised, but really okay. Did Debbie say anything?" I added.

Cara looked puzzled.

"Not a word. In fact, we haven't spoken to her. She called our folks, but then had to take off. Her father's not well and she had to get home."

"I see, well that's too bad. That cop nearly got me," I went on, "he had me in his sights and was starting to bring his stick down on my head, but at the last second I dove at his feet and he only grazed my shoulder." I reached up and touched my right shoulder in automatic imitation of Schneiderman's gesture. Schneiderman gave me a thumbs up sign.

"Your diving block," he exclaimed, recalling the Ryder game. "The one you used on us to take out my interference. God, I remember that. You stripped me naked. It's all I could do to make it to the sideline."

"Well with that cop's club coming down, I was pretty desperate." I said. "I had to do something or end up in Bellevue."

"That was quick thinking," Schneiderman said. "I always thought of you as a guy who uses his noggin."

Then the three of us walked back to the center of the room. People were still milling around there. I was looking for an exit.

I located the main doors and started for them, but Sidney Rosenhaus was blocking my path. He was talking to Schneiderman's father—actually seemed to be haranguing him. One of King R's hands rested on Mr. Schneiderman's arm.

"They are good kids," Sidney Rosenhaus was saying, "but dumb. Naïve. Excuse my French, but the mayor of New York doesn't give a crap about how many signs you are carrying on your back. Or"—here he poked a finger toward Mr. Schneiderman's mid-section— "how many complaints you file. All your complaints, all your marches, the whole kit and kaboodle of this we-the-people stuff is *bupkus*. It's shadow boxing. It's swinging at air. Listen to me. Don't waste your time with *hazorai* like this. It's bunk. Only one thing moves the ball," he went on. King R held up a hand and made a rolling gesture with thumb and forefinger. "Do re mi. Show me a hundred of your best people, your best sign makers, and I'll match that with one *schmekler*. Do you know what greases the wheels in this town, what gets them spinning?" Mr. Schneiderman did not know.

"*Schmeckle* dust. That's what. Do you know what *schmeckle* dust is?"

Mr. Schneiderman did not know that either.

"Moola, scratch, mookie, cash on the barrelhead. You've got to have it flying out of your pockets if you want anything done in this town. You think you can take on Mackel, take on Tammany? You can't take on Tammany and their boy, Mackel. He can have you in the clinker before you can get out those doors over there. And don't think you will walk like these kids did. You are a big fish. Mackel can have you getting the runs from prison food for months if it suits him. You can't mess with him or the Tammany goons who put him in his seat. What you need," King R went on, "is to call in your marker, get every warm body, including your *mackatumin* on your side and raise a war chest. You need connections to bring in the cash."

At that, Schneiderman's father looked forlorn.

"Good idea," he said, "but I'm fresh out of connections. Mackel is putting out the word that I am disloyal and not to be trusted. He's already turned a lot of people against me."

With a wave of a hand King R tried to banish Schneiderman's fears.

"Not to worry. I have enough connections for the two of us. You are out of a job, right, flat out on your rear end? From what I've heard, Mackel kicked your ass good."

"I guess so," Mr. Schneiderman said.

"So you need a job, a place to hang your fedora, as they say. And you are a DA yourself, I understand?

"For twenty years."

"Okay, listen. The governor is not going to do anything because the mayor is Tammany and he'll get on the phone and say, nix, no deal for this guy Schneiderman. He doesn't know how to play ball. They rub each other's backs, see. These boys are first class *schmecklers*. They know the rules of the game, and they won't interfere with the other's boondoggles. But I talk to both of them all the time and they have taught me one thing. Do you know what that is? They want to get re-elected. They like the fact that when the time is right I come up with big bucks. And do you know what else? I build playgrounds for the mayor. Hizzoner really likes that. It gets him in good with the PTAs. Just last week he called and asked me to build in the Bronx. He needs help up there. 'Manhattan is my town,' I told him. 'I know,' he says, 'but we got an urgent need up in Riverdale. The Chinese are moving in around upper Broadway, the Dyckman area, and there is a big vacuum up there. Their kids got no playgrounds to run around in.'

"'Suddenly you care about the Chinese?' I said to him.

"'They vote Democratic,' he told me. 'We need that block in our column.'

"So I helped him out, and now I've got connections in the Bronx. If you hear of any openings either up there or in Manhattan—the mayor owes me big in Manhattan—just give me a buzz. Maybe I can give you a hand."

"Why thank you very much, Mr. Rosenhaus," Schneiderman's dad said. "That is very generous of you."

"Call me Sidney," King R said. "We are sitting in the same boat. Both our kids are mischief makers."

Henry was standing alongside his father and spotting me, he waved and came over.

"Jonathan, long time no see. When are you going to visit us at the Plantation?"

"Soon, I hope."

"Well, good. We hope so, too. What are you reading these days? I'll have to prepare for one of our stimulating conversations."

"Actually, not too much. I've been busy running around town."

"So I hear. I understand that you are quite the sprinter."

I looked at Henry. He smiled.

"Debbie called to tell me about the arrests. She said Cara and Schneiderman had been busted. Naturally I asked about you, too."

"And?"

"She told me that you got away without a scratch."

"I was lucky," I said. "I nearly got my brains splattered by a mad dog cop."

"But you didn't," Henry said in a tone that made me want to lay him out on the stationhouse floor. "You used your speed to good advantage. Cara tells me that you are really quite a fast man all around. Didn't you nearly outrun Schneiderman for a touchdown?"

"Not quite. He caught me."

"Yes, well you managed to outrun him this time. I understand that you were nowhere to be seen when he and Cara got nailed by the fuzz."

I was searching my mind for properly nasty retort, perhaps offering congratulations on a perfect imitation of Pound's smugness, but I was slow on the uptake and before I could come up with anything, Cara was at our side with Ken Masters in tow. He was holding her hand and I had to restrain an impulse to administer a well-placed karate chop.

"You two busy dissecting Eliot again?" she asked Henry.

"Not this time. But we hope to have a long poolside discussion on that subject, don't we, Jonathan?"

"Absolutely," I said.

Cara touched my arm and gestured toward Masters.

"You two know each other, right?

"We met briefly at your party," I reminded her.

The mannequin looked puzzled.

"Did we?" Then he remembered. "Oh yes. As I recall, that was the time you got sick and had an accident on the rug."

Cara gave him a mock punch in the ribs.

"Don't be so rude, Ken," she said. "You are going to hurt Jonathan's feelings."

Again she reached out and this time lightly touched my hand.

"Don't listen to a word he says, Jonathan," she declared, looking pointedly at Masters. "Ken Masters is just a natural boor."

"So I've noticed," I said.

A few yards away Schneiderman was talking with his father and spotting them there Cara went over to say good-bye. She shook his father's hand, kissed Schneiderman on the cheek, and then leaned forward and whispered something in his ear. Schneiderman smiled and nodded, but said nothing. Cara then turned, walked quickly back to me, and pulled me aside.

"Look I've got to go now," she said. "Thank God you are all right. Please do me a favor. Go home and get some rest. And call me tomorrow. We need to talk."

"I'll do that," I said. "And thanks."

Then Cara took Ken's arm and they headed for the wide double doors at the front of the stationhouse. Cara's parents were waiting there. Greeting their daughter and the Sheepman with what I thought were words of affection, the four of them walked into the street.

I followed them out. On the way to the subway I had visions of the big cop, the sumo wrestler, coming after me with his nightstick, about to crush my skull. Diving at his feet, I cut the legs out from under him with a perfect rolling block and he comes down hard, crashing into his partner and bringing him down as well. I quickly realized, though, that I was just trying to shore myself up, trying to escape from the plain truth; that out of fear of getting hurt I had abandoned my friends. I thought, then, of Schneiderman and of how, instinctively, he had hurled himself against the big cop, and I felt ashamed. And then, unbidden, a memory arose: it was of the time when Schultz, the super of our building, pushed his way into our apartment and accused me of throwing matches out the window—I was innocent of this crime—and of how my father had stood up to the Nazi. My father was barely five-foot-seven and Schultz was at least six-foot-two and massively built, but my father stood toe-to-toe with him, ordered him out of our apartment, and if he didn't move fast enough threatened to give his big schnoz something to think about.

I was about eight when this happened and, recalling it, I felt a fresh wave of shame at the thought that my father; even my daydreaming, strictly noncombatant father, had refused to yield to a bully; had, in fact, risked his neck to stand up for me.

At the corner I stepped off the curb and nearly got hit by a lumbering mail truck making a sharp right turn. The traffic cop in the center of the road yelled at me to wake up and watch where I was going. Chastised and feeling stupid, I was determined to keep my wits about me and to concentrate on my route. Making sure to read the street signs, I made my way to the nearest subway station, got on the number four express train to Manhattan, and managed to block off all further fantasies of kicking ass until I was safely home.

Chapter Eight

I tried calling Cara several times the next day but got no answer on her phone until, just after ten at night, she picked up.

"I can't talk now," she said in a voice that sounded rushed and agitated. "We just got back from the beach and I found out my grandmother in Philadelphia is ill and in the hospital. I'm getting ready to go down there."

"At ten at night?"

"My folks don't want me to do it. They say it's not necessary, that she's not in serious danger, but she's all alone and she's hurting. She needs someone with her."

"That is awfully good of you."

"It's not good. It's what needs to be done. People find all kinds of reasons not to have to put themselves out, not to do the right thing because, basically, they don't want to make the effort. It's uncomfortable. They have to get off their butts at ten o'clock at night after a hard day at the beach and they don't want to do that. They don't want to discomfort themselves, so they simply don't. My folks claim that Grandma doesn't need them. Well, I say the hell with that bullshit. If you are selfish and lazy, admit it. Don't feed yourself a line and don't try to get me to buy into that kind of self-deception."

"How will you get there?"

"There is an eleven o'clock train. I'll be at the hospital by one in the morning."

"Will you be okay?"

"You sound like my father, always worrying, always with the dire predictions. When I told him I was going no matter what, he wanted to call a car service so I would not get raped on the way down there. 'Dad, I can take care of myself,' I told him, but, of course, he doesn't believe me, actually needs not to believe me so he can still be my protector."

"I can understand that," I said. Cara cut me off.

"Look I've got to go. I've got to get on the subway if I'm going to make that eleven o'clock train."

I started to say, "I'll be rooting for your grandma," but she had already hung up.

I didn't hear from Cara for three days. I left messages, but she did not call back. Then when I got home from school after basketball practice one evening, there was a note on my bed.

Call Cara, no matter what time tonight.

I dropped my books and went straight to the hall phone. My mother had heard me come in and met me there. She looked pale.

"Is something wrong? Is it an emergency?"

"I don't know, Ma."

"Her parents not well?"

I shook my head. "It's her grandmother. She's been sick in the hospital."

My mother nodded with understanding. I could tell that she was thinking of her own mother who had died suddenly of a stroke three years before.

I wanted privacy, but my mother stood by, her heart heavy with foreboding that the worst had happened, while I dialed Cara's number. When she answered, Cara's voice did not sound grim.

"Hi," she said.

"How's your grandmother?"

"She's good. It was pneumonia, but they got it under control and she's home now."

"That must be a relief." I signaled to my mother that everything was okay, and mouthing, "thank God," she reluctantly retreated to the living room.

"It is. She's a real trooper. It meant a lot to her just to see my face."

"I'll bet." It would mean a lot to me to see your face, too, is what I wanted to say, but I held back.

"Good control," Mel said when I told him about my restraint. "When someone's had a fright, a near trauma, you don't want to bring yourself into the picture too early. Remember, at those times you have to be an ear and an ear only. What you feel, what you want to say, these are irrelevant. If you had made that cutesy remark of yours, it would have set you back a minimum of two months. But you are learning," he added. "I can see that this relationship is maturing you."

"Thanks," I said. "I hope you are not the only one who thinks so."

"I've got big news," Cara was saying. There was a playfulness in her voice and I imagined her sitting on her bed, smiling at the thought of what she was about to say. There was a moment of silence before Cara spoke again, and a sudden chill took hold of me. Cara's voice had the same quality, carried the same lilt, as did my cousin, Millie's, when, unable to contain herself when I called one day, she burst out with the news that she had just gotten engaged to Myron Kornbluth, a rabbinical student from Rochester, New York.

Could it be, I thought, with rapidly rising pulse, that the mannequin had made his move, had put a lock on Cara, as Mel predicted he would try to do, and claiming his place as heir apparent to King R's uptown empire, had pinned her? Was she really telling me that she was engaged to the Sheepman, that by playing the game right she had achieved her goal of securing her blanky with a marital tie?

"Are you sitting down?" Cara asked.

"On my mother's best slip-covered chair. Shoot."

"It looks like you are going to have a new teammate."

"What?" For an instant I thought that Cara was speaking in code; that she was letting me know that she was breaking up with me and, out of sympathy, was suggesting a replacement. Very likely her sidekick, Debbie, who had the build and charm of an offensive lineman, I thought, or possibly Joan Karpowitz, her big-bosomed campaign manager who looked and spoke like a younger version of Golda Meir.

Cara paused for a moment, making me wait. Then, with barely restrained relish, she made her announcement.

"Stan Schneiderman is transferring to Harmon. He's going to be your teammate. It's practically a done deal."

I heard, but did not comprehend. The words simply did not register. Schneiderman coming to Harmon? Schneiderman, Harmon's arch enemy, defecting to us, the team he mocked, trampled on, ran roughshod over, and sent back to our locker room with tears in our eyes?

"Is he flying in with Rudolph Hess?" I asked. The whole idea seemed preposterous, a Cara fantasy, or, perhaps, a dream that stayed with her and got confused with the real world. The Brooklyn fiasco had taken a lot out of her, I knew, and then there was the scare over her grandmother and the last minute trip to Philly. Probably she has not come back to herself, I thought, and is vulnerable to all kinds of imaginations. Most likely this latest fantasy had something to do with her obsession with rescuing people, I figured, and now she was fixed on the Schneidermans and getting them out of Brooklyn.

"There is no way Ryder would let Schneiderman go," I protested, "he's their whole team—all of their teams. My God, we would have to give up Buckstein to get him."

Cara scolded me, "Don't be mean," she said. "I know this is a huge shock. Even King R couldn't believe that after twenty years Schneiderman's dad would just pick up and move his family out of Brooklyn. But if you think about it for a minute, this is a fantastic opportunity. Picture it. The two of you together. What an incredible combination. Tannenbaum and Cousy teaming up. You guys could break every record in the books."

"We'd have to survive each other first," I said.

"Don't even think like that," Cara protested. "The two of you are going to be great buddies. Didn't I always say so? You are kindred spirits. Actually, the three of us are. We constitute a triumvirate, an unstoppable combination."

I had visions then of endless coffee klatches with Cara and Schneiderman, the two of them sitting head to head in some espresso bar and plotting a march against Gristede's or the A&P for exploiting their salespeople or firing a Latino store manager. This kind of thing had little appeal for me. I admired the two of them for wanting to get out there and raise their voices against real abuses, but somehow taking to the streets just wasn't my thing. Right now, though, I kept my mouth shut. Clearly this was not the time to share my feelings with Cara or to have her lecture me on one's civic responsibilities.

Besides, I needed to know just how real this whole Schneiderman thing was.

"Are you absolutely sure about this?" I asked. "This isn't just an idea or a plan for some time in the future? You are certain that Schneiderman is coming to Harmon?"

Cara's voice took on a sharp tone. Clearly she was offended by my question.

"Yes, I'm sure," she snapped. "Much as your literal minded Harmon men may think so, I don't make things up just to please myself. My father helped Schneiderman's dad with a contact and he got hired by the Bronx DA. The guy used to work for Mackel and he hates the son of bitch. Can't stand his bloody guts and was salivating at the chance to stick it to him by hiring someone the idiot just axed. So the whole family is packing up and moving to Riverdale. They've had it with Brooklyn and the stench coming out of Mackel's office. They need a change, and it turns out Riverdale is perfect for them. It's ten minutes to the new job. There is only one hitch. Schneiderman's grades aren't stellar. In fact, they pretty much stink. It turns out our boy is more at home shooting pool or doing the samba on the floor of the Copa than he is logging time in the Ryder library. When it comes to getting grades, he is nowhere. He's still rattling around on his own goal line and your admissions people are making a thing about his not being Harmon material. But Sidney says pressure is on to take him anyway. Your alumni jocks are peeing in their pants at the idea of Schneiderman in a Harmon uniform and they are putting pressure on your headmaster, offering big bucks for a new building, that kind of thing. Right now it's a negotiation, but King R says that cash talks and building funds talk even louder, so in the end the good old boys will get their man."

At that point Cara's mother called her for dinner and we had to hang up. Back in my room I thought about what she had said and it struck me as true. Our alumni group was loaded with arthritic old timers who showed up at our home games, sported outsized maroon and white buttons, made a lot of noise shouting instructions from the stands, and wrote angry letters to the board when Harmon had a losing season. Before home football games you could spot half a dozen of them on the sidelines, taking turns playing quarterback and tight end, scampering a few yards, cutting sharply, and making key receptions.

Each year this contingent put up big bucks to fund scholarships for a couple of star athletes recruited from local public schools. Every fall at least two strangers with builds like Jones Beach lifeguards would appear on campus, set school records on the gridiron, show up in classes for a couple of months after the football season, then vanish silently into the Bronx streets from which they came. For our alumni, landing Schneiderman was on a par with the Giants snatching Sammy Baugh from the Redskins, and I had no doubt that they would go all out to get him. This meant not only a full scholarship, but extras like passes to Palisades Amusement Park and tickets to see the Rockettes at Radio City Music Hall.

Convinced now that the impossible was actually going to happen; that in a matter of days or weeks Schneiderman, Ryder's version of the Lip, would be donning the maroon and white of Harmon, I tried to picture him, not as the target of a well-deserved helmet in the ribs, but as one of us, teammate and buddy, who from now on would be lining up shoulder to shoulder with me as we took on the snub-nosed kids from All Hallows and Fordham Prep, teams that counted on Harmon, with our squad of well-padded noncombatants, to be an easy win.

What would it be like, I wondered, to run interference for Schneiderman, to spring him loose with a cross body block instead of trying, with a rocket strike of my own, to nail him behind the line and smash him to the ground.

And on the basketball court, what would it be like to feed him the ball as he faked out his man and sprinted for the basket; or, on a fast break, to lay in an easy two points after he hit me on the fly with one of his signature precision passes?

At night, to my surprise, I would dream the unimaginable; the two of us as buddies who sat together on team bus trips, worked on a game plan to upend Trinity, the league powerhouse, and, on off hours, talked about our strategies with girls. In these dreams Schneiderman was worldly and knowledgeable, a man about town who had psyched out the prep school scene, had a particular know-how with Finley coeds, and who passed along his secrets to me as easily as, with his rifle arm, he could hit me with a perfect strike whenever I managed to break into the open.

"It's natural," Mel explained over hamburgers at Starks Restaurant when I told him what I had been dreaming. "Take a guy like Sugar Ray Robinson. Do you think the Sugarman spends nights dreaming of his pals down at Stillman's? No way. Ask him and he'll tell you that what he dreams of is playing poker with Jake LaMotta or shooting pool with Rocky Marciano, two guys he's badmouthed and who would be all too glad to bash his head for him. What you have here is built-in protection, the mind's way of turning our fears of getting castrated, totally pulverized, into parlor games. It's a genetic thing, old as history. Look in the Bible. You'll see what I mean. Do you think Abel had no idea what his mad brother was up to, had no notion that the guy was out of his mind with jealousy? No way. They practically lived in each other's skins. But he didn't want to know, couldn't let himself know. Did he dream of the big fellow slicing him up with a hunting knife? Not a chance. What the kid dreamed of was working with the big guy on a woodcarving project."

I told myself that Mel was right, that my reaction was perfectly normal, that my dreams simply reflected a wish for peace, a wish to avoid a clash with someone who, for years, had lived in my head as nemesis number one. And I told myself that in this situation a nervous gut was totally normal, that when Durocher crossed the Brooklyn Bridge and landed in Coogan's Bluff, even veterans like Hubbell, Maglie and big John Mize got palpitations and dreamed cover-up dreams. Still, though, I could not shake the fear I felt at the thought of Schneiderman being at Harmon; the shock—like running into Leo the Lip on the lunchroom line—of encountering him on our turf.

The mornings were particularly bad. As soon as I awoke, my stomach started in with a series of acrobatics and I could get nothing down for breakfast. A couple of times at school the cramping got so bad I had to see the school nurse who scared me by taking repeated pokes at my midsection and talking all the while of the dangers of acute abdomens. Mel, though, pooh-poohed that idea.

"What you've got is a case of gut memory," he declared. "At the mention of Schneiderman's name your intestines go into high alert; they are ready for a rocket strike."

Things eased up for me, though, when after two weeks there was still no sign of Schneiderman. Then, one morning, when I got to school a few minutes early, I stopped in at Tillman's office to visit with Laura, who officially held the title of secretary to the headmaster, but who was hired, I was convinced, because at ten paces she had a Betty Grable rear end and the moves to match. For reasons that were entirely mysterious, she had taken a shine to me and from time to time, as part of my four-year master plan that culminated in Laura giving herself to me on the floor of her cubicle as a graduation present, I would stop in for a chat.

That morning Laura was in a conspiratorial mood. When I stuck my head in the door she waved me inside, then put a finger to her lips and nodded toward Tillman's office.

"Big doings in there," she whispered, "A major pow-wow."

"Oh yeah? What's up?"

She shook her head.

"Top secret. Can't say. But I can tell you one thing. You are going to be one happy guy when all of this was over."

"I can hardly wait."

She did not have to say more. I knew that the Schneidermans were in there negotiating with Tillman and that King R's prediction would undoubtedly come true. With alumni money behind him, Schneiderman was sure to be admitted. And before much longer, I thought, I was bound to run into him on campus. There he would be, unmistakable even at a distance as he crossed the campus with that long, easy stride of his. And it seemed some kind of devilish irony that overnight, with a stroke of Tillman's pen, Schneiderman, the Flatbush firebrand, would become not only an instant Harmon man, but our most prized possession.

In fact, it did not take long for a deal to be struck—rumor had it that the Harmon side was forced to throw in season tickets for the

Knicks—and it did not take long for Tillman, like that lunatic Stoneham bragging to the world that he had lured the Lip out of Brooklyn, to announce his latest acquisition.

It happened on a Monday morning with the whole student body seated in the auditorium for our weekly sing. This was a Harmon tradition. Each week began with all the grades gathered together to raise our voices in song. Under the tremulous baton of Mr. Nagler, Harmon's walking mummy, who was said to be the oldest extant Latin teacher in the Western Hemisphere, we spent an hour belting out college fight songs and folksy favorites like "Dinah" and "Row, Row, Row Your Boat."

That Monday, though, things were different. When I entered the auditorium I noticed that the movie screen, on which the lyrics were flashed, had not been lowered. Instead, we were confronted with an open stage, bare except for two heavy wooden chairs placed a few feet apart that looked as though they had been imported from a Venetian palace.

I settled into my seat and took care to place my book bag under my feet so that it would not slide away. As I leaned down, I felt a tap on the shoulder. Mitch Sternheim, Harmon's direct connection to Las Vegas, was sitting next to me and I imagined that he was trying to get my attention so that he could give me the morning line, hot off the wire, on Sunday's Giants-Eagles game. When I did not immediately respond, he followed up with a sharp jab to the ribs.

"Do you see who is up there?" he whispered. "Somebody's got it in for you. What odds would you have given that you'd ever see a scene like this at Harmon?"

I looked up. Walking on stage from the wings, looking all formal and solemn, was Tillman, closely followed by Schneiderman in a gray three-button suit. They seated themselves on the throne like chairs and, arms folded, stared out at the audience. Then after a couple of minutes, Tillman rose and motioned for silence. He had a way, whenever he spoke to the student body, of infecting the room with indefinable anxiety. Part of Harmon lore was the tale about an announcement he had made in assembly one winter morning. The weather report had predicted a heavy snowstorm due the following day. Regarding it as his duty to forewarn the students, Tillman stood at the podium and, dead pan, addressed the entire school.

"I am told that we are in for severe weather tomorrow," he began, "and that the subway system may be shut down. Well, gentlemen, I can promise you this; if the subways don't run, you will."

Now once again Tillman was going to make an announcement but, surprisingly, and unlike any other time in recent memory, he was smiling. So unexpected was this change, so out of character, that seeing the headmaster up there grinning, actually looking happy, evoked further unease in the audience. For my part, I knew what was coming but I still found myself sharing the general feeling of apprehension. And at one point I had the fleeting thought that Tillman's smile was a total put on; that it was the fair weather before the storm, a ray of light before his face clouded over and he hit us with some dire announcement; that study hall time would be doubled or a new set of examinations had been invented.

Tillman motioned for silence and, instantaneously, the chatter stopped. Then in a tone that was decidedly genial, as surprising as his smile, he began to speak.

"Gentlemen," he began, "I have postponed this morning's sing in order to make an important announcement, an announcement that I know will please you as much as it does me. We are very fortunate to have a new student at Harmon. It would be more accurate, however, to put the word, new, in quotations, for many of you already know and admire this person. This is especially true of our athletic teams who— dare I say it—have come not only to admire and respect this individual, but to fear his remarkable prowess on the fields of play.

"I hasten to add that this reaction has nothing whatever to do with the character of the man. Not at all. I can say without fear of contradiction that he is a most praiseworthy individual. No, this response has solely to do with his prodigious talents as an all-around athlete. I know, therefore, that you, our student body, will join your administration in extending the warmest possible welcome to the newest addition to our Harmon family. So without further ado, let me introduce you to an individual whom I have no hesitation in characterizing as Harmon's gain and—sad for them—the Ryder School's loss, Mr. Stanley Schneiderman."

Tillman then motioned for Schneiderman to rise and, as he did, his face now turning crimson, the entire student body rose with him and led by Tillman himself broke into applause that lasted a full minute. On stage, Schneiderman looked like a shy Lou Gehrig receiving the crowd's ovation on his final day at Yankee Stadium. He smiled weakly, jiggled his feet a couple of times, slowly raised an arm in acknowledgement of the tribute, then unsuccessfully tried to signal the audience to stop. When the applause finally tapered off and we were back in our seats, Tillman made a show of shaking hands with Schneiderman, clapping him on the back, and leading him down the three steps to the auditorium floor. Then the two of them walked up the center aisle to the rear exit, all eyes on Harmon's most exciting acquisition since we managed to outmaneuver Trinity and land Alex Siegel, a six-foot-two power forward and bona fide nephew of Bugsy Siegel, when he decided to transfer from Bronx Science.

After assembly I found Schneiderman waiting for me just outside the auditorium doors. He was sweating and he looked traumatized.

"My God, did you hear all that?" he asked. "That Tillman is some piece of work. Pure Barnum. I haven't heard that much bull since I was suckered into a side show at Coney Island. You've got a real huckster in your front office."

"Tillman can spin a yarn," I agreed. "With him, you've just got to hold your breath until the hot air blows off. But I thought that he meant what he said about you and how proud he is to have you here."

"So proud he nearly caught my nose in the door he was trying to slam on me last week. 'Your boy doesn't have the grades,' he kept telling my dad. 'Simply doesn't have the grades. We have our standards at Harmon. That's what makes us who we are.' He practically booted the two of us out of his office and if it wasn't for half a dozen fat cat alumni waving pledge cards in front of his face, I'd be lining up for Finley."

Hearing that, all at once I had a heart-stopping vision; Schneiderman once again playing against us, only this time wearing the orange and green of the Finley team as he slashes off a tackle and heads for the end zone. And in the stands a figure with rust red hair and a Hepburn profile raises a fist, leaps to her feet and, laughing and clapping hands, waves a Finley banner with joyous abandon. The appearance of this vision, totally unbidden, unnerved me and it took a few seconds of deliberate effort to delete these images and to focus again on the present moment.

"Anyway," I finally went on, "don't get scared by Tillman. He's got a thing about standards. Talks endlessly about the Harmon mission to maintain them. The truth is the man lives in a dream world. He imagines he is running some top drawer English prep school. He's blinded himself to reality. This is no Eaton on the Hudson. The school is full of guys who know more about making book than reading one. Of course there are a few outsize brains in every class, but the rest of us just slug through. The key here is to be a team player, do what the old goats want in the classroom, and keep up with whatever they throw at you. If you play by the rules, you should have no trouble at Harmon."

When I spoke those words I had no doubt that they were true. There was no question in my mind that Schneiderman had a golden touch, that inevitably he would be a winner at anything he set out to do. It never occurred to me that there was a reason for his academic troubles at Ryder.

It did not take long, though, to recognize that there were plenty of reasons for them. When it came to the classroom, it was clear that Schneiderman was not going to break any scoring records. In fact, it was evident that he was struggling with a problem that could very well break up what Cara had labeled the dazzling duo, Harmon's answer to Tannenbaum and Cousy, before it even got on the court. As it turned out, Schneiderman's schedule put him in three of my classes, and it was in Spanish, the first one that we had after assembly, that I realized that something was wrong.

The Spanish teacher, Mr. Deutsch, was a short, sallow man who was German by birth and, rumor had it, a Third Reich sympathizer. In the lunchroom and the corridors we mocked him with Nazi salutes and goosestep imitations. In class we sat motionless, petrified with fear, dreading the four words, spat out in cold steel fury, "Take a minus, Sonny," with which Deutsch condemned and punished any *dumkopf* guilty of committing an error in grammar or pronunciation.

Spotting the new boy, Deutsch quickly put him to the test and his face grew gray as Schneiderman not only stumbled over a simple translation, but spoke the kind of Puerto Rican accented Spanish, picked up on the streets of Flatbush, that Deutsch loathed. In his class, use of anything other than pure Castilian Spanish evoked rapid-fire denunciation accompanied by a double minus that immediately lowered a final grade by a good five points.

To us it was an amazing act of self-control, on a par with Fiorello La Guardia keeping mum in front of a microphone, that Deutsch contained himself in the face of a performance that offended every Aryan cell in his body. In a voice straining to control an impulse to vilify the offender and to spit out a record number of minuses, he ordered Schneiderman to sit down, took out his grade book and, in red ink, wrote in his name, followed by two large X's, clearly indicating a student headed for deep trouble. Then he began to mutter to himself in German, words that Mel, sitting just to his right in the front row, translated as, "donkeys who spray manure ought to be kept in their stalls."

Math class was not much better. Mr. Killigan, the math teacher, who stood six-foot-two, had a bushel of white hair, and looked and acted like Mark Twain, made a practice of putting an algebra problem of his own devising on the board each day. Then, in a low and menacing voice and wagging his finger from side to side, he would intone "eeny, meany, miney, moe," ultimately pointing to a student whose task it then was to proceed to the board and, in front of the class, attempt to solve the problem.

The choice, however, was not always as random as it appeared. Killigan had a running battle with a student named Walker, a wise-cracking squash player known for his daring in taking on teachers and giving as good as he got. This at Harmon was an extremely dangerous practice, and those who tried it often found themselves not only sweating it out in Tillman's office, but punished by a week's suspension from school.

Killigan was more tolerant than most, however, and unlike many of his humorless colleagues, seemed to enjoy jousting with Walker. The day before Schneiderman arrived in his class, Killigan had called on Walker, not this time to solve an algebra problem, but to explain to the class just what it meant to circumscribe a circle. Walker's response was instantaneous.

"I really wouldn't know, sir," he said, in a tone that was flat deadpan, "I'm not Jewish."

Like Deutsch, Killigan immediately tested Schneiderman, but more gently, and with a good deal more tact. Forgoing his usual selection process, he asked Schneiderman if he would like to try his hand at solving the day's problem. Quite deliberately, Killigan had made it a comparatively simple one involving trains traveling in opposite directions at different speeds. It was the kind of elementary problem that the class had worked on at the start of the term.

Looking as though he was trapped in his own end zone, Schneiderman glared at me with an expression that clearly was one of fear. It was the first—and I believe the last—time I ever saw him frightened. I gave a slight nod of my head and pointed my chin toward the blackboard. He got my message. He had to get up there. Once Killigan made his choice of student, there was no way out. No one bucked Thomas Killigan.

At the board, Schneiderman stared at the problem for a good two or three minutes. Then, indecisively, he began to set up an equation. A few stifled laughs made their way through cupped mouths. He was clearly on the wrong track. Quickly Killigan moved in, erased Schneiderman's efforts with a single swipe of his eraser and, talking all the time, compared the approach that Schneiderman was using to his taking a snap from center and racing toward his own goal line. Then, with quick strokes, he wrote out the correct equation, handed a fresh piece of chalk to Schneiderman, and ordered him to demonstrate how to solve it.

Schneiderman's first moves were promising. He seemed to know what he was doing and Killigan stood alongside watching and nodding. But then Schneiderman bogged down on the matter of negative numbers. It was obvious that he hadn't the slightest idea what to do with them. Making a few futile guesses, he tried changing their signs and moving them to the other side of the equation. Nothing worked. Finally, he reverted to staring at the board. More laughter broke through. Killigan turned to the class with an expression of silent warning. Then, like a referee stopping a fight, he took the chalk from Schneiderman and holding it high, asked if anyone could help out our new student.

First to raise his hand was Dorfman, a slight, freckled-faced quiz kid with whom, since ninth grade, I'd been vying for number one spot in the class rankings. Dorfman was good at everything—he had set a Harmon record by being teacher's pet simultaneously in three subjects—but mathematics was his natural language and his facility in algebra was such that he could easily have taught the subject himself.

At Killigan's invitation, Dorfman rose from his seat, strode to the board, picked a piece of chalk from the rack and, with stunning speed, solved the equation. Then, indulging himself—he relished the role of teacher to his peers—he gave Schneiderman a tutorial on the handling of negative numbers.

After class I waited in the corridor for Schneiderman who had been summoned to Killigan's desk for a talk. When after ten minutes he emerged from the classroom, he looked pale and was carrying a sheaf of papers.

"Remedial stuff," he said, holding up the stack and looking distinctly unhappy, "Killigan says I'm starting back on my two yard line and I've got the whole damn field of algebra to cover in a few months."

"That is a lot of territory," I said softly. I was trying to put as much empathy into my voice as I could.

"He said I might do better to drop out right now. 'No need to be a hero,' is what he said, but if I decided to stay in the class, I'd need a lot of help. He wasn't mean, but what galled me was the way he put everything in football lingo. Why the hell does everyone around here speak football to me? I feel like some brainless ringer hired to push bodies around."

"People here remember you as the guy who scored the winning touchdown against us," I said. "And they have this vision—Mel says it's become a mass obsession—of you doing the same thing for Harmon." I gave him a pat on the shoulder.

"You should be flattered. You've become our instant white hope."

"At this rate I'll be lucky to get on the field before they put me on probation."

Just then I noticed that Dorfman was standing a few feet away in the corridor. Now he came up to Schneiderman.

"I can keep you on the field," he said. "I'd be glad to work with you, bring you up to speed."

Schneiderman seemed taken unaware. For an instant he looked confused. Quickly he glanced at me, then turned back to Dorfman.

"Thanks a lot," he said. "That is really kind of you. I may take you up on that offer sooner than you think."

"Do that," Dorfman replied in the tone of cool superiority that invited one to bash his face in. Suddenly, I found myself stepping forward.

"Actually that won't be necessary, Dorfman," I said. "I have already arranged something with Schneiderman here. We'll be working together."

"Well bully for you," Dorfman replied. "You know how to move in quickly, don't you?" Then, turning to Schneiderman: "Lucky you that you have such a brilliant tutor, but if he comes up short, drops the ball again, if you know what I mean, I'll be on the sidelines."

"Thanks, " Schneiderman said. "It's good to know I can call on you."

When Dorfman was gone, Schneiderman looked at me with an expression half puzzlement, half amusement.

"You really swept me off my feet," he said. "I had no idea you cared."

I could feel the heat in my face.

"I couldn't see you getting caught up with that creep. A couple of hours with him, and you'd be on the first train back to Brooklyn."

"Did you actually mean it?"

"What?"

"That you'd work with me?"

"Sure, if you'd like."

"Thanks. I feel like you are the only one running interference for me. I appreciate that."

"Now who's using football lingo?"

"You're right. I've caught their bug. Anyway, thanks. After today's showing, it's pretty obvious that I'm going to need all the help that I can get."

"It's a deal then."

We shook hands and I headed for my next class. I was already late and I knew that I'd get a dressing down, a demerit and, very likely, extra study hall time, but somehow none of that mattered. I felt good, unusually strong, strangely immune to any punishment that awaited me.

Basketball practice was held every weekday afternoon as soon as school let out. Usually just the team and the coaches showed up at the gym but that afternoon there must have been fifty students in the grandstand and half a dozen more milling around outside, waiting for Schneiderman to arrive.

We had agreed to walk over to the gym together, a distance of perhaps two hundred yards from the main building, and promptly at three I found Schneiderman sitting on the lawn outside the front door. He was chatting with Dorfman who had a large ruled tablet in front of him and was jotting down some figures. I tapped Schneiderman on the shoulder.

"We'd better head out," I said. "Your fans are waiting for you."

Schneiderman smiled, "Okay. Let's go. I would not want to be responsible for a riot."

He got up and shook hands with Dorfman.

"Good to chat with you," he said. "And thanks for the tip, we'll be in touch."

I tried to get a look at what Dorfman had been writing, but he had already stuffed the pad in his book-bag.

"Pretty persistent guy," I said as we started across the football field for the gym.

"He wanted to show me a couple of things about balancing equations," Schneiderman replied. "I think he wants to feel useful."

By inviting you to *shtup* him in the ass is what I wanted to say, but I kept my mouth shut.

For a while, we walked in silence. Schneiderman's stride was not the same easy, ground-covering glide that was his trademark. He was walking slowly, as though the day had drained him.

About halfway across the field a thought occurred to me and I just blurted it out.

"It must be totally weird for you to be putting on a Harmon uniform."

"Like sleeping with the enemy."

"I know what you mean." I said. "It's damn hard for us not to think of you as this Ryder steamroller who is always trying to flatten our asses. I just hope nobody on the court today gets confused and tries to take a poke at you."

"I'll be watching my back," Schneiderman said.

We suited up in the locker room, then walked out together and on to the court.

Mike Mueller, the coach, was waiting for us. Mueller had come to Harmon some dozen years before, fresh out of Springfield College where he was a starting guard on a team that won a Division Three college championship. That credential and the fact that Springfield was known as the birthplace of American basketball—legend had it that it started there, using peach baskets as hoops—landed him the job of heading up the basketball program at Harmon.

Mueller was hard working, earnest, and unimaginative. For a decade our teams had used the same strategies; pick and roll on offense and a collapsing—and often porous—zone on defense. Despite this and because our school managed to attract a fair number of city kids who grew up playing schoolyard basketball, we had fairly decent teams. The prior year we were in contention for the league championship, losing out to Trinity in the final game of the season. And this year the pundits who covered high school sports for the New York papers gave us a fighting chance to upset Trinity and take the crown.

Until Schneiderman appeared on the scene, all eyes were on me as the key to Harmon's season. Our team's leading scorer, I also had the most assists and anchored Mueller's sputtering offense from my right guard position. A lot of people, though, including coach Mueller, had serious doubt about my ability to go the distance without falling into a slump. That was my pattern. Typically I would start off fast, score in double figures for perhaps half the season, and then go into a free fall. In the last half of the past two seasons I averaged less than eight points a game and committed a barrel full of turnovers.

"It's a neurosis," Mel said, "self-castration, pure and simple. You can't stand being a winner. You have the best set shot and are the best ball handler in the county. Every year you start out as everyone's choice to make the All-City team, but if there is any trouble at home, if your father's business is on the rocks again, or he gets himself into another stew"—Mel was the only one I told about the IRS problem—"you start missing easy layups and you begin to shoot like a blind man."

"And you shoot from the hip with your two bit analysis," I retorted.

"Okay. Be a deaf mute if you like. That's fine with me. But unless you take a good hard look at what you have been doing, you'll continue to torpedo yourself and bring the whole team down with you."

"What's your solution, trade in my dad for a new model?"

"No, trade in your thick skull for a little insight. What you need to do is to work with yourself, recognize the pattern, and finally get it into your head that scoring in double figures won't cause your dad to kick the bucket."

I made a sour face and a yanking motion, pantomiming yanking Mel off his soap- box stage, but I heard him and I knew that in some way he was right. Actually my guilt was far from an unconscious matter. When my dad got into trouble, my feelings of guilt were exacerbated by the anger—and the despair—that I felt when, with his business clearly headed for disaster, he pretended that his troubles amounted to a minor accounting error or a temporary cash flow problem.

In what way this plaguing guilt was affecting me, on the court or off, I did not really understand. What I realized, though, was that although I hated Mel's uninvited comments and would gladly have treated him to a thorough head bashing when he started in on me, I also trusted his intuition. Mel had a way—mysterious to me—of sniffing out self-deception and zeroing in on what a person was trying to hide from himself.

If self-scrutiny was what I had been avoiding, and what Mel was pressuring me to employ, Schneiderman's arrival at Harmon and his instantaneous ascension to brightest star in the Harmon horizon got me off the hook. Now all eyes shifted to the new boy. If our team was going to make a trip to the County Center and the league championship game, clearly it was Schneiderman who was going to get us there.

When, at our first practice together that afternoon, the two of us walked onto the court—Schneiderman deliberately let me go first— Coach Mueller greeted us with a thoroughly atypical grin. Like Tillman, Mueller rarely smiled. To do so might have given the impression that he was confident of a winning season and, like many doomsayers in the coaching profession, he did not want to have to eat his words. Now, however, he was acting like a man whose horse had just come in. As we stepped on the court, he rushed over from the sidelines to greet us or, more exactly, to greet Schneiderman.

"Welcome, welcome," he said in a voice that sounded like a PA announcer. "Welcome to Harmon. We are delighted that you are joining us, aren't we, Jonathan?" He turned to me with a deliberately wide smile. These were the first words Mueller had spoken to me in a week.

"Absolutely," I said.

"Yes, we all feel that way," he added. "We believe that you have the stuff to make a huge difference to our team, don't we, Jonathan?"

"We do," I said. "We definitely do."

"Ever since I got the good news—it is still hard to believe—I've been thinking, actually staying up nights thinking, and what I'd like to do," Mueller went on, "is to pair you two as a duo, forward and guard, both on the same side and overload any zone defense we come up against. We'll out-maneuver them and always have one of you free to drive to the basket and make the easy layup. What do you think of that idea?"

It all sounded too easy, too straightforward, one of Mueller's appealing but ultimately unworkable strategies. The coach was clearly enthusiastic about his own plan, though, and neither of us wanted to spoil his mood so we nodded our ascent as he outlined the offense that he wanted to install.

Spurred on by this affirmation, Mueller immediately organized a scrimmage, the first team, with Schneiderman and me at right guard and forward, against the reserves. Before we got started Mueller gathered our opponents around him and ordered them to test us, to mimic Trinity's rough and tumble style, and to give Schneiderman and me no quarter.

The player assigned to guard me was a kid named Bahary, the son of a diplomat from Egypt, who at a distance and with his shirt off, looked for all the world like the image of a barefooted warrior inscribed on an ancient Egyptian funeral vase. Bahary was tenacious in guarding me. His hands were forever in my face and whenever I moved he was there, matching me stride for stride and trying to hedge me in and prevent me from cutting toward the basket. Despite these tactics, and with the use of head and shoulder fakes I had learned from Al McGuire himself at a basketball clinic in the Catskills, I managed to shake him and break free a handful of times.

Whenever I did, Schneiderman spotted me and hit me with a perfect pass right on the numbers. Taking the ball on the move, I was able to drive in for a layup or score with a running one-hander from around the circle. Within a short time I was in double figures and at first Mueller was elated. Every time I hit a basket he pumped a fist and, from the sidelines, called out throaty words of encouragement. But then, when he realized that Schneiderman was not scoring himself but was continually passing off and feeding the ball to me, he became agitated.

"Shoot," he called out when Schneiderman had the ball, "throw it up. Let's see the one-hander," and such entreaties. When these had no effect and Schneiderman continued to pile on the assists, Mueller blew his whistle, came on the court, and addressed his new player directly.

"Don't be shy, fella," he said, "no need to be shy just because you're new. We are counting on you to be our high scorer, our number one offensive thrust, if you know what I mean. So if you have a clear shot, take it. Go for it."

Schneiderman listened, nodded, and on his next two possessions hit two quick buckets on soaring set shots from outside. But then, as though he felt uncomfortable in the spotlight, he quickly slipped back into his previous role as director of the attack and feeder to his teammates.

On the sidelines, Mueller began to curse under his breath. Then he blew the whistle again, stomped onto the court, and announced a change in the teams.

"We'll mix you up," he said. "I want you two"—he pointed to Schneiderman and me—"on opposite sides. I want you to play against each other. Jonathan, you guard Schneiderman here and keep him bottled up. Schneiderman, I want you to pretend you are back at Ryder. You are playing us for the championship and you want to make Jonathan look like a tangle-footed chump.

"Just play him like you always have," he added. "Forget you are at Harmon. Just do your regular stuff. You've never had trouble handling Jonathan."

This last comment burned me and I set out to guard Schneiderman so that he had no space to shoot. I played him up close, harassing him with a hand in his face, and when Mueller wasn't looking—he was refereeing this part of the scrimmage—bumped him when he tried to break away and sprint down court. Despite my best efforts, though, Schneiderman managed four buckets, two running one-handers, a daring hook shot from the key, and a long set shot, practically from half court, that swished through the net as though guided by radar.

We had been playing for about twenty minutes when, abruptly, Schneiderman called for a time out, approached Mueller, spoke with him briefly, and then trotted off the court and headed for the locker room. Puzzled and a bit unnerved by his sudden departure—I felt some need to shepherd him around that first day—I wanted to follow him downstairs. Mueller called for a substitute, though, and insisted that we play another ten minutes.

When, finally, he blew the whistle to end the scrimmage, I dashed down to the locker room. Schneiderman was already dressed and on his way out. A light rain had started and seeing that the new man had no rain gear, Andy Potsalis, the locker room attendant, had rummaged through a pile of discarded clothing and had come up with a battered St. Louis Cardinal baseball cap. In his haste to leave, Schneiderman had left it on the bench next to his locker. Realizing what must have happened, I grabbed the cap, ran to the door, and caught Schneiderman just as he was on the way out. He thanked me, set the cap on his head, and with a jaunty gesture of appreciation, tipped it to me. He started out again, then turned back.

"By the way, you were good out there, Jonathan. Really good. Half the time I couldn't move. You really had me bottled up."

"You managed a few good moves yourself," I put in. Schneiderman smiled and thanked me. He seemed to value my opinion and be genuinely appreciative of anything complimentary that I said about him. Given the way I viewed him—I often felt that his skills as a ball handler and shot maker put him in a different league—this surprised me. I was pleased, though, and after he'd left I found myself repeating his words, hanging on to them.

Before heading out again, he reached out and touched me on the arm.

"Let's talk later," he said. "I'll call you tonight." Then he was gone.

I was curious about where Schneiderman was going and why he'd had to cut out early. He wasn't the sort you asked that kind of question, though. There was something private and contained about him, a reserved quality that acted as an invisible wall. It wasn't that he was unfriendly, not at all. He was quite approachable in school and in the locker room he made a point of chatting with his teammates and joining in the fun when they did imitations of Mueller. Nonetheless the wall was there, and unless he specifically let it down and invited you in, you knew to keep your distance.

Chapter Nine

To my surprise he did call. I was in my room working on one of Killigan's more satanic homework problems and waiting for my mother to announce dinner when she knocked on my door.

"Phone."

"Who is it, Ma?"

"A man. A boy. I didn't get the name. He said he was with you this afternoon. What were you doing this afternoon?"

"Nothing dangerous. It must be Schneiderman."

"Who?"

"A new friend, Ma. He's not a drug addict, he doesn't smoke cigarettes and he's an A-plus student."

"Your father will be glad. You know he worries about bad influences. He's started to worry that your friend, Melvin, is a bad influence; that he sneaks cigarettes and is pushing you toward girls."

"He is absolutely right. Melvin is a terrible influence. Guys who hang out with him can get a social disease. That's why I've switched to this fellow, Schneiderman. He has good habits."

"I'm glad to hear that. The truth is you can't be too careful these days."

"I know, Ma," I said. "that's why I do a background check on every new kid meet."

I walked into the hallway, took the receiver, and hunched over so that my mother could not hear.

"Are you free tonight?" Schneiderman asked me straight off.

"I have a date with Killigan."

"Your taste in men leaves something to be desired. The guy is a pure sadist. I've got a migraine from staring at the Rube Goldberg contraption he devised for the homework assignment. Can you get into it at all?"

"I've been trapped in a maze full of no exit signs for the last half hour." I replied. "I need a rescue helicopter. I'm flying blind myself. But if you want to come over, we can take a shot at cracking the code."

"You are a life-saver. Thanks. I'll be there in an hour."

It was just after seven when Schneiderman arrived. He had shed the gray suit that he wore to school and now was dressed in sports jacket and open-neck shirt. On his head was the beat-up St. Louis baseball cap, making him look like a Cardinals fan who had taken a wrong turn in the road.

When I greeted Schneiderman at the door, he extended a hand. I took it and ushered him into the apartment. My folks were still at the dinner table which was set up in the foyer as, years before, they had commandeered the dining room as a badly needed second bedroom.

I introduced Schneiderman, first to my mother. My father sat in his chair, waiting.

"Hello," she said, not warmly. Her smile was polite, unenthusiastic, the kind of smile she reserved for gentiles and strangers. That was my mother. She was nothing if not cautious, and now she was being her extra-cautious self, especially suspicious of anyone new in my life. I could see that she was wondering just who this new fellow was, where I had met him, whether he was a smoker, and in what direction he was likely to lead me.

Before I could turn to him, my father was on his feet, shaking hands and grasping Schneiderman by the elbow before I finished the introduction.

"Welcome to our home, Stanley Schneiderman," he said. "It is a pleasure to meet a friend of Jonathan's, particularly a new friend. Some of the others—I won't name names—are not the best influence, if you know what I mean. Come sit," he continued. "You'll have some food with us. There is plenty left." I could tell immediately that my father was being his company self. This was not the father I saw every day, the father I found so hard to talk to, who, for long stretches of time was lost in his daydreams. This was someone else, a man who came alive when we had company, who told stories, played the genial host, and carried on in ways that at times caused me to want to leave the room with embarrassment.

Schneiderman smiled and tried to beg off.

"Thanks so much, Mr. Manheim," he said. "That is awfully generous of you. But, actually, I've just had dinner."

"Then you'll have dessert. When my wife serves meatloaf, it's a rule in our house, only one dessert is allowed. Did you ever hear of Junior's Cheesecake? In this category, it is the number one product in the country, bar none. Taste it, you'll see what I mean. What I want to point out is the combination, the pairing, as they say. Meatloaf and Junior's is an unbeatable combination. I made the discovery accidentally, serendipitously, as they say, and I've kept them together ever since. When you find a match like that, you hang onto it."

"Actually, I know Junior's very well," Schneiderman broke in. My dad loves the place. His office is a block away. I am actually from Brooklyn. Don't let my cap throw you off. It's something I picked up this afternoon and I've gotten attached to, but I'm no redbird fan. I'm strictly a Flatbush product, born and bred in the shadow of Ebbets Field."

"Then you know what kind of special place this is," my father said. "This is not something your average person understands. In Brooklyn you have the whole world in one area. One geography has it all and it is a world that gets along. You've got no camps to lock up Japanese people in Brooklyn. Japanese, Chinese, Puerto Ricans, the Hasidim, they all get along, eat each other's foods and on Sunday all the families make a day of it at Prospect Park."

Schneiderman nodded and politely agreed. But he flashed me a look that signaled what other friends had said outright; that they didn't know what to make of my dad.

"And I'll tell you something else about Brooklyn," my father went on. "There's no better vacation spot. This is probably the number one secret in America today. People insist on schlepping to Puerto Rico, Hawaii and for what? Once you've seen a half dozen palm trees and spent three bucks for a piña colada, the show is over. If you want beach, what I say is come to Sheepshead, come to the Brooklyn shore. And Coney is beach plus, if you know what I mean. At Coney you've got beach, you've got ocean, and every weekend you've got a carnival that's better than the Mardi Gras."

Schneiderman smiled. "That is something I've never heard before," he said. As he spoke, he retreated a step as though instinctively putting more space between himself and someone not quite right in the head. Unfazed, my father kept pace with Schneiderman, positioned himself in front of him, effectively cutting off any escape route, and began to talk with him as though there was no one else in the room. Schneiderman listened politely, nodding at intervals, and from time to time, responding with a remark that promptly elicited a fresh flood stream of observations and commentary.

My mother and I, outsiders, sat across from each other, watching and exchanging glances. Left out of the conversation, I found, to my surprise, that I was quite upset. In fact, I had to fight off a growing feeling of resentment at being excluded by my father's insistent focus on Schneiderman.

My father was going on now about the Brooklyn shore, recounting how as a young man he would walk the beaches, pail and shovel in hand, and when he spotted activity in the sand, get on hands and knees and dig for clams.

"And do you know something else," he said to Schneiderman, "sometimes when I walked I made up poems, actually wrote quite a few poems to this lady here," he pointed with his chin at my mother. "Can you imagine a fella like me, for forty years a peddler in hardware, writing poems? It's hard to believe such foolishness."

"I don't think that is at all foolish," Schneiderman put in. "There is nothing foolish about poetry. I have an aunt who writes poetry and she is a remarkable person. Poets are very special people." He turned to my mother, who was sitting passively at the end of the table, taking in the scene.

"You agree with me, don't you, Mrs. Manheim?" he asked. My mother seemed startled by the question. She twisted in her seat. Her face lost color.

"It was a very nice thing to do," she murmured. Then she looked at me for a clue should more questions be forthcoming. I shrugged, not sure myself what to expect.

"There you go," Schneiderman said to my father. "You really impressed the lady. I'll bet that's why she married you. She knew you were a different kind of guy."

My mother was staring at me, eyebrows raised, and I was afraid that she might make a puncturing comment. I avoided her eyes, concerned that a return glance would be interpreted as encouragement.

After his discourse on our unappreciated borough, my father had fallen into silence. He seemed to be lost in memories. Then, all at once, he awoke, recalled that Schneiderman had said something about having left Brooklyn, and wanted to know if that was really true.

"Do I understand that you are no longer a Brooklynite?" he demanded. "Did I hear that right?"

"That's right. My dad needed to leave. We moved three weeks ago."

"To where?"

"Riverdale. Didn't Jonathan tell you? I'm at Harmon with him. We're teammates now."

Actually I had mentioned this to my parents soon after Cara broke the news about Schneiderman transferring to Harmon. I was so upset, so discombobulated by what I'd heard, so in need of a sympathetic voice, that I broke an inviolate rule of mine: never give family more than name, rank and serial number, and blurted out the incredible tale. Seeing my agitation, my mother had made an appropriate face, and my father, although distracted by his own worries—that afternoon he had received another missive from the IRS—had made sounds that indicated his understanding of such aggravation. It was clear, though, that he had not really understood, had no idea how something like this can shock the system. I tried to explain with an example. I said what happened was like Father Coughlin, the Jew-hating demagogue and my father's arch nemesis, renting a cot and moving into the living room, but the example so agitated my father that he forgot all about my situation.

Now, though, some of what I'd told my folks seemed to be coming back to him and he began to get the picture. He looked at Schneiderman.

"Are you Schneiderman, the roughneck?" he demanded.

"I'm not sure what you mean."

"The fellow who tried to decapitate my son?"

"Actually, I think it was a mutual effort."

My father disagreed. "Couldn't be," he said. "Jonathan is not that kind of fighter. That is not his nature. You barreled into him and stole the football, isn't that so?"

"Do you mean the time I tackled him and he fumbled?"

"That was no fumble. If an eighteen wheeler smacks into you on your way home from the A&P, you are not going to hold onto your groceries."

Schneiderman laughed. "You flatter me. I'd say it's more like being hit in the tush by a creaking two wheeler, but I understand where you are coming from. You are Jonathan's father. You are being a dad."

My father was clearly pleased by this comment.

"Well I try," he said. "When you have your own aggravation it is not easy, but I try. Listen, you have to understand something. The time we are talking about, that was the first pass Jonathan here caught in the big leagues, if you catch my drift, so you don't like to see an occasion like that spoiled."

"Of course. If I had known that, I wouldn't have touched our boy here," Schneiderman replied.

It was hard to believe what I was hearing. As I sat listening to my father speak, I felt confused. I had no idea that he kept track of what I did on the field. He never said a word to me and if he ever mentioned our team, it was only to offer condolences after we'd been bushwacked by Fordham Prep or one of those other Catholic school powerhouses. Now, though, it seemed that he'd been keeping a record of my performances and I wondered if he grasped the sorry truth; that in three seasons on the J.V. I had managed only half a dozen receptions, most of which were five yard pitches that hit me on the numbers as soon as I had crossed the scrimmage line.

I wondered if my father had put his buddy, Sugarman, up to spying on me. Could it be that the rumor about Sugarman—that he was a weekend scout for the Giants—was deliberate misinformation;

that, in fact, sitting next to my father at our games, doing his dirty work, he was actually recording the number of my fumbles and missed tackles? And if my father had discovered that his son was an all-thumbs receiver, what else might he know?

Although seemingly preoccupied with his own aggravations, was he, in fact, more attuned to me than I had imagined? Known for his intuition with customers—he could identify quick payers and procrastinators at a single glance—had his radar detected my concerns, my preoccupations? Did he know about Cara and me and East Hampton? Had he picked up, not only that I had lied about going to Rockaway, but, more important, that this outing was no excursion? Had I somehow given away the truth; not only that Cara and I had made out madly, but that I had come within inches of being the recipient of oral stimulation? I began to look at my father with fresh eyes.

He was not looking at me, though. He was focused on Schneiderman, talking to him about me as though I wasn't sitting a foot away, an arm's length from both of them.

What amazed me, too, was that my father had started to speak about an upset of his own, actually admitted that he had worries. I knew from my mother that things were approaching a crisis, that the IRS was moving in quickly, and that unless my father came up with a payment plan for the taxes he owed, there would be prosecution, but he never let on to me that there was so much as a cloud on the horizon. Everything was in control, he claimed. Whatever bookkeeping problems there were would be taken care of.

Now, however, he had acknowledged to a stranger, to Schneiderman of all people, someone who until a month ago ranked number one on my list of personal persecutors, that he had his own aggravations. What magic, I wondered, did Schneiderman possess that could elicit such a confession. Perhaps it was a genetic thing, I thought, a talent inherited from his father who, no doubt, had made a career of prying secrets out of mafia henchlings. Although I wanted to break into their conversation, ask my father questions and force him to focus attention on me, I held back. Besides, I was curious as to what else, what other secrets, Schneiderman might elicit.

Appeased by Schneiderman's easy manner and his humor, my father had turned to querying him about his family.

"Schneiderman is a familiar name," my father remarked. "I think I've heard of the Brooklyn Schneidermans. Is your father in paints or roofing materials?"

"My dad is a DA. He worked in the Brooklyn office for twenty years and we lived on Jay Street. Then he got into a fight with his boss, Mackel, and we had to leave."

"Mackel," my father responded. "I know Mackel. That fellow is a number one putz. I used to have a branch office in Brooklyn and the creep tried to close me down for owing a couple years back taxes. Can you believe something like that?"

"That's him," Schneiderman said. "He goes after the little guy and lets the Tammany crooks walk."

"Your dad made a good move," my father declared. "You don't want to work with a *gonif* like that."

"That's what my dad says, too."

"Well he's right. One thing I've learned in this business, if you want to know a customer, what he is really like, forget about balance sheets, credit ratings, how fast he pays; stuff like that. Just look eye to eye. What you see there is like an x-ray, a fluoroscope. Did you ever buy shoes and see your feet under a fluoroscope? You can see right through to the bones. If you know how to look in the eyes, you get a surprise. You can see a man's heart, see what it's made of. First thing I tell my crew, look in the eyes, you'll see the heart. It's our firm's mantra, if you know what I mean."

"I do, that's the kind of thing my father would say," Schneiderman put in. "He has let people go who have gotten into trouble because he believed they were good folks who had made mistakes. He wasn't out for convictions, but if someone is really a crook, he won't stop until he puts them away."

"He sounds like a good man," my father said. "Someone with heart. A man like that has a lot to teach a son," he added. "Isn't that right?"

Schneiderman did not answer right away.

"I've learned some things from him," he replied. "When he's had the time." I thought I detected a note of anger—or was it bitterness—in Schneiderman's voice, but I said nothing.

"I can't say that I have taught Jonathan very much," my father went on. "Frankly he is more his mother's boy. She's been the biggest influence. My wife is a good woman, very smart and educated way beyond what I've managed, but I've tried to show him character, show him how to play his cards straight up, no finagling, no cheating. I've tried to teach him what I said about heart. Assess by the heart. But to do that you have to let the other guy look in your eyes, too, do you know what I mean? One thing about Jonathan, you can always look in his eyes. He's very open, very straight that way."

"I've noticed that," Schneiderman said.

I had been upset at my father speaking of me in the third person, but now, at this unexpected compliment, I felt embarrassed; embarrassed and strangely guilty, as though I didn't deserve any praise from my father. And I worried that, privately, Schneiderman was laughing at his naiveté. I wanted to say something, to diminish what my father had said, but I was afraid to appear as foolish as he was acting, so I kept my mouth shut.

Now having discovered that Schneiderman's dad was a DA and that he had trouble with Mackel, the same SOB who gave him non-stop heartburn over a paltry few years back taxes, my father felt allied with the older Mr. Schneiderman, felt him to be a brother under the skin, and he wanted to know more about him.

"So how long was he in Mackel's office?" he wanted to know.

"Twenty years. He started right after law school."

My father did some rapid calculations on his fingers.

"That's when I was in Brooklyn," he announced. "Actually, I'm pretty sure I heard of your dad. Wasn't he the one who went after the numbers racket?"

"That's right. You've got a good memory, Mr. Manheim. That was one of his biggest cases. He hated those guys for ripping off the poor."

"I'm pretty sure I saw his picture in the *Daily News*," my father said. "Splashed all over page four when he put away a slew of mafia hoods."

Schneiderman nodded. "We kid him about that. He hates the *News*, calls it a fascist rag, but he keeps a clipping of that story in his wallet."

"Why not," my father said. "In his line of work you don't get a lot of kudos. Complaints, yes, criticism, yes, but *nachas*, this you have to supply for yourself.

"I'd like to meet your dad," my father added. "Maybe one day you'll bring him over."

Schneiderman responded quickly. "He'd like that," he said. "He'd be honored to meet your family."

My father's attitude surprised me. I had never known him to take a particular interest in my friends' parents. In fact, the opposite was the case. When I had friends over, he wanted to be the parent, the storyteller, the center of interest. He never said as much, but I knew he felt inferior when he heard that a friend's father was a college graduate, had a prestigious position, or had money. And he handled these feelings, as he did so much in his life, simply by ignoring their existence. Now, though, he was all ears, eager to hear more about Schneiderman's dad, who, it seemed, had become an instant hero of his.

"Is that your dad's specialty," my father asked, "racketeers and hoodlums?"

"Actually, most of his cases are white collar crime. Crooks in business suits. He handles a lot of embezzlers and tax cheats."

"There is one under every bush," my father agreed. "Everywhere you look, there are *schnorers*. The problem is, the feds go after the wrong ones. They let the big cheats go and hound the little guy who is having a few problems meeting deadlines."

Schneiderman immediately picked up the clue.

"I know what you mean, Mr. Manheim," he said. "My father has said the same thing. He's helped dozens of people who are in that boat. He knows how to talk to the IRS, smooth the waters if you know what I mean; arrange payments, get those monkeys off folks' backs."

"He knows how to do that?"

"He does it all the time. Listen, if you have a particular interest in this subject, why don't you speak with my dad? It's a specialty of his and he loves to talk about it. In fact, you'd better get set for a non-stop lecture. Once he gets started, you are in for a mini course on tax law."

"Your father wouldn't mind talking with me? I wouldn't want to impose. He has his own *tsouris*. I would hate to be any kind of a burden."

"Are you kidding? Talking about someone else's problems would be the best thing for him. For someone like him, there is no better tonic."

Schneiderman got to his feet.

"Look," he said, "let me call him right now, see if he is free to talk."

"You'll interfere with his supper."

"No problem. He'd rather talk than eat."

Schneiderman looked around, spotted the phone in the foyer, and dialed.

Apparently his father answered, and for a minute Schneiderman spoke to him in a lowered voice, so that, sitting at the dining room table, we could not make out the words. Then he turned toward my father and held out the phone.

"My dad wants to speak with you."

My father hesitated. His face flushed and he got up awkwardly. Then he came forward and took the receiver.

"Hello, Mr. Schneiderman, this is Eli Manheim, Jonathan's dad." Then with the phone in hand he turned his back on us and took a few steps toward the rear of the room so that we could not hear.

Schneiderman motioned to me to get up. "Could we go to your room, Jonathan?" he asked. I nodded, understanding his meaning. He followed me down a long narrow corridor, the kind they have in old pre-war apartments. The last room at the far end was mine. We went in, me first, Schneiderman following, and closed the door.

"Thanks," I said.

"For nothing." Schneiderman replied. "My father is delighted to have an audience."

For the next hour we tried to work on Killigan's lunatic homework assignment. It was so complicated—devising fiendish homework problems was Killigan's special talent—that it took twenty minutes and repeat readings just to grasp what he was getting at. Schneiderman's concentration was not great. He gave up after stumbling a few times while grappling with the text and he simply laid down his pencil when it came to formulating an equation. I was able to make some headway and thought for a while that I was on the right track, but then bogged down when my attempts to solve the equations I had set up ran aground.

"We'd better call Dorfman in from the bullpen," Schneiderman teased.

"No way. I'd rather run up the white flag and fall on my sword in Killigan's class."

"You're jealous?"

"Of what, a muscle-bound calculator?"

"The guy is a genius."

"A genius who has the charm of Mortimer Snerd."

"As a matter of fact, Snerd is a big hit with the Finley girls. The other day on the subway I heard that next to the Harmon boys he is the dummy they would most like to curl up with."

"I'm not surprised. Snerd is a doll compared to Dorfman."

We wasted a lot of time *kibbutzing* that way and more time with Schneiderman filling me in on his misadventures as a student. It turns out that he had trouble learning from an early age, never did well in school and, over the years, had exhausted the patience of a half dozen tutors.

"What can I tell you," he said, "I'm doomed to be an auto mechanic or a gigolo. My dad will have to outfit me with a disguise to avoid embarrassment. I'll probably end up in exile someplace in Idaho.'"

"Not to worry," I said. "I hear they have great basketball out there. With your talent, you are a cinch to make it big with the Idaho Spuds."

"Thanks for the compliment. But with my school record it's a lot more likely that I'll be digging potatoes for a living. But if you can get me through Killigan's obstacle course, who knows, maybe I could land a job doing the books for the Boise general store."

Then we got into more of Schneiderman's childhood. I was curious to know what it was like to be a DA's son and whether he got to know any criminals.

"Did you ever hear of Meyer Lansky?" he asked.

"The mob boss and murderer?"

"That is one hat he wears. Under the other he is the sweetest guy in the world. He is like your good uncle Otto. Just ask, and he'll turn the city upside down to do you a favor."

"Like rubbing out Dorfman?"

"He could arrange that if I asked. But if you met him, you wouldn't believe he could rub out anything more than yesterday's socks. He is your neighborhood do-gooder, with an armful of gifts for anyone who comes to his home."

"You actually went to Lansky's place unarmed?"

"Hung out with him. His son, Peter, was in my class at Ryder. A gang of us used to go over to his apartment every weekend to watch football. For a long time he had the only TV set in the neighborhood. Peter's place was our second home. At some point during the game Meyer would come in to say hello. He knew all of us by name and he had a little gift for everyone. I owe my whole baseball card collection to Meyer Lansky."

"Your dad knew about this?"

"A lot of times he would pick me up there after the game. He and Lansky understood one another. Lansky knew if my father could get the goods on him he would put him away for life, and my father knew that at any time Lansky could have him fitted with a pair of cement boots. But they also respected and trusted one another. My dad knew that when it came to me and the other kids, Lansky was absolutely trustworthy. He totally protected us. And Lansky knew that my father would never take advantage of their social connection to pull a stunt on him. Nothing was ever said. They never spoke about rules, but they lived by them. You have to get to know my dad.

He's got his problems, I can vouch for that, but when it comes to his job, he tries to be fair. He makes a point of listening to everyone, to all sides of a story. That's one thing he's taught me. Take your time, get to know a person before you judge. Don't assume anything. A lot of the time you'll be wrong."

"Great advice but pretty hard to follow, at least for someone like me who is convinced that ninety percent of the population are assholes."

"Viva the other ten percent. But I know what you mean. I'm the same way. I'm ready to take out a contract on half the world, starting right now with your pal Killigan."

"Throw in Dorfman and it's a deal."

Just then my father opened the door without knocking.

"Now that is a man," he blurted out as he came in. He walked over to Schneiderman, reached out, and shook his hand. "Your father is a prince, did you know that," he asked. "An absolute prince. He gave me a complete course on the IRS, every in and out, every angle. Right away he understood my situation and gave me a blow-by-blow plan to get them off my back. This is a man who should be mayor of New York. He knows how to listen to people."

"When he wants to, he can be very helpful," Schneiderman agreed.

"Absolutely," my father continued, "this is strictly a five-star individual. With the right PR and the right people in his corner, he could be our next Little Flower. He has the touch. I told him, 'Schneiderman, you have the magic, the sex appeal. Don't waste it. Don't spend it chasing hoodlums.'" Now my father again took a step toward Schneiderman. "In this life the worst thing is to waste talent," he said. "It's the absolute worst. Talent doesn't stay forever and it doesn't come back. 'You're a natural,' I told your dad. 'Play your cards right and in a couple of years you'll be boss of Gotham.' Do you know what Gotham is?" he asked Schneiderman. "It's this whole damn city, including Staten Island, which is *persona non grata* for me. 'When you're the boss you can have the pleasure of running Mackel right out of town,' I told him, 'and I'll be first in line to help you.' He was appreciative of that."

"Did you manage to sign him up as a candidate, Dad?" I asked in as light a way as I could. I felt a need to say something, to try to divert my father from what was becoming an unstoppable—and totally embarrassing—monologue.

"He's got a lot on his plate right now," my father answered seriously. "The man has a lot of aggravation. But he told me he would think about it when he cleared out the dreck in his head and got himself settled. He is definitely going to think about it and call me."

I could feel my face redden. As my father carried on I kept looking at Schneiderman, trying to determine if he thought him as much of a fool as I did. There was no sign of that, though. In fact, Schneiderman seemed to be enjoying my father's free associations. I wanted to quiet him, though, and for him to leave us alone.

"I'm glad things worked out for you, Dad," I put in. "We can talk about all of this later on. Right now we are behind on a bitch of a homework problem." My father got the message.

"Not to worry," he said. "You two go right ahead. I'll be right inside if you want more information." Then with a parting comment, he turned to Schneiderman.

"I can see you are like your father," he said. "A solid citizen. I am glad you and Jonathan have gotten to be friends. You can be a very good influence, keep him on course."

"I'll try to do that, Mr. Manheim," Schneiderman replied. After my father was gone, he broke into a soft chuckle.

"He's a card," Schneiderman said. "He knows how to put it on. But there is something kind of sweet about him, too. Or am I wrong?" I dodged the question.

Finally we got back to Killigan's puzzle. I worked on it, pretty much alone, for about the next twenty minutes. Sitting next to me, Schneiderman threw in an occasional suggestion—reliably off the mark—but as the minutes passed I could feel him growing restless.

"You've just about got it," he said at one point, looking over my shoulder at the calculations I had jotted down. "Why don't we quit now? You can finish up later."

"What's the rush?"

"I've got an idea."

"About what?"

He looked at his watch. I noticed that it was the kind of cheap model that they sold in drugstores.

"We've still got time to catch the last show."

"What are you talking about?"

"The stage show at the Roxy. They say it's a humdinger, the best of the year. If we hurry, we can just make it."

"You're mad. Killigan and my father on the same night must have done it. You've gone off the deep end."

"I'm serious. We've been chasing our tails around this maze for over an hour. We both need a break, a short trip for a little well-deserved entertainment."

"This is a school night and it's already late. The only trip I'll be making tonight is to the kitchen for a bedtime Oreo cookie."

"Spoken like the model student we all know you are. Listen, if you are not careful that tight halo of yours is going to give you migraines."

"I'll take my chances."

"What about taking a chance on having some fun. That would be a novelty."

"Okay. I'll gamble on a Saturday night date with you."

"You are putting things off. Tonight is our night. The show ends tomorrow. This is our last chance. Look," he added, "if we take off now, we'll be back in two hours."

"There's no way. My mother knows when I get up to go to the bathroom. She figures each trip will cost a couple of points off any exam I have the next day."

"Don't worry about her. I'll speak to your mom. I'll convince her that a serious homework problem has come up and to solve it we need to leave the house for a couple of hours."

"It won't work. My mother is descended from purebred paranoids. She can smell fish stories a mile away."

"Leave it to me," Schneiderman said. He left the room and was back in ten minutes.

"Let's go," he said. "It's all set."

"What did you do, bribe her with an Israel bond?"

"I told her that we had come across an impossible problem, one of Killigan's humdingers, and that you were very worried that it might show up on tomorrow's test. I explained that we could get help from my uncle Mike who is a genuine math whiz—this is true by the way. The problem, I said, is that he lives in the Bronx and that you didn't want to ask permission to go out so late, that you didn't want to upset her. I explained that I volunteered to speak to her because I saw how worried you were getting and I knew she wouldn't want you to get sick over a math problem."

"How did that go over?"

"Like Barnum trying to sell sideshow tickets to Hadassah. But I think the part about your getting sick got to her. She started asking me a lot of questions. What is my uncle's full name, where exactly does he live, is he married, things like that. Then, finally, she asked how long we'd be gone and when we expected to be back."

"What did you say?"

"A couple of hours. I explained that we would have to go by subway and then spend time with Uncle Mike and that this time of night subway travel can be very slow."

"You're a genius. Cara told me she thought you had a lot more white matter than the average jock but that it had been dormant for a long time and needed stimulation."

"And did she volunteer to do the stimulating? I hear she has a talent for arousing flaccid brain cells."

"She was talking about street smarts. Her dad is like that, a street fighter without a lot of education, so she knows the type."

"Well please tell her she can improve my education anytime she wants. I'd be glad to be her latest project."

We tossed aside our books, I grabbed my NY Giants team jacket—purchased through a special radio offer—and we were off. We half walked, half ran to the 96th Street station and a few minutes later were sitting side by side on a downtown local.

I never went out on a school night. This was an unspoken taboo in my family and I was curious as to whether Schneiderman made a habit of this kind of thing.

"I get restless being home," he said. "Things can get pretty tense there, so I make a point of getting out when I can."

"What about your schoolwork?"

"The answer is self-evident."

"Where do you go?"

"Often to the movies. Sometimes to listen to some jazz."

"Alone?"

"Uh huh. I don't mind that. I'm kind of a loner, actually."

This surprised me. Schneiderman had an easygoing manner about him and I imagined him having lots of friends. He must have sensed what I was thinking.

"I can be friendly enough," he put in, "but it takes me a long time to make a real friend. I have a hard time trusting people. I don't know why. Maybe it's because my dad is always talking about the vicious things people do to one another."

I couldn't imagine having a father like that. My dad was just the opposite. He trusted everyone, including all the wrong people.

At that point we had reached our stop and had to break off the conversation. I made a mental note, though, to continue on the way home. I wanted to learn as much as I could about this fellow Schneiderman who, it seemed, had something mysterious about him.

Five minutes later we were standing in front of the famous Roxy Theatre, one of only two Broadway houses that, for one price, offered both a first run Hollywood film and an hour-long stage show featuring a big band and several headline performers, many from the vaudeville circuit. On the current bill were the Stan Kenton Orchestra, the comic Morey Amsterdam, straight from an engagement at the Concord Hotel in the Catskills and, as an added attraction, Bojangles Bill Robinson, tap dancer extraordinaire.

We were too late for the last showing of the movie, a June Allyson-Jimmy Stewart comedy, and the lady at the box office solemnly informed us that the price of admission was the same, movie or not, and that there would be no refund for the stage show alone.

Accepting these conditions, we dug into our pockets for a dollar and a quarter apiece, took our tickets, and entered the grand lobby of the Roxy Theatre, a showplace that, in my imagination, looked to be the great hall of a Venetian Palace transplanted to Broadway.

Hanging from the gilded ceiling, three outsized crystal chandeliers illuminated the large, elegantly decorated entryway. Thick pile maroon carpeting, extremely soft to the step, extended the length of the lobby. The walls were covered in red and gold fabric upon which, at regular intervals, appeared dark blue shields, like the coat of arms of some royal family.

In addition to its grandeur, the Roxy's huge lobby emitted a certain glow, a feeling of warmth and welcome that enveloped us as we hurried toward the large doors that led to the inner theatre.

We had just reached our seats when the lights dimmed and, arising phoenix-like from some underground vault, the stage itself appeared and on it, illuminated by converging beams from a trio of spotlights and filling the theatre with its brassy big band sound, was the Stan Kenton Orchestra, led by the great man himself.

As soon as the band started, Schneiderman began a rhythmic tapping of his feet in time to the music.

"This is great," he whispered, turning to me. "Isn't this great? Aren't you glad we came?"

Actually, I wasn't entirely sure—I couldn't quite shake the anxiety I felt about the undone Killigan assignment—but there was something about Schneiderman's enthusiasm that caused you to want to agree with him.

After leading the band through two instrumental numbers, Kenton brought on his female vocalist, a short but shapely blond named Connie Collins.

"She's new," Schneiderman whispered, "recruited from the Les Brown Band."

"Oh."

"Wait, you'll see. She's another Jo Stafford."

In fact, Connie was good. She had a large voice, and belted out two Hit Parade favorites, "Anapola" and "Yes, Sir, That's My Baby" to the enthusiastic approval of the audience.

Next came the comic, Morey Amsterdam, short and penquin-like, who did ten minutes of Borscht Belt *shtick*—have you heard about the bagel manufacturer who was so cheap he sold his leftover bagels as toilet seats to midgets?—followed by the *piece de resistance*, the phenomenal Bojangles Bill Robinson.

After tapping his way across the stage, climbing and descending a stepladder, Robinson spun, twirled, and shuffled over to a lone chair on stage that he circled several times then picked up and danced with as though it was Ginger Rogers herself. After each maneuver, all of which involved much fancy footwork, the audience burst into spontaneous applause.

"He's better than Astaire," Schneiderman said, leaning over toward me. "If he wasn't a black man, you'd see him on screen with the real Ginger."

"Very likely," I agreed. Schneiderman spoke these words with surprising intensity; in fact, with more than a little anger, and I could not help wondering if, as a ringer from Brooklyn who was with us at Harmon, but not really one of us; who the faculty regarded as little more than a hired hand, he thought of himself as someone like Bojangles, a performer who, no matter how talented, would always remain an outsider.

The stage show lasted for quite a bit longer than the scheduled hour, and it was well after eleven by the time we headed for the subway. I found myself checking my watch every few minutes. I pictured my mother sitting up, listening with rising panic for the doorbell, berating herself for being so foolish as to allow her son to go off with this Schneiderman fellow whose mysterious uncle could very well turn out to be the famous Arthur Avenue axe murderer who was terrorizing the Bronx.

Seeing my growing agitation, Schneiderman volunteered to come home with me and speak to my mother before I made my appearance.

"If she sees you first, she'll be convinced you are bringing home a corpse."

"In that case, we'll walk in together as buddies who are very much alive."

"Believe me, you don't want to be there. She's liable to come after you with an axe of her own for corrupting the young."

"I suppose you're right. I can't take the risk. If I end up with a concussion, I'll be off the team and Tillman will have no more use for me."

We went on like that all the way to the subway, *kibitzing* with one another in an effort to ease my anxiety.

The uptown train was practically empty and at my request we took seats near a door just in case the Bronx killer had decided to move to Manhattan.

Schneiderman seemed perfectly calm and I was curious about how he pulled off what I gathered were fairly frequent nighttime excursions.

"Do your parents know where you go nights?" I asked. I imagined that Schneiderman's nocturnal outings were strictly undercover operations.

"Absolutely. As long as I stay in school, my folks are okay with what I do. They have troubles of their own, big troubles that preoccupy them, so they leave me pretty much alone." Just for a moment—and barely detectable—his face seemed to collapse into an instant of sadness. He recovered, but something remained of that moment in what he said next.

"That probably sounds great to you," he said, "and sometimes it is. I like the freedom, but there are times when you begin to wonder if anyone really cares."

"I'm sure that's not true," I said.

"I don't know. My folks are pretty much into themselves. My mother has been depressed for years and with the trouble they are having now, it's a lot worse. She just withdraws and sits alone with a glass of whiskey, listening to classical music. She's never been able to cope with my father. He dominates her and she retreats. I can't seem to reach her, especially with what is going on now."

This was the second time that Schneiderman alluded to some big trouble in his family and I found myself wanting to know what this was about, but I didn't ask. There was something about him that warned you not to intrude, not to invade his privacy. So I waited, but now he had shifted ground and was talking about his father.

"The man is a walking contradiction," he was saying. "You won't find a greater humanitarian and at the same time someone so totally involved with himself. He is into every good cause you can think of and some you could never think of. Whatever he does, though, he is right there watching himself do it. He doesn't need a mirror. He acts and watches himself acting at the same time. I can tell you this takes a lot of energy. Maybe that is why he gets so wrapped up in himself."

"I think I know what you mean," I put in. "My dad is different. He's no crusader, but a lot of the time he seems out of it too. He comes up with these nutty schemes to make money and then he gets lost in his daydreams."

"I'll tell you something about your dad," Schneiderman said. "He is a lonely man. I could feel that when I was listening to him carry on over at your place. He's been shut out in your family. It's you and your mother together and he's the outsider. I'm sure that you are aware of that."

"He leaves himself out," I replied defensively. I could hear a note of criticism in Schneiderman's voice. "No one can reach him."

"Probably because he feels he's not wanted. By the way, what did you make of the fact that he keeps such close tabs on your football career?"

"My mother says my being a ball player gives him a kick. It's something to talk about at the corner bar."

"Did you ever think that you might be selling him short? My guess is he knows that you don't welcome his interest, that you'll rebuff him if he lets you see that he wants to be involved.

"Listen," Schneiderman went on, "I know that feeling well. At school people think of me as a popular guy, the jock always surrounded by a bunch of kids. Sometimes that's true, but it doesn't mean much because I can't believe that anyone is really interested. Maybe that is why I know how your dad feels."

Schneiderman's comments about my father were making me uncomfortable, so I took this opening to ask more about his family.

"We looked terrific on the outside," he said, "but we weren't ever really close. My mother tried, but mothering was not her thing and she was terribly awkward at it. Most of the time she turned me over to black maids to raise. I was closer to them than to her. If I marry a lady from Harlem, you'll know the reason why.

"When I was a kid my folks would go out three, four nights a week, so I got pretty used to being alone. Then when my mother got so depressed, she just kept to herself and I didn't have her then either. Now she manages to get to the hospital, but that's about it. The rest of the time she sits alone and broods."

"Is someone sick in your family?" I found myself asking.

Schneiderman did not reply but looked at me in a way that seemed to scrutinize my face. Then it appeared that he was about to say something, perhaps to explain, but in the end, he didn't.

"We'll talk about it another day," is all he said. And then added, "Tonight is not the time. Tonight is strictly for fun."

The word was strange to my ears. Fun was not something we spoke about in my family. I cannot recall my folks ever saying that they had fun at anything, or wishing me a fun time. We didn't think that way. My parents' idea of entertainment was an evening of cards, gin rummy or hearts with two or three other couples. Once a month it was our turn to host the event. Then my mother would give the apartment a thorough cleaning, order in deli with potato salad and cole slaw, supply soft drinks and a dozen rugelach from the local bakery, and settle in for the evening. Coming from the living room, I would sometimes overhear the sounds of laughter and *kibbutzing*— one of the rare times I heard happy noises in our home.

As for me, my nights out—strictly on weekends—consisted of hanging out on Broadway with Mel and a few other friends, occasionally traveling to the Garden for a basketball or hockey game— City College and the New York Rangers were big in those years—and ending up at Tip Toe for a late-night sandwich. Sometimes I had a date—usually a pretty disastrous affair—with Myra or some new girl whose name a well-meaning, but clearly blind, relative had given me. Those evenings, too, ended up at Tip Toe where Mel conducted a thorough postmortem exam.

"We ought to do this again soon," Schneiderman was saying, "and maybe next time we ought to invite Cara. We could have an outing of the triumvirate."

"I don't think this is her thing." I said. "The Roxy's not likely to book the Russian Army Chorus anytime soon. Besides she'd probably spend the evening trying to organize the ushers."

"Maybe so," Schneiderman said, "That girl is a puzzle. She's a terrific person, always out there working for the underdog, ready to walk her feet off to try to put things right. But somehow it seems as much for Cara as for anyone. She reminds me of my dad that way, but I might be wrong. She's probably not as self-involved. Anyway, she's an interesting puzzle, someone I'd like to get to know a lot better."

I was impressed and a little scared by what Schneiderman said. He seemed to have a handle on Cara, to understand her in a way that surprised me for someone with a jock mentality. And I wondered just how well, on their marches and demonstrations—Korvettes was their current target for trying to get away with paying less than the minimum wage—these two were getting to know each other.

We sat in silence for a while. We were both exhausted, both overstimulated. We needed a few minutes of quiet to absorb it all, absorb all that happened that night.

Then as we were approaching my stop, Schneiderman renewed his offer.

"Are you sure you don't want me to come upstairs with you? I don't mind taking the heat for our spending so much time at my uncle's."

"All you would get is the frost. The heat is reserved for the prodigal son who has let himself be misled by strangers. She wouldn't say anything to you outright. It's her policy to be polite to guys, even no-goodniks like you. But don't expect an invitation to dinner anytime soon."

"Maybe I can woo her with an extra-large cheesecake."

"Not likely. She's not in love with Junior's the way my father is. You'll probably have to work through him. He's got a thing for you anyway."

We said good-bye at the 96th Street station, and on the walk home I tried to recall the technique Ellery Queen used to slip unseen into a suspect's residence.

Upstairs I let myself in the front door with my key, slipped off my shoes, and began to inch my way toward my room. As I reached the foyer, a light snapped on and my mother advanced on me like a cop making a collar.

"It's nearly midnight," she announced. Her words were heavy with accusation.

"I'm sorry, Mom. We stopped at Tip Toe and I lost track of the time."

"Your friend lost track, too?"

"I guess so. We were planning for our next game."

"You were planning how to play basketball at 12:00 a.m.?"

"We were absorbed."

"While you were absorbed, I was getting ready to call emergency rooms."

"I'm sorry, Ma."

"This new friend of yours is trouble. He talks nice, but he is a bad influence.
Next time he'll have you coming home with the milkman. I don't want you to see him again."

"You're upset, Ma. He's really a good guy. He worries about my health. That's why he made sure I'd be prepared for Killigan's exam."

"What he got you into is a lot of trouble. Not getting sleep is what will get you good and sick. I don't want you to see this boy again."

"We'll discuss it in the morning. I have to get to sleep."

"Okay, but I mean it."

"I'll see you in the morning, Ma." I waved at her and continued on to my room. I thought she would come after me, but I guess she was just too drained from the night's aggravation. I got into bed, fell asleep instantly, and dreamed of being on stage at Radio City where, with my partner, Gene Kelly, I am performing a tap routine. In the dream Kelly looks a lot like Al McGuire, the great St. John's playmaker.

After we've received a tremendous ovation from the audience,
McGuire leads me through the stage door and onto a basketball court
where, with infinite patience, he teaches me his infallible technique
for sinking a layup.

Chapter Ten

After that evening, Schneiderman and I spent a lot of time together. A few nights a week he would arrive at my house after practice so that I could help him with the brain twisters that Killigan's fiendish mind devised for that day's homework assignment. Sometimes—usually over my mother's strong protests—I made the trip back to the Bronx to work with Schneiderman at his house, but he did not encourage this. It turned out that his parents did not get along that well and he did not want me to be a witness to their unhappiness.

The problem, as Schneiderman saw it, was that his father had inherited a hypercritical gene from some malcontent in his family. It was as though he was programmed to be dissatisfied with everyone and everything around him. This trait did not endear him to his co-workers and bosses, and he was already in trouble with the DA at his new job. Schneiderman's dad had let it be known that in his opinion the chief was too soft on the petty thieves and Mafia soldiers who were intimidating the citizenry of the Bronx. He lobbied—not always pleasantly—for more arrests, more prosecutions, and fewer plea-bargains.

"It's not that he's wrong," Schneiderman told me, "his judgment is usually on the mark. It's that he has no tact, no sense of timing, and no ability to read other people. When he is convinced that he is right—which is most of the time—he becomes a bull charging at whoever is in his path. He puts people on the defensive and ends up trampling on their feelings. His bosses don't take too kindly to this approach and sooner or later they ask him to leave. He is at it again in the new office and unless he can put a rein on himself, we'll be packing up again and heading for God knows where. There aren't endless possibilities and my dad is running out of options."

"That is pretty scary. What does your mother say?"

"That's just it. Not a hell of a lot. She tries to reason with him and when that doesn't work she ends up pleading, but that just upsets him and they fight. When it comes to his own behavior, my father is a blind man. He can't see a thing."

Actually, I had witnessed this kind of scene a couple of times when I was at Schneiderman's house. His father would come in late, usually after we'd eaten, looking dapper—he was quite a handsome man—and act very friendly to me and Schneiderman. Often he had a joke or a story to tell, and for about a half hour he was thoroughly entertaining.

Then something would irritate him, usually some chore not done by his wife, and he would become angry and sarcastic. His anger fed on itself, rising to new heights every few minutes until he was in a rage that threatened to turn physical.

One time—I'll never forget this—I became the target of his wrath. The two of us were alone in the living room and he was complaining about his boss who had refused to investigate a corrupt city agency.

"They take bribes from developers and hand out contracts to the ones who come across with the most moola," he was saying.

"And the DA won't investigate?"

"Not enough evidence," he claims. "Says I am on a fishing expedition."

"That doesn't sound right. I suppose you've gotten some hard evidence?"

Suddenly Schneiderman's father turned on me.

"Are you doubting me? Of course I have evidence. Who do you think I am, some shyster who is just looking to smear people? These characters are the worst, the lowest. They are out to make a buck, period. That's all that counts, and they don't care how they get it. They give contracts to *gonifs* who use substandard materials and build crap houses. And, believe me, they couldn't care less. If there were a fire, these buildings would go up like cardboard. A dozen people could die and these idiots would call it an act of God or some other bullshit. And that would be the end of it. There would be no consequences. They get away with murder."

"That's horrible. Is that really true? Have you seen that kind of thing happen?"

"Don't be naïve, Jonathan. The trouble with you kids is that you don't want to know what is going on. You don't want to see the dirt that is right under your noses. You and Stanley just want to play your games, play ball, chase girls, do whatever gives you a kick. But when it comes to the rotten side, to corruption, cheating, abuses, you don't want to know about them. You look the other way."

I wanted to protest, to say that wasn't true, that I cared a lot about those things; that, in fact, I was in on the demo in Brooklyn that tried to save his neck. But I'd seen enough of Schneiderman's father to know not to tangle with him.

Schneiderman was with his mother in the next room. Hearing his father's raised voice, he hurried in, appraised the situation, and in a matter of minutes, with few words spoken in a soothing way, was able to calm his father down. This was a talent of Schneiderman's. There was something about him, a rare ability—I'd not seen it in anyone else—to speak to the injured part of a person, to make him feel understood.

This was a trait—to me it had a touch of magic—that I admired and envied and sometimes, when my mother became upset with my father for not recognizing that Rome was on fire, I tried to imitate Schneiderman's approach. Inevitably this would end up infuriating my mother.

"Just butt out, Mr. Buttinski," she would say. "You don't know what is going down here. I live with a man who wears blinders twenty-four hours a day. More than a whole stable full of horses. You are telling me to be reasonable. Well, let him be the reasonable one. Even half a reasonable person I could live with. I'd settle for that. Then maybe you could have yourself the calm mother you are always *hocking* me about. But there is no way to reach this man. This is not somebody who lives in this world. He lives on Mars, sits in his chair on Mars reading his paper. Just try to bring him down. It's impossible. You could *plotz* from trying."

At that point I would usually give up, figuring that I hadn't yet mastered Schneiderman's technique, and that to really learn it I needed more time watching him in action.

In the evenings, when Schneiderman and I were supposed to be tackling madman Killigan's latest invention either at my place or his, we would usually squander most of the time talking. If we managed to get in a half hour solid work we counted that a good night's effort. Mostly we talked about the team and coach Mueller and the music scene in New York—and girls. Sometimes, though, we talked about the problems we had living with our parents.

It wasn't my style to open up to people. In that way I took after my mother who by nature was suspicious of the world. But Schneiderman's easygoing manner and his refusal to judge people—his whole life he had heard stories of the way that people, often innocent people, were condemned in the court of public opinion—drew me out.

Mostly I complained about my folks. I once read a poem whose first line stated flat out that parents fuck you up. They don't mean to, the poet said, but they do. That was a view with which I concurred, and in my talks with Schneiderman I supported that contention with what I considered to be irrefutable evidence.

"I am going to tell you something," I said one night, "but you've got to swear that you'll never tell a soul. My mother will murder me if she finds out I told you. To her this is something you never talk about.

"Before I was born, she had a child, a girl, who died at birth. I don't think my mother ever got over it."

"And you were the replacement, the hope of the family, is that right?"

"Right. I'm the bright star who is supposed to make up for everything. And on top of that, my mother doesn't think I'll live long enough to do it. She's convinced that a strong breeze will do me in. She has my windbreaker out anytime the temperature drops below seventy.   "

"Houdini would have a tough time breaking out of chains like that," Schneiderman put in.

"It would be impossible. He couldn't do it. He'd be no match for my mother."

Schneiderman suggested a tactic that he found useful in his own family. The mind-easing fib like the story he'd concocted about our needing math help from his uncle in the Bronx. In the case of agitated mothers like mine, he claimed, this was more effective than a dose of Phenobarbital.

It took me time, but I learned and applied Schneiderman's method with quite a bit of success. As a result, the fights with my mother diminished and the range of my excursions with Schneiderman widened. They included one memorable night spent at The Blue Note, where as a result of a connection that Schneiderman's father had with him, I met and shook hands with Dizzy Gillespie.

Schneiderman had a few things to say about me and my father as well.

"This distance he keeps, his refusal to share, hurts you," he said. "I get that. I felt the same way about my dad. And my guess is that you do what I used to do—still do sometimes—go on the attack, trying to avoid more pain by lashing out first."

Schneiderman's words surprised me. He did not use psychological language the way that Mel did. His vocabulary was closer to the plain talk of Durocher himself. But like The Lip who, rumor had it, was the only one who understood moody Duke Snider and could zero in on what was troubling the Duke, Schneiderman had a feel, a kind of sixth sense, for what people were really like behind their masks.

"Maybe you should ask yourself the same questions I finally had to ask myself after years of being furious at my dad." He continued. "Do I understand this man at all? What would I be like if things were reversed and I had to deal with a kid like me?"

Schneiderman's comments upset me and caused me to want to protest that it was he who did not understand; that he wasn't in my family and he didn't know what it was like for me to have to deal with a father like mine. But, somehow, I couldn't shake off what he had said. There was something about the way, in a few words, he had summed up the trouble that my father—and in fact the three of us— were struggling with that was compelling, that resonated with something inside of me and that, try as I might, I could not quite dispel.

To get rid of the discomfort that Schneiderman had caused me, and to turn the tables, I turned the conversation back to his family and quizzed him on what troubles he was having. To my surprise, Schneiderman was quite open about his situation.

His father's preoccupation with criminal activities, Schneiderman said, his dedication to battling wrongdoing—that of others, never, of course, his own—made him inaccessible to his own family.

"He has always worked twelve, fourteen hours a day minimum," Schneiderman said, "and that includes a lot of weekends.

"You've had a father who insists on living in the clouds," he observed, "I've had one who insists on riding his hobbyhorse off in all directions."

At one point, Schneiderman said he realized that his father was more than a little crazy and that whatever stability there was in his family—and there wasn't much—would have to come from his mother. Timid and frightened as she was, she was the only parent he could rely on.

What struck me about Schneiderman and where we were so different, was in our reactions to our fathers. For reasons I could not fathom, he seemed to bear no resentment toward his.

"My father is a mad man," he declared. "Certifiably manic at the very least and a lot of the time totally into himself. But the fact is, despite his madness, or maybe because of it, he's done some very good things. He's a fighter who has always been on the side of the little guy and I admire him for that."

We spent a lot of time talking about girls, too, and in that department Schneiderman surprised me. I thought of him as one of those super jocks, the ringer type, who always ends up with the prettiest girl in the room but apparently that was not the case.

"I've never really had a proper girlfriend," he confessed. "I can't seem to settle on one. I guess I'm your typical rolling stone, on the move all the time, but never ending up with anybody." He had thought about this situation, he said, and he decided that it had to do with trust.

"When my mom was upset she withdrew from us," he explained. "She just pulled away. I tried to get close to her, but I never knew when she might go into one of her states and disappear again. So I got cautious with girls. I expected to be burned and I wasn't going to let that happen. Maybe that's why I've never had a proper girlfriend."

I was surprised, but I believed Schneiderman. From what I'd seen of his mother, she could have played one of those depressed Swedish types that I'd seen in foreign films, the kind that is always brooding and unhappy and I could imagine that Schneiderman had learned to keep a safe distance from her.

But I wasn't sure that things weren't different now. From what I had seen of his relationship with Cara, it looked like it was getting pretty close; closer than he had described with other girls and, as far as I as concerned, a bit too close.

The three of us sometimes met after school to hang out at the Madison Avenue Coffee Shop or share donuts at a Horn and Hardart's. At these times I often felt isolated, left out of the powwow that Cara and Schneiderman would hold when they met.

Cara was always talking about the evils being committed in this country, the exploration of working people and such, and as a self-described activist she was on the lookout for fat cat companies that had done some grievous thing; fired workers without cause, locked out union members, things like that. Then she would organize what she called a demo, essentially a protest march, against that company. A number of her friends from Finley worked with her to stage these marches, but somehow—maybe because she had organized the demo against his father's Tammany fink boss, she managed to recruit Schneiderman as one of her chief aides de camp. She tried to bring me in, too, and I did help out with a number of chores, but I realized that this just wasn't my thing. I tried, but I couldn't throw myself into the spirit of these protests the way that others did so, when it came to planning demos, which is what Schneiderman and Cara mostly did, when we met, the two of them huddling together over coffee and scheming like a couple of Sacco and Vanzetti's. I just sat and watched, feeling very much the outsider who had to control himself from busting in and breaking up their huddle.

I was never quite sure why Schneiderman had gotten involved. It was true that Cara had gone to bat for his father, and I figured he felt he owed her for that. But I kept wondering if there was more to it. Schneiderman made no bones about liking Cara. I remembered, when he first met her, how impressed he'd been with her energy and her ability to get things done. It was true that he'd had some reservations then and had wondered if she was another self-involved do-gooder like his father. But I hadn't heard him speak that way for months. In fact, now he had nothing but good things to say about her.

"She is the real thing," he told me, "a straight shooter. What you see is what you get. There is no bull." And he would always point out that Cara was reliable in a way that a lot of girls weren't. With the kind of mother Schneiderman had, I figured that meant a lot to him.

"She's a looker, too," he added. "She has style. The guy who gets her"—here he smiled and nodded in my direction—"will be a lucky son of a gun."

I wasn't sure what he meant by that. Was he simply saying that he knew of my interest in Cara and that if I landed her as a girlfriend he would regard me as one lucky guy? Or was he hurling a challenge at me, letting me know that he, too, was interested in her; that he was in the race and that he was hoping to beat me out and be that lucky guy?

It is not that I distrusted Schneiderman. He had always impressed me as a straight arrow, not the kind of person who is ready to slip a knife between your ribs. But I also knew that he was fiercely competitive, and I had the bruises to prove it. When he went after something he wanted, he went all out, with the force of one of his rocket strikes. And at this point I wasn't sure that he didn't regard Cara as fair game and me in the way that he did when he was playing for Ryder; as a respected opponent whom he intended to demolish.

I kept all of this to myself, though. This was not a conversation I was ready to have with Schneiderman. Right now, dealing with the

Sheepman was challenge enough. I did not want to face the possibility that I might have to take on an ass kicking Durocher-type as well.

Chapter Eleven

"It is working," Mel said over hamburgers at Starks. "The strategy is definitely working. It is just as I thought. Your personality is bringing out all of her perverse qualities. The idea of making love to an all thumbs receiver is proving irresistible. In the battle of the fetishes you are becoming more compelling than the Sheepman."

"You are just saying that."

"I am serious. The trend is absolutely clear. When this thing first started, it took our Miss Finley three days to return your call. And you had to make a reservation to buy her an egg cream. She was all caught up with Mr. Photoshoot and his *Redbook* cronies. There was no room at the inn. Now she's done a total one-eighty. Looks like she finally got wise to the fact that old Kenny boy has been using her as a beard and she's gotten tired of playing Santa. That and the fact that King R has his eye on you for the dinette division has given you an edge. Play your cards right and before you know it she'll be putting the Sheepman out to pasture."

"Can't we give him a little shove, convince him that the grass is greener over at Myra Herz's backyard?"

"You can't rush these things. Patience is the name of this game. Disillusionment takes time. It proceeds in stages. My guess is that our gal is still in the early phase. Rage hasn't set in yet. But when it does—by the way, Jonathan, for future reference a woman's greatest fury is at being duped, not scorned—the mannequin won't know what hit him. He'll get the boot and be out the door before he can take off that fag coat of his. At that point we move in to fill the vacuum."

"Good thinking," I said. "I'm all for filling any vacuum I can find, especially if it belongs to Cara Rosenhaus."

"Being a smart ass will get you nowhere. This is serious business. If you want King R's mantel passed on to you, you've got to follow the plan."

"When do I rush in to fill the gap?"

"You don't rush in. You move slowly. With all deliberate speed, as they say. You begin by calling our Miss Finley every night. Ask about the Korvette demo, let her know that you are with her all the way, that you are working on a placard that will skewer the fat cats up in the boardroom. If King R answers, be friendly. Ask about his playground. Show an interest. Tell him you'd like to come along on his next visit. Take a leaf from his book. Do a little *schmeckling*."

"That is not my style."

"Your style will land you a bride named Myra Herz and a top spot in Herz's Herring Emporium."

Mel was convincing and his plan worked out as he predicted. Cara seemed pleased that I called, and from then on we chatted most nights. Sometimes she was the one to reach out, and once she surprised me by calling quite late. It must have been ten-thirty and I was already in bed when my mother came in looking distinctly unhappy.

"It's your girlfriend," she said, "and no apology for calling so late."

"It's probably a crisis, Ma," I said. "Maybe her grandmother had a relapse."

"God forbid." The thought of a relapse instantly erased my mother's anger.

Actually Cara's voice sounded sad.

"Hi," she said, "did I wake you?"

"It's okay."

"I just thought I'd say hello. I was thinking about you and I missed you."

"I miss you, too."

Cara had not been that open with me before and I was thrilled at hearing those words. But Mel had warned me not to let a moment like this go to my head, that it was all part of what Cara was going through, part of letting Masters go. He called it stage one of the disillusionment process and he advised me not to ask her about the Sheepman.

"It won't be long now before the fairy's cover is blown," Mel promised, "and she realizes that it is really King R that he's had the hots for."

Actually it happened faster than I thought. We'd been talking nightly for just a couple of weeks when Cara asked me out on a date.

"We haven't really had a proper date," she said. "We're overdue."

I was surprised and excited by her taking the initiative this way and I immediately called Mel with the good news.

"It's a start," Mel said. "You are definitely on course. But don't expect to *shtup* her. It's a big jump from the Sheepman to Sleeping Beauty. It's got to be a shock to the system. In these matters you have to be biologically-minded. Think of the body. Always consider the body. When the body has been shocked, you have to wait for a bit. Give the organs time to settle down, time to realign. A lot of relationships never get off the ground because the timing is wrong. When people ignore body rhythms, there is always trouble."

In this I thought Mel was being overcautious. Cara had been increasingly friendly to me over the phone. She was thrilled that I volunteered to march in the Korvette demo, and I was hopeful that once we got together the combination of the Sheepman vacuum and the revival of her old tenderness towards Number 86 would carry the day.

That week, though, I had trouble concentrating on school. I kept thinking about our date and, especially, having private time with Cara. I had a picture of the Rosenhaus apartment in my head and in class I found myself calculating the distance from one of the Rosenhaus living room couches to her bedroom.

I had trouble on the basketball court, too. Our team had been doing well in recent weeks. We'd won four straight games and people were beginning to talk about the dynamic duo, Schneiderman and Manheim, who were burning up the league. In a special section on our prep school league, the *Telegram* had profiled our team and predicted that we would win the division title.

It is true that Schneiderman and I worked well together. We anticipated each other's moves, connected on key passes, set up effective screens, and hit a good percentage of our shots from the floor.

The week before my date with Cara, though, I couldn't concentrate. In a league game against St. Paul I flubbed passes, shot miserably, picked up three personals in the first quarter, and managed only two free throws the entire first half. Exasperated and hoarse from screaming at me, Mueller yanked me five minutes before the end of that period.

The way I was playing threw Schneiderman off his game, too, and at halftime we were behind by ten points. When he came off the court, Schneiderman made a beeline for me. He was sweating, his face was flushed, and he was furious. Schneiderman did not like to lose, and we were losing pretty badly.

"What the hell is wrong with you?" he demanded. "You are lousing up every damn play. Why don't you just hand them the game and get it over with? What the hell is going on, Jonathan?"

I couldn't respond. I felt myself close to tears.

"I don't know." I finally managed. "I'm totally off. I can't do a freaking thing out there."

Seeing how upset I was, Schneiderman immediately backed off. Now he spoke softly.

"What is it, Jonathan? What's troubling you?"

"I don't know. Nothing."

Schneiderman sat down next to me on the bench, reached out and touched my arm.

"Come on, out with it. We're pals, right? We can tell each other everything."

I could not help smiling.

"It's stupid."

"It's about Cara, isn't it?"

Schneiderman had intuition about these things and he knew how to read me. For a moment I said nothing. I wasn't keen on letting him know what I was up to with Cara. I wasn't sure what his interest was, where he was coming from when it came to her, but I had a need to talk, to unburden myself. I told him about the date and how I couldn't stop worrying that I'd make a total hash of things.

"Look, Jonathan," he said. "This is not a hundred yard dash. You're in a marathon. Whatever happens Saturday night is not the whole race. You've got a long way to travel with this lady. Think about where you want to be six months from now."

Where I wanted to be in six months was the place I wanted to be now, ensconced in Cara's bed, but I did not say that. Somehow, though, Schneiderman's words calmed me. I don't know if it was what he said, or his tone, or the fact that he seemed to be solidly in my corner and not jealous, but listening to him I felt less knotted up, more relaxed. And when I thought about Saturday night, I no longer experienced fear. In fact I began to look forward to Saturday night with rising confidence.

My plan was to hit up my father for a twenty—if he had it he was always ready to stake me to a night on the town—add the few dollars I had saved from my allowance, and take Cara to a French bistro on East 86th Street where you could get a duck leg and the trimmings for under ten bucks. Then I imagined we would go back to her apartment, settle down on one of the plush Rosenhaus couches, and resume what we had begun in Cara's East Hampton bedroom.

She had other ideas. When I arrived, she announced that we were going across town to the Thalia for the eight o'clock show. It seems that in the past few weeks she had developed a huge crush on Vittorio DeSicca and had set her mind on our seeing *The Bicycle Thief.* I was disappointed, but hoping for some smooching in the dark, when we got inside I grabbed seats in the last row of the shoebox theatre, where I figured we would be comparatively inconspicuous. Cara wasn't playing, though. There seemed to be something on her mind— stage two of the disillusionment process I imagined—and for most of the movie she sat apart from me, upright and aloof, inviting no touching of any kind. In fact, until the closing scene, the only physical contact we had was a brushing of fingers when, simultaneously, we reached for the bag of popcorn that we shared.

There was one promising moment, though. During the last wrenching scene, Cara closed her eyes and leaned her head against my shoulder. I managed to stroke her face a few times until, without speaking, she pulled away and resumed her upright position. Although I'd been on good behavior, had been careful to give her plenty of room and to follow Mel's rules of engagement for ladies traversing the disillusionment syndrome, I still worried that I had done something wrong. Perhaps I hadn't shown enough enthusiasm for Cara's projects—I couldn't help contemplating my flat feet when I volunteered to join the Korvette's march—or, worse, that with her intuition she had sensed what I had in mind for the evening and was offended by my insensitivity to her emotional condition.

In fact, it turned out that Cara was bursting with rage at the Sheepman and had been nursing anger at someone else as well. I did not learn about this last grievance—she kept it to herself the whole evening—until I was about to leave.

Earlier that evening, her target had been Masters. We were barely settled on a couch back at her apartment and I had—gently—reached for her hand when she pulled away and began a diatribe that went on for close to an hour. Ken Masters, she hissed with a vehemence previously reserved only for CEOs with self-awarded stock options, was a total phony.

"The guy doesn't give a fig about raising the minimum wage or anything else about the way working people get treated," she said. "If he was running Korvette's I guarantee you in a month he'd turn the place into a sweat shop.

"He pretended to be interested in my body," she declared, fixing her eyes on me as though I were the criminal—was there a warning here I wondered—"but what he really wanted was to have Sidney *shtup* him in the ass."

"Disgraceful," I said, agreeing with her assessment. "It's what Mel and I suspected. With that fruitcake coat of his and his modeling for ladies magazines, we had him pegged from the start."

"Well, I wish one of you had sounded the alarm."

"I wanted to, but you were so into him there was no chance."

"We both had a thing for Sidney," Cara lamented, "That's what blinded me. What about you?" she asked suddenly. "Are you in love with my father?"

"He's cute," I said, "but a little too hairy. I prefer a smoother look."

"Like Schneiderman?" she put in. I looked at her. I was startled.

"Why do you bring him up?"

"I don't know. Maybe because I think of you two guys as always connected, in your own ways really into each other. Somehow you seem like brothers under the skin."

"You must be high on the Good Book. You've got us confused with Cain and Abel."

Cara laughed a light laugh. It was the first time that her mood lifted. Soon she was back to Masters, however, and she went on at length about her feeling of utter betrayal, a preoccupation that, according to Mel, heralded the arrival of stage three of the disillusionment process.

It wasn't until I got up to leave an hour later that she brought up Schneiderman again. This time it was with an angry outburst that totally surprised me. I had no idea that she'd had enough contact with him to arouse such feelings.

"What kind of person is your friend, anyway?" she began.

"What do you mean?"

"I just want to know. Is he the kind of guy who, if he gets the chance, will fuck you over?"

"I don't know about that." I said, "but he's spent many hours trying to crack my skull if that counts for anything. Why do you ask?"

"I can't figure him. For a while I thought he was a total sweetheart, but he pulled a real number on me. He was supposed to help out with the demo, check out the Korvette neighborhood and chart our march route, but he never showed up. I wonder if I had him all wrong."

"Maybe something happened and he couldn't call," I found myself saying.

"You really are brothers aren't you?" Cara retorted. "Of course now that you are teammates, I suppose you have to defend him."

"Look, I have no idea what happened," I said. "But I suspect he'll have an explanation. Anyway I'll try to find out when I see him at practice."

"Don't tell him I said anything. I don't want him to know that he upset me."

I did not know what to make of that statement. Was this pride, or was Cara hinting, as Mel suggested, that her rage at Schneiderman had other sources. In any case, I didn't want to think about that now or to bring the matter up with Cara. For much of the evening she had seemed preoccupied with her hurt and anger and I was having a tough enough time just getting through to her. I had no intention of introducing another complication into that dispiriting picture.

I was about to leave and, in fact, had my hand on the doorknob, when all at once I had a flash memory. I pictured Schneiderman's face and the look of sadness that came over it when, a few weeks earlier, he had mentioned that there was some kind of trouble—serious trouble I gathered—in his family. I turned back to Cara.

"I just thought of something," I said. "A while ago Schneiderman mentioned that his family was having some kind of difficulty. Maybe that is why he didn't show up."

"What kind of difficulty?" Cara wanted to know.

"I have no idea. He just let it drop that the family was going through a hard time. He didn't say anything more."

"And you didn't ask?"

"I didn't think it was any of my business. He didn't volunteer and I didn't want to pry." Suddenly Cara turned on me. Her facial muscles tightened and her voice became sharp.

"What are you talking about?" she demanded. "This has nothing to do with prying. This has to do with caring. How do you know there is not some kind of crisis? This family could be in a lot of trouble. The fact that a person is too shy, or too embarrassed, to spell out what is happening doesn't mean they don't want you to know. If Schneiderman really didn't want you to know anything, he wouldn't have mentioned it at all."

"I frankly didn't think of that," I said. "To me, asking questions would have been butting in. I don't feel comfortable doing that."

"Being concerned about your own feelings doesn't strike me as the way to have a friendship," Cara remarked.

My face flushed. I realized that she was right and I was embarrassed. But wasn't there something to the idea of not being intrusive, of taking one's cue from the other guy? Cara didn't seem to get that. As Henry had indicated, when Cara was convinced of something that was it, there was no other way of seeing it. He had learned that lesson and, presumably, so did Cara's friends. I understood this about Cara and it did not stop me from loving her, but I was having a hard time with this part of her.

"Look," Cara was saying, "we can't simply ignore the Schneidermans. Who knows, there might have been an emergency. The family is new to the area. They might have needed help."

"I'll find out whatever I can," I responded, sounding I suppose, a bit tentative. I did not know what to make of the sudden turn from fury at Schneiderman to pressing concern for him and his family.

"Please do that," Cara replied. She seemed to be struggling to contain her impatience. "And if it's just too hard for you, don't worry. I'll do it. I need to have a few words with Stan anyway. I need to find out what is going on."

I left the apartment feeling really down, bummed out, as the expression goes. I realized that I'd rationalized the whole exchange with Schneiderman, that, in truth, my reticence was disguised self-interest and that I'd not acted as friend. That bothered me, but what really had me down was the conviction that Cara had lost all respect for me. I had missed my chance to show my credentials as a compassionate man, a man ready to reach out to people in trouble, and I was desperately afraid that, as a result, Cara had relegated me to her black list; had lumped me with Father Coughlin, J. Edgar Hoover, and the mannequin as callous opportunists.

Later that night Mel called, and when I told him what had happened, he tried to calm my anxiety.

"You got the backwash from the Sheepman fiasco," he declared. "Probably you and Schneiderman both. What Masters did left Miss Finley furious at men, and since you were the one male at hand at the moment, you got the overflow. At that point Cara's mind equated any male figure with a betrayer, so she launched a preemptive strike. Women in that situation often do that kind of thing."

I appreciated Mel's efforts but he seemed to be stretching to make me feel better. As it turned out, though, he might have been right. To my surprise, Cara called me the next day, and although she didn't apologize directly for turning on me, she was clearly reaching out and trying to make it up. She even went so far as to ask me out, suggesting that we get together that night and have the dinner date that we'd missed. When she was inclined to do so, Cara was expert at grabbing hold of a dream and hauling it into the real world.

I made a reservation at the 86th Street French bistro, but when I arrived to pick up Cara she vetoed that choice on the grounds that the French were anti-Semitic and collaborators with the Nazis. Instead she opted for a Ninth Avenue Turkish restaurant (Turkey, she explained, was one of the few countries willing to take in the Jews after they were expelled from Spain in 1492) where she was known—I suspected she and the Sheepman had made this one of their favorite haunts—and greeted by name.

At dinner Cara told me that she had decided to throw her hat into the ring and run for student council president at Finley. Her campaign committee met regularly at this very restaurant with the owner, Itamar, a former activist in the old country, lending his expertise as political consultant.

This connection proved fortunate for me because, as a gesture of support for Cara's candidacy, Itamar took ten percent off our check. Since I was a little short of cash—the place was pricier than I was used to—this concession allowed me not only to pay the bill with impressive casualness, but to leave a couple of dollars tip.

Back home, for the better part of an hour Cara seemed her old East Hampton self; warm, playful, sexually aggressive. We settled into a plush Rosenhaus couch right away, and after no more than ten minutes of above the waist petting she reached down and unzipped my fly. I had worn my best *Fruit of the Loom* undershorts in preparation for this moment, and as a result of almost daily visualizations of this very scene, was psychologically prepared for what was to follow.

After first fondling, then extracting, my penis from within the folds of my shorts, Cara slowly lowered her head toward my crotch. Then, all at once, when she was inches from making contact, she stopped suddenly, sat up, and held her head as though stricken by a piercing migraine.

"Oh my God," she cried out, "I just had a vision."

A paralyzing fear gripped me. I imagined that as she approached ground zero and glimpsed my organ, an image of the Sheepman's big dick had risen up before her.

Now Cara had her eyes closed and was shaking her head as though to rid herself of the frightening image.

"You saw something?" I asked. She nodded.

"Schneiderman's face. He was crying."

"What?"

"He was grief stricken. Something terrible has happened."

"What are you talking about?" I felt angry, confused. My penis was slipping back into my shorts with alarming speed.

"Is he all right?" Cara persisted. "I want to know."

"Who?"

"Schneiderman."

"Why in the world were you thinking of him? He's fine, more than fine. He hit for double figures in yesterday's game. He was a one-man show."

"I mean personally. Is he all right, not terribly distraught?"

"Not as far as I know."

"And his family. What about them?"

"I haven't heard anything." I was becoming more confused by the minute.

"Anything new about his mother?" Cara asked. I shook my head, but the look on my face, poorly masked puzzlement, gave me away.

"You do know about the mother," Cara said in a tone that seemed to carry a warning. "You did manage to ask, didn't you?" A panicky feeling seized me.

"Actually both of us were so caught up with practice and the game and everything, we never had a moment to talk."

Cara looked at me in a way that reminded me of King R's face when he held forth on Harry Truman. Then she started to button the blouse that, a few minutes before, she had unbuttoned and thrown back to expose her breasts.

"Well just in case you might like to know, Stan's mother has become seriously depressed. Apparently she's in a bad way."

"Worse than usual? I know she's been depressed for a long time."

"According to Stan, a lot worse. For the past few weeks she's barely said a word; just sits in a chair staring at a book, but not really reading. Stan says she's been unreachable."

"That's terrible. I saw her a while ago and she didn't seem that bad. Do you know what happened?"

"Apparently she's been drinking heavily. I understand there is trouble in the family. Stan didn't say exactly what, but obviously it's something really worrisome. Anyway, Stan thinks the constant stress of the situation just got to her and she tried to anesthetize herself with more and more alcohol. That's what pushed her over the edge. She is being treated with medication, but so far that hasn't really helped. Stan is really worried. He says if she doesn't pull out of it soon, they are going to have to hospitalize her for shock therapy."

"Jesus. That is scary. When did you find this out?"

"The other day. After you left I called Schneiderman and asked him straight out what was going on."

"And he told you just like that?"

"Just like that. He would have told you, too, if you had asked. Actually he wanted to talk. He's isolated. He needs friends."

I said nothing. I felt deeply ashamed. There wasn't anything more to say. I wanted to apologize to Cara, but I knew that would be stupid. It wasn't Cara who I needed to apologize to. The guilt I felt was plastered on my face and resounded in the silence, but Cara did not attempt to ease my pain.

"Anyway," she went on, "how is your friend doing in school these days?"

"I'm not sure, but I don't think too well. He showed me a couple of tests that he got back. Both D minuses."

"And did you volunteer to help?"

"I've worked with him on math homework and he knows he can call on me if he wants to. "

"That's not the same as offering to help. Look, Schneiderman's a guy with pride. He's not going to come begging to you. You've got to be out front in these things."

"I didn't want to assume anything and insult him."

"You and your insult *mishegas*. While you are worrying about insulting your pal, he'll be tossed out on his ear. No matter how good he is on the basketball court, they'll boot him if he fails a couple of subjects. Your august institution is not going to lower its standards for an import from Brooklyn."

"Are you saying that I can do something about that?"

"Of course you can. Both of us can do a hell of a lot. What we need is a plan, a definite schedule of tutoring, not some anemic offer that you don't mean anyway."

I felt insulted by this remark. I wanted to protest, to say that my offer was genuine but that it was Schneiderman who wasn't really interested. But I didn't want to start a fight.

"You have something in mind?" I asked. Cara shook her head as though she were dealing with a rather dull child.

"If the two of us pitch in," she said, "we can make a difference. I'll take English and history. Why don't you take math? I'm not very good at that and that's where he's having most trouble."

"What if he refuses help?"

"We present the plan as a *fait accompli*. No discussion. No choice. And we get our message across plain and simple. He works with us or the management trades him back to Brooklyn. It's up to him."

Cara's attitude startled me. I was unused to that kind of unvarnished directness. In my family no one made decisions. And if we were compelled to make one, it took months of agonizing rumination along with predictable bouts of diarrhea in one or another family member, to get to that place.

"I like your idea," I said to Cara, "especially the *fait accompli* part. You are right. If we leave it up to Schneiderman to ask for help it, will never happen." I looked over at Cara. Her face had taken on that determined look that I knew well from watching her plan an action against some union busting outfit, and it struck me then that there were very few people like her.

"You are a really good person," I blurted out, "not too many people would make this kind of effort." Why I felt moved to say this just then, I have no idea. It was a thought that arose in my mind as I listened to Cara talk about the obligation one has to intervene when a friend is in distress, and I wanted to tell her what I was thinking. Did I also sense an opening in this situation, a chance to make a comeback and to restore myself in Cara's eyes? Perhaps. But if so, it didn't work.

"She has been around *schmecklers* for too long," Mel said later when I told him what had happened. "She can smell trumped-up morality a mile off."

Perhaps that is what happened. In any case, at the door Cara was cool, her voice even. She stood a couple of feet away and maintained the distance. I stepped forward and tried to give her a good-bye hug, but she held me off. Then she spoke in a flat voice, a deliberately flat voice, the kind of voice teachers use when they have reached into their reservoir of patience once too often and come up empty.

"I've been thinking, Jonathan," she said. "We need a moratorium right now. I don't want you to call me for a while. We need a break."

I wanted to argue, to protest, to prove to Cara that this was the totally wrong approach, that what we really needed was more contact, a lot more contact, but I could tell from her voice that the issue was closed.

"Okay," I said. "If that is what you want."

"What I want is to know that we think alike, that we share the same values. And you need to think about what you are willing to do for Stan, what the friendship means to you. One thing I can tell you though. If somebody doesn't start working with him soon, our boy will find himself riding the A train back to Brooklyn."

I nodded, "I'll do that," I said.

Cara was speaking in the straightforward, unemotional way that she did when she felt irritated. The warmth that I prized, that she had been displaying toward me recently, was gone. Clearly she was troubled by my failure to reach out to my friend, a gesture of caring that would have been second nature to her.

There was no point in staying longer, so I said good-bye and left. Once on the street I felt a terrific heaviness on my chest. There was no doubt in my mind that at this point I was sitting squarely at the top of Cara's black list and that there was no way off, no redemption.

When he learned about it, Mel tried to put what happened into perspective.

"These things mean a lot to Cara," he said. "She'll go all out for a friend and that's admirable, no question. But she can be an absolutist. For her there is no other way. Your personality is different. You have your own way of helping. Don't let her make you feel guilty. With someone like Cara you have to stand your ground. She only respects men who take her on.

"If you want to get back in the game, you've got to jettison that *dybbuk* inside you, the one that does a *mea culpa* whenever someone stubs a toe."

"I've been trying to ditch my mother if that's what you are getting at," I retorted, "but let me tell you this is no easy task."

Mel nodded in agreement. "It's a job and a half," he said. "These mother images are tenacious. When you are not looking, they will slip in under your guard and start directing traffic from inside your gut." Then Mel reached out and put a hand on my shoulder.

"Look," he said, "you put yourself in a bad place, but the ballgame isn't over. You pulled a bonehead play but if you keep your noggin screwed on right, you can make a comeback."

"It's probably too late," I said. "You should have heard her voice when she spoke to me. Cool as a chilled glass. It made me think that she's already got her eye on someone else. Either that or she is in the process of resuscitating the mannequin."

"I doubt that," Mel replied. "By my calculations, he still upstages you on Cara's shit list. And if you play your cards right, that's where he'll stay."

"The first thing you need to do," Mel went on, "is to get out of yourself. Do some good works. Get hold of Schneiderman and drill math into his thick skull until he starts dreaming equations and can handle any curve ball that Killigan tosses at him. Show our Miss Finley that she's wrong; you only pretend to be a selfish shit. Behind that façade beats the heart of a loyal March of Dimes donor."

After that, I didn't lose time contacting Schneiderman. I buttonholed him after practice the next day and straight out offered help with his math homework.

Schneiderman was grateful—and puzzled. "Thanks," he said. "That is really generous of you. And I'm sure I'll be taking you up on your offer. But what is going on? Did you and Cara have a powwow and decide to make contributions to Harmon's neediest case? She called me about the same thing."

"No way," I said, "We have no connection with the UJA. This is strictly self-interest. I want a championship ring on my little finger, so I need you to stay on the team. And Cara needs you to case the Korvette neighborhood."

"I see," Schneiderman said. "Well okay. I'm glad to do what I can for you guys."

As it turned out, Schneiderman needed a good deal of help—math was definitely not his thing—but the problem was finding times when we could work together. Cara had already preempted after practice time, and each afternoon she showed up at the gym, stationed herself on the sidelines a few minutes before we came off the court, and snared Schneiderman as soon as he had showered and dressed. Several times he tried to escape, pleading prior commitments or a GI upset, but Cara held firm and insisted that he put in forty-five minutes minimum four or five times a week.

By comparison I was hopelessly lax. Schneiderman and I met some evenings at his place or mine, but we were both tired by then and by the time we schmoozed about the team, the coach, our last game and our next opponent, there wasn't a lot of time left to work.

We made some headway, though. I was able to show Schneiderman an approach to setting up and solving equations, and I thought he was beginning to get it. I even gave him a fair shot at passing Killigan's course. But his concentration wasn't great and he often claimed fatigue, called a time out from our drills, and returned to his favorite topics, basketball and jazz. I heard a lot about the downtown jazz scene and after a while I wasn't sure who was tutoring whom. Soon I became almost as expert as he on the city's premier jazz venues, and on any given day could tell you who was appearing at the Downbeat or the Village Vanguard.

We talked a lot about girls, too, and I told Schneiderman a bit about my troubles with Cara. "She's a handful," Schneiderman said, "and a lot of the time I'd like nothing better than to walk her over to the East River, pick her up, and dump her in. She's a taskmaster, incredibly persistent and headstrong. It is like trying to get away from a grizzly. If I ever miss a session with her, she won't let go. She insists that I come over to her place to make it up."

"She invites you over there?"

Schneiderman nodded, "It's impossible to say no. She'll hound me until I make up the time."

That did not sound right to me. Schneiderman, who could break the tackles of three-hundred-pound apes, was portraying himself as helpless against pint-size Cara Rosenhaus. That didn't wash, and I wondered why Schneiderman wanted me to believe that story.

It occurred to me that there might be a lot more to this tutoring gig with Cara, more to his going to her apartment for makeup sessions than he was acknowledging. And it struck me, too, that perhaps I had Schneiderman figured wrong, that in truth he was more like Durocher than I had imagined; and that like the Lip, who was known for pulling stunts like changing his lineup at the very last second to confuse the opposition, he might not be playing with his cards face up.

Chapter Twelve

It was early November then and although we had played just a handful of games, it was clear that our team was going to make a run for the league championship. Not only had we beaten Hackley and St. Paul's handily, but to the surprise of the pundits on the *Telegram* and *News* who covered high school sports, we'd breezed past Iona Prep and Collegiate, two teams that had trounced us the year before.

Like a gift to Mueller from some God who had a soft spot for embattled high school coaches, Schneiderman energized us, his natural leadership—it was as much a part of him as his easy stride—providing the spark that propelled us from our usual place as respectable also-rans to the top of our division.

Schneiderman's skill as playmaker and anchor, his steady hand, also made the difference. He was the most selfless player I had ever seen. When the ball came my way, I automatically glanced toward the basket, looking for an opportunity to shoot. Not Schneiderman. He would hold the ball, dribble once or twice while he sized up the defense, and then, faking a move in the opposite direction, suddenly rifle a pass to a teammate cutting for the basket. I don't know how many assists he had that season—it was surely a league record—but as the result of his feeding me for easy layups and short one-handers—I was his favorite target—I began to average better than twenty points a game. That was twice as many as I'd scored the previous season and I got a lot of publicity in the local papers as a rising star, an all-league prospect and, as one writer put it—Schneiderman would not let me forget this—a choice recruit for one of the Ivy's.

And it was not only Schneiderman's deft ball handling that sparked our offense. For his size—he was no more than five-foot-ten with his arch supports in place—Schneiderman was the best rebounder I had ever seen. When he spotted a shot angling off the rim, he would coil, bend at the waist, and then soar into the air as though propelled by a trampoline. With arms extended he was able to reach within a foot of the basket, and with his large hands—in childhood he was nicknamed Paws—he would snatch the rebound from much taller, but comparatively leaden-footed, opponents.

Mueller pressed him to shoot more, continually calling from the sidelines for him to throw one up—he was deadly from around the key—but Schneiderman played his own game, preferring to hit me or Hank Schultz, our six-foot-two forward, when we executed a pick and roll and managed to put daylight between ourselves and the defender. There was something modest, almost shy, about the way that Schneiderman played, as though he were a guest on our team; a guest who felt as though he didn't quite belong and wanted to keep a low profile. By mid-November we still had not played Trinity, the best team in the league and the one favored to take the title for the second consecutive year. The previous season they had simply run away with the trophy, beating us twice by sizeable margins each time.

For a couple of weeks before the Trinity game Mueller held special practices that extended well past six o'clock and caused us to trudge the half mile to the elevated train—ours was the last stop on the Broadway line—in darkness.

Each practice culminated in a scrimmage, the first team against the reserves, with the latter wearing specially ordered green and yellow "T" shirts—Trinity's colors—and running plays of theirs that Fred Kahn, the student manager whom we sent to scout our opponent, had scribbled down on half a dozen index cards. For these intra-squad games Mueller officiated, donning a regulation referee's jersey and blowing an official whistle.

It was during one of those scrimmages—we'd been practicing against Trinity's defenses for about an hour—when Schneiderman asked me to step over to the sidelines.

"Do you remember a while ago I asked if you could come with me on a short trip?" he began.

"Uh huh."

"Well, could you come with me now?"

I was taken by surprise. I looked over at Mueller who had collared Phil Mankoff, a reserve center, and was jawing at him for two sloppily thrown passes.

"Right now?"

"In ten minutes. I'm going to have to leave then."

"What about Mueller? The man is not going to be pleased at our cutting out of practice. And he doesn't seem to be in the mood to be crossed."

"I'll take care of Mueller."

I didn't know what to say. The idea of just walking out of practice scared me. Mueller could be nasty, and the last few days he had been on my case for a series of missed layups.

Schneiderman read my hesitation.

"Look," he said, "It's okay. I'm used to going alone. Don't trouble yourself about it."

"No, I want to go," I put in quickly. "Just let me know when." I was terrified of Mueller—he was quick to bench players who didn't toe the line—but I had given my word and I had no intention of letting Schneiderman down.

"I'm going to speak to Mueller now," Schneiderman said. "When I give you the nod, we'll hustle down to the locker room."

"Okay."

I watched from the foul line while Schneiderman approached Mueller. When the coach grasped what was afoot, a gloomy expression, half anger, half pout, settled over his face. With his eyes averted, he asked a few questions, glanced quickly in my direction, and then, after another brief exchange, simply shrugged unhappily.

The scrimmage resumed and I scored a couple of quick baskets. Then Schneiderman was fouled by an over-eager scrub and he hit two free throws. At that point he signaled to me, called out to Mueller that we were leaving, and we headed for the locker room. We showered and dressed quickly and within a quarter hour were out the door.

"Where are we going," I asked.

"You'll see."

Side by side we walked to the subway, hardly talking, and took the train to Washington Heights. Then we headed west to the bus terminal. Schneiderman was a fast walker and it was all I could do to keep up with him.

At the terminal I followed Schneiderman onto a bus that crossed the George Washington Bridge and headed north into Rockland County.

When we were seated, our hips touching intermittently as the bus bumped over rough roads, I asked again.

"Can you tell me where we are going now, or is this one of those mystery bus rides?"

"You'll see in a couple of minutes." Schneiderman replied. "I want you to meet someone."

At the Spring Valley station Schneiderman signaled to me and we got off. Then we walked a good half-mile to what, from a distance, looked like a college campus. There was a large expanse of lawn, wide walkways, and a number of red brick buildings scattered at a couple of hundred yard intervals. The sign on the heavy iron gate made clear that this was not a college, but a state hospital. Just before we reached the entrance Schneiderman stopped, turned to me, and spoke a few words.

"I have a sister in here," he said. "I asked you to come because I want you to know her."

I felt honored by what he'd just said and I wanted to tell him so, but it seemed too corny to actually say something like that.

"I'll be glad to meet her," was all I could manage. Then, out of pure awkwardness, I asked if there was a children's hospital on the grounds.

"They have a building for children," Schneiderman replied. "It's a warehouse for kids that families can't cope with." Then, after a pause, he added, "mostly psychotic kids and the brain damaged."

"I see." I said. It struck me then that Schneiderman might be taking me to see just such a child and I found myself suddenly frightened.

With Schneiderman leading the way, we passed through the entrance, closely watched by a uniformed guard who peered at us from within a pint-sized gatehouse. Then, after a short walk, we entered a squat five-story building that stood several hundred yards away in the right hand corner of the campus. I followed Schneiderman down a long corridor, painted hospital green, and into an elevator with a badly scratched up interior.

We got off at the top floor. Directly in front of us was a nursing station staffed by an attractive young clerk-receptionist and two nurses' aides, all black women. The receptionist, Grace, smiled a greeting when she spotted Schneiderman coming off the elevator. Her voice was upbeat.

"Hello, Mr. Schneiderman," she called out, "nice to see you again."

"Hello, Grace." He introduced me, turning to one side and waving me forward as though I was a celebrity.

"Grace, this is my friend and teammate, Jonathan."

"Well hello, Jonathan, and welcome. So you are teammates!"

"We are on the same basketball squad."

"Wonderful. You two look like quite a combination, "she laughed, "do you do that Globetrotter razzle dazzle?"

"Not quite like that," I said.

"Well, I'll bet you both are terrific," Grace went on. "Someday I'd like to see the two of you on the court together."

"It would be our pleasure," I put in.

Grace turned to me. "So you are keeping your friend company today?"

I nodded.

"Well that is good of you. He usually comes alone and that's not easy, if you know what I mean."

Before I could respond, she went on.

"Do you know our little patient, our little jewel?"

"I haven't met her yet."

"Well, she is a doll. Just a sweet, sweet thing, isn't she, Mr. Schneiderman?"

"Absolutely. She is a great kid. That's why I wanted Jonathan to meet her." Grace turned to me.

"Well you are in for a treat," she said. "This is a special day for you."

Schneiderman's voice turned serious.

"How is she doing today, Grace?"

The receptionist glanced in the direction of the aides who were sitting together at one corner of the nursing station and one of them, a short, rotund woman with a husky no-nonsense manner, stepped forward. She nodded at Schneiderman and began to speak in a low-pitched, restrained voice, well practiced at delivering bad news.

"Right now your sister is sickly, Mr. Schneiderman," she said. "We've let your folks know and they came by this morning. Looks like she has caught pneumonia. The doctor's been here and she's on antibiotics, but she's not responding as well as we'd hoped. These children have a hard time with pneumonia. It's serious with them. We are watching her closely and are doing our best by her. I just thought you should know." Schneiderman looked stricken. He said nothing, but indicated with his head that he understood.

"She's weak, but you can see her," the aide went on. "She may not speak much, but she'll be glad to see you."

"She is always very glad to see her brother," Grace put in.

The aide motioned to us and we followed her through thick double doors that led to the wards. We passed along a wide corridor that smelled of disinfectant and into a small, perfectly square room that contained what looked like an oversized crib. In it I could see a blue blanket and, beneath that, the body of a child whose auburn hair was visible above the cover. It was late afternoon by then and the room was in shadows.

Schneiderman approached the crib, stood silently for a moment, then leaned in and whispered a greeting.

"Hi sweetie."

I stood behind him, making sure to give him plenty of room. I felt scared and out of place.

The child's eyes remained closed for a moment longer. Then they opened and, slowly, she rolled her head in the direction of her brother's voice. When she saw Schneiderman, she smiled a weak smile that clearly took some effort.

Schneiderman moved closer, reached in, and took hold of the hand that now lay outside the blue blanket. Then, with his other arm, he signaled to me to approach.

"Sweetie, I've come to see you, and I've brought a friend who very much wants to meet you. This is my friend, Jonathan. He's on our team. He is one of our very best players." The child's smile seemed to broaden, as though it was reaching out to me. Her body did not move.

"I hear Mom and Dad were here this morning," Schneiderman went on, "and the doctor, too. We are all here for you, all here to help you get better."

I thought I saw the child's hand move slightly, as though it was trying to grasp Schneiderman's hand more tightly. Her body did not stir.

"She's very weak," Schneiderman whispered to me. "She can't move much, but she understands everything."

"I can see that."

For several minutes Schneiderman stood over the crib, silent, just holding his sister's hand. I felt a need to say something.

"What is her name?" I whispered.

"Evelyn."

"She really is beautiful."

Schneiderman again leaned over the crib. "Jonathan says you are beautiful, Evie. And that is not just anyone saying that. Jonathan is known for his taste in women, so he should know."

The child's head seemed to move ever so slightly.

"She says thank you, Jonathan. That is very kind of you. I'm glad you could visit."

"I'm glad I came," I called out, as though by raising my voice I could get through to her.

Schneiderman then turned back to me, "Would you mind if we stayed just a little longer?" he asked. "I'd like to sit with her for a while."

"That's fine," I said. "I'm in no rush." In fact, that was not true. I had a ton of homework to do, including an English writing assignment, and I was anxious at the thought of getting home after seven. I'd have some explaining to do, especially if my folks had to wait dinner for me, and—this was something that regularly infuriated my mother—she ended up serving a meal that was either overcooked or lukewarm.

I was ashamed of myself, but the truth is I wanted to get out of there. I said nothing, though, and for what seemed like a very long time, Schneiderman simply sat alongside his sister's bed, looking at her but not speaking. Then, finally, it must have been a good ten minutes—he signaled to me that it was time to go.

On the walk to the bus stop we barely spoke. Schneiderman's head still seemed to be back in the hospital room and I did not want to intrude. Finally, though, I asked him how long his sister had been in that condition.

"It's been two years. It was meningitis. It came out of nowhere. She was perfectly fine before that. You should have seen her, Jonathan. She was the liveliest little kid you can imagine. Full of fun. Then, practically overnight she became a rag doll."

"How horrible." I didn't know what else to say. I didn't have any siblings. The story that I'd heard over the years was that after she had a stillborn child, my mother tried once more to get pregnant when I was three, had a miscarriage, and gave up. I always wanted a kid brother or sister—I would dream of the two of us being a team and cooking up tricks to play on our parents—but from early on I knew there was no chance of that, so I pretty much settled the matter in my mind and took what advantage there was in being an only child.

What I could not imagine, though, was having a perky little sister and then having something like this happen. As we walked to the bus station I tried to think about it, to put myself in Schneiderman's place, but I couldn't. My mind would not let me. Instead I kept thinking of home and what excuse I'd give my mother for being so late. I couldn't say I was out with Schneiderman. Ever since the Roxy escapade she had banned him from the house as a decidedly dangerous influence, on a par with Mitch Sternheim, who peddled Camel cigarettes from a book bag he kept permanently stowed in his locker.

Schneiderman didn't speak again until we were seated on the bus. He seemed to need time to absorb the visit, to live with it, and in his own way, to bring it to an end.

He must have done that because when he spoke next he was on to something else entirely. It was as though we'd never made the trip, never seen what we'd seen.

"Looks like I'm in hot water," Schneiderman announced as we sat side by side, our hips again sliding and bumping as the bus made its way back long the same pitted road.

"In what way?"

"Your man, Tillman, called me in today. Pulled me out of class and straight out issued a warning. Just like that, no preliminaries. I'm failing, he told me, and if I don't pull my grades up this marking period, I'm off the team. I'll have my choice of watching the games from the stands or getting myself a box of Band-Aids and helping the assistant manager in charge of boo boos. Either that, or Tillman will be glad to give me a personal recommendation to the coach at DeWitt Clinton. He even hinted that life at a public school might be easier on my nerves."

"He was that blunt?"

"Almost. He tried to throw in a few sugar cubes here and there. Claimed he was a fan of mine, that he admired my team spirit—a sign of good character he said—and that he wanted to see me keep playing. He even offered to set me up with tutors. But the message was clear. I'm not cutting the mustard. I am on the brink of probation, and unless I do a quick about face and quit being the poster boy for the peanut brained ringers that Harmon imports, I'll be watching you do your star turn from the stands."

"Tillman must have really gotten to you," I said. "You have forgotten who the star is around here. What are you going to do? You can't let the bastard simply drop you."

"Tillman is not a bastard. He is what he is, a guy whose one claim to fame is running a top-rated school and who means to keep it that way. He is not going to risk his place in the Sun to win a couple of basketball games."

"Well, then, we'll just have to turn you into a blue ribbon scholar so Tillman can claim bragging rights for discovering this Schneiderman character from Brooklyn, knocking the Flatbush out of him, and making him into an Ivy League contender. This is not going to be easy, though," I added, "trying to teach algebra to another Leo the Lip is on par with trying to get Casey Stengel to cozy up with Hamlet."

"If anyone can do it, you can," Schneiderman replied. "You are definitely the man for the job. Just make sure you spend enough time with your student so that some of that IQ of yours rubs off."

Over the next couple of weeks we worked at Schneiderman's place—my mother's ban on him still held—and actually made some progress. Both of us put in more time and, to my surprise, Schneiderman called a moratorium on his nighttime outings and, most nights, made himself sit at his desk for a couple of hours. The result was that he began to get the hang of algebra and now, instead of flunking Killigan's tests by historic margins, he came within striking distance of passing.

"You are definitely rallying," I said to him. "Stick is there and you've got a good shot at pulling this thing out."

Schneiderman was less optimistic.

"You can't always play catch up," he said. "If a team gets too far behind in the fourth quarter, it won't be able to close the gap. Even if they rally, it will be too late."

"Maybe that team hasn't been taught how to come from behind," I said. "Maybe what it needs is a good tutor."

Schneiderman smiled. "It's possible," he allowed. "Sometimes one-on-one coaching makes a big difference."

The Trinity game was a couple of weeks off now and I had developed a problem that was quickly souring Mueller on me. In fact, he said if I didn't shape up, he'd make me suit up with the scrubs.

The problem was that I was continually missing easy layups. The truth is I'd been having this problem for a couple of months. It seemed to start about the time that Schneiderman came over from Ryder and steadily worsened to the point that it had become a rare event for me to hit a straightforward layup. With each passing day, and each flubbed shot, Mueller was becoming more agitated. At one point he threatened to sit me down until I could get a handle on my mechanics.

"The problem is not mechanical," Mel declared after watching me miss half a dozen shots in practice, "it's Oedipal. You are suffering from a bad case of pizzazz envy."

I knew what he meant and somewhere inside I knew he was right, but I found it hard to admit. Mel was talking about the fact that I had begun to imitate Schneiderman's flying trapeze style of going in for a layup; only, as Mel reminded me, I wasn't Schneiderman.

What he would do when attempting a layup was to leap into the air, curl both legs under him, and seem to sail toward the basket like some kind of flying beetle. It was a dramatic move that when successful—which in Schneiderman's case was almost all the time— drew shouts of cheers from the stands, but it was not one reproducible—at least by me.

I could execute the leap and the curling of the legs, but because of the speed with which I propelled myself forward, my shot regularly struck the backboard with too much force. Typically it would carom off the board, hit the rim, and bounce away, usually into the arms of an opposing player.

Mueller was being driven mad by the missed shots, which regularly cost us half a dozen or more points, and he threatened repeatedly to bench me if I didn't straighten myself out.

This I had trouble doing. What started as stubborn determination grew into a habit, then a compulsion. After a couple of months of imitating Schneiderman's style, I no longer had my own. Whenever I left the ground now my legs would automatically curl beneath me. I could no longer control them. They seemed to have a life of their own.

Even Mel, who prided himself on his psychic powers, was stumped. His suggestion that when I jumped I should imagine myself a polio victim, my legs encased in steel braces, did not do the trick. Nor did his alternative suggestion that in the midst of a game I picture myself the target of mafia hit men, my feet treated to a pair of concrete boots.

"It's self-destructive," Mel finally decided. "You have some crazy need to do yourself in. Look where you've put yourself," he added, "you are on the verge of taking up permanent residence on the Harmon bench. You must be suffering from terrible guilt. Have you committed any carnal acts lately?"

"I wish." Actually the first thing that popped into mind was my persistent, if unsuccessful, efforts over the years to *shtup* Myra Herz, but I said nothing about this.

"This has got to be about your pal, Schneiderman," Mel said. "I have a hunch that you are still playing the Ryder game, still trying to nail him for the hit he put on you."

"What are you talking about? What has the Ryder game got to do with now?"

"Everything," Mel retorted. "Your mind is pulling a number on you, putting up a decoy, convincing you that you are an innocent, just one of Schneiderman's teammates who admires his skill and wants to learn his moves. What you can't face is that you have it in for the guy. You are still mad and it's not only about the Ryder fiasco, Schneiderman's wing-ding style has got the Finley girls screaming and it makes your flat-footed set shots look like plain vanilla pudding. Take a hard look at yourself. What you'd really like to do—and what you are punishing yourself for—is your wish to get Schneiderman under the boards, give him the business, and send him straight to Mt. Sinai."

I looked at Mel. His face was flushed and he looked like a madman who had just stepped off a street corner soapbox. Over the years I had heard Mel spout many crazy ideas but now he seemed to have gone over the edge.

"Will you please do yourself a favor, Melvin," I said, "and check yourself into Bellevue. I'm afraid you are beginning to hallucinate." But Mel held his ground.

"It's you, my friend, who is in need of a shrink. You are totally out of touch with yourself." For serious symptoms like mine Mel recommended a strict Freudian—only deep analysis, he said, had a chance to reach me—but I ignored his suggestion. As far as I was concerned, my problem was not psychological, but mechanical. What I needed, I was convinced, was a sharp eye, a coach who could watch me in action, spot what I was doing wrong, and help me correct the mechanics.

Schneiderman tried to help out by collaring me one afternoon after practice and attempting to straighten out my thinking. Although it might look impressive, he said, his flying maneuver was not something to emulate. He had picked it up from some fancy dan player at the Central Park courts and it had become a habit—a bad habit. It made sinking a layup much tougher and he was sorry that he had ever gotten started with it. No talented player, he said—he actually put me in that category—should want any part of it.

I heard what Schneiderman said but at that point I could not unglue myself. I was stuck in a pattern I could no longer change. Recognizing this, and that I needed more help, Schneiderman took me aside one day after practice.

"It's time for a little reverse tutoring," he declared. Then he insisted that I remain on the court for twenty minutes every day after practice so that he could watch me try to break the habit and correct me when I relapsed.

To do this, he had to make Cara wait to begin her own tutoring. She objected strongly, making clear that she had a lot more important things to do than sit on her hands and watch Schneiderman waste his time on a lost cause—she pointedly did not speak directly to me—but he simply ignored her and insisted on carrying out his plan.

With a referee's whistle in hand, Schneiderman watched and counted while I performed a drill of thirty consecutive layups. If, as I made my jump, my legs began to curl, Schneiderman would sound a shrill blast on the whistle. That meant that I had fallen off the wagon and had to repeat the shot. With nothing better to do, Cara reluctantly kept score and tapped on her clipboard when I had reached the required thirty goal mark.

After a week of this drill I had pretty much broken through and had returned to my old form. This meant no leg curls, no flying beetle moves, just my plain Jane style; the drive to the basket, the leap with outstretched arms, then the soft release so that the ball angled off the backboard and eased into the basket.

During practices Mueller watched me closely, scrutinizing my moves during warm-up drills and keeping a close eye on me whenever I had possession of the ball. Mostly he watched from the sidelines, but even at a distance I could feel his eyes on me. And I sensed, too, his skepticism, his doubts about the genuineness of my conversion, his expectation that I would revert to my misguided ways, continue to miss easy layups, and cost us ball games.

After a week, though, in which I was near perfect in the layup department, he allowed himself a backhanded compliment.

"You're doing better," he announced one day after practice. "The legs aren't folding up. What did you do, put them under a pants' presser?"

"Actually I steamed out the wrinkles in the *john*," is what I wanted to say, but didn't dare.

"Schneiderman and I worked a lot on the problem," is what I did say, "and I think we finally got things straightened out."

Mueller smiled.

"Schneiderman helped you undo Schneiderman?"

"Something like that."

"Well good for him. But from now on, make sure you don't try being him again," Mueller warned me. "If you start in with the fancy Dan moves, you'll be sitting down until you grow warts on your ass."

He was as good as his word. In scrimmages, if I was pressed hard by a defender, forgot myself, and put up a shot a la Schneiderman, Mueller would give a blast on his whistle, point an accusatory finger at me and, without a word, wave me to the bench.

In the end, though, he must have believed enough in my rehabilitation to start me against Trinity, the league defending champion and the odds-on favorite to repeat. At that point both teams were undefeated at 8-0, but Trinity was rolling over its opponents and we were struggling to win our games. Mueller called a team meeting and made it very clear that if we had any idea of taking the title we would have to play a lot better than we'd been doing; and unless we got lucky and Trinity had an off day and got beaten by someone, we would have to win both of the games we were scheduled to play against them that season.

In the first game things were touch and go right down to the wire, and Mueller's decision to bring me back from oblivion seemed to be a brilliant stroke—according to the *Hilltopper*, in a class with the best stratagems of Nat Holman, City College's famed guru.

Right from the opening minute I had one of my best games ever. I hit my trademark long set shots like Tannenbaum himself, scored on several running one-handers, and put in a string of layups without so much as a single curl. I felt like a new man, like a junkie who had kicked the habit and was possessed of new energy.

The game was a toss-up all the way. The teams were evenly matched on almost every count and the score remained so close that in the last ten minutes the lead changed hands five times. In fact, if the final whistle had blown thirty seconds before it did, we would have been celebrating in our locker room with bottles of Coke and Seven-Up overflowing their caps and spilling onto the cement floor. And there would have been a toast to Schneiderman who, with a single daring move, not only stole the ball, but very nearly the game as well.

With less than a minute remaining and the score tied, Trinity took possession and moved up court deliberately, looking to set a screen and get the ball to McManus, their ace, for a final shot at the buzzer. Anticipating that strategy, Schneiderman waited just inside the lane. Then, just as the ball was thrown and McManus was stretching for it, he swooped in like an attacking hawk, batted it away, seized it on one bounce, and rifled it down court.

I was there. Knowing Schneiderman's thinking and his skill as a ball hawk, I sensed what he was going to do. When I spotted him starting his move, I took off for Trinity territory. I grabbed Schneiderman's heave at the foul line and, all alone now, went in for the easy two points. A yard or so from the backboard, I made my leap. My jump was high—when I released the ball I was just a couple of feet from the basket—but as I went up, my legs, as though triggered by some automatic spring, folded under me.

My momentum propelled me toward the basket and as I reached up with the ball I had the flash thought that I must look very much like Schneiderman as he sailed in for a layup. I tried to position my arms to put up a soft shot, one that would just touch backboard and ease into the net, but I was moving too rapidly for full control. The ball struck the board above and just to the left of the basket, circled the rim, then fell to the side and into the hands of McManus who, cursing Schneiderman, had raced down court after me.

Cupping the ball with one giant hand, he whirled and, like a javelin thrower, hurled it the length of the court. At the other end a Trinity player, caught flat-footed by Schneiderman's steal, stood watching the action a few yards from our basket. Seeing the ball hurling toward him, he reached high and managed to snare it. The force of the throw nearly knocked him off his feet. Regaining his balance, the player whirled, dribbled twice, launched himself into the air, and, with a fluid, easy motion, laid the ball in for the winning score.

The Trinity bench erupted. The reserves poured out onto the court, jumped on the backs of their teammates, and raised fists to the rafters. A cadre of priests appeared from somewhere and joined the celebration. One or two went down on their knees, offering up thanks to the Lord. At a distance, we watched in silence, then filed off the court like men going to a hanging.

In the locker room, Mueller said nothing. He just stared at me with cold hatred. None of the other players spoke to me, either. As I passed them on the way to my locker, they looked away, kept their eyes on the floor, or pretended to be preoccupied with getting into their clothes.

Only Schneiderman approached me. He said nothing about what happened. As I sat on the bench in front of my locker, he simply reached down and touched my shoulder.

"We'll get them next time," he said. "We've got their number. Next time out we are really going to kick ass."

I tried to smile, to acknowledge Schneiderman's words, and to thank him for them, but I couldn't. I felt numb. I was sitting scrunched over, staring at the floor, but seeing nothing. In response, all I could do was to reach up and touch Schneiderman's thigh as he stood over me. It was all I could manage.

Chapter Thirteen

I was bummed out for weeks after the Trinity fiasco. In an article on famous goats, the *Hilltopper* ranked me right up there with Charlie Root and Mickey Owen, and Mueller continued to freeze me out. For days he wouldn't talk or even look at me. If he had anything to say, he'd get Fred Kahn, our manager, to convey the message, which, unfailingly, was some sarcastic remark about the astounding progress I was making.

At every practice Mueller would make me sit on the bench for a good hour before letting me in on a scrimmage. When I got in, though, I played well. After what happened I watched everything I did, moved deliberately, and did not take a shot until I was in the open and a couple of feet from the basket. As a result, I was a steady scorer—fed regularly by Schneiderman's passes—and I made sure to play tight defense.

My teammates felt the steadiness of my play and its consistency, and along with Schneiderman, I became an anchor for them. My return to form and to my old place as a team leader seemed to give all of us a boost after the depression that set in following the Trinity game. In practice, the whole squad, including the scrubs, began to show more spirit and hustle. A new feeling of hope was in the air and when the astonishing news broke that Trinity had lost a game, had been upset by lowly St. Paul's, hope slid quietly into optimism. And then, as we grew sharper in practice, a feeling of inevitability set in; the conviction that we were destined to destroy Trinity next time around and to relieve them of the league title.

Then something happened to Schneiderman. Suddenly—it seemed almost overnight—his play fell off. He began to make mistakes; double dribbles, walking violations, errant free throws that he had never made before. And his passing, always pinpoint accurate, became chancy. Sometimes he hit his man as he broke for the basket, but often now his pass was off-target, thrown behind his man or too far ahead, leading to an easy interception.

This was not like Schneiderman, but no one knew what was wrong. And Schneiderman wasn't saying. He simply looked preoccupied; preoccupied and glum. We were used to his leaving practice early once or twice a week, but now he cut out an hour early almost every day. In the midst of a scrimmage, sometimes even before there was a break in the action or a time-out called, he would simply give Mueller a sign with a wave of his hand, walk off the court, scoop up his warm-up jacket from the bench, and disappear into the locker room. Once, between scrimmages, I came down after him, only to catch a glimpse of him, his St. Louis Cardinals baseball cap sitting backwards on his head, disappearing out the door.

For several days, Mueller said nothing. He simply watched Schneiderman slipping and looked worried, but kept his distance. But then, one afternoon, he called Schneiderman into his office before practice—he had a glass enclosed cubicle at one end of the gym—and I could see the two of them talking, Muller shaking his head and looking more concerned than ever. When he came out, Schneiderman simply rejoined the first team—we were practicing free throws at that point—and said nothing to anyone.

For a good while—it must have been close to a week—Schneiderman shared nothing with me either. It was not that he was unfriendly. He spoke with me after practice and several days a week we walked to the subway together, talking mostly about the team and Mueller and his strategy for our next encounter with Trinity. He was subdued, though. I had to initiate conversation and unless I kept it going with comments and observations, it would tend to die out and we would walk in silence.

I suspected that things were not going well with Evie and that is why he was leaving early every day, but I didn't want to bring up the subject without some sign that I could do so. And none was forthcoming. Whatever was happening, Schneiderman was keeping it to himself. That, I had come to learn, was typical of him. He was not a confider. Whatever troubled him—and you could tell he was troubled from the glum expression on his face when he was alone and thought no one was watching—he kept to himself. Schneiderman was the kind of person who was embarrassed to talk about his worries, almost as though it was a failure to have any; and he didn't invite you to ask either. Sometimes I wanted to break in, break through his reserve, and tell him it was all right to have worries, all right for things not to be going well, but I never did. It seemed too risky. And in a strange way, Schneiderman seemed too fragile.

Now I wanted to ask about Evie, ask about how things were, but for several days I just observed Schneiderman and said nothing. I didn't want to intrude and I don't think I wanted to know, either, in case things were really bad.

Finally I spoke to Cara one afternoon at the gym. Since her outburst, she had remained distantly cool toward me, speaking minimally and letting me know that she was still angry, but at least she had begun to speak—for over a week she simply stared at me— and that was enough for me to approach her. Although I did so a bit warily, preparing myself for a second eruption, I managed to ask if she knew what had come over Schneiderman, if what I suspected, that Evie had taken a turn for the worse, was so. Cara looked at me for a moment before answering. No doubt she was wondering why I was asking her that question, why I, supposedly Schneiderman's pal, did not know what was happening. Finally she nodded.

"She's in a bad way. They don't know if she'll pull through this time."

"That's what I was afraid of." Cara's expression took on her schoolmarm look.

"Have you spoken to Stan?"

"It's been on my mind a lot. But I haven't yet. I didn't know if I should. I didn't know if he wanted to talk to anyone."

I could feel Cara's disapproval. She seemed on the verge of lashing out at me for my hesitancy, my passivity, but she must have thought better of doing so. When she spoke, her tone was restrained.

"He'll definitely want to speak to you," she said. "But you have to go to him. He's not someone who can reach out."

"I realize that."

"Well then?" She looked at me as though I was a kid reluctant to start his homework and made a shoving motion with her hands.

The next day after practice—it was not a good one; the whole team seemed lackadaisical in response to Schneiderman's mood—I walked straight to his locker and sat down on the bench next to him while he was changing. I reached out and touched his shoulder.

"It's Evie, isn't it?" Schneiderman nodded.

"How did you know?"

"It's written all over your face. How bad is she?"

"It's bad. She's critical. The doctor says it could go either way and we have to be prepared."

"That's tough."

"The damn thing is, there is nothing I can do. Nothing anyone of us can do. I go to the hospital almost every day and all I can do is sit there. Sit there and watch, and—please don't laugh—pray. I don't believe in God. I never could believe in the idea of God. Yet I pray. Isn't that idiotic?"

"Not at all. I gave up God right after my Bar Mitzvah and I'd pray, too. In fact, that's exactly what I'm going home to do."

"You're as crazy as I am."

"Look, it couldn't hurt. In case we both are wrong, at least we've kissed the right tush." Schneiderman smiled.

"You've got more of a practical head on your shoulder than I thought."

"Look, if you want company, I'd be glad to take the bus with you again."

"Thanks. I don't think so. Right now I'd rather be alone."

"I get it. But if you need me for anything, just ask." He reached out and touched my knee as I was sitting astride the bench.

"Thanks. I'm glad you came over."

"Me, too."

I didn't hear anything for two days. Then, one night, while I was struggling with another Killigan brain twister, the phone rang. I raced in and got it before my mother could answer.

"The fever has broken. She's coming through. She's going to make it."

"That's wonderful. How great. What great news."

"I thought you might want to know."

"Might want to? Are you kidding? I would have murdered you if you hadn't called."

"Well, lucky me that you don't have to. By the way, could you spare an hour?"

"Tonight?"

"I thought we could go out for a little celebration. Have a drink or a Tip Toe sandwich."

"No Roxy?"

"We'll do that when she comes home. And tack on the Apollo in Harlem."

"My mom will be thrilled."

"What about tonight?"

I felt on the spot. Clearly Schneiderman wanted to go out, to have some company, to unwind a bit after the agony of the past week, and I wanted to do what he wanted; but I did not see how I could manage it. I had tons of homework yet to do and, besides, I had no reason to take off suddenly.

"I'd love to meet you, but I don't know how I can get away."

"Come on. Use your imagination. Make up a story. Tell your mother you left a crucial piece of homework at a friend's house."

I hesitated.

"She'll see through me."

"Not if you are definite enough. The trick is to be convincing."

"Okay. I'll try. But if I don't show up, send a locksmith. They are liable to padlock my room."

I did get out, though, by staging a near perfect imitation of a panic attack. All at once from my room I let out a horrific cry followed by a long groan. Then I struck at the wall and mimicked the sudden onset of tachycardia. Rushing into my parents' bedroom, I half screamed, half choked out, that I had left my bio assignment at Mel's and that I was sunk without it. Then, before the barrage of questions and protests could be launched from my mother's side of the bed, I turned, grabbed a jacket from the hall closet, and was out the door.

We had arranged to meet at Tip Toe and when I arrived Schneiderman was already there, sitting at a table in the rear, two bottles of beer in front of him. How he always managed to get himself alcohol was a mystery I never solved. But he did it, either by ruse or bribe, and he was always ready to buy me a drink. Now as I sat down across from him, he flipped off the bottle cap and poured two glasses.

"Drink up, he said. "Drink to a happy moment."

I lifted my glass.

"Let's hope it's more than a moment, that the good news is permanent."

Schneiderman shrugged.

"We don't know. Right now it's good, but the situation is touch and go. There's no predicting."

"But right now things are good," I insisted.

"Right. So we drink to now, to the moment, and don't look ahead. That will be our motto. Keep your eyes on today. Tomorrow there is bound to be trouble."

"Are you expecting bad news?"

"It is not that. I have no idea what is going to happen. We could get a call that she didn't make it. She survives or she doesn't. That's where Evie is. But think about it. We're not so far from the same place."

"We're not?"

"Not really. Right now Evie is balanced on a thin rope. Our balance is better but something could come along and topple us, too. When I was at Ryder, a kid in my class came down with meningitis and was gone in forty-eight hours."

I had never heard Schneiderman talk like this. I wondered if he'd had a couple before I'd arrived. Or was this some dark side, some part of him I'd never seen that was coming out now, being driven to the surface by what he and his family were going through?

"Are you okay?" I asked.

"I'm fine. I'm celebrating, having a drink with you. I'm okay now. It's just that all of this has finally gotten to me. I haven't really allowed myself to take it all in. Maybe I couldn't until now. But do you know something? Your friend has started to think for a change."

"But you are being so morbid."

"Not morbid. Real. I've been thinking about what is real, what we don't let ourselves think about; at least I never did until all of this wiped away the bullshit."

I nodded. "I can understand why you didn't. In this situation I probably wouldn't either. But ordinarily I don't have that problem. I think a lot about what is happening in my life and I usually have a pretty clear picture of what is true and what is not."

"Actually, that's not my impression, Jonathan. From what I've seen, you fool yourself a lot of the time. You have a need to see people your own way, the way you want to see them and that can blind you. You don't realize it, but your take on people is often way off base."

"What are you talking about? Who do you mean?"

"Your father, for one. You treat your father like shit."

"Where did you get that from?"

"It's obvious. You look down on him. You and your mother. You think he is a *putz* because he is struggling to stay afloat."

"You don't know what you're talking about. You have no idea what my father is like. Talk about reality, this is a man for whom reality doesn't exist."

"He has problems, true. Big problems, I'm sure. And I know he gets lost in his own troubles. But how often have you even tried to talk with him, share what is going on with you, maybe invite him to see you play? He's awfully proud of you, you know? He keeps track of your statistics."

"You seem to have a lot better relationship with him than I do."

"Because I don't live with him, so I don't judge him. I judge my own father. By the way, he is doing it again, antagonizing this DA, saying he is a wimp who won't prosecute a jaywalker. If he keeps it up, he is sure to get the boot."

"Can you do anything about it?"

"I've spoken to him, but it's no use. The man is totally driven. So do you know what I do? I accept him with his craziness. That's what I do. And I love him the best I can."

"I knew you were an unusual guy, but I didn't know you were actually J.C."

"That's just the point. I'm not. And when I look at myself, what am I? I'm pretty much of a bust."

"What are you talking about?"

"I'm a jock. That's what I am. A guy who can play ball, period. You see me. I'm barely literate. I read like a retard and my math skills are sixth grade at best. What is my future going to be? A career as a perpetual ball player, the kind of overgrown kid who will still be playing in the Parks Department handball tournament at age fifty? If I don't make it in college ball and get some asshole of an alumni to give me a job, I'll be selling shoes at Macy's."

"You'll have a touch with the women," I said, "You'll probably be salesman of the year." My attempt to lighten things didn't work.

"And that is another thing," Schneiderman went on, "I don't really have friends. Admirer's, yes. Acquaintances who don't know a thing about me, plenty. But I have a hard time making friends. You see me, I'm pretty shy when it comes down to it. Like I told you, I've never had a proper girlfriend. I'm not sure I'd know how to relate to one."

"We are pretty much in the same boat there," I put in quickly, "my batting average in that department wouldn't qualify me for the grapefruit league."

"You have Cara."

I felt like laughing out loud, but thinking about Cara and where I was with her just hurt too much.

"Where have you been? She barely speaks to me."

"Because you are an asshole. You don't read her properly. You keep offending her, trampling all over the things that are important to her. She wants you to be a hero, but a lot of the time you act like a self-centered Harmon turd."

"She told you that?"

"Not exactly. But she hinted."

When I heard that I felt as though I'd been knifed.

"I suppose you are her real hero?"

"Sometimes she idealizes me, but she doesn't know me. And I'm staying out of it. It's your game to win or lose. But if you get booted or drop out, I'll probably take a shot. But frankly, I don't think I'm in her league."

We sat for an hour just talking. I did not know what to make of what Schneiderman was saying. He seemed to have some need to put himself down. I felt like reaching out, saying something supportive, but I didn't know if that was the right thing to do. Finally—it was after ten by then—I told him that I'd have to get back or my mother would have me in solitary every night for a year.

Luckily when I got home she was already asleep and I slipped into my room unnoticed. I couldn't sleep, though. I kept thinking about what Schneiderman had said and, somehow, it troubled me.

"What you heard," Mel said when I told him about the evening, "was guilt speaking. His sister nearly died. She is very damaged and could go at any time. Schneiderman is a survivor. He's healthy and he's a big *macher*. He's Harmon's hero. All the coeds adore him. Half of them have photos of him in their wallets. How is he going to face the difference the enormous difference, between himself and the kid lying in a hospital bed? He needs to knock himself down just to keep going. Otherwise the gap is just too great; the guilt is too much. Incidentally, this is why he is lousing things up on the court. It's all part of the same thing."

"I never thought of that," I said, "I should have said something, shown him that I understood."

"Better not," Mel said. "In situations like this, a person needs to work things out for himself, find his own balance and his own solutions."

What Mel said seemed right to me although, privately, I thought that perhaps what Schneiderman was saying was actually so; that he was able to look at himself squarely in a way that few people I knew could do. Nevertheless, I was impressed with Mel's insight. A few months ago, when we were at a party and he had too much beer, he had confided in me that he had been in therapy for over a year. I wasn't surprised given the crazy man that he was. But I thought now that whoever his shrink was, he must be one smart guy. Obviously Mel was learning a lot from him. And I figured if things fell apart for me; if Schneiderman didn't come out of his funk and start playing like himself, and if Cara kept up the deep freeze, I might just give the guy a ring.

Chapter Fourteen

Two weeks had passed since Cara called a moratorium—sent me packing, in Mel's words—and when I wasn't preoccupied with Schneiderman's state of mind—I monitored him for signs of progress at every practice—I was preoccupied with strategies for getting back with her.

My plan depended on a quality I'd observed in Cara; her willingness to forgive. She was a hothead, no question, with a temper like King R's, and she could be as tough and unyielding as he was. If she was on the outs with someone—she had waged a two-year battle with a Dewey supporter in her class—she could be implacable. She kept the fight going and looked for every opportunity to take a shot at her adversary. In fact, after the break-up with Ken Masters, she lost no time letting the world know what a complete asshole he turned out to be.

But if the other fellow made a gesture toward her, offered any kind of apology—a simply "sorry" would do—that ended the feud. Cara never held a grudge. Even when her best friend, Debbie, turned against her during her campaign for Council President, and, out of pique for some slight, spread the word that Cara was a collector of Red Army songs—information that her opponent used to brand her a dangerous communist—Cara took her back into the fold as soon as Debbie expressed regret for her actions.

This was what I was counting on; Cara's readiness to forgive. I figured if I did a *mea culpa*, acknowledged my error in not making sure to find out about the trouble in Schneiderman's family and offering to help; in short, not being the good and responsible citizen that Cara thought everyone should be, I'd be granted a reprieve and could slip back into my old place.

In fact, that strategy was pretty successful. Cara responded quickly to my apology and her voice regained its warmth. She said she understood—she claimed to know me pretty well—and even tried to make me feel better by relating an incident in which she herself had behaved callously toward Clarence, the doorman, by failing to inquire after his mother when the old lady was confined to bed with a broken hip.

But she did not offer to see me, and when I suggested that we get together, she had an excuse—a mid-term poly-sci exam—as to why she could not spare the time.

"You were on the right track," Mel said when I laid out what I had done.

"So far, so good. But you didn't go far enough. What you need to do is to show her that you've changed. Tell her that you've been dreaming about the Boston Tea Party and that you now realize that tyranny can't be overthrown by a person sitting on the bench. She'll like that. And throw in examples of the new you. Tell her about the hospital visit to Schneiderman's sister. That is the kind of good works she is looking for. And the tutoring. Don't forget to mention all the tutoring that you've been doing with Schneiderman. No need, though, to spell out the results."

Mel was right. When I called a few days later and told Cara what I'd been up to, she was definitely impressed.

"Seems like you've really gotten off your duff," she said.

"Well I've thought it over," I replied, "and I realized that if we hadn't dumped that tea, we'd still be under the Brits' heels. And probably victims of English anti-Semitism," I added for good measure.

"No question," Cara said. "Behind their façade, the English are bigots. When you come across people like that, you can't reason with them. You have to act fast and take them down."

"Absolutely," I agreed. "The colonists had it right. Sitting on their tushes wasn't doing them any good. They realized that they had to get moving and kick some ass."

"I've never heard you speak this way," Cara said.

"Well, frankly, I'm tired of being a bench warmer," I replied. "I've decided to get out there and butt heads. By the way," I added— the idea to say this just popped into my head as a way to firm up my image as an activist—"I've been working on a sign for the Korvette demonstration."

"Really? What is the message?"

"You'll see when I'm done." Actually a few nights before I had dreamed of constructing a huge ten-foot placard that read *Korvette cuts throats, not prices,* and presenting it to Cara as a peace offering. "I can tell you this, though," I added, "it is going to shake up those fat cats in the front office. They are going to feel some real heat on their tails."

"That's terrific," Cara said, but her voice sounded flat, lifeless, without emotion. Certainly there was no sign of the enthusiastic response that I'd been hoping for.

"Is something wrong," I asked. "Isn't this what you've wanted from me, to get more involved? You are always going on about the importance of having effective signs, about how they are the voices of the march and all that."

"I know. And yours sounds wonderful. Only..." Cara's voice trailed off, then stopped.

"Only what?"

"Jonathan, the demo is over. We had it yesterday. It was scheduled for yesterday."

"And you didn't let me know?"

"I didn't think you were interested. You've never shown much interest in demos—demos just aren't your thing. Isn't that what you've said, more or less always said, that your flat feet couldn't handle them?"

"How could you know that I haven't been to a podiatrist?" I countered. "I told you I'm a new man."

"I'm really sorry." She sounded genuinely remorseful. "I guess I chose the demo date before I had a chance to meet the new you."

"Well, I'm upset."

"Don't be. I'll make it up to you next time. Tell me about your sign," she went on in her warmest voice.

"It's not that important."

"*Au contraire.* It's very important. I want to hear about it."

I told her, and she more than made up for the earlier lame response.

"That's brilliant," she said. "It gets straight to the heart of the matter. These Korvette characters are the worst kind of cutthroats. If we hit them again, I'll have you right out front as our number one sign bearer."

"I'd like that," I said. "But I want you with me. The two of us out there together."

"It's a deal," Cara said.

"By the way," I asked, "how did yesterday's demo go?"

"Actually great. We really put it to them. And we got some terrific PR. NBC did a segment on us."

"How was the turnout?"

"Terrific. Our whole crew showed up. Even your pal, Schneiderman."

"Schneiderman was there?"

"He was one of the first on the scene. I think he wanted to make up for not showing up last time. Anyway, he worked his tail off, both at the demo and at the party afterward."

"There was a party?"

"Just a little gathering. Wine and cheese. I had the gang over to my house to celebrate our victory."

"Schneiderman came to your place?"

Cara's tone changed. All at once she sounded defensive, defensive and annoyed.

"Yes, Stan came to my place along with everyone else. In fact, he helped serve. He was really great about lending a hand."

"I'll bet he was. Three cheers for him. Schneiderman is not dumb. He knows how to play the game."

"You sound jealous," Cara responded. There was irritation in her voice and I could tell that she was warming up for a fight, so I backed off.

"I'm not jealous. I'm just upset that I missed everything, that no one thought to call me."

Cara nodded. Her voice became conciliatory.

"I'm really sorry about that, Jonathan. It was my oversight. I'll really try to make it up to you next time."

Maybe it was because she really felt guilty, I was never really sure, but the next night Cara rang me at home. My mother summoned me to the phone.

"It's the girlfriend," she called out, not without a touch of sarcasm. I let that pass without reacting, but privately I wondered what my mother knew. I had told her nothing about my troubles with Cara, but she was pretty sharp in picking up on my moods and putting two and two together.

When I reached the foyer to get the phone, my mother was still nearby. She was busy rearranging figurines on a living room shelf but had stationed herself so as to be able to eavesdrop on my conversation. In as obvious and dramatic way as possible, I picked up the receiver, stretched the cord as far as it would go, backed into a hallway, and shut the door. I had no intention of letting my mother know my business, especially when it came to girls and, most especially when it involved a conversation with Cara, who, for all I knew, might be calling to give me the boot.

I was wrong. In fact, Cara's manner threw me off balance. She could not have been friendlier.

"Hi, Jonathan," she began, "how are you feeling today?"

"I'm okay."

"I was really concerned about how upset you were yesterday. About the demo and all. I'm really sorry about what happened."

"I've gotten over it. It's all right."

"I'm glad you feel that way. I hate to see you so upset."

"It's really all right."

"Good. Well, listen, I've got an invitation for you."

"To what?"

"A party. A birthday party for Sidney. It's his sixtieth. We are throwing him a bash out in Westchester."

Through a business connection, the Rosenhaus' had rented out the Rye Bath and Tennis Club for the occasion.

"And you want me to come?"

"Absolutely. Sidney particularly asked for you. 'Invite Pancho,' he said. 'I want to get him out on the court and beat the pants off of him.'"

"That sounds like your father."

"That's Sidney's sense of humor. But don't mind him, it's his way of being affectionate."

"I'll bet." Pancho was Pancho Gonzales, the great tennis champion with the lightning serve. King R had started calling me that—to rattle me I was sure—during our last tennis match when I frustrated him by managing to hit two aces in a row.

"No, really. He thinks very well of you; calls you an interesting young man with a lot of promise."

"As what, a ball boy?"

"Don't knock yourself. No, he really means it. Those were the exact words he used, 'interesting' and 'promising.' Of course he thinks that you are still pretty raw and need a lot of work, you and your tennis game both, but he sees potential. He thinks you have what it takes to be a winner."

"Should I be flattered?"

"Absolutely. Sidney never has anything good to say about my boyfriends. You are the first one."

At the word, boyfriends, I felt a momentary thrill, like the first time I found my name posted among those who had survived Mueller's cuts and made the varsity squad.

"Well please thank him for me. And tell him if he wants to work with a hunk of raw material, I'm his man."

"I'll tell him. He'll be thrilled. Nothing will make him happier than to have a boyfriend of mine to work on."

At that moment a scene flashed in front of me. I am in my wood-paneled Harlem office, chairing a meeting as chief of King R's rapidly growing dinette division. But I quickly blot out that picture lest Cara catch on to what I've been imagining.

"And, by the way, I agree with him," Cara added.

"About what?"

"That you have what it takes; that you'll be great at whatever you do."

"From you that is high praise."

"I mean it," Cara said. "One thing you can say for Sidney," she went on, "he can spot raw material when he sees it."

"Well thank you," I said, "I had no idea that your father had any interest in me."

"That's another thing about Sidney," she said, "he is full of surprises. So will you come to the party?"

"I'd be delighted."

Actually I was very pleased, pleased and surprised that Cara and King R wanted me at a family celebration.

"It was the East Hampton weekend," Mel said when I told him about the invitation, "that was the key. You made quite an impression. You triggered a lot of dreams."

"I did?"

"Absolutely. The father found himself a new tennis partner and just maybe the successor he's been looking for. And, Henry, the brother, finally got himself a set of ears, and pretty sharp ones at that. You probably don't realize it, but you made a lot of friends."

"What about Cara?" I asked. I could not imagine why, but I valued Mel's take on things.

"Looks like she is willing to give you another shot. You've sold her with the new your idea. She is curious to see who this person turns out to be."

"So am I."

"Listen, you are making progress," Mel said, "any invite from Sidney Rosenhaus is no small potatoes. Just don't mess it up," he added. "When you are on the court, remember to play hard and lose gracefully."

"Don't worry, I haven't beaten the man yet. He's a human backboard. He gets everything back. If he doesn't manage to exhaust you chasing his bloopers, he will drive you batty trying to get a shot by him."

"Well you've got to hold on to your sanity and stay cool," Mel said. "Remember, this is an investment. Two sets with Sidney Rosenhaus are worth a couple of rungs on the King R corporate ladder."

"I'll try to keep that in mind," I replied. "But I can't guarantee what this Pancho character will do. If he gets frustrated enough, he is capable of committing mayhem."

The party was the following Saturday, and for a few days beforehand I felt energized, revved up, my head awash with imaginings about the occasion and what might happen, especially afterwards when Cara and I could be alone and I could demonstrate just how well I could live up to my potential. One thing bothered me, though, kept nagging at me throughout the school day and just wouldn't leave me alone; what Cara had told me about having had people over after the demo. I kept picturing Schneiderman in her apartment, relaxing, having fun, flirting with Cara and her playing up to him. Despite all that I knew; that the party was hardly a party at all, nothing more than drinks and snacks, just Cara's way of saying thank you to everyone who supported her efforts, I kept picturing Schneiderman and Cara together, talking, laughing, and if he stayed on after everyone had left, who knows, perhaps celebrating by falling into a clinch.

I tried to forget all that, put it out of mind as so much foolishness, but the imaginings kept coming back, haunting me, so I decided, finally, to mention something to Schneiderman. Perhaps I was looking for reassurance. I don't know.

One afternoon after practice I stopped by his locker.

"Hi." Schneiderman looked up and smiled.

"Hi, Jonathan." He motioned for me to sit down. "How are you these days?"

"More important, how are you? How is Evie?"

"So far, holding her own. We've got our fingers crossed."

"I'm really glad things are better. I've noticed you seem more relaxed."

"For the time being."

"Well let's hope it's for longer than that. By the way, I heard you were at Cara's demo the other day."

"Yeah. I felt I owed her some help. I skipped out on her the time before."

"I would have been there myself but I didn't know about it. She never told me."

Schneiderman scanned my face. Then his voice took on a softer tone. "I think she had the idea that you weren't interested, that this just wasn't your thing."

"She could have let me decide."

"I suppose. But look, don't be upset, I think she didn't want to put you on the spot, make you feel guilty if you didn't want to come."

"Maybe. I'm not sure what really happened. I'm never sure what Cara is up to. How did it go?"

"What?"

"The demonstration."

"Oh. Well, very well. There was a good turnout and the crowd got in the spirit. A lot of folks joined in, simply came forward and joined the line. We even got radio coverage on the six o'clock news."

"Very impressive."

"I tell you, that Cara is something. She is a fantastic organizer. It took a hell of a lot of effort to put this thing together."

"I understand that there was a party afterward."

"Kind of. Very informal. Some of us went over to Cara's for drinks."

"A victory celebration?"

"Sort of. It was Cara's way of acknowledging the hard work the group put in to bring this off. It was very thoughtful of her. People really appreciated the gesture. In fact, everyone agreed that she did a terrific job all around."

"I heard that you were pretty terrific yourself, that you were a tremendous help."

"Who told you that?"

"Guess?"

"That was nice of her to say, but the truth is I wasn't any more helpful than anyone else. We all chipped in. That is the only way these things get done. It was a real team effort."

"Well Cara thought you were extra special. I'm sure she showed her appreciation. When she likes someone, Cara can be very warm."

"I don't doubt it. Well, she certainly thanked me enough times. She is very generous that way."

I realized that I couldn't go farther with this conversation without tipping my hand. There was more, a lot more, that I wanted to know, but I did not want to put Schneiderman on the spot—he had enough on his mind—or run the risk of looking pathetically insecure, so I let the matter drop.

Sidney's party was to begin at four in the afternoon, but to leave enough time for Cara's mother to do a final check on the arrangements and for the big tennis match to take place—King R issued a challenge to me as soon as I arrived at the apartment—we left the city at noon. Before he sent for the car, King R made it clear that I was to sit up front with him.

"It's my birthday," he proclaimed. "I get to choose. Jonathan and I need to talk so we can settle world affairs, isn't that right, Jonathan?"

"Sure thing, Mr. Rosenhaus."

"Sidney. Call me Sidney. You are family now. You call me Sidney and I'll call you Pancho. How is that?"

"Fine."

"By the way, how is that big serve of yours?" King R asked.

"I haven't played much."

"Good. Then you should be pretty rusty. When that first serve of yours comes in, it's a ball buster, right up there with Gonzales."

"Thanks, but it's not very consistent."

"That's what I'm counting on, my boy. Inconsistency is what I thrive on. When I see that a competitor is inconsistent, that he keeps changing his marketing approach and his price list, I know I have him on the run."

"Well I don't think you are going to have much trouble with me."

King R turned to Cara.

"Listen to the fellow. Mr. Modesty. He can't get the ball over. He's no competition. Well I can tell you this is just the kind of character you've got to watch out for. These guys are the ones who will beat the pants off you and claim it was all a fluke."

Cara laughed. "You've got his number, Sidney," she said. "You've got our boy pegged."

We'd been on the road for just a few minutes—we were just approaching the East River Drive—when King R threw out his first question.

"So what do you think," he asked, "did FDR betray the Jews?" I wasn't prepared for this. To get myself ready for another encounter with King R, I had read some more about Truman and had boned up on Wilkie and Dewey as well, but I didn't expect to be hit with something so loaded.

"That's a tough question," I replied. "I think he might have done more."

"More what?"

"Let more Jews into the country."

"And why didn't he do that?"

"I'm not sure, really."

Sidney Rosenhaus glanced over at me as though I was the dullest boy in the class.

"Because first and foremost FDR was a politician, that's why. People forget that when it came to politics, he was one shrewd operator. He knew where the power was. He didn't want to alienate the white establishment in this country. He was no fool. He knew very well that the Rockefellers and the Morgans and the Fords were anti-Semitic. They didn't want a bunch of refugee Jews brought into this country, and FDR went along with them. He needed them on his side."

"Are you saying FDR sold out the Jews?"

"He would never have acknowledged that. He always had good rationalizations for his policies," King R replied, "but in fact, yes, that is exactly what he did."

"It's hard to believe," I said. Actually I did not want to believe what Sidney Rosenhaus was saying. For my family, and all my friends' families, FDR was our savior, the greatest, most beloved hero of our times. I had never before heard a word of criticism spoken against him.

"FDR was everyone's hero," King R declared, "that is why he could get away with so much. But the fact is, he was responsible for hundreds of deaths. He had a lot of blood on his hands. Believe me, a man like Abraham Lincoln would not have behaved that way. Lincoln was a politician, too, a master politician, but he had a big heart. And he listened to his heart. People say that FDR had a pretty big one, too, but it wasn't steady. You couldn't always rely on it. When it came to Jewish refugees who were out in the cold, who desperately needed a home, it just shut off. Do you know what Lincoln would have done? He would have welcomed the Jews. He might not have liked them anymore than he liked blacks, but he would have welcomed them. He would have opened the gates and thumbed his nose at Rockefeller."

"Or he might have brought him around, persuaded him to see his point," I put in. "Lincoln was great at doing that."

I had read a lot about Lincoln and I wanted Sidney Rosenhaus to see that, to see that I was an informed person. King R glanced at me.

"That's a good point," he acknowledged. "In that way Lincoln had more *sekel* than FDR. When it came down to it, he was tough. He stood his ground, but he also knew how to work with people.

"I'll tell you something else, Pancho," he went on. "In this life you've got to walk a line between being tough and having a heart. If you don't know how to be tough, you'll find yourself out on your ass, shut out of everything you want. But you can't trample on people either. Do you know what I mean? In my business I am always walking the line. I've got rules, strict rules that everyone's got to follow. You can't work for me unless you are willing to play the game."

I wondered if King R was sending me a message, letting me know what would be expected of me if I joined Rosenhaus Furniture, but I said nothing. I just listened.

"What I do is I apply the TR method," he went on. "Do you know why I call it that?" This was a rhetorical question. "Because of Teddy Roosevelt," King R explained.

"TR is Teddy Roosevelt. That is the Roosevelt you want to follow, not the one that shuts gates on Jewish people. Do you know much about TR?"

I had to acknowledge that I didn't.

"We haven't gotten to him yet in history," I explained.

"Well, get to him, then," King R replied. "Everyone needs to know about TR. He was the best, our best leader. He gave us a way of working and a way of living that if you pay attention, will carry you far. Basically the man was kind, you couldn't find a more generous man, but he didn't take guff off anyone. And he didn't indulge people and make them weak. He made his crew buckle down and that is the way I operate. Ask my people. They will tell you how it is. I don't accept excuses. Don't try to make excuses to Sidney Rosenhaus. It won't fly. My people know that they have a job to do, and they do it. And I reward good work. Everyone in my company gets good money and everyone is covered head to toe. No one has to worry about getting sick. You get sick and we take care of everything, soup to nuts. But when you are healthy, you work and you produce."

I was getting the warning and it was making me nervous. Clearly King R was a taskmaster, just the opposite of my father who gave people a week off if they had the sniffles.

"Those are the rules," King R declared. "I operate by rules, my TR rules I call them. And let me tell you something, my folks respond. They like rules. People want rules. They like to know where they stand. Do you agree with me?"

"Actually, I'm a rules person myself," I said. "I always like to know where I stand."

"There you go. That is what I am telling you. Your average person is a scared person. He wants direction. Do you know what a good boss is? A good boss is someone who has a compass in his head and tells you where you are, tells you where you are and where you need to go. That's the kind of boss people want to work for."

"I'll remember that," I said, only half aware of my effort to reassure Sidney Rosenhaus that in me he had a man cut from the same mold.

"Good. Then you've learned something today, Pancho. You have learned something about managing people. And would you like to know how I handle competitors?"

I made an assenting sound, but I'm not sure that King R heard it.

"Well, it's simple," he went on, "simplicity itself. No scheme, no strategies, no fancy footwork. I declare war, that's what I do. I go all out to put the other guy out of business. How do you like that for straight talking?"

"That's what business is," I replied. "The survival of the fittest."

As Sidney Rosenhaus was speaking, I thought of my father and how different he was from King R. Instead of battling Seidman, the hustler who was cutting into his business, and going right after him, undercutting his prices and knocking him out of the game, my father managed to convince himself that Seidman was no challenge at all.

"The man can't see what is in front of his face," my mother complained, "what a blind man can see, he is blind to. 'Not to worry,' he tells me, 'There is no problem.' His customers are loyal, he says. He has customers who have been with him thirty years. Meantime the loyal customers are flocking to Seidman and your father is giving me unsigned checks for household expenses."

It made me mad to think of my father in this way. And when my mother stirred me up with such talk, I wanted to storm into the living room, rouse him from his chair, confront him, and force him to face the truth about what was happening to his business—and to us. At other times, though, I had the fantasy of stepping into the breach and joining him in the business. Working with my father, I would supply what he needed, the no nonsense guy who would take on Seidman while he did his thing, talk on the phone and schmooze with customers.

Now as I sat alongside King R and compared my father to him, I felt a wave of humiliation about who my father was. But then I remembered something. I recalled the talk I'd had with Schneiderman and what he had said about his dad; that he was a difficult man, an opinionated man, and, at times, an impossible one, but he was who he was and Schneiderman was doing his best to love him anyway. Somehow, recalling that conversation and thinking about Schneiderman and the way that he put things, straight out, no frills, no contorted thinking, had a calming effect on me. I felt less tense and I was able to focus again on what King R was saying.

"The name of the game is winning," he pronounced. "In my business every day is a battle. You win or you lose, period. There is no in-between. That is a lesson I learned from my father. For you this message hasn't sunk in yet, am I right? You don't know what real competition is. You haven't had to face it yet, isn't that right?"

"I guess not the way you mean it, anyway."

"That's because you haven't been exposed. Fellows like you live in a make believe world. It's games and fun. You don't know about scrambling for a buck." Sidney Rosenhaus then glanced quickly at me and, perhaps concerned that he had hurt my feelings, he switched to a friendlier tone.

"It's not your fault," he put in, "that's the way kids are today. You are an okay guy. A little soft, maybe, not toughened up yet; too much mother for your own good, but basically okay. My daughter thinks you are okay and so do I. A hell of a lot better than that other creep, anyway. But when we get on the court this afternoon I'm going to try to demolish you, kick your ass good. If I can help it, I won't give you a point. And that is what I expect you to do to me. We'll be in a war. Competition is warfare and don't let anyone tell you different. But once I've taken the prize, that is enough. I don't need to crush a man, break his spirit. In my business if I win a territory, drive the competition out, I'll reach out to the other fellow, offer him a job or a fair payout even if I don't have to. I'll never see a man go hungry."

"That is good of you," I put in.

"It's not good. It is right. That is something my father taught me. You have to do what is right, even if it costs you. Take Lincoln. Do you think Lincoln loved the slaves, that he turned them loose because he cared so much about them? He truth is, Lincoln didn't particularly like black people. If he had his way, he would have shipped then back to Africa—that is how much he loved them. He freed then because he needed them on his side, needed them to win the war, but also because he knew it was the right thing to do. Lincoln had a conscience. That is what touched people. He held the conscience of the whole country in his head. People sensed that and they respected Lincoln for it. That is what made him a great president. He represented the best of us."

At that point we were just crossing into Westchester. King R was still carrying on, now about Jefferson Davis, who he claimed exemplified the flawed conscience of the South. I tried to listen and to respond every few minutes, but the ride had made me drowsy and I had to pinch a thigh at regular intervals to stay awake. A couple of times I nearly drifted off, but whenever I closed my eyes I heard Mel's voice in my ear, rousing me, calling to me to keep alert and reminding me that a great deal, perhaps my whole future, was riding on the way that I handled Sidney Rosenhaus.

The Rye Beach and Tennis Club was a large, sprawling building—it had formerly been a banker's mansion—set on an expanse of lawn that sloped gently toward the Long Island Sound. Off to one side of the entrance, on the front lawn, was a perfectly manicured putting green, and on the other, at a distance of perhaps a hundred yards, an Olympic-size swimming pool and poolside bar decorated in a Caribbean motif, whose specialty was rum punch and other tropical drinks. On the other side of the building, just visible between a pair of maple trees, was the tennis complex, six green composition courts, a pro shop, and leaning against the metal fence that enclosed the area, an assortment of long-handled brushes and rollers.

Sidney Rosenhaus parked the car in the visitors lot and we made our way back to the front entrance. A large porch circled the house, and from it one had a sweeping view of the Sound. Standing there, we could see a cluster of sailboats about a half mile from shore. They were circling each other, getting in position for the club championship race.

Cara's mother wanted to sit for a while and have a drink in the lounge after the long drive up, but King R was impatient to get on the courts.

"I've got a date with Pancho here," he said. "This could be a long match, right Pancho?"

I nodded, "Absolutely, a fight to the finish."

King R then ordered his wife to hold the drinks until later.

"You girls can toast the winner when we come off the court," he said.

Cara was standing alongside her mother. She looked at me, winked, and pantomimed, raising a glass, "to the victor belongs the spoils," she mouthed.

At first it didn't look as though there was going to be much of a match. I started off badly, making one error after another, and King R took the first three games easily. I hadn't played for several weeks and my timing was way off. My big weapon, my first serve, would not come in for me. Seeing this, King R moved in to just a few feet behind the service box and racked up points by taking my weak second serve on a high bounce and smashing his return deep to my backhand. Whenever he scored in that way, King R would grin and point his racket at me in a way that irritated the hell out of me. I now could understand why, as Cara once said, quite a few of his competitors wanted to kill him. King R took the first set, 6-2, without raising a sweat. His strategy was simple; keep the ball on the court and let me make the errors.

"I see you are a little rusty, Pancho," King R said after he hit the winning volley. "I don't want this to be too easy. See if you can give me more of a game."

I said nothing in reply, but I was mad, mad and feeling humiliated all at once. Before the start of the second set I reviewed everything my teacher at the Central Park courts had taught me—he claimed to have given the same advice to Helen Moody when she was starting out. The first thing was to slow down, take my time on my serves, make sure that my feet were aligned correctly, and take care to toss the ball no more than a foot or so over my head. As I got ready to start the second set, I heard my teacher's voice speaking to me, slowly, calmly, repeating these directions to make sure that I got them right.

Across the net King R moved into position to receive my serve. He crouched low, began to bounce on the balls of his feet, and grinned an infuriating, self-satisfied grin.

I went into my serving motion and hit three cannonballs that had King R fanning the air and cursing under his breath.

"What did you do, sneak in a box of Wheaties behind my back," he called over to me after I had taken the first two serving games at love.

"Actually, it's the can of spinach I carry around with me," I called back. And immediately worried that I had been smart-alecky.

I won the second set, 6-1, and would have shut out King R except for the fact that toward the end of the set I lost my touch and double faulted three times.

The match was the best of three. Whoever took the third set would walk off the court the victor, with the right to be toasted by the Rosenhaus ladies who were watching from just outside the fence. We got ourselves ready for the big test. I was feeling revved up—my heart was spinning toward a tachycardia—and in an effort to calm myself, I did a couple of stretches. On the other side of the net, King R made a show of changing racquets, then thumping the strings of his new weapon to test its resiliency.

King R did not like to lose, especially to a kid whom he suspected of *shtupping* his daughter, and he was prepared to employ whatever tactics, psychological or otherwise, that would give him an edge.

The set began slowly, with each of us feeling the other out and probing for weak spots. King R's strategy was unchanged. He played defensively, not going for winners but concentrating on keeping the ball in play and waiting for me to make the inevitable error.

That approach paid off and King R won the first three games by simply outlasting me. Playing the retriever—an indefatigable retriever—was a role he had perfected over many years of making himself into a stonewall. No matter where I placed my shot, he somehow managed to get to the ball and send it back, mostly as infuriating deep lobs that caused me to backpedal and, all too often, flub my return. As he regained the upper hand, King R's good humor returned and he began to tease me, suggesting that I send out for another can of spinach and making similar needling remarks.

I knew that he was trying to rattle me and throw me off my game, a tactic that in my case often worked, but this time the needling caused me to buckle down, hit stronger ground strokes, and switch to a more aggressive net game. Once again my serve started to come in and I ran off four straight games with the loss of only a couple of points.

What happened to me after that I am not sure. Perhaps I was discouraged by King R's tenacity—he refused to fold when I had him on the ropes—perhaps I simply ran out of steam, or possibly without my being aware of it, I was heeding Mel's advice to think about my future and to make sure that I walked off the court a loser. In any case, once I'd taken the lead, my game pretty much fell apart. I double-faulted twice in a row, reverted to total inconsistency on my first serve, and on my second fed King R such puff balls that he had no trouble angling his returns into the corners for clean winners.

Emboldened by fresh success, King R changed tactics and launched a surprise net game. After hitting deep to my backhand, every so often he would chug to the net like a creaking Toonerville Trolley, hold his racquet head high, and make quick work of my floating returns.

In the end, King R rolled over me in the final three games and took the deciding set, 6-4. When it became clear that he was on the way to winning, King R cut out the needling and, instead, surprised me by calling out words of praise on the few occasions when I hit a winner and took a point.

On the way back to the clubhouse, King R put an arm around my shoulder. "You don't have the killer instinct, Pancho," he said "That is your problem. You had me, but you couldn't finish me off. You were too afraid of yourself, too afraid of being a killer. Well, I can tell you one thing, in this life you've got to be able to finish off your opponent. If not, you can be sure that you'll be the one done in. You'll learn, though," he added. "I don't doubt that. I can see that you have the instinct to go for the jugular. You just have to be less afraid of that side of your personality."

The party was a grand affair. There was an incredible buffet, including lobster tails, prime rib, a colorful array of vegetables, some steamed, some roasted, overflowing bowls of salad, and platters of parsley potatoes, all arranged in neat rows. There was an open bar stocked exclusively with top brand liquors, and music was supplied by a five-piece Lester Lanin combo that regularly played the debutante party circuit.

After dinner there were speeches by friends, family, and a few officials from the Parks Department, one of whom called King R the Robert Moses of the city's playgrounds. On the personal side, he was praised as a devoted husband, caring father, and loyal friend. Cara spoke of him as her model, the person she most admired—and most often fought with. That got a laugh, as did Henry, who cited his father as his number one—and only—patron.

When the dancing started I could not wait, finally, to take Cara in my arms. Before I could approach her, however, I had to engineer an escape from Henry, who buttonholed me as soon as dessert was finished, steered me to an adjacent room, and insisted that I settle myself into a large armchair as he recited verse by verse his newest find, a little known Pound poem that, surprisingly, was pro-Semitic. He planned, he said, to write a letter to *The Times* about this literary discovery and offered me the chance, if I was interested, to be co-author. It took pleading an upset stomach to make my getaway, but when I did, Cara was already on the floor with King R. I thought of cutting in, but I heard Mel's voice warning me not to sabotage myself, so I waited.

When she was free—King R was called back to his table to say good-bye to some city officials who were leaving early—Cara came straight to me, pulled me up, and led me to the floor.

We danced non-stop for over an hour. Cara was a graceful dancer. She was a graduate, mandatory for every properly brought up East Side child, of the famous Viola Wolf Dance Academy, at whose monthly socials the boys were required to wear dark suits and carry white gloves, the girls to wear their best party dresses. I held her close and she just eased into my arms. The festive atmosphere suited her and she was in a good mood. And to my surprise—I hadn't expected it given our history—she seemed happy to be with me.

"Thanks for being so good to Sidney," she whispered to me as we held each other and moved slowly to Lanin's rendition of "Always."

"I didn't realize that I was."

"But you have been, absolutely. You've been a saint the way you listen to him carry on. You seem to have endless patience. None of us can listen that way. And, by the way," Cara added, "Sidney was really pleased by the tennis. He appreciates your attitude, that you seem glad to play with him, and that you go all out to make it a real game. You may not realize it, but Sidney is a lonely man."

"I wouldn't have guessed that. He seems so outgoing."

"That's his façade. He knows how to be the glad hander. He's great at that and at playing the big philanthropist, but the fact is he doesn't have real friends. He is surrounded by people who take from him, so he appreciates genuine kindness. And he says that you are a kind man."

"Really? Well I like him and I am glad to play with him."

"He likes you, too, you know."

"Really?"

"Absolutely. He sees something special in you. Maybe you remind him of some part of himself. Anyway, I think you are more of what he wanted in a son."

"I'm flattered."

Cara leaned into me, and placed her face close to mine. "Just keep it up, Jonathan," she whispered, "some very good things could happen."

It was after midnight by the time we got back to Manhattan, but Cara invited me up to the apartment. Her mother objected, saying that it was too late to have a visitor, but Cara insisted.

"Just ten minutes, mother. Jonathan needs a cup of coffee to keep him awake on the way home." In the kitchen we hugged for a few minutes, just stood next to the kitchen table and held one another. Then, taking me by the hand and motioning for silence, Cara led me into her room. As soon as the door was closed, we kissed, a long open-mouthed kiss. Then I cupped my hands on Cara's breasts. In response she leaned into me, thrusting her breasts into my open hands. But when I reached back and began to unzip her dress, she stopped me.

"Not now. The witch will be sounding off at any minute." Sure enough, just seconds later, Cara's mother called out from the hallway.

"Cara, it's nearly one o'clock. Jonathan has been here over a half an hour. It's time for him to go home now."

At that moment Cara's face was nestled in my neck. She lifted it long enough to call back a reply.

"Okay, Mother. He is just leaving." Then she took a step back, made a sassy face, and thumbed her nose at the bedroom door.

We kissed for a few more minutes until Cara whispered that I'd really better get going before the witch came knocking and things heated up. I nodded.

"Okay."

Slowly, still wanting to hold on, we let go of each other. Then, arm in arm, we walked into the hallway. At the front door I reached over, took hold of one of Cara's shoulders, and turned her toward me. In return, she moved in close and lifted her face, and we kissed a final light kiss on the lips.

"To be continued," she said.

On the street I could not calm down. My entire body felt wired, as though something in me had shifted into overdrive and had gotten stuck there. I had not felt so high since the time that I scored an even two-dozen points against Hackley and the *Telegram* featured a photo of me going up to tap in a rebound. I felt an urge to find a phone booth, call Cara, and right then and there arrange our next rendezvous, but I controlled myself. I did not want to press my luck.

Chapter Fifteen

There was bad news and good news. The bad news came first in a phone call from Schneiderman. It was about eight in the evening and I was in my room cramming for an American history test. My mother called to me from the foyer and when I reached the phone she handed it to me without a word. The sour expression on her face let me know who was calling.

"I'm sorry to interrupt," Schneiderman began, "I know you are in the midst of studying for a big exam but I thought you'd want to know what's happened. I got my semester grades today."

"And?"

"It's not good news. I am off the team."

"You are kidding. What are you talking about?"

"Just what I said. I didn't make the cut. My grade average came in under the wire and they are putting me on probation. I flunked Killigan's final and got a D in math for the term. That finished me off. I was actually running a C-minus average, even in Killigan's course, thanks to you. But the D dropped me into purgatory. You know Tillman's rule. Anything below a C-minus means automatic probation. So you'd better fine-tune that radar shot of yours," he added, "you are going to have to carry the team."

I said nothing. I felt as though someone had walked up to me and, suddenly, without warning, delivered a crushing blow to my abdomen. I wanted to say something supportive, something to ease the pain that I knew Schneiderman must be feeling, but I simply could not speak. Of course I should have been prepared. Anyone looking at Schneiderman's record could have predicted that this could happen. But I did not expect it. Somehow I had convinced myself that he was in pretty decent shape, that he had come a long way, and that the work we did together was enough to pull him through. When I felt contained enough to speak, I asked Schneiderman what had happened on the final.

"It was a disaster from the opening bell. The first problem totally threw me. I couldn't get a handle on it and I started to panic.

Once that happened, the game was over. I couldn't think straight and everything fell apart. Everything you taught me flew out the window. I ended up making a mess of the whole exam."

"What rotten luck."

"Luck like that comes to my kind of mind, I'm afraid," Schneiderman replied. "Actually Killigan was pretty decent about the whole thing. No scolding, no put down. He simply wrote on my test booklet that he was sorry to have to fail me, that I had been doing a lot better in the course, but that there was simply no way to give me a passing grade on this exam."

"Shit. I thought you were going to make it, that what we did together put you on the right track."

Schneiderman was quick to reply.

"Look, I hope you are not blaming yourself for this. This was my screw-up. You've been an A-plus tutor, as good as they get. Without you I'd still be down at the bottom of the barrel. I'd never have gotten this far."

"Thanks for saying that, but the fact is you didn't make it. I didn't manage to pull you through."

"Look, what's done is done," Schneiderman said, "There's no point in doing a postmortem at this stage of the game. What you've got to do now is get yourself over to the gym as often as you can and practice that long distance shot of yours. It's going to be crucial. With the kind of pressure defense Trinity is going to throw up, we are going to have to depend on outside shooting."

I heard what Schneiderman said, and for the next week I was pretty good about working on my set shot. I forced myself to stand alone on the court for ten minutes before and after regular practices and fire away from different angles. And my diligence paid off. I was becoming an eagle eye, able to hit consistently from all over the court. But, somehow, my heart wasn't in it.

I was feeling depressed, depressed and strangely empty. What happened with Schneiderman—our losing him—hit me harder than I expected. And I realized how much I had come to rely on him, on his steady presence, his calm leadership, the deft way that he brought the ball up court and directed our offense. I felt as though there was a vacuum, a giant hole right in the center of our team—and in our lives—without Schneiderman. He and Mueller both kept telling me that I could fill it, that if I just played my game I could more than make up for his absence, but I did not feel that way. I felt as though I was being asked to lift a couple of hundred pound weights and even though I was being reassured that I could do it, that I had the requisite strength, I knew the truth; that there was no way that I could meet that challenge. And worse, I found myself feeling resentful toward Schneiderman, angry at him for letting us down, for being a total washout who had not used what I'd spent hours trying to teach him. And as a result of his obtuseness we were now a damaged team, a ship suddenly deprived of its captain that was sent into battle against the toughest outfit in the league, one that—we heard it through the grapevine—had vowed to eat us alive.

"Look it's understandable," Mel said when I told him how I felt. "That is the primitive mind at work. Forget about reality. We know what happened. Schneiderman struck out. Killigan threw him a couple of curves and he couldn't hit them. It's not his fault. He is simply not a curveball hitter. You know that, but your unconscious doesn't. It feels betrayed, let down, screwed over. And you are naturally angry. You worked your butt off with him and he didn't come through for you. But do you know what? Even deeper down, you blame yourself. You think you should have pulled it off. You should have made it happen. If you were any good, or more accurately, if you really wanted him to pass, you would have seen to it. You would not have let him fail. But that kind of attack on yourself is too painful to tolerate so you blame Schneiderman instead. For someone like yourself, this is natural. It is the way the aboriginal mind operates. It casts off blame as fast as it can."

I knew that Mel was right, that what I was experiencing was an old and familiar reaction, a need to blame others for my inability to rescue them, but I couldn't help feeling it just the same. I felt cheated and undermined, as though Schneiderman had deliberately screwed up to make me look bad, to show me up as the inept teacher and lousy friend that, privately, I felt myself to be. I tried to root out such thoughts, to drive them from my mind, but they kept returning. All that day I was in a total funk and at night I barely slept. I was afraid of being visited by bad dreams.

Then, like a lightning bolt, the good news arrived. I heard about it the next morning between my government and English classes. I was standing in a fourth floor corridor with a group of students waiting for the classroom door to open when Schneiderman came dashing up the stairs, pushed through the crowd, and found me.

"Touch me, Jonathan," he ordered, reaching for my hand. "I want to make sure I'm real."

I poked at his chest.

"The front feels pretty solid," I declared. "If you are a fairy, it doesn't show."

"I just want to make sure I'm not dreaming or have gone totally bonkers."

"You don't look a tad crazier than usual. What's up?"

"You'll never guess. A total shocker. Headline news. A first in the history of this venerable institution."

"Let me guess. Well let's see. Harmon pulled off a trade with Finley; you and Buckstein for the stars of their JV badminton team."

"The people at Finley are not that stupid. They know that they can do better than that." I nodded. "Okay then, I've got it. Tillman worked out a package deal with the Giants. You and Durocher both get shipped back to Brooklyn for cash payments of fifty bucks a head."

"Nope. The original trade was a strictly no refund, no return proposition."

"Well then I give up."

"You won't believe this. Killigan called me in this morning, me and this other flunky, Larry Stone."

"Called you in for what, forty lashes?"

"Not a one. Actually the opposite, an olive branch, a stay of execution. Can you believe this? He started out by saying that he'd been thinking about the two of us. At the beginning of the term we both looked like lost causes, pretty hopeless cases. And Killigan told us that he had pretty much written us off. But we surprised him. We both made comebacks—mine thanks to you—and pulled ourselves up to C-minus averages. But then both of us tanked on the final. That made Killigan take a second look at his exam; that and the fact that even the smartest guys didn't do so well, and he realized what a brain twister he'd come up with. So in light of everything, and to acknowledge the progress we'd made, he decided to give the two of us another shot. He's made up another test and he's willing to substitute the grade we get on it for our lowest exam grade of the term. And that includes last week's final."

"That's incredible. Did you make the diagnosis of dementia on the spot?"

"I kept my mouth shut. If it's hardening of the arteries that gets me back on the team, I'm asking no questions. After we kick Trinity's butt, I'll send Killigan an IOU for a neurology consultation."

"Actually I think something else may be going on," I put in.

"What's that?"

"I think you have a secret admirer in Killigan. I caught sight of him in the stands several times this season. My guess is it troubles him that it was his exam that put you on the sidelines."

"At this point I need all the guilty teachers I can get. If this actually works, if I do okay this time around, I'll personally autograph my exam book and dedicate it to Killigan."

"He'll be touched. It will be a memento to remember you by once he hangs up his noose. By the way," I asked, "when is this event taking place?"

"Tomorrow."

"Tomorrow?"

Schneiderman nodded. "There is no choice. Tomorrow is the final day for teachers to make any changes in their grades. As it is, Killigan is going to have to go to Tillman and explain what he's up to. He is breaking rules and Tillman is liable to give him a hard time."

"Killigan knows how to handle Tillman." I said, "that is not going to be the problem. An exam tomorrow is. How in the world are you going to get ready by then?"

"I guess we'll have to pull an all-nighter," Schneiderman replied. He looked at me but I said nothing. This was the first night in weeks that I would not be under the gun. During the exam period I had felt intense pressure to excel. Tillman had made it clear that our first term senior year grades were really important; that they often spelled the difference between getting into an Ivy League school or having to settle for a Colgate or a Lafayette. So every night after practice I forced myself to hit the books until after midnight, and by now I was exhausted. I was looking forward to an evening of shameless indulgence; having a large, and special meal—my mother had promised a post-exam pot roast for the occasion—listening to my favorite radio programs for a couple of hours, and, in bed, reading the brainless paperback mystery that I had bought myself as a rare treat.

But here it was, a miracle; an unimagined opportunity, a chance to raise Schneiderman from the dead. The idea, though, of giving up my one night of relaxation, a night I had been looking forward to for over a month, was giving me a throbbing headache. I knew that I should have responded to Schneiderman's announcement with enthusiasm, enthusiasm and an immediate offer to help get him ready for the exam, but I just couldn't get the words out.

"That is great news," was all that I could manage. "The second time around should be easier. I know that you'll come through this time."

If Schneiderman expected anything more, he gave no sign of being disappointed. While, earlier, he had hinted at the idea of our having a cram session that night, he did not follow up on this and ask for help, and I held back from offering any. I told myself that he would be all right, that since he'd had a taste of a Killigan final he now knew what to expect and, undoubtedly, would do much better this second time around.

I could not fool myself, though. I knew that Schneiderman still had major areas of weakness and that if stumped by one of Killigan's devious brain twisters, he might very well panic and crash again. I attempted to put this thought out of my mind but it kept coming back, and I was unable to concentrate on my classes. My conscience kept after me, nagging at me all morning, and by midday I decided that I had to find Schneiderman and offer to work with him. The thought of my relaxing in bed with a crime novel while Schneiderman sat alone in his room struggling to set up equations—this was still his *bête noir*—while fighting the temptation to throw in the towel and focus instead on the new Stan Kenton album that he had just purchased, was too disruptive to ignore.

I decided that I would catch him that afternoon before basketball practice—he was now helping Mueller as a kind of assistant coach—offer to work with him for as long as needed, and not take no for an answer.

It was a couple of hours later—I recall the clock on the study hall wall read just past eleven—when I was summoned to Tillman's office. Laura, Tillman's secretary, sent a student messenger to fetch me. The note that the kid handed me was terse—and alarming.

"You have an urgent telephone call." I spring out of my seat, hurdled the stairs, and made it to the office in under two minutes. All the way I imagined the worst; my mother run over by a truck on the way home from the A&P, followed by the second worst scenario, my father stricken with a heart attack and, at that very moment, being wheeled into the E.R. at Mt. Sinai.

When I reached the office, I tripped on the threshold and nearly fell into Laura's lap. Fending me off with one hand, she helped right me with the other. Then she handed me the phone.

"It's some young woman," she said, "she says it's urgent." Laura's face was skeptical, as though this might turn out to be a student prank. It was Cara.

"I'm terribly sorry to bother you, Jonathan," she began, "but I had no other way to reach you."

"You scared me. I thought my mother was hit by a Parcel Post van."

"I'm sorry. I didn't mean to frighten you. I just had to reach you."

"What's up?"

"Another invitation from Sidney."

"You got me out of study hall to tell me about an invitation from your father?"

I knew that Laura was listening—she was making faces at what she had heard so far—so I shrugged my shoulders and tried to look puzzled.

"You don't understand," Cara was saying, "this is big. This is no country club lunch. This is big time stuff. The city is honoring Sidney. The mayor is going to present him with a medal It's a black tie affair at the Waldorf, the annual Parks Department fund-raiser. Sidney needs an answer right away."

"Let me get this straight. Your father is inviting me to a black tie dinner in his honor and that is why you called me at school?" Laura's face registered disgust. She was motioning for me to get off the phone. I risked Tillman emerging from his office at any moment and catching me in the act. If he did, there was a good chance that Schneiderman would have company on the bench.

"That's right," Cara said, "Sidney has taken a table. It probably cost him five thousand bucks. The wife of one of his cronies has come down with the flu and so they can't come. He's invited us instead. But he needs an answer now, right away, *toute de suite*. If we can't make it, he's going to call other friends. Everyone wants to be there."

"When is this grand affair?"

"Tonight. That's the whole point. Why do you think I'm calling you now? It's tonight."

A sudden panic took hold of me.

"Tonight?"

"Tonight. T-o-n-i-g-h-t. Get it?"

"Yes, I get it. I'm just floored. I didn't expect anything like this."

"Me neither. But Sidney really wants us to come. He called me especially to tell me to invite you and to get an answer right away. Her said to tell you that he thinks you'll really enjoy the evening, that it is a real opportunity. He wants to introduce you to the mayor and a lot of other muckety-mucks."

"He said that?"

"Just a few minutes ago. He got hold of me as soon as he heard of the cancellation."

"I don't mind him calling me at school," she added, unable to resist getting in a jab.

"And he really wants me to come?"

"What did I say?"

"I'm just surprised. And honored. Really honored. Please tell Sidney I said that. I'd love to come, only...."

"Only what? You have other plans?"

I had to think fast. If Cara knew the truth about Schneiderman's situation and that the makeup exam was to be held the next day, it was likely that she would withdraw the invitation on the grounds that my duty as his friend and tutor was to be at his side at this critical time.

I did not disagree with that. It was precisely for that reason that I'd decided to offer my help. Now, though, that I knew that King R had expressly asked that I be invited, that I was truly wanted, I found myself taken over—possessed—by the idea of being with Cara on this special occasion and of being recognized, not only as her boyfriend, but as part of the Rosenhaus family.

I felt, too, that Cara really wanted me to come. It was not in her nature to be sentimental about her father—she was much more comfortable dueling with him—but I sensed that his being honored in this way meant a lot to her. Clearly she could have arranged to go alone, but I knew she had called me because she wanted me to share this special evening with her. And I did not want to turn her down. I had to admit to myself, too, that the chance to be alone with Cara after the event—her parents had been invited to spend the night at the mayor's residence—had its own appeal.

I had the strongest impulse to simply say yes to Cara, to accept the invitation without another word and not to let this chance—Mel later called it a game changing offer—slip by. But there was Schneiderman. Out of my feeling for him as well as a deep sense of obligation—somehow I felt him to be my responsibility—I had concluded that I needed to be with him, to work alongside him as he faced this critical challenge.

I knew what to do, but I could not do it. I kept thinking about the evening, about being with Cara, about *kibitzing* with King R, and about being part of the Rosenhaus clan. And the more that I pictured that scene, the more I found myself wanting to accept the invitation, to accept it and simply put Schneiderman and his troubles out of mind. I could not do that either, though, and, as a result I felt totally stymied. I could not respond. My head was throbbing and I felt stabbing pain in my abdomen, as though someone had taken a knife and sliced into my intestines. On the other end of the line, Cara was waiting. For several seconds we did not speak. Cara did not break the silence but I could hear a light tapping sound, the sound of her fingers drumming against a tabletop and I knew that she was growing impatient.

"Actually I was planning to work on a paper tonight," I finally said. "I'm really late getting it in."

"I thought you were finished with everything," Cara replied, "that the semester was over."

"It is. But I got so loaded up preparing for exams, I had to take an extension on my final English paper. It's due tomorrow."

"Well that is too bad. It would have been a fun evening. I'll tell Sidney. He'll be disappointed, but it will be okay."

"Will it?"

"Sure. Sidney knows what work means. He respects hard work. He'll understand."

"What about you? Are you very disappointed?"

"I'll live. It would have been a ball, a real putting-on-the-dog evening. I haven't been to one of those in years. But it's okay. I understand. If you can't make it, you can't make it."

"You could go alone."

"I could. And I might. But I think I'd feel awkward. This is the kind of occasion you want to share with someone. It would have been fun to be with you."

"I know," I said. "I feel the same way. I really want to come."

Cara did not reply. There was silence for a moment. Then I began to speak and what I said just came out of me. I had no idea where it came from. The words just appeared in the space between Cara and me, as though put there by some alien creature.

"You know something?" I said, "Screw my English paper. I'm blowing it off. I'll turn it in when I turn it in. If I get marked down, so be it. I'll survive."

"Are you sure?" Cara asked. "This doesn't sound like you."

"It is now. I'm breaking out. The people are breaking their shackles. I've been a grubby grind long enough. I'm sick of it. Tonight sounds like a blast. Let's do it."

"Are you sure? You won't blame me if you get a B on your paper?"

"No recriminations. I'll risk it. Tell Sidney to count us in."

"What about a tux? Do you have one?"

"No, but I have a blue suit direct from the plain pipe racks at Barney's. A gift from my folks."

"Great. You'll meet hizzoner in style."

I was excited, more excited than I'd been since the Giants swept the Dodgers in a twi-night double-header the summer before. I was excited, that is, for about ten minutes. Then the panic returned. I was going to see Schneiderman at practice within the hour and I had to come up with a story that would get me off the hook. Before Cara called, I was going to make him an offer that he could not refuse, one that, among other things, would cause him to think of me as his benefactor, as the guy who saved his ass from the fire. Now I had to lie, to invent some airtight excuse that would deceive Schneiderman and prevent him from seeing me as the traitor, the turncoat that I felt myself to be. I tried to think of what I could tell him, what kind of story to invent, but I could think of nothing that sounded plausible. The idea of something happening to my parents, my mother struck down by a speeding truck or my father a heart attack victim, would not fly.

Schneiderman would quickly discover the truth. The catastrophe clearly had to be more remote—that is, not checkable—but still urgent enough for me to have to cancel. What that might be, I had no idea.

Then I found myself propelled by another urge, an urge to do something for Schneiderman. I felt a need to offer compensation for my defection, something to ease the disappointment that I was inflicting and—not least—to provide Schneiderman with some tools, a makeup kit as it were, that he could use to dig himself out of the hole he was in.

My next subject, Spanish, was held on the third floor. I was making my way to class along the third floor corridor when, all at once, I found myself turning around, breaking through the crowd of students that had formed behind me, and heading for the stairwell. I climbed the stairs to the fourth floor and, breathless, re-entered the study hall and returned to the seat I'd occupied before being summoned to Tillman's office.

In the half dozen years I'd been at Harmon I had rarely cut a class. In all that time I can think of only two occasions when I did so, both because I felt ill prepared to take an exam. But now I was cutting Spanish with hardly a thought as to what I was doing. I was consumed by the idea that I had an urgent task to accomplish and not much time—forty minutes by my watch—to complete it.

I opened my book bag and extracted the algebra text that we used in Killigan's class along with some loose-leaf paper. Then, for the next ten minutes, I took notes on the various kinds of problems—and their solutions—contained in the chapters covered this past semester. The remainder of the time I gave over to composing problems of my own, similar to those in the book, but also including my version of the snares and traps that Killigan stayed up nights inventing.

This was no easy task. To be useful to Schneiderman, I had to supply answers as well as questions and by the time the bell rang ending the period, I had completed only three problems. This necessitated my doing the unthinkable; cutting two classes in a row. Strangely, though—Mel said that I was in what he termed a reparative frenzy—I was totally unconcerned about the offense I was committing. Tillman had a zero tolerance policy for unexcused absences, and I knew that if he found out I ran the risk of being benched alongside Schneiderman, but I gave no thought to that possibility. I was totally focused, like a religious scribe at work, on the task I had set myself. And by the end of the second study hall period I had my full complement of six problems—a mini-test in itself—neatly written out and ready to present to Schneiderman.

My plan was to catch him before practice and present him with the sample problems as an aid to preparing for the makeup. I knew that he would not ask me about working with him. He never asked for favors. That was a kind of credo of his, and I don't think that he expected any favors to be done for him. No doubt he would assume that, for whatever reason, I just wasn't available to tutor him and he would ask no questions. Whether, on his own, he would be able to buckle down and get himself to work on the kinds of problems Killigan was likely to throw at him was another matter. I expected that he would give up after being thrown for a loss a couple of times, but my hope was that out of a feeling of obligation to use the gift I'd given him he would hang in there long enough to tackle the half-dozen sample problems. Schneiderman was that way. He was extremely grateful for anything you did for him and he always tried to reciprocate in some fashion. In this case that meant sitting still long enough to review the material I prepared and, hopefully, to absorb the method of solving problems that I had carefully outlined.

I couldn't keep my mouth shut, though. I suppose it was guilt that took over, or my wish for Schneiderman's approval, but when I found him in the gym I did not do as I intended; say a few encouraging words and hand him the practice problems. I felt a need to explain why I would not be available to work with him, to excuse myself, and to feel reassured that he understood.

Before I knew what was happening, I found myself making up a story, telling Schneiderman that I'd had a call from my father and that his sister, my aunt Min, had suffered a stroke, a serious stroke, and had been taken to a hospital.

"She's critical," I explained. "It's touch and go. The whole family is going to the hospital tonight. I was planning to help you get ready for tomorrow," I added, "but I'm afraid that it won't be possible. I won't be getting home until late. I'm sorry about that."

If Schneiderman saw through me, had any idea that I'd invented this family crisis, he gave no sign of catching on. To the contrary. Having had firsthand experience with serious illness, he was entirely solicitous.

"My God, don't apologize," he said, "of course you have to be with your aunt. She's going to need all the support she can get. And please don't worry about me. I'm going to nail my ass to my chair tonight and review everything we've done."

I handed him the sheets of practice problems that I'd written out.

"I thought these might help," I said. Schneiderman was caught by surprise. Puzzled, he took them, saw what they were, then looked at me.

"When did you do these?"

"After I got the call and realized I wouldn't be available tonight. I had a couple of free periods," I lied.

Schneiderman stood there, leafing through the papers and just shaking his head. Then he reached out, put his arms around me and gave me a hug. I felt the power of his arms, which pressed hard against my rib cage. We remained that way, Schneiderman's arms wrapped around me, for another moment. Then he stepped back and grasped me by the shoulders.

"Thank you," he said.

I couldn't look at him. I simply nodded and touched his arm in response. Then murmuring a quick, "Good luck tomorrow," I headed for the door.

Chapter Sixteen

I went straight home. On the walk to the subway I felt a headache coming on, a dull ache that soon became a throbbing pain behind my eyes as I replayed all that had just happened; the story, the lie I'd invented—and pretty well botched—Schneiderman's efforts to reassure me that he would be all right, and at the end, the way that he reached out to me. Somehow I could not get that last moment out of my mind; Schneiderman's strong arms around me, his expression of thanks.

By the time the subway platform was in sight, the headache had spread to both temples so I stopped in at the candy store at the bottom of the hill, ordered an egg cream, and asked Benny, the owner, if I could borrow two aspirins.

"What's the matter, Johnnie?" he asked, handing me two aspirins from a bottle that he took from under the counter, "You afraid of that Trinity gang? Let me tell you, you boys are the better team. Between you and your pal, Schneiderman, you won't find a better combo in the city. When you two are clicking, no one can touch you, believe you me. The only thing that this Trinity outfit has over you is up here." He pointed a shortened, arthritic finger at his forehead. "It's the Jewish victims thing," he declared. "This is your greatest enemy. Teams like Trinity know it, they sense it, and they play it for all it is worth. Why do you think they hand out crosses as standard equipment to these guys, big silver crosses. imported straight from the Inquisition? To hypnotize Jewish teams, that why. They figure that one look at five of these things coming at you, like five exterminators moving down court, and you fellows will be finished. You will be right back in the ghetto, running from the Cossacks. And it's true," he added, "a lot of good Jewish teams, solid teams, have been licked on the spot. They freeze up and they can't get untracked. They are beaten before they start.

"What you've got to do," Benny went on without pausing for a breath, "is beat these guys at their own game. You've got to out-pray them. Look, first thing you do when you come out of the locker room is form a *Minyan*, go to center court, hold hands, and say a *brucha*. It will help if you light a couple of candles to make it look like *Shabbos*. Believe me, this will scare the bejesus out of those Trinity goys. They won't know what is coming off. They'll think you are putting curse on them with some kind of Hebrew ritual, and they will freak out. You'll give them such a case of the shivers, they'll be throwing air balls all night. They'll be totally knocked off their game."

"That is a hell of an idea, Benny," I said. "I'll pass it on to our coach."

"Tell him it's from me," Benny put in. "Tell him I grew up in a neighborhood where the Irish toughs beat up the Jewish kids every day. Tell him I've been studying psychological warfare my whole life."

"I'll tell Coach Mueller," I promised, "he's very psychologically-minded."

Sitting in a near empty subway car—the only other passenger was a Finley kid with a green pallor who looked as though he was being sent home from the nurse's office—I wondered what to tell my parents, how to explain my sudden appearance hours earlier than usual. My first inclination was to make up another story, concoct a sudden stomachache or something. I was afraid the truth would bring on Gestapo-like grilling by my mother, but I realized I just wasn't up for another lie. Besides, I figured I would need my mother's help to press my suit, which I hadn't worn since a cousin's wedding over a year ago and which I had relegated to a rarely frequented spot somewhere in the back of my closet.

As it turned out, my folks were very good—secretly thrilled I thought—about the whole thing; about the invitation, and about me, their son, being part of such a gala event.

"This Mr. King R must think very well of you to invite you to such a grand affair," my mother said, beginning to fish for information.

"We get on pretty well," I replied.

"And I imagine you must be on very good terms, very friendly with this Cara," she added, continuing to troll.

"We are good friends," I said in as flat a way as possible, hoping to put an end to these excursions. My mother simply shifted ground.

"And the mother also must be favorable," she put in, "otherwise she would put in a veto."

"She tolerates me," I replied. "That's about it. Actually I don't think she likes any of Cara's boyfriends."

"This I understand," my mother said, "when it comes to a child, anyone not family is an *auslander*. But you, they are already treating as one of theirs."

"Not quite," I protested, "but I think they are getting used to me."

When he heard the news, my father came straight to my room. I had put on fresh underwear to prepare for any eventuality—what Cara had told me about having the apartment all to herself had stayed in my mind—and I was about to try on my freshly pressed suit when he appeared, looking excited.

"Is it true what your mother said?" he asked, "that you are going to meet the mayor?"

"That's what they tell me, Dad, I guess we'll see."

"This is a big honor," my father said, "something special. Your whole life you will remember this moment."

"I hope I'll remember a lot more than that," I said.

"Get a picture," my father persisted. "I'd like to have a picture of you shaking hands with the mayor."

'I will if I can," I said, "but I don't think that shaking hands with me presents the photo op the mayor of New York is looking for."

"Well it should," my father lectured, "how often does he get to meet one of the best basketball players in the city?"

I ignored my father's comment and turned to face him directly.

"How do I look?" I asked, trying to strike a cool David Niven pose. My father took a step back and looked me over, head to toe.

"Perfect," he declared, "like a model from *Esquire*."

I could feel my face redden—I'm not sure why—and my father quickly changed the subject. He reached for his wallet and extracted a money clip containing a roll of bills. He withdrew a twenty and held it out to me.

"A night like this, you travel strictly first class," he announced, "you'll need money in your pocket."

I shook my head and held out an arm in protest. "Thanks, Dad," I said, "I really appreciate the offer. But Cara's folks will be taking care of everything."

My father nodded but continued to hold out the money.

"You are their guest," he said. "This I understand, but you still need to have cash on you. Every car needs a spare tire. Suppose on the way home the lady wants to stop off for a drink, a little nightcap. Or she decides you should take a buggy ride around the park. On these special occasions a lot of women get that idea. You have to be prepared. If you've got a spare tire, there's no worry. You'll be ready for anything."

I accepted the twenty and slipped it into my wallet.

"Thanks, Dad," I said, "this is really generous of you."

"Don't mention it," my father said, "just have yourself a grand time."

I was a little late getting out of the house so I did take a cab, something I almost never did. But I heard my father's words in my ears and decided for once to listen to him. And I told myself if there ever was a time to splurge, this was it. Besides, if the Rosenhaus' were out front waiting for me—Cara called to say they would be going downstairs shortly—I did not want to arrive on foot like the plebian West-Sider I felt myself to be. I wanted to arrive in style.

When the cab pulled up, the Rosenhaus' were standing under the building's awning looking for all the world as though they were about to step into the society pages of the *New York Post*. They looked elegant. King R wore a perfectly tailored tuxedo—its style made him look ten pounds lighter—to which were added the festive touches of a plaid bowtie and matching cummerbund. Sarah Rosenhaus was stunning in a satiny—looking forest green gown—I could see now what a beauty she must have been when they married—and Cara, in a pearl white, off-the-shoulder, chiffon dress, was lovelier than I had ever seen her. Catching sight of her as the cab drew to the curb, I had a sudden flash memory; my first glimpse of her at the Ryder game, the angular Hepburn profile, the flowing rust-red hair, the energy and high spirits that seemed to flow from her as she bantered with the Sheepman. And I felt the same rush of excitement that came over me that afternoon when, lining up for the kick-off, I caught sight of that face in the stands.

As I got out of the cab, Cara came forward to meet me and took my arm. We walked that way, arm in arm, the few yards back to where her parents were standing, Sidney Rosenhaus seemed genuinely glad to see me. He extended a hand and when I took it, he placed his other free hand over mine as a gesture of warmth and welcome. Sarah Rosenhaus nodded and offered a thin smile. Cara stood close to me and, again, took my arm as King R signaled to Clarence, the doorman, to summon the limousine— provided by the city as a courtesy to its distinguished guest—that was waiting at the corner.

Clarence opened the door and, standing alongside him, King R then took over and directed us to our places. He ordered me to sit in the back with the ladies while he took the jump seat. As soon as we started out—the limo had barely left the curb—he turned to face the back seat.

"The minute we get there I am taking you two"—he indicated Cara and me—"to see the mayor. He draws a crowd and we don't want to have to stand in line. You'll like him," he continued, now speaking directly to me. "He is a good man. Not that he's always right, far from it. He's stubborn as a jackass. But he's got the right instincts. He's not one of those shyster politicians and, believe me, that counts for a lot. I've mentioned you to him already and he's looking forward to meeting you. He is a basketball fan. He follows all the games, so you don't have to be shy around him. I've noticed that you tend to be on the shy side," King R added, "but I can tell you with the mayor there is no need. He's the kind that goes out of his way to be friendly so don't hesitate to speak right up."

I didn't think that Cara noticed my face redden—we were sitting in near darkness—but at King R's words, she reached over and gave my hand a playful squeeze.

"What about me, Sydney," she called out, "I'm shy too. Aren't you going to give me a pep talk also?" King R chuckled.

"You I don't worry about," he said. "You know how to turn it on. Before the night is over, you'll have the mayor endorsing your Senate campaign."

"Don't be mean," Sarah Rosenhaus piped up.

"Who's being mean?" King R shot back. "I'm complimenting her. You take it as a compliment, right Cara? As far as I'm concerned, a woman who doesn't know how to get around a man is no woman at all. Isn't that right, Jonathan?"

"Absolutely," I replied. I squeezed Cara's hand and she snuggled up against me. "That's just what I always say. If a woman can't get around a guy, she doesn't have what it takes. I couldn't agree with you more."

"Well that's one thing we don't have to worry about with these ladies," Sidney Rosenhaus pronounced. "We have a couple of experts here."

King R was as good as his word. As soon as we arrived at the Waldorf—the dinner was being held in the ballroom which was already packed with guests sipping cocktails and reaching for the circulating hors d'oeuvres—King R led us through the crowd to a spot near the dais where the mayor was in conversation with a giant of a man who looked a lot like Dolf Schayes, NYU's star center, but who turned out to be the Manhattan Borough president. As soon as there was an opening, Sidney Rosenhaus introduced us and for the next five minutes the mayor focused exclusively on Cara and me, as though we were the high rollers he was counting on to refurbish the Central Park Zoo. Clearly, Sidney Rosenhaus had briefed him on the two of us, but even so I was impressed by the amount of information that he had at his fingertips. Right away he asked Cara how her campaign for Council president was going and he commented approvingly on her wish to have a career in politics.

"We need women leaders," he said, with a conviction that sounded genuine. And then he added in a way that, surprisingly, did not seem to embarrass Cara, that he'd heard that one day she would like to run for the Senate. And here, too, he was approving.

"Do you know, we've never had a female senator in this state," he remarked. "And it's about time we did." And spontaneously, and again quite convincingly, he volunteered to help her any way that he could. "When the time comes," he said, putting a hand on Cara's arm, "make sure to contact me. No doubt I'll be out to pasture by then, but I can give you some tips. Politics is about being tactical; tact and tactics. Remember those words. You've got to know the right people and you've got to know how to handle them." Cara, who made a thing of disliking and distrusting politicians, remained silent for a moment. Then, catching herself, she thanked him for his offer.

Hizzoner then turned to me.

"I understand you are a whiz on the basketball court, Jonathan," he began, "one of the best in the city." I shook my head and muttered some denial—I could feel my face redden again—but, undeterred, the mayor persisted in singing my praises.

"They tell me you are another Sid Tannenbaum," He said, "with a deadly set shot, and that you are the mainstay of the Harmon team." I wanted to disagree again and to mention Schneiderman's name, but at that point I could not get out more words so I just stood there with a red face, not meeting the mayor's eyes and feeling myself to be about as articulate as Mortimer Snerd.

"I understand that you've got a championship game coming up," the Mayor went on, continuing to impress me with what he knew, "How do you think Harmon is going to make out?"

"They are going to kick Trinity's butt," Cara put in suddenly, "and this man here"—she jabbed a finger close to my forehead, "is going to be the reason why."

"I have no doubt," the mayor said, and he wished me he best of luck. "I'll make a point of following the game," he added, "and your exploits."

"Thank you, sir," I managed. "I'll do my best."

The mayor nodded and then, responding to an aide's tap on his forearm, turned to another well wisher who, it turned out, was the head of a municipal union. Just before Cara and I headed back into the crowd in search of our table, I overheard the mayor, in his most convincing voice, praising the newcomer's leadership of local 1099.

We found Cara's parents sitting at the head table along with a number of City Hall officials, including the deputy mayor and controller. King R was engaged in lively discussion with the parks commissioner, but when he spotted us he motioned to us to join the group. Two places had been saved for us not far from where the mayor and his wife would sit and I thought that Cara would be pleased by this arrangement. When we took our seats however, ushered to the table by a bosomy female staffer, her face took on a distinctly glum expression.

"Is something wrong?" I asked.

"We'll have to look at him all night," she replied in a half whisper.

"What's wrong with that?"

"It's demoralizing. He's such a goddamn pro."

"So?"

"So I'll never be like that. You saw him in action. He's a master manipulator. Not a wrinkle. Smooth as a baby's ass. In ten minutes he had me in the U.S. Senate and you an all-city superstar. He calls what he does tactics. Do you know what the right name is? *Schmeckling*, that's what. It's a fancy name for *schmeckling*. It comes easy to him. He's a natural at it. I'm not. I could never do that. It's not me. If someone acts like an asshole, I'll call him an asshole. When it comes to those things, I can't keep my mouth shut. So if that is what it takes to make it in politics, I might as well pack it in right now. I couldn't get elected dog catcher."

"You are not being fair to yourself," I protested, trying to calm Cara's agitation. You may not be a *schmeckler*, but you can be damn tactful when you want to be"—*which is not too often*. I thought to myself, but didn't say.

"Look at the way you organize demonstrations," I added. "You are the leader, no question. You get everyone to behave and carry out their assignments. That takes skill—and tact. Plenty of tact. You have to deal with a lot of rough characters, and you get them all to cooperate. You have to know how to talk to people to do that. Besides," I added, "you know how to handle Sidney." This I said in a half whisper so King R, sitting a few feet away, would not hear me. "You can have him eating out of your hand. And that is something even FDR would have trouble doing."

Suddenly Cara leaned over and planted a kiss on my cheek. "You are really sweet, Jonathan," she said. "You are a real sweetheart."

The dinner was surprisingly good; shrimp cocktail, a mixed garden salad, squab with julienne potatoes and string beans, and a delicious parfait for dessert. This was my first taste of squab—ours was a strictly roast chicken family—a fact that I kept to myself for fear of giving the impression—which I was convinced Sara Rosenhaus had of me anyway—of being a West Side rube who, gastronomically speaking, had not ventured beyond the boundaries marked by Zabar's on the south and Barney Greengrass' appetizing emporium a half mile to the north.

The after-dinner speeches, though, were slow torture; one overweight, balding official after another—Cara whispered to me that the mayor must have deliberately surrounded himself with Oliver Hardy types to make himself look good—making the obligatory bows to their boss and to the honored guest of the evening. Carried away by his own oratory, the deputy parks commissioner hailed King R as the angel of the city's playgrounds whose wings touched the lives of thousands of children before finally settling down and launching into an interminable recitation of the remarkable achievements of his own department.

We were an hour and a half into the program—I was fighting sleep and my bottom hurt from non-stop sitting—when Cara quietly edged over toward me.

"Do you want to leave?" she whispered.

"Can we?" I glanced over at King R. He seemed to be listening intently to the speaker, perhaps in reciprocity for the kudos he had received.

"I don't want to offend your father," I said.

"Wait here," Cara replied, "I'll speak to him."

Cara got up from her chair and very quietly made her way to where King R was sitting. Coming up behind him, she whispered into his ear. A half minute later she inched her way back toward me.

"It's okay," she said. "we can go. Sidney said he'd take off himself if he could. And we can have the limousine. He and Sarah are leaving with the mayor."

At that point I felt exhausted just from the effort of trying to stay awake, but the idea of snuggling with Cara in the back seat of a limousine seemed just the right prescription to revive me.

"Terrific," I said. "I could definitely use some private time with you."

Cara nodded, "I was thinking the same thing."

In the limo, Cara leaned up against me and rested her head on my shoulder. For most of the way home she was quiet—unusual for her—and seemed preoccupied with something. I felt that she did not want to talk, so, until we were close to home, I said nothing. I just let her rest. But there was something about her prolonged silence that troubled me and made me anxious.

"Is anything wrong?" I finally asked.

"I'll tell you later," Cara half whispered and again fell silent. Her reply increased my anxiety. In my experience, pretty much limited, it's true, to transactions with Myra Herz, an evasion like that usually spelled trouble. It foreshadowed a later announcement, always spoken with deliberate gravity, that we needed to break up; that she had thought things over and had concluded that we were incompatible; that a Gemini and a Cancer—she was the former, I the latter, simply could not mix. This, she would add, was confirmed by the fact that she no longer felt passionate when we kissed, a sure sign that we were not meant for each other.

In Myra's case this announcement was usually made after I had not called her for a week or if, as sometimes happened, I had to break a date. Most often a determined effort on my part to call more often, to take her to a movie she wanted to see, and, if she remained stubbornly intransigent, to surprise her with a hand delivered bouquet of flowers, repaired the damage and caused her to call the calling off, off, as the song goes.

With Cara, though, I knew things would be different. If, for some reason, she was put off by something I did, or something about me—I was fearful that my West Side status, or lack of status, had at

last come home to roost—that would be it. There would be no
changing Cara's mind, no way to assuage her and get back into her
good graces. My fate would be sealed. I would end up sharing a
pasture with the Sheepman. That is just the way Cara was.

After some time, perhaps five minutes, she remained silent. She
It was with a good deal of anxiety, then—I could feel my heart
moving into tachycardia range—that I followed Cara into the
apartment.

For some time, perhaps five minutes, she remained silent. She
simply flung herself onto a living room armchair and continued to look
preoccupied. I sat down across from her on a matching chair and
waited. I did not understand what had brought on this mood, but I
sensed that it was best not to ask. There was something that radiated
from Cara, a tenseness that felt vaguely menacing, that caused me to
give her space. I could sense anger in her silence and I was afraid, if I
spoke—or misspoke—that she would lash out at me.

After a couple of more minutes, Cara's body seemed to relax a
bit, but she clearly remained troubled by something. Finally she
spoke.

"What did you think of tonight?" she asked.

"It was okay," I replied, trying to guess what she was getting
at. "Kind of fun. It was interesting to meet the mayor and all the big
muckety-mucks and to see how they operate. It was an education."

"Did it make you think about anything?"

"Like what?"

"I don't know. What you want to do with your life? What is
important to you?"

"Not really. Most of the time when I was awake, I was
thinking about sinking set shots and beating the pants off Trinity.
What did you have in mind?"

"I don't know. I suppose I wondered if you could see yourself in
Sidney's shoes twenty years from now."

"Not likely. Playgrounds aren't my thing. Seesaws make me
sick to my stomach and I'm scared to death of the monkey bars.
Besides, when it comes to good works, I'm no Sidney Rosenhaus. The
health of New York City is not something I worry about. It doesn't
keep me up nights. As for kids, as far as I'm concerned, if they have to

use a little elbow grease because their swings are a bit rusty, that's okay with me. I don't consider that a tragedy." As soon as I had spoken those words, I felt anxious. I was afraid that I had come across as a callous Republican. If Cara thought that, she kept her feelings to herself.

"Well, if you are not into improving where you live, what are you into?" she persisted. "How are you going to give something back?"

"Frankly, I'm not at the giving back stage," I replied. "I'm still trying to figure out how I am going to live my own life."

"Well how *are* you going to live your life," Cara asked. "What are you planning to do with yourself?"

Her voice had begun to take on a challenging tone.

"Well now that you ask," I said in as light a way as I could manage, "I was thinking of applying for prince of the dinette division. I understand there is an opening." Cara answered without smiling.

"It's a possibility," she said. "If I talk to Sidney, it probably could be arranged. But tell me something," she added, "is this what you really want? Are you sure of that?"

Cara seemed to read my mind. The truth is, I was totally confused—and anxious—about my future. I couldn't deny that landing a berth with Sidney Rosenhaus had lot of appeal—King R seemed to take care of everybody—but the very word, business, had become anathema to me, I just couldn't imagine myself in business. That was my father's life, and to me it spelled only trouble.

"I don't know what I want," I said. Somehow Cara's question—and the whole evening—had unleashed something in me and I wanted to share my worries with her. "The only thing I know is that I don't want to end up like my father, working six days a week, always short of cash, struggling just to meet the payroll, and half the time having to hustle to keep a step ahead of the IRS. It's not a life."

"Sounds horrible. Has it always been like that?"

"For as long as I can remember. But if you ask my father, he'll tell you a different story. As far as he is concerned, he's had cash flow problems, that's all, and they are going to get straightened out in short order. For him, short order can mean a week, a month, a year.

It depends on his mood. But after a while, you get the message. Short order is a mythical time. It never comes."

"How sad. Can't you talk with him, help him to see what is really going on?"

"You don't know my father. Reality is not his bag. His reality is what he invents. He's very creative that way."

"And you've had enough of that kind of creativity, isn't that it? You want the opposite, to know where your next paycheck is coming from." There was something in Cara's voice that put me on the defensive, that sounded a bit condescending, but I let it pass.

"I guess so. I've seen enough tight rope walking for a while. I'll stick with terra firma. So if peddling dinettes isn't my thing, it will probably be law school for me. It's respectable, it's a living, and it will let my mother sleep nights. What about you?" I asked. This focus on me was making me uncomfortable. I felt that Cara was sizing me up as mate material and I wanted to get out of the spotlight. "Are you going to take the mayor up on his offer?"

"That's just it." Cara said. "What went on tonight really threw me. Just watching that man at work, the way he played us, it made me sick to my stomach. I nearly barfed on the spot. If that is what I'd have to do to get elected, I'll opt out right now. You saw it for yourself. It's all about money, money and kissing ass." Cara got to her feet, took a few steps, and stood over me. She was agitated and getting more so by the minute.

"Why do you think the mayor of New York City was all over us, doing his tushy-kissing number on two kids from nowhere?" she demanded. She did not wait for an answer. "Because of Sidney Rosenhaus, that's why. And not Sidney Rosenhaus, the playground maven. It is King R, the deep pockets contributor, that he was sucking up to. He probably figured that playing up to us for ten minutes was worth a good twenty-five thousand. And he's right. He'll get Sidney to cough up at least that much. I don't want to live that way," she added. "Sucking up to a bunch of fat cats so they'll reach for their wallets at the end of my act. And where does all of this get you anyway?" she asked. "No matter how successful you are, no matter how much money there is in your coffers, you are going to feel bankrupt. You are going to feel like a whore. Look, these people aren't in the business of filling war chests for nothing. They want their favors. They want you to suck their dicks. I'm not into that game."

I felt a sudden alarm when I heard that. Was this an indirect reference to me and my prospects for the evening? I decided to play it cool, to ignore Cara's last remark, and to await developments.

"I know what you mean," I said, "personally I felt the same way about the show hizzoner put on, but if you want to be a winner, that's the price you have to pay. There is no other way."

"Except to opt out, to refuse to play." Cara's words surprised me. I had never before heard her talk this way. Quitting was not her thing.

"You can't do that," I said, "you were born a politician. You've wanted to be in politics since you were in diapers, and probably before that. You are going to be New York's first lady senator. It's in the cards."

"Well, the cards are going to have to be shuffled," she replied, "I never realized what a dirty game I'd have to play. I'm going to drop out, forget the whole thing."

"What would you do instead?"

"An honest job. Teaching, maybe, or working at the UN; or, if I get adventurous, maybe doing a stint with a relief agency in Africa. After a few years I'll probably get married to some lawyer and end up doing my politicking at the local PTA."

"Somehow that doesn't sound like you," I said. "It's not a fit. You'd end up running demos in the schoolyards and putting the kids on picket lines. Besides, you can't quit politics now. The country is headed for tough days. We are going to need a brain like you in the Senate. If we were married," I added as a final note, "I wouldn't let you quit. It would be an injustice to the people."

While she was talking, Cara's agitation had propelled her to move. She walked the length of the living room a couple of times. Now she stopped, came toward me, and kissed me lightly on the lips.

"Thanks," she said. "I needed to hear that."

Then she took a step back and, reaching out, cupped my face between her hands.

"By the way," she said, "that could happen."

"What?"

"You know, the husband bit. You are looking as though you could fit the part."

"Really?"

"Absolutely. Didn't you say you would end up in law school?"

"Uh huh."

"And didn't I say that I'd end up marrying a lawyer?"

"You did."

"Well, there you go. A perfect match. In fact, two perfect matches. You and me, and you and Sidney. Just think how thrilled he'll be. He'll have a son, a son-in-law, and a tennis partner he can beat the pants off all rolled into one. Even if you don't do the dinettes, he'll probably put you on the board of directors and throw in an apartment as a wedding present."

"Where?"

"Either down the street or around the corner. Sidney likes his family close."

"Makes sense. That way when we get the call, we can be ready to head out to the Hamptons in a matter of seconds."

"You've got it. You are really getting to know the man. Well, how does it all sound?"

"Terrific. You, me and King R. What more could a man want? You've got to promise me one thing, though, no quitting, no copping out, and no PTA. You go for the brass ring."

"Okay. If you say so. I wouldn't want to disappoint my husband. Especially since he's already laid out money for a campaign button. But look, we can't get married cold," Cara added with much concern, "we need out try things out first."

"What did you have in mind?"

"Guess."

Before I could answer, Cara threw herself on me. She was strong, and for an instant I felt as though I'd been hit by one of Schneiderman's rocket strikes. The impact knocked me backwards and onto a red velvet couch that stood just behind me. Cara landed on top of me and pressed her mouth against mine, a long smothering kiss that ended only when I needed to come up for air. Then we lay side by side, holding each other, giving each other small kisses, periodically breaking into giggles, and not needing to speak. Our bodies were pressed up against the back of the couch and my arm was pinned beneath me. With some maneuvering I was able to free it and I caressed Cara's breasts and ran my hand along her thighs. Then I reached under her dress and stroked her genital area through her panties, trying to locate her clitoris so that I could exert steady pressure on it as Mel had instructed me to do. At first I couldn't seem to find it, the little button, as Mel called it, and I worried that in Cara's mind my clumsiness as a lover would earn me no better than a D, or Buckstein-like, rating. When, though, after a few panic filled minutes, Cara began to emit soft moaning sounds, I figured I was in the right place.

Things were developing well—I felt on course—when, suddenly, Cara halted the proceedings. She reached down, moved my hand off her panties, and pressed her body against mine.

"Let's go slowly," she said, "It's a lot better that way. Right now we need some pillow talk."

At that point we'd been on the couch for close to an hour and that seemed slow enough—in fact, agonizingly slow—to me. Besides, it seemed to me that Cara had things backwards. As far as I knew, pillow talk came after, not before the deed. That's when the lovers were supposed to lay back, relax, and share a cigarette. I had brought a pack of Lucky Strikes just for that purpose. I said nothing, though. I did not want to risk unsettling Cara and precipitating one of her moods.

"Talk to me," Cara whispered.

"About what?"

"About you. Tell me your dreams."

"Do you want to turn this into a porno flick?"

"I mean your daydreams. Your hopes and wishes. I want to know who you really are."

"You mean you prefer to make love to Sid Tannenbaum?"

Cara smiled. "He's your real love, isn't he? That's my true competition."

"Well he's got a better outside shot than you do."

"Well, then, I'll just have to practice I couldn't stand being beaten out by another Sidney. Will you teach me so that I can compete with this Mr. Tannenbaum—or is the name really Schneiderman?"

I felt a bolt, a sudden shock pass through me when Cara mentioned Schneiderman's name. I didn't know what she meant, what she was getting at—I suspected there was a lot on her mind about Schneiderman and me—but I didn't want to get into any of it, so I deliberately ignored what she had said.

"After the Trinity game I'm all yours. I promise we can practice anything you like."

"That's what is really on your mind, isn't it?" Cara replied. "That's all you can really think about." She was smiling, but she sounded disappointed. "Well, what do you think? Are you going to win? Can you beat those guys?"

"They are tough," I said. "A really tough outfit, but if we play our best, we've got a shot."

"Without Schneiderman?"

The sound of his name again—and Cara mentioning him twice in the space of a couple of minutes—had an unnerving effect on me. I wondered why she kept bringing Schneiderman up, but it seemed best not to ask.

An image suddenly arose in my mind, a picture of Schneiderman sitting at his desk, struggling with the problems I gave him. Whether it caused me to say what I did, I do not know. Mel claimed that the *dybbuk* in charge of Jewish consciences had snuck upon me—but I found myself telling Cara the truth, telling her all about what was happening.

"Schneiderman may get to play after all," I said. "Things have changed. There is a real possibility."

"What are you talking about? I thought he was on probation."

"He is. He is supposed to be. But there's been a reprieve. It's a miracle. He has a second chance. I can't believe it myself." I explained what Killigan had done and his offer of a second exam, with the implied promise that if Schneiderman passed the makeup, he'd pass the course. Then he'd be off probation.

"That's incredible," Cara replied. "Unbelievable. At Harmon? Tight ass Harmon? There has got to be a mistake. Either that, or this Killigan character has gone off the deep end."

"That's what I thought, but apparently he is no more crazy than usual. Personally, I think he has a thing for Schneiderman. But, hey, if Killigan gets off by playing the savior and pulling Schneiderman back from the brink, that's okay with me. We want him back anyway we can get him."

"Any algebra exam, makeup or not, is going to be a big hurdle for Stan," Cara put in, sounding a realistic, but deflating note. "When is this exam anyway?"

"Tomorrow morning."

"Tomorrow? A few hours from now? That's impossible."

"Impossible or not, that's when it is. That's when it has to be. Tomorrow is the last day grades can be changed. Killigan has to get the change in by noon or the whole thing is *kaput*."

"But that is ridiculous. There is no way that on his own Stan Schneiderman has a ghost of a chance of passing another version of the exam he just flunked. You know Schneiderman. You are his math tutor, for God's sake. You know how brain dead he is when it comes to numbers. Half the time he still has trouble with arithmetic. If he doesn't memorize an equation cold, he'll get it all wrong. He'll invent something that looks like a diagram of a quarterback sneak. To have any chance at all, he'd need somebody right there, at his side, working with him right up to the opening bell."

"You haven't seen him recently," I replied as evenly as I could. "He's not that bad. I've spent a lot of time helping him, and in the last couple of months he has come a long way. He's much better than he was. Anyway, tonight there was no choice. I had to come with you guys so I did what I could. I gave him half a dozen practice problems to work on. I think he's got a good shot at passing."

Maybe it was the way I put it, but hearing this, Cara's voice took on an edge.

"You had to come with us guys, is that what you said?"

"You invited me to a dinner honoring your father. That is no small matter. You called me at school about it. You wouldn't have done that unless you really wanted me to come with you. You also made it very clear that your father wanted me to be there. With that kind of invitation, there was no way I could turn it down."

"But didn't you hear me say that if you were busy, if you already had other plans, that would be all right; that Sidney would understand completely? And that I would, too?"

"I heard you, and I appreciate your not wanting to pressure me, but I knew that you really wanted to go, that you would have been very unhappy if you had missed this special night. And I didn't want you to be disappointed."

"So is that why you did not mention Schneiderman's situation and the exam tomorrow? Because you didn't want to make me feel bad for making you an offer you could not refuse, for luring you away from what you had your heart set on doing; sitting in a room all night tutoring Stanley Schneiderman for a makeup exam he is likely to fail anyway? Or is the actual truth that it was you who really wanted to be there tonight? Look, I understand. It was a chance to get closer to Sidney, to show him that you really care. And it was an opportunity to meet some big players in the city, people with influence. Who wouldn't be tempted? But you had an obligation."

Cara was putting me on the defensive, stirring guilt that I was trying to keep under wraps. And she wasn't getting the whole story.

"Of course the chance to be with you, and to share this special occasion with Sidney and the family was tremendously appealing. Frankly, I felt flattered that you asked me. I had never been to an affair like this, so I thought it might be fun. But if I didn't think you really wanted to go, that it was important to you to be there when your father was being honored and that if I refused the invitation you would have been terribly disappointed, I would have declined. And I would have told you why."

Cara shook her head.

"Jonathan, you are not being honest with yourself. You are rationalizing. I think you know me. And you know that the one thing I value is honesty. I try to be honest with people and I expect them to be honest with me. I hate deception of any kind, especially self-deception. It is the most dangerous kind of dishonesty. The fact is, you knew very well that if you had told me the truth I would have withdrawn the invitation on the spot, regardless of what I personally wanted. That would have made no difference.   As far as I am concerned, when a friend has a need, that is the number one priority. That is what counts, and all that counts. You know that without help Stan is all over the place. He can't concentrate for more than ten minutes at a time, and when he does he gets confused.   His mind begins to transpose numbers and letters and things get jumbled up pretty fast. Whenever I've worked with him that problem comes up front and center. It arises right off the bat. But you know that. And you know that to make headway he needs someone to sit with him and help straighten things out. So did you really think that giving him a bunch of problems and leaving him alone to struggle with them was really going to be helpful? Or was that just your way of trying to ease your conscience? To buy it off, so it wouldn't trouble you when you were sipping champagne at the Waldorf?"

"You are being totally unfair," I retorted. "You are building a case without knowing the truth. The fact is, if you hadn't pressured me the way you did, telling me that Sidney thought of us first, that he really wanted us to come, and that he needed an answer right away, I wouldn't have agreed. You can believe that or not as you choose. And by the way, maybe it's really you who is not looking at yourself. Maybe that is something you need to do, too."

For a moment, Cara said nothing. Then she shook her head.

"You just don't get it, do you, Jonathan? You don't see what you've done. I don't think you have any idea of how ambitious you are, how you fool yourself into thinking that you are this sweet, considerate fellow. I guess you fooled me, too. Well, I hope that your friend, Stanley, passes that exam tomorrow. Otherwise you—even you—may have to deal with a hell of a lot of guilt."

I protested, said again that she was being unfair, that what happened tonight was a two-way street and that we needed to talk about that, but she cut me off.

"I really don't want to talk about this anymore," she announced. "There is no point."

I tried to tell her that we needed to talk about it, that it was important, that we needed to straighten this thing out, but she made a quick waving motion in front of her face like a fight referee signaling that the end had come.

"I said I didn't want to talk about it." Her voice was firm, angry. "I'm finished."

Then she turned away, and with a short nod of her head, pointed toward the door.

"You'd better leave," she said, "I'm tired. I want to go to bed." Then, without another word, she started out of the room. As she reached the foyer, she turned around to face me.

"And by the way, too bad you didn't score tonight. With my parents away, this was your golden opportunity, wasn't it? Or are you going to tell me that I have it all wrong, that this wasn't part of your calculations?" Without waiting for an answer, she walked quickly to a side door that led to the rest of the apartment, slipped inside, and closed the door behind her. I thought of following her, yelling at her that she had it all wrong, that she didn't understand the bind I'd been in, but I realized that it was no use. Once Cara had a fixed idea, there was no reaching her. So I walked out.

At that point, my headache had returned full blast, my eyesight had turned blurry, and in the dim light of the hallway I could barely make out the elevator bank. I pressed the call button, but the elevator did not appear quickly and I felt too agitated to wait. I headed for the stairwell and, walking like a misprogrammed robot, made my way down the ten flights. Reaching the lobby, I appeared suddenly through the rarely used door to the stairs. The two doormen on duty stared at me as though I was an intruder who somehow had gotten into the building. And one of them, a burly fellow, started toward me, but then Clarence recognized me and called him off. I didn't look at them. I looked straight ahead and kept walking. Outside, the weather had turned chilly. My head was throbbing and my vision remained blurry. I felt as though I had been smashed in the back of the head with a two-by-four, and after walking just a block, felt a vague nausea coming on. But I kept walking, feeling dizzy and slightly sick to my stomach, until I got home. On the way, I tried to puzzle things out, to take in all that had happened, but my mind wouldn't cooperate. The throbbing pain in my head was just too great and all I could think about was taking to my bed.

Chapter Seventeen

As soon as I got home I went to the medicine chest and took two aspirin immediately followed by a double Alka Seltzer, a remedy for intractable aggravation passed on to me by Mitch Sternheim, who first used it during an economic slump when sales of the Turkish cigarettes that he kept in his locker hit an all-time low. I also tried it—with some success—after Myra Herz got mad at me during a petting session, abruptly terminated the hand job she was giving me, and precipitated a painful case of blue balls.

Although I was exhausted—what happened with Cara had totally drained me—I slept fitfully. It was just after three a.m. when I awoke with palpitations and the thought that it might really be over; that Cara might have put me out to pasture with the Sheepman. Out of pure agitation, I dialed Mel's number. I felt guilty waking him at that hour, but he had let it be known—this was the physician in him—that he was on twenty-four hour call for emergencies, so I knew that it would be all right.

When he heard the story, Mel responded in a way unheard of for him. He was silent. When he finally spoke, there was uncertainty in his voice.

"This is a tough one, Jonathan," he said. "This is not going to be an easy fix. Ordinarily our Miss Finley is very forgiving. If you hurt her and apologize, she is okay with that. She doesn't hold grudges. But injuring a friend is different. That she is not going to forgive so easily. That violates one of her principles. Disloyalty to a friend really goes against her. We could be facing a long road back."

Mel's words threw me. I could usually count on him to be upbeat, to come up with a strategy, even a cockamamie one, that inspired hope.

"So I'm washed up," I said.

"Not necessarily. No need to dig out Myra's number yet. I simply said that it would be a long haul. If you recite enough *mea culpas*, she'll probably come around."

Mel's first recommendation was to do nothing; to wait—and pray.

"If Schneiderman comes through, you are half way home. What you did won't seem so self-serving after all. Cara will have to acknowledge that despite everything, you managed to save the day. That should help a lot."

There wasn't much comfort in Mel's words. Although I continued to hope against hope that Schneiderman would pull it off— after I hung up the phone I even threw up a prayer to whomever was up there—I couldn't quite get myself to believe that it would happen. And I was upset, also, by Mel's referring to me as self-serving. Even he, who fancied himself a psychologist, obviously did not appreciate what I was up against, how incredibly difficult the whole situation was for me.

"Look, don't take offense," Mel replied when I called him on what he'd said. "I'm not blaming you. Far from it. You had an offer that was almost impossible to refuse. A leg up with King R and a night with Cara Rosenhaus; that's a combination even Rabbi Joshua— the name Mel insisted on using for Jesus—would have had trouble turning down."

Later that morning Mel called back.

"I've been thinking," he said, "repentance is your best shot. Repentance and confession. It's time to haul out the old falling on your sword routine. But you have to do it the right way. If you're not convincing, you'll be out there sharing pastureland with the Sheepman."

"*Hara-kiri*'s not my thing," I replied. "My mother says I have a sensitive stomach. Besides, this wasn't just my doing. This whole business was very much a two-way street."

"You know that and I know that, but in Miss Finley's mind you are a culprit who has turned on a friend. There is no question that she's got you in the turncoat category, right up there with Benedict Arnold, the quisling Petain, and Tokyo Rose. Your only chance to reverse things is to own up to your part, take responsibility for what you've done, and don't try to fudge it. A touch of self-castigation wouldn't hurt either. But whatever you do, you can't phony it up. She'll see right through you."

"I get what you're saying," I replied, "and you're probably right, but I can't do it. I am not going to be the fall guy here and take all the blame. Cara was the one who called. She came to me, she and her father, with this gilt-edged invitation, this once in a lifetime opportunity to be present at the coronation when Sidney is crowned king of the swing set. She came bearing this big red apple and now she condemns me for taking a bite. Little miss innocent over there refuses to look at herself. As far as she is concerned, she's done nothing. She's set herself up as judge and jury and I'm the one up on charges. Well if she thinks I am going to buy that scenario and plead guilty, she has another think coming."

For a moment there was silence on the phone. Then Mel replied.

"What you say is true," he responded. "All true. The lady definitely tempted you. She came with an apple all right, a big shiny apple, and it's true she held it right under your nose. But you still could have told her no thanks; that you'd love a bite but that apples give you hives. In a situation like that, allergies can come in handy."

The news came through the next morning. Schneiderman called to tell me.

"It didn't work out," he announced, "and I didn't even come that close. I got two points lower than first time. I'm sorry I let you down."

I felt a sudden numbing of my body and, at the same time, a throbbing sensation in my chest.

"What happened?"

"I screwed up about halfway through. I was fine until then. The practice problems you gave me were great. They really set me up for the first half. Everything looked familiar and I was on a roll. Then old Satchel Page over there started pitching curves; curves and change ups; he threw in problems I'd never seen before. I got confused and I guess I clutched. Anyway, the last half of the exam was a big zero. I kept throwing up air balls and hitting nothing. It was a total disaster. Afterwards, Killigan just handed me back my test book and shook his head."

"He didn't say anything?"

"Nope. The look said it all. He went out on a limb for me and I let him down. He was not happy."

"You didn't let anyone down," I said. "You tried your best. I feel like I'm the one who let you down. I should have been with you the night before."

"For God's sake, don't blame yourself, Jonathan. What you did was an enormous help. I can't imagine what I would have done without those sample problems. They kept me in the game, at least for a while. Besides, you had no choice; not when there's a crisis in the family. By the way, how is your aunt doing?"

I froze and said nothing, managing only a noncommittal sound. With all that had happened, I'd forgotten about Aunt Min. Schneiderman followed up quickly.

"I mean she made it, didn't she?"

I grunted. "She's hanging in there."

"Is she still critical?" I made another grunt-like sound.

"So you'll be at the hospital most of the day," he declared. "I know what it's like when someone is that sick. You want to be with them as much as possible. I couldn't have taken it if something had happened to Evie and I wasn't there. Do you want me to let Mueller know that you won't be at practice again today? "

"Thanks," I said. "It's awfully good of you to offer, but you know what? My folks are going to be at the hospital all day so I can spare a few hours right now. I don't want to let the guys down." I didn't let on what I also wanted to say; that I felt furious at Schneiderman for letting me down; furious that he turned out to be a total washout who managed to trash every effort I'd made to help him.

"Are you sure?" Schneiderman asked. "It's going to be tough on you if anything happens."

"I know," I said, "but I'm going to have to take a chance."

"Okay, but don't forget that we are talking about a game. No matter what happens this season, in the end it's about a game. It's not about real suffering. If I were you, I'd think pretty hard about the choice I was making."

After that conversation—when it came to hospitals, illness and such, Schneiderman had a way of waxing philosophical—I wanted to call Mel and tell him what trouble I was in, but that would have meant confessing the mad story I'd invented. I was frankly too embarrassed, and too angry at myself for concocting such a lie to make the call. Besides, I was afraid that he would advise me to come clean, confess the truth, and make a fresh start with Schneiderman— probably good advice—but not something I could do and still face him.

The only course I could think of was to keep the story going, at least for a few more days, until I could announce—I had already practiced a tone of surprised relief—that a miracle had occurred, that my aunt had not only survived but that she had made a remarkable recovery; so much so that the doctors were sending her home that very day.

That strategy, I figured, would get me off the hook but, in fact, it proved a lot more difficult to pull off than I imagined. For Schneiderman, hearing about my aunt must have awakened all his feelings about his sister and the regular pilgrimages he made to the hospital. And he must have assumed that I was as committed as he was to making hospital visits. Not a day went by that he did not ask about my aunt and whether I had been at the hospital. And since he was well schooled in such matters, he also inquired about her diagnosis, about the medications she was taking, and about the nursing care that she was receiving.

I could only respond with generalities, generalities and vagueness—which, I think, made him suspicious. And on a couple of occasions I made tell-tale slips, such as complaining of having to work all night on an overdue *Macbeth* paper while forgetting that in an earlier conversation I had made a point of mentioning that I'd spent the evening visiting my aunt.

Schneiderman never called me on these slips and I was never sure whether or not they registered—or what he knew. He gave no sign of doubting me, but when I made these kinds of mistakes he would give me a look—a kind of puzzled stare—that made me wonder just what he had picked up and what he was keeping to himself.

My worst fear, though, one that kept me up nights, was that he would spill the beans to Cara. I had no doubt that when she heard that Schneiderman had flunked the makeup, she had called him, as she had done before, to express sympathy and to offer help. Doubtless they talked about what happened, and I worried that in recounting everything Schneiderman might have told her about my aunt and the excuse I gave him. That, I knew, would finish me off. There was no way that Cara would forgive a lie of that magnitude. That would put me right up there with the forked-tongued Senator Bilbo on her black list; a place from which there was no possibility of redemption.

I comforted myself, though, with the thought that such a scenario, while possible—Cara could wheedle information out of a deaf mute—was unlikely. Schneiderman did not strike me as a gossip. I had never heard him pass on a rumor about anyone. He had once told me, in fact, that one of the qualities he most admired in his father was his dad's ability to keep his own counsel. Marvin Schneiderman never talked about a case, not even the sensational ones that made headlines. And I found myself hoping against hope that in this respect Schneiderman took after his old man. I was relying on this being so because the strategy I was developing depended on Cara knowing nothing of the story I'd invented. That was my only chance, I figured, of being recalled from the dead.

At night, in bed, I was assailed by endless thoughts of Cara; what she was doing, what mood she was in, whether she had started to see someone else—horrific images of the Sheepman making a comeback tortured me—that made sleep impossible. And when I did drop off, the few hours of shut eye I managed to get were filled with dreams of being with Cara in a ballroom—Mel interpreted this as a wish to return to the golden moments of the Waldorf evening—holding her in my arms, kissing her and, finally, our making love on a plush Rosenhaus sofa that conveniently dropped from the ceiling at precisely the right moment.

Then all the next day my head would be filled with ways to make contact with Cara; calling her, sending a telegram, hiring a messenger to deliver a handcrafted note of apology, any means of breaking a silence that was becoming unbearable.

The only relief I got from this bombardment was during basketball practice and that because the tumult taking place there filled my head to capacity.

When Schneiderman broke the news to him, Mueller fell apart. After hearing the first time that Schneiderman was headed for probation, he had sunk into a near psychotic depression—he was mute for two days—but came alive, in fact soared into a near-manic state, when he learned of Killigan's offer of a makeup. Somehow Mueller managed then to convince himself that all would be well, that Schneiderman would breeze through the second time around, and his key player, our team's anchor, would be available to carry out his plan of booby-trapping an overconfident Trinity team.

Now, however, crushed by the realization that Schneiderman was irretrievably lost, he again plunged to the depths. This time, however, what brought him back and once more set him soaring was a scheme that his brain had managed to concoct in some kind of self-righting maneuver.

Mueller's idea, given Trinity's superior height—they had a couple of inches on us at almost every position—was to outrun them.

"We'll asphyxiate them," Mueller explained. "They won't be able to breathe. They'll get the bends chasing our tail. And while they are trying to come up for air, we'll be rolling up points."

It was a great plan, except that it didn't work. We were not runners. Our offense had always been a deliberate one. When we had possession of the ball, our style was to set things up, execute rehearsed plays, and wait to take the open shot. When in practice we tried to change and become a fast break team, we fell all over ourselves. We fumbled the ball, double-dribbled, threw passes away, missed shots, and generally looked like the Finley girls playing with gloves on.

In the missed shot department I was the leading culprit. Unexpectedly, and frighteningly, like a drunk suddenly tumbling off the wagon, I found myself relapsing. Thinking I was cured, Mueller had devised a fast break, an attack that, most of the time required me to charge down court and take a long pass a few feet from the basket. Then my task was to drive in and put up a layup for an easy two points.

It didn't happen. Like a sneaky virus bursting out from its hiding place, my symptoms returned in full force and I missed more than a half dozen consecutive layups. My shots hit the rim, caromed off the backboard, overshot the basket, or simply fell short of the mark. From the sidelines Mueller watched, counted the misses, and came to a rapidly rising boil. When I flubbed my last shot, he bolted from the sidelines, grabbed me by the shirt, put a fist under my nose—I had nightmare visions of Cara bursting out laughing at my flattened palooka schnoz—and ordered me off the court.

For the rest of practice I sat alone on the bench—no one dared talk to me—folded into myself, shrouded in black gloom, and assaulted by memories of the Ryder game and of being benched for the retard, Buckstein. It seemed that every time I looked up I caught sight of Bahary, my replacement, snaring a long pass, leaping into the air, legs flailing like a mad dancing Turk, and hitting his layup. It seemed to me then that the ground had suddenly given way under my feet and that I had been cast down to the bottom of a vast pit, with Cara and Mueller standing with their backs to me at the rim. Totally paralyzed, unable to move a muscle, I lay helpless. I could do nothing to reach them.

When practice was over—Mueller had not looked at me once since throwing me off the court—I pulled myself up and was starting for the locker room when Schneiderman caught hold of my shoulder from behind. When I turned, he fired a basketball at my mid-section. I barely got my hands up in time to block it and prevent a direct hit.

"You are not going anywhere, Jonathan," he said. "You are getting back on the court right now. We are going back to the drawing board." I wanted to refuse, to tell him that I was in no mood for more frustration, and walk away. But I didn't. There was something in his voice, a quiet authority that one simply didn't argue with.

I stepped back on the court, and with Schneiderman watching, took the ball, drove for the basket—and missed the layup. And for the next half hour, despite Schneiderman's coaching, I continued to be off the mark, my shots either striking the rim or angling too sharply off the board.

After my last miss, Schneiderman retrieved the ball and walked toward me. He said nothing until he was very close, no more than a couple of feet away. And when he spoke, he kept his voice low. What he had to say was clearly private.

"I heard about that night," he said. "Cara called, told me about the dinner." He reached out, touched me on the shoulder. "Look, don't sweat it. It's all right. I understand what happened, with the invite and everything. I probably would have made the same choice."

That was all he said. Then he toosed me the ball for another try.

At first I didn't get it. I was expecting to hear more instructions, more corrections about the placement of my arms and the like. It took a moment for Schneiderman's words to register. Then I could feel my face flush and I could not look at him. I wanted to say something, to explain what a fix I'd been in, how I'd been ashamed to admit what I had done so I made up an excuse, a dumb excuse, to cover my tracks. I wanted to say how sorry I was about the whole thing, but I couldn't speak. I couldn't get the words out. I was too embarrassed. Simply nodding, I turned away and continued the drill, with Schneiderman again observing and coaching.

Late into that practice session things finally began to come together. Following Schneiderman's instructions, I began to regain my form and by the end of that session I was scoring pretty consistently.

"He's almost back," Schneiderman said to Mueller. "We'll continue to work and he should be okay by Saturday."

That was the day of the Trinity game. Mueller was skeptical.

"I dunno," he said. "I dunno if I can take the chance. The boy is unpredictable. Under pressure he could fall apart. I'm tempted to start Bahary."

Schneiderman shook his head.

"Bahary is not in the same class," he said. "Against Trinity you have to go with your best."

I was not sure what Mueller would do. During practices he watched every move I made. The constant expression of wariness on his face often morphed into a scowl, particularly if I showed the slightest sign of slipping. I was preparing myself to be relegated to the bench again, but somehow—I surprised myself—I didn't care that much. My mind was elsewhere. I was preoccupied with Cara, with what she was thinking, with what she had taken away from her conversation with Schneiderman, and with the meaning of her continued silence.

Behind Mel's back—I didn't want to risk another critique—I had tried several times in the past week to call Cara. I never got her. Each time the phone had been answered by a different person. Once it was the maid, another time Cara's mother, both of whom were cool and curt. Cara was not at home, I was told, and they didn't know when she would be returning. Each time I left a message asking her to call, but she never did.

One time I got King R. For a moment he did not seem to know who I was. Then he caught on and, cordially enough, asked after my tennis game, but he made no mention of East Hampton or another match. And he declined to take a message. He was terrible at taking messages, he said. He could be relied on to get things ass backwards.

"But let me give you a piece of advice, Pancho," he said. "If my daughter is giving you a hard time, be persistent. She doesn't like to admit it, but she's like her mother. She wants to be courted. But if you've had an argument and you're wrong, admit it," he added. "Be big about it. Stubborn guys like me get her dander up."

On my last try I got Henry. Hearing my voice, he expressed pleasure at the chance to bring me up to date on his latest project. He had had a change of heart, he explained. After a dozen years of being a Pound man, totally devoted to Ezra, he had inexplicably fallen out of love with him. His new man was Hopkins. Did I know Gerard Manly Hopkins, he wanted to know, and his innovative "Spring Rhythms"? I had to admit that I hadn't been reading Hopkins lately.

"Well you must," Henry said. "This is high art; very sophisticated, in its own way in a league with Eliot."

"Really," I said. "I wouldn't have guessed that."

"Absolutely," Henry declared. "There is no question about it. Hopkins is not known to many of our contemporaries. Even the critics pass him by. But he is the best. You can take my word for that."

"I do," I said. "I know what kind of taste you have." Henry then invited me to a Hopkins reading that he was planning, but under the circumstances I had to defer my answer. Then, figuring I could lose nothing, I told Henry about the trouble I was having with his sister.

"Don't let it get to you," Henry counseled. "Probably the situation is temporary. Cara is on the outs with half the world. That's her nature. She can't help it. Just keep telling her she is right, one hundred percent right. That is the magic word. You've heard the phrase 'I'd rather be right than be president'? Well it was invented for my sister. Just say the magic word and the gates will swing open. And when you are back in her highness' good graces, don't forget the reading. You'll love Hopkins." I didn't leave a message with Henry. There was no point. I knew there wasn't much chance of it getting delivered.

A full week had passed since that fateful night at the apartment, and in that time I had developed a catalogue of roving physical symptoms that, without warning, shifted from heart to stomach, to urinary tract, including the prostate, which had flared up with acute inflammation. Within an hour's time I could be assailed by palpitations, cramps, and groin pain in no particular order, and sometimes in repeated waves. I was totally miserable and because of that misery—and a growing feeling of desperation—I confessed to Mel that I had broken the rule of abstinence.

"I'm not surprised," Mel replied. "I expected as much. When it comes to women, you have no discipline. But now that you've gone this far, there is no turning back. You have to go all the way."

"What are you talking about?"

"She knows you called and that you are still interested. This removes any anxiety on her part that she has gone too far, that she's alienated you, and that, this time, you've packed it in for good. So you've got to turn that liability of yours, your impatience, into an asset."

"Sounds like a splendid idea," I agreed. I wasn't sure I was following Mel's thinking, though, and my puzzlement must have shown on my face. He looked at me and shook his head slowly, a gesture reserved for pathetic cases.

"Look," he went on, "now that you've initiated contact, you've got to follow up with action. You have to be forceful, take charge, insist on seeing her, and don't take no for an answer. You've got to get over to her place on the double, bang on her door, collar her, and don't let her get away. Let her feel your passion. It's the only way she'll respond."

"What do I do about the doormen?"

"Screw the doormen. Handle them. Bribe them, sweet talk them, use a body fake and slip by. Do whatever it takes. But make sure you get hold of Cara. Make her feel your strength and the force of your personality. Let your desire hang out."

I wasn't sure just what Mel meant by that, but I pretty much got the picture. To pull this off, I needed a touch—actually more than a touch—of Bogie in my approach. Cara prided herself on being an intellectual and, no doubt, when I confronted her she would want to start an argument. Like an Oxford debater, she would begin to lay out her reasons for shutting down our relationship. "This is my thinking," she might begin, but I would cut her off right there.

"I don't pay you to think," I would retort, a la Bogart to Bacall and, recognizing the change that had come over me, she'd have to contend with my take-no-prisoners approach.

So for the second time since I spotted Miss Finley in the stands—and fell in love with that face—I boarded the crosstown bus, determined to find her and press my case. And I set myself to take on anyone, including any white-gloved sentry at the gate, who tried to dismiss me as a washed up West-Sider.

This time I did not have to travel far. Although I obtained a transfer in case I needed to switch to the Madison Avenue line and cruise the streets in search of Cara, I had no need for it. After I got off at the Park Avenue stop, I walked a few blocks north to 90th Street. And that is when I spotted her. She was just getting out of a cab that had pulled up in front of her building. I was at the corner, and summoning my old Cavalier's speed, I took off and caught up with her just as she was about to enter the lobby.

"Cara," spontaneously, without thinking, I called her name. She turned quickly, and seeing me behind her, looked distinctly apprehensive.

"Jonathan, what are you doing here?"

"I've come to see you. We need to talk. I'm not going to be shut out"—I heard Mel's voice in my ears—"I'm not your wimpy Sheepman"—for an instant I thought of saying sheepish Sheepman, but the alliteration seemed too pretentious—"and if you think you can stonewall me, you've got another think coming."

Cara gave me a surprised look.

"I'm not stonewalling you, Jonathan. I just don't want to see you right now. There really isn't anything to talk about."

"But there is," I protested. "That is exactly the point. There is everything to talk about. We really didn't talk that night. We left everything up in the air. I didn't have a chance to explain. There is a lot that I need to say."

"I really don't know what more there is for you to explain," Cara replied. "What you chose to do speaks for itself." Her voice was firm, even, not unkind, but sounding a bit like a teacher having to repeat to a protesting student why it was that she had to discipline him.

"Cara, look," I persisted, "this is important. You don't really have the full picture. Everything happened so fast in your apartment, I really couldn't think. I couldn't describe what it was like for me to make this decision, what I went through when you called. I need to do that. It's important for me, for us, that you hear me out. I need just a few minutes of your time, no more than a couple of minutes. You owe me that."

Cara responded gently, "Okay, Jonathan. If you have something more to say, I want to listen. I don't know if it will change anything, but I want to hear you out."

She started into the lobby and gestured for me to join her. Clarence was on duty. As we approached, he stood aside, smiled and, addressing us as a couple now familiar to him, offered us one of his hearty greetings.

Chapter Eighteen

I followed her into the elevator and we stood side by side in silence.

"I'm having dinner out with my folks tonight," she finally said, "so I'm not going to have a lot of time."

"A few minutes is all I need," I replied.

In the apartment Cara led the way directly to her room and shut the door. Then she sat on her bed, actually perched on the edge, and waited. I stood a couple of feet in front of her. She had said that she wanted to hear what I had to say, but the expression on her face, unmistakably skeptical, made clear that she did not expect me to come up with anything she had not heard before.

I had rehearsed a speech, with editing by Mel, but now that I was actually in Cara's room and had her attention, just about everything I planned to say seemed to have vanished from my mind. It was as though my worst fear; that I would be on stage in front of a packed audience and draw a complete blank, was coming true. Sensing my anxiety, Cara tried to help.

"You said you needed to tell me something."

What came back to me then was the sound of Mel's voice and his repeating the word, apologize.

"What she wants to hear is your owning up to what you did and apologizing," he had insisted. "That's the only thing that might get through to her. Arguing, fighting over who's to blame will get you a quick date—with Myra Herz."

It was the same advice King R had given me, and keeping that counsel in mind, I started off pretty well.

"Look, I'm sorry about this whole thing," I began. "The truth is, I had every intention of working with Schneiderman. In fact, I was ready to give up my night off to do it. But your invitation threw me off. The idea that your father asked me to come and really seemed to want me there, and the way that you spoke about the evening, what a great time it would be, and your adding that we could be alone after the dinner; all of that just threw me off. I lost my balance. You should know I didn't intend for it to turn out this way."

Cara nodded while I was speaking and when I'd finished she added a thought of her own.

"I've been thinking about what happened," she said, "and I can see that your problems with your father had a lot to do with this. You wanted Sidney to make up for the father you don't have. I get that. And I can understand how the idea of an event like this; a black tie dinner and a chance to get in with Sidney and to meet a bunch of big shots would be awfully tempting."

She seemed to be coming around, getting on my wavelength, and I wanted to solidify this way of thinking.

"That's right," I said. "It was a huge temptation, but it was also more than that. You made it sound like a once in a lifetime opportunity, a make it or break it situation with your father, that everything depended on my showing up."

"Perhaps you wanted to hear it that way, Jonathan," she countered. "If you recall, I said very plainly that Sidney would understand if you could not make it. He appreciates that a person may have other obligations. I do, too. I told you not to worry if you were already committed to something else, that it was no big deal."

She was repeating the argument she'd used before and it was obvious that she still did not understand, did not appreciate the bind I'd been in. There was no doubt that she had wanted me at King R's dinner, very much wanted me to be there with her. She did not want to be unaccompanied at such an occasion. Anyone who'd heard her phone call to me would have gotten that message. It was unmistakable.

I reminded her of this and also of something pretty important that she seemed to be minimizing.

"I was trying to please you," I said. "I wanted to do what I knew you wanted."

"I understand that, and I appreciate it, too. Don't think I don't. I knew that you had me in mind and wanted to please me, but was that the main reason for your decision, or was that secondary? Think about it, Jonathan. Wasn't the chief thing, really, what you said before, that the temptation was huge, that you didn't really want to pass up the chance to get in with Sidney and be part of our family? If you are honest with yourself, wasn't that it?"

"That was part of it, sure. I don't deny that. But it wasn't the whole story. I really didn't want to disappoint you. You don't seem to get that."

"Jonathan, I get it. I really do. But I don't think you are taking a hard look at yourself, really looking honestly at why you did what you did. And, look, I'm not condemning you. Probably most people would have made the same choice. I am not condemning self-interest. Everyone struggles with that. But where you come out in that struggle makes a difference. A few weeks ago Javits' office called and asked if I'd like to volunteer in the Press Office. A friend of my dad wanted to do him a favor and recommended me. Sidney said it was a terrific opportunity to get in on the ground floor with that organization and if I did a good job for them I'd be in a position to get some kind of appointment later on. That was damn appealing, especially since Jake is an okay guy. I've met him, and, basically, he is a good man. But he's on the wrong team. To win, he has to play ball with the right-wingers. Without them, he'd be in trouble and he knows it. So he is in their pockets. I couldn't be part of that set up."

"So you refused. You fought your temptation and I didn't, is that it? You are on the side of the angels and I'm the corrupt sinner who should be wearing a couple of scarlet letters. Is that what you are telling me?"

Cara's pious attitude was getting to me. No doubt she was a highly principled person and all that, and I very much admired her for that quality, but she didn't hesitate to let you know about it, and I was tired of being reminded that I didn't come up to her standards.

"Jonathan, I'm not condemning you. Far from it. And I'm not being critical. I'm just saying that you made a certain decision for your own reasons and you need to own up to that. You are going to have to live with what you did and you are going to have to face Stan Schneiderman. I don't envy you that."

"And you are going to have to judge me. Is that what you mean, or have you already done that and decided that I'm an unworthy lout?"

"Please, Jonathan, I don't think anything like that. I understand what happened and I understand why you did what you did. And I don't judge you. Please believe that. But I've had to think about all of this. I've had to think hard about it and what it means to me. It hasn't been easy and, frankly, I'm still uncertain about where I stand on what happened that night. But I know that it is important and that I'm not going to be able to move ahead with us until I figure it out."

"So you are saying that because in your mind I made the wrong decision; the decision to accept your invitation and still try to provide help for Schneiderman, help that I thought had a good chance of getting him through the exam, that you can't bring yourself to see me? Is that what I'm hearing?"

"Jonathan, I'm not saying that, and I don't mean that. What I am saying is that I don't know what I want to do. I feel very confused. It upsets me, but frankly, I no longer feel that I know who you are, who the real Jonathan Manheim is. Sometimes I feel that we are very different people, that we have very different values and when it comes down to it, want very different things, but I don't know. I'm confused. I need more time to think, to try to sort things out."

Hearing Cara speak this way, I found myself irritated—irritated and impatient with an attitude that, just beneath its surface of reasonableness and honesty, its frank confession of uncertainty, contained a distinct note of moral superiority. No, she wasn't judging me, she said, but of course she was; judging and assessing whether or not I was a bad character—as opposed to her self-denying purity—and whether she could allow herself to carry on a relationship with someone so morally questionable.

I was about to say some of these things to Cara—and privately tell Mel's voice to go to hell—when I spotted it, a shapeless gray baseball cap embroidered just about the peak with the intertwining letters, SL, the logo of the St. Louis Cardinals. It was on Cara's night table, resting up against the base of a reading lamp. For a moment I did not recognize it. Then I remembered, and it was as though someone had wound up and smashed me under the diaphragm with a two-by-four. I felt a stabbing pain in my gut and, at the same time, I became dizzy and had trouble focusing. I said nothing, but Cara immediately sensed that something was wrong.

"Are you all right, Jonathan? You look strange."

I did not answer. I simply took a step forward, reached behind her, seized the cap, and held it in front of her face.

"This belongs to Schneiderman."

"I know," Cara responded evenly. "Stan forgot it when we had the wine and cheese party after the demonstration. I have to return it to him. I keep meaning to do that, but it's been slipping my mind."

"I see. You forgot, so you just keep Schneiderman's cap next to your bed. But tell me something, do you usually hold parties in your bedroom? Is that why he left it in here?"

Sarcasm was not my style. In fact, it was a weapon I thoroughly disliked and very rarely permitted myself to use, but now I found myself so agitated, so hurt, that I couldn't hold back.

Cara immediately knew what I was experiencing, and although she was angered by my response, she made an effort to calm me.

"Jonathan, don't be so suspicious. We were all in the living room. Stan left the cap there. I brought it in here so the maid wouldn't toss it in the sports closet. Things have a way of disappearing in there."

"I see," I said. "That makes sense. And it's been sitting here right in front of your eyes for how long? If I remember correctly, that party of yours was quite a while ago."

"Jonathan, please, I told you what happened. And that's the truth. Frankly I've had a lot more important things on my mind than making sure that a beat up St. Louis Cardinals baseball cap that probably couldn't survive the trip anyway gets returned to Stanley Schneiderman."

Cara was speaking in the direct, no nonsense manner that she used when she was trying to explain a simple fact to someone who, for whatever reason, wasn't getting it. And it was clear that she wanted to dispose of a matter that, to her, required no further discussion. To me, however, she was behaving like someone who had something to hide and who was attempting to conceal a secret by getting away from the subject as quickly as possible. Cara was good at that. In conversation, when she no longer wished to pursue a particular topic, she would employ a device that she had learned from King R. She would interject a comment that was not really on point but that was close enough to it so that she appeared to be continuing the discussion while actually taking it in a new direction.

Cara was starting to do that now. She began to describe the party, who was there, and how much people drank.

"We must have polished off three bottles of champagne," she was saying. "Everybody got high. I was surprised that more people didn't walk out without their belongings."

I wasn't going to go for the bait and let her off the hook. Cara prided herself on being honest, a straight shooter, but she had a politician's heart. She knew how to get around people. I realized that she was trying to throw me off the track, to divert me from pursuing the matter of Schneiderman's cap, which was practically in her bed, and from discovering the truth about their relationship.

As I stood there observing her sleight of hand tactics, it struck me how stupidly blind I had been. I had been unable to see what was evident to anyone who spent even five minutes with Schneiderman and Cara when they were huddled together in one of their planning sessions. I had blinded myself to what was happening in front of me because the thought of these two teaming up, of these supposed friends betraying me and Schneiderman once again beating me out, was simply intolerable.

It was obvious, though, if I had only been able to piece things together, that Cara and Schneiderman had gotten closer by the day. His flunking Killigan's final had brought out all of her rescue fantasies. She was intent on saving him from perdition—being shipped back to Brooklyn—and once Cara made someone a personal project, there was no stopping her. She threw herself into the task— in this case, no doubt, into Schneiderman's arms—with the eagerness of a child on Christmas morning.

Both Cara and Schneiderman, I realized, knew how to be deceptive. They were both good at it. Each in his or her own way came on as being a caring person, generous and unselfish and, in a sense, that was true of both of them. But that was only part of the story. The other part was a very different matter. Both were fiercely ambitious people. When they wanted something, some prize, they went all out. There were no restraints. Cara was very much like her father in that respect. By his own admission, King R was out to destroy the competition. He made no bones about that. And Cara could be the same way. When she ran for Council president, she decimated her opponent, branding her Finley's own Bilbo because in the locker room the girl was overheard to refer to the family maid as the *schvatzer*.

As for Schneiderman, when it came to cutthroat tactics, he was right up there with Durocher, who regularly ordered his pitchers to dust off opposing batters. And like Durocher, Schneiderman was all smiles when his team was winning. If they fell behind, though, and were threatened with losing, he was quick to dig into his bag of dirty tricks. He had no compunction about using his elbows under the boards, grabbing an opponent's jersey from behind and, if the latter was about to sink a crucial basket, launching a rocket strike that would send that poor devil crashing to the floor.

It was true, too, that Schneiderman had admitted having a thing for Cara, and although he had said that he would hold back and not approach her while I was in the picture, I had no doubt, given his drive to win, if Cara came on to him and he saw a chance to move in and cut me out, his unquenchable thirst to beat out his old rival would take over and overcome any pangs of conscience he might have over breaking that implied promise.

"Maybe that's the explanation," I said, turning to Cara, "all the champagne you guys consumed." I was not going to let her dodge the issue. "You probably got so high you blanked out half of what happened that night. Do you think it's possible that you and Schneiderman actually were here in your bedroom together and that I found his cap on your night table because he did leave it here?"

Cara just shook her head.

Jonathan, please. Nothing happened. Not anything like you are implying. As I said, Stan was incredibly sweet that day and enormously helpful. So when he was leaving I gave him a goodbye kiss. And he kissed me back. That was it, that was my great betrayal, the unspeakable act of kissing my boyfriend's best friend because I appreciated how hard he worked and all he'd done for me. That's all there was to it. I took it for granted that you were my boyfriend, not Stan Schneiderman, and I thought you knew me well enough to know that I'd never cheat on the person I'm involved with.

"I think this whole business has gotten to you; Sidney's dinner, the makeup exam, you're upset about it all. It's affecting your mind. You seem determined to hang on to this crazy idea of yours. I have never seen you like this. Your mind is operating on this one track and you won't get off of it."

"And you obviously want to get me off that track as soon as possible. You'd also like me to believe that there is something wrong with me. That would be a neat way of making everything my problem. I've noticed that that is something you are good at."

Now Cara turned away from me and walked toward the door. When she spoke next, she sounded tired and discouraged.

"There is no point in this, Jonathan," she said. "Believe what you want. Obviously that is what you are going to do. I'm exhausted. I really can't discuss this anymore. You had better go now."

I knew what Cara was up to. I had seen her operate this way before when she wanted to end an argument. Accused by a friend of having done something hurtful, she would refuse to discuss the accusation. She would simply shut down and stop responding. That way she avoided looking at herself and what she had done. She had no interest in hearing about that kind of thing.

This is what she was doing now. It was clear that no matter what I said, regardless of the evidence, the smoking gun that I held in my hand, she was going to stonewall me. I remembered then what she had once told me about the power of denial. We had been discussing a newspaper item about a government official who had been arrested by the FBI on suspicion of being a Soviet agent.

"If I were in that guy's shoes," Cara had said, "I'd deny everything and just keep denying it. If you do that long enough, you can get people to doubt themselves and to back off."

This was her tactic now, but there was no way that she was able to see that. If I confronted her with what she was doing, with the tactic she was using, she would become enraged and we'd end up having a blowout. I nodded my head in agreement.

"You're right," I said. "There really is no point in trying to have a discussion with someone who refuses to discuss anything. I'll be going now," I added. I started for the door. Cara had opened it and was standing alongside it, not looking at me.

"Maybe you ought to think about your behavior and how you handled things tonight," I threw out as I passed her. She did not respond and continued to avert her eyes. Then, after I had barely cleared the threshold, she shut the door hard behind me.

Chapter Nineteen

On the street I felt dizzy and thickheaded, but also revved up. Although I was thoroughly discombobulated—and frightened—by what had just happened with Cara, I also felt oddly good. Mel claimed that psychotic denial had set in, but I don't think so. For once I had stood up for myself and hadn't wimped out. I had caught Miss Finley, the great moralist, the voice of the people, in a bald-faced lie. She had tried to pull a cover up, but what actually happened was clear.

After she dumped me—Mel was probably right; she was looking for a reason to give me the boot—Cara had called Schneiderman with the excuse of extending condolences and had turned on the charm. And he had responded. It was obvious from the beginning that they had a thing for each other, and when Schneiderman thought I was out of the picture—no doubt Cara made sure to inform him that we were finished—he had moved right in. That didn't surprise me. He had told me that he was right on my back and that if Cara and I broke up, he'd be right in there, taking his shot.

The speed of it all shocked me a bit, I had to admit, but that was Schneiderman. He was like the Lip, who was known for making bold moves; who, when he spotted Jackie Robinson taking a big lead off third, immediately flashed him the sign to steal home. They were men of action.

Let them have each other, I thought as I boarded the crosstown bus. They are two of a kind, both opportunists—my mother's favorite word to describe people she did not like.

My good mood—for a while it became a Mueller-type mania— lasted until after dinner. Then everything hit me and my world just caved in. I felt a terrible emptiness, just an enormous pit where my gut used to be, and by bedtime I had plummeted about as far down as I'd ever been. Then I did something strange. I sought out my father— he was already in bed—and asked him to come in and sit with me. And then I told him the whole story.

For a long time—it must have been close to an hour—he just listened. Then when I had finished and pretty well exhausted myself recounting all that happened, he quietly offered a few words.

"With women you never know, Jonathan," he said. "When it comes to the heart, to matters of the heart, even your best ladies, the most reliable, will try to pull the wool over your eyes. This has happened to me; not with your mother, she doesn't think this way, but with others when I was young. So you had a right to question, to have a raised eyebrow, so to speak. Maybe this Cara was telling the truth, maybe not. From what you've told me, it's very possible the two of them, she and your friend Schneiderman, have been in cahoots. You had a right to ask, to want to know. But I can tell you one thing. If the lady is unhappy with what you said, if she calls it quits, you will not be out of business. Not someone like you. You are the type women go for, not only smart, but a ball player. The ladies always go for ball players. You see them lining up outside Ebbets Field after every game, waiting for the players to come out, even a short fellow like Pee Wee Reese. Next time after a game when you leave the gym, take a look around. Win or lose they will be there, good-looking girls wanting autographs or, better still, a few words with you."

I thanked my father for what he'd said. It didn't help a great deal, but I knew that he was trying and, in turn, I wanted to reach out to him, to say something more, to include him in my life, perhaps invite him to the Trinity game. But somehow, I couldn't get the words out. I felt too awkward, too embarrassed, so I simply said goodnight and got into bed.

The next day's practice was the last before we faced the Trinity juggernaut, and I knew that if I didn't get some shuteye, I'd give an all thumbs performance and, no doubt, end up on the bench watching Bahary hit the mark with his pretzel jump shots. But I couldn't turn off my mind. I kept seeing images of Cara and Schneiderman making out on one of the Rosenhaus' plush couches. And in these scenes Cara didn't stop the action; didn't hold on to her panties at the last minute. And there was no mother, either, to blow the whistle. Fortunately— Mel said it was the dream censor springing into action—before they could go all the way Cara's face faded and was replaced by a likeness of Myra Herz. The last thing I remember, in fact, was Myra and Schneiderman going at it in what looked like the Frick Museum. Then I drifted off to sleep.

There were two days left before the Trinity game and we still had no battle plan. After junking his fast break strategy, Mueller went in the opposite direction.

"We'll slow it to a crawl," he announced. "Play a possession game. We'll hold the ball and move it around, but we won't take a shot until we've got the easy layup. We'll frustrate the hell out of them, make them foul us, and throw them off their game."

That strategy did not work. As it turned out, it was our team that was thrown off. We were used to a certain rhythm, a certain tempo, in executing our plays and the sudden slow place disrupted our offensive scheme. We mistimed our screens, bungled our give and go plays, and were off target on our passes. After a half hour of this, Mueller gave up.

"What we don't need is a bunch of Buster Keatons in slow motion," he said.

Later in the practice, though, he came up with what, in his judgment, was a brilliant plan. Approaching Schneiderman, who was watching from the sidelines, he threw a practice jersey at him.

"Suit up," he ordered. "You are going to be our Trinity." I knew that he was referring to McManus, Trinity's one-man team. Mueller's idea was to put Schneiderman on the practice squad, instruct him to mimic McManus' moves, and set up a game condition scrimmage, the starting five against the scrubs.

"We'll have to get a ruling on this." Fred Kahn, our manager, piped up. "I'm not sure that someone on probation can practice with the team."

"Tillman is in his office a thousand yards from here," Mueller replied. "What he doesn't know, he doesn't know. It's not going to bother him."

Freddie looked doubtful.

"I'm not sure about the legality of this," he said. "We could get in big trouble with the league."

Mueller turned to the players who were milling about, waiting for some action.

"Will somebody please grab this wimp and soak his head in a bucket of water," he pleaded. Then he motioned to us to form a circle around him.

"The best way to lick this Trinity outfit is to know their moves," he explained, "and especially to psych out their big man, McManus. If we can shut him down, we've got the game. So I'm going to ask Schneiderman here to turn himself into McManus, be McManus for this afternoon. Schneiderman here," he continued, "knows the beanpole, has played against him and has studied his moves, haven't you, Stan?"

Schneiderman looked noncommittal. "And," Mueller went on, "Schneiderman here is in the same class, the same league. Both are play makers with similar styles, so we'll know what we are up against." Then Mueller turned to me.

"Jonathan, I am putting you one on one against McManus here," he announced. This evoked some murmurs of surprise from the group since the real McManus had a good eight inches on me.

"He's got the height," Mueller acknowledged, "But you are quick, and you can play defense when you want to, and you can jump. If you stick close to him, keep your hands in his face, and go up with him when he goes for rebounds, you've got a chance to hold him down, hold him to single digits. And that will be the key. If we shut down McManus, we shut down Trinity. He's pretty much their team."

"I'll do my best," I said.

"Okay, good," Mueller said and, leaning forward, continued to instruct me. "Today I want you to practice real tight defense, Jonathan. Play Schneiderman tough. Don't give him an inch. When he has the ball, crowd him, don't let him drive the lane. The idea is to contain him, keep him under wraps. Then he looked at Schneiderman. "Stan, I want you to go all out. Turn on the burners. Make this fellow"—Mueller swept an arm in my direction—"work to stop you. Be McManus. And don't be afraid to use your elbows under the boards. That's what he does. And Jonathan here has got to be prepared for him."

Schneiderman didn't say anything. He just nodded in reply.

Mueller then called for the ball, strode to center court, and placed his whistle to his lips. The teams lined up on either side of him and, as in a regular game, the players shook hands with their opposite number. Schneiderman gripped my hand and grinned. "Don't forget, I'm McManus," he said, "go all out. Play me tough and don't hold back. You are going to have to do that against the real article."

The tap went to Schneiderman who immediately spun, whipped the ball to Bahary who had streaked down court, and Trinity was out in front, 2-0. In the first period that is pretty much the way it went. Schneiderman was all over the court, grabbing rebounds, firing perfect passes to teammates cutting for the basket, and hitting three running one-handers in a row. On all three scores I had fallen for his body fakes and he had managed to gain the step on me that put him in the open.

A couple of times after that, when he slipped by me and drove in for a layup, I caught up with him, and getting a hand on the ball from behind, managed to deflect his shot. Both times, though, I got called for a foul and Schneiderman made both free throws to give him more than a dozen points before the half was over.

Starting the third period, the scrubs were out front by four points and Mueller was becoming agitated.

"You are not playing defense," he shouted at us as he gathered the starting team around him, "You are letting them run all over you. Play this way against Trinity and those suckers will eat you alive."

He turned to me, "Schneiderman is making a fool of you, Jonathan," he said. "He is running circles around you. Think McManus, for God's sake. You are not going to get away playing like a Finley fag against him. Move in close, crowd him, force him to the outside, don't give him wiggle room."

I said nothing, merely nodded, but Mueller's words stayed in my head. They stung.

In the second half I moved in on Schneiderman, crowded him, angled myself to block any inside move, and if he tried to spin away, I was right on his heels, matching him step for step.

Twice I managed to poke the ball out of his hands, grab it, and whip it down court to Seligman, our fleet-footed center, who laid it in for two points.   Another time I intercepted one of Schneiderman's bounce passes, sped to the free throw line, stopped short, and fired a two-handed Tannenbaum set shot that whistled through the cords without touching the rim.   By the end of the third quarter we had caught the scrubs and were ahead by a half dozen points.

Schneiderman was becoming frustrated, and in the final period he turned aggressive. He used his elbows under the boards and, a couple of times, knocked me backwards when I started up for a rebound. When he had the ball, he passed less and took more shots himself, often using a head fake and then driving the lane.   I continued to be right on him, playing him practically chest to chest, but he scored several times, tricking me by starting to dribble, then stopping and leaping high to sink a one-handed jump shot. With five minutes to go the score was tied.

Schneiderman called a time out and huddled with his team. When they broke and took the floor, their strategy had changed. Now they were in a zone defense, following the ball and trying for an interception.   In response, we went into our zone busting offense, whipping the ball from one to another and looking to spot the free man. I stationed myself in the right corner, took a bounce pass from Seligman, and was open for a clear shot.   Just as I was about to release the ball, though, Schneiderman appeared from nowhere. Roaming in the zone defense, he tracked the ball and swooped in on me with both arms raised high. I tried to arch my shot over his head, but he got a hand on it and managed to deflect it. Then he grabbed the skidding ball, dribbled the length of the floor, and sunk a layup to put the scrubs ahead by a basket.

There were less than two minutes left on the clock when it happened. I took a pass just beyond the circle, and spotting a slight opening to my left, faked right, and drove for the basket. A couple of yards from the hoop, I leaped, extended my arms to ease in the layup and, perversely—it hadn't happened during the entire scrimmage— my legs curled. My shot hit the board, bounced onto the rim, seemed to cling to it for an instant, then fell away.

My jump had carried me a few feet to one side of the basket. From that spot I watched the ball and set myself to try to snare the rebound. Schneiderman was a foot in front of me, crouching, tracking the ball, also ready to spring. As the ball came down, the two of us went up at the same time, Schneiderman in front, me just behind him. Schneiderman's leap was higher, but the ball came down just behind him and he had to reach back to grab it.

The momentum of my leap carried me forward, and as Schneiderman arched backwards, I smashed into him, my right shoulder catching him high on the back. The force of the blow spun him around. He twisted, his legs kicked out, then he dropped straight down. He landed flat on his back, his head striking hard against the wood floor.

Mueller blew his whistle, made an exaggerated thrusting motion with his chest, and called me for charging from behind. I protested the call, yelling at Mueller that we were both going for the ball, but he shook his head, repeated his pantomime of the foul, and held up one finger, indicating that Schneiderman had one free throw coming. He started toward our basket, players from both teams trailing behind him.

Schneiderman was still down. He lay as he fell, flat on his back, his legs partially bent. He did not move. Now one of his teammates walked over to him and extended an arm to help him up. Then, abruptly, the player dropped to his knees and called out for Mueller.

"Coach, get over here," he shouted, "Stan's hurt. He's not moving. He looks out of it."

Mueller turned, dropped the ball, and ran to Schneiderman's side. He and Fred Kahn, who, hearing the call for help, grabbed his first-aid kit and sprinted onto the floor, reached Schneiderman at the same time. Both dropped to their knees. Mueller called Schneiderman's name, then administered a light slap to his face. There was no response.

"We better not touch him," Fred advised, "this could be serious. It could be his neck." Mueller nodded, and putting his face close to

Schneiderman's, called to him again. Getting no answer, he turned and shouted over his shoulder.

"Call for an ambulance. Someone, quick, call for an ambulance."

In less than ten minutes the ambulance arrived. I heard the wail of the siren, first at a distance, then almost on top of us. There was no direct road to the gym, so when he reached the school grounds, the driver had to shift into low, sound his horn continuously, and head straight across our playing field, while clusters of runners and soccer players scattered for cover.

Fred Kahn was at the door, holding it open. Two attendants jumped from the back of the ambulance. Then, reaching back inside, they grabbed some equipment and rushed into the building. It was the same emergency team that showed up at Cara's place when I passed out at her party.

The young woman reached Schneiderman first. She took in the situation, then leaned down and called to him. He had regained consciousness now, and, in reply, he mumbled something, but his words were slurred and she could not make out what he was saying. He still had not moved. The other attendant took Schneiderman's vital signs, then called in on his walkie-talkie, "We've got a man down here at the Harmon gym. Looks like a neck injury. He is not moving."

"Use the brace," a voice crackled back. "Don't take a chance with a neck." Then another pause and some static, the voice came through again.

"Can he be transported?"

"I think so."

"Okay, then. Brace him, put him on a stretcher, and get him here as fast as possible."

"Will do."

The female attendant returned to the ambulance, brought back a neck brace, and working together, the two of them eased it in place. Then with Mueller's help, they lifted Schneiderman onto a stretcher. Then they wheeled him out.

I stood at the door and watched them go. When Schneiderman was in place and the ambulance doors were shut, the driver backed up, made a sharp turn, and steered the ambulance onto the field. The siren shrieked and they pulled away.

No one spoke to me. I stood alone for several minutes. Then Mueller came up from behind.

"Tough break," he murmured. We were silent for a while. Then I turned to face Mueller.

"It was an accident," I said. "We were both going for the ball." Mueller nodded, "I know," he said, "but you were overeager and you fouled him. You reached over his back trying for the ball, and you rammed him. I had to call it. But you're right. It was an accident. Try not to take it too hard." I didn't say anything. I just walked away.

The gym had emptied out and I sat alone on the bench. Immediately after the ambulance left, I had the impulse to rush out, follow it to the hospital, and be at the Emergency Room when the doctors examined Schneiderman. But I could not move. I felt paralyzed and I just wanted to be alone. I didn't want to see anyone or talk to anyone.

I sat in the empty gym for close to an hour. I was feeling nothing, but my mind was throwing up images of that last play; the missed shot, the ball spinning on the rim, my watching, crouching, then springing—and crashing into Schneiderman. And then, somehow, a memory from the Ryder game arose in my mind. It was after my fumble and Schneiderman had made the recovery. I saw myself diving at him, ramming him, my helmet cracking bone, and him lying there, not moving. Quickly I turned away from that image and thought again of what had just happened on the court. Mueller was wrong. There was no foul. I wanted to find Mueller, buttonhole him, and prove to him that he had missed the call; that there was no way that he could see the whole play from where he was standing. But I didn't try. I knew it would be no use.

On the way to the subway I felt like an automaton. I took my usual route across the Harmon playing field and down the long hill to the station. But I saw nothing and I was unable to think. It was as though I'd been smashed on the back of the head with a two by four, my brain had gotten scrambled, and I was still suffering the effects of that blow.

There was a dull, steady ache low in my forehead, just over my eyes, and I felt so drained that I had to stop walking and rest for a couple of minutes at the bottom of the hill. There was trouble on the tracks and close to a half hour wait for a train. When one finally came, I rushed in, found an empty seat, shut my eyes, and tried to sleep.

As soon as my eyes closed, my mind, which moments before, had seemed totally empty, was suddenly filled with images, past and present, that appeared in quick succession, like pictures in a slide show.

First I saw Schneiderman in our living room, engaged in a conversation with my father, paying close attention to my dad, and responding thoughtfully to what he was saying. Then I saw myself as a younger teenager walking away from the dinner table while my father was carrying on in his usual way, reinventing history or forecasting a rosy future for his collapsing business. I remembered that I had thought him a fool then and although I said nothing, my behavior in leaving the table—I would offer a lame excuse about having loads of homework to do—spoke for me.

Then I saw myself in the Harmon locker room, a Cardinals baseball cap in hand, running after Schneiderman who had left it on the bench next to his locker and was heading out the door. And I recalled that, for some reason, he had a habit of doing this—Mel said that in Schneiderman's unconscious wearing a St. Louis cap was like being traded away from Brooklyn—and that I had teased him about it, diagnosing his school difficulties as being due, not to a learning disorder, but to a rapidly advancing case of dementia. And then—the next image that appeared gave me a stabbing pain under the diaphragm—I saw myself with Cara in her bedroom. Agitated, she was denying my accusation, insisting that I had it wrong, that there was a kiss, that's all; that the notion of betrayal was my idea and that I seemed to need to believe that. And I pictured myself fighting with Cara, not believing her, and walking out.

The last image that appeared—thankfully nothing else followed—again took place in the locker room. I was talking with Schneiderman about Cara, trying to get a line on what was going on

een them. And I remembered that Schneiderman was out front
out his feelings for her. He told me flat out that he really liked and
dmired Cara, and that he envied me being with her. And that if we
broke up, he'd be first in line to take a shot. His meaning was clear.
If I were still with her, he would do nothing. He would make no play
for her as long as I was involved. And I knew at the time that he was
telling the truth. I hadn't the slightest doubt about that.

There were no more images, but at that point a wave of shame
came over me and I could feel a burning sensation on my face. I slid
down in my seat, half covered my face with an arm, and must have
made some odd grimacing movements, too, because when I looked up,
the four other people in the car were all staring at me as though I was
in the throes of the DTs.

To escape from what I was feeling, what had come over me, I
closed my eyes and tried again to sleep. In fact, I must have dozed off
for a few minutes because, when I awoke, I immediately understood
what had been happening. It was as though, as I slept, all the images
that had assailed me had come together, had fused, and, putting
pressure on my brain, had forced into my consciousness an awareness,
a truth, that had been rising to the surface but that until then I had
managed to block out and keep at bay.

I understood then what had happened on the court, and knew
now that Mueller was both right and wrong. He was right that there
had been a foul, but wrong that it was Schneiderman who was the
target. It was not Schneiderman whom I was attacking; it was who I
saw in him, saw reflected in his eyes and could not bear to see; an
image of myself, the small-minded, envious person and disloyal friend
that I had become. It was that image, that reflection, that I needed to
obliterate. And I grasped, too, the trick that my mind had played on
me; how, to ward off the guilt I felt over what I'd done, the injury I'd
caused, I needed to experience Schneiderman as the enemy, needed to
believe that it was he, not I, who had betrayed our friendship.

The pain stayed with me, the pain and the waves of shame,
that, like aftershocks, continued to assault me until I could take no
more and somehow, mercifully, just before I reached my stop, my
brain managed to shut them down.

As soon as I got home I called the hospital.

"Mr. Schneiderman is in surgery," the lady at the informati‍‍ desk reported. "We have no other information." I tried twice mor‍‍ later and got the same reply.

I remained in my room the rest of the evening. My mother came in with food, but I had no appetite. I had an urge to speak to Cara, to get a word of comfort from her, but I did not want to take a chance calling her. I had no idea how she would respond at this point, and I was in no mood to risk one of her harangues.

I did speak with Mel when he called, but his efforts to reassure me, to insist that what happened wasn't my fault, somehow rang hollow. I got off the phone quickly.

About then my father came in to sit with me. He didn't say much, just a few words. Mostly he just sat in silence in a corner of my room like the Orthodox do when comforting a mourner. They just sit with him to let him know that he is not alone. Just their presence, the knowledge that they care, makes a difference.

Before he went to bed, my father came over to me, reached out, and touched my arm.

"It could have been the other way around," he said. "Easily the other way around. And you wouldn't have blamed him. You would have understood."

I nodded. I didn't believe him, but I appreciated the effort. The Trinity game was the next afternoon and I knew that I had to get some sleep. With Schneiderman out, it was up to me to take over and anchor the team. And I knew if I wasn't in decent shape I'd botch everything and make a fool of myself. But I couldn't sleep. I dozed on and off, but mostly my mind went to the past, to times with Schneiderman—and Cara.

I felt pretty beat in the morning and the last thing I wanted to do was face a hungry Trinity team that was set to devour us—and spit out the pieces. I tried to think through Mueller's strategy, the plan of attack that we had rehearsed, but I couldn't concentrate and, in any case, without Schneiderman leading the offense it was unlikely that we'd be effective in carrying out the plan. I decided, finally, that we'd